mela

multi-ethnic literatures of the americas

AMRITJIT SINGH, CARLA L. PETERSON, C. LOK CHUA, SERIES EDITORS

The MELA series aims to expand and deepen our sense of American literatures as multi-cultural and multi-lingual and works to establish a broader understanding of "America" as a complex site for the creation of national, transnational, and global narratives. Volumes in the series focus on the recovery, consolidation, and reevaluation of literary expression in the United States, Canada, and the Caribbean as shaped by the experience of race, ethnicity, national origin, region, class, gender, and language.

THE GRAND *Gennaro*

THE GRAND *Gennaro*

Garibaldi M. Lapolla

EDITED AND WITH AN INTRODUCTION BY
Steven J. Belluscio

RUTGERS UNIVERSITY PRESS
NEW BRUNSWICK, NEW JERSEY, AND LONDON

Library of Congress Cataloging-in-Publication Data

Lapolla, Garibaldi M. (Garibaldi Marto), 1888–1954.
  The grand Gennaro / Garibaldi M. Lapolla ; edited and with an introduction by Steven J. Belluscio.
      p. cm. — (Multi-ethnic literatures of the Americas (MELA))
  Includes bibliographical references.
  ISBN 978-0-8135-4568-4 (hardcover : alk. paper) — ISBN 978-0-8135-4569-1 (pbk. : alk. paper)
  1. Italian Americans—Fiction.   2. Immigrants—New York (State)—New York—Fiction.   3. Italian
Americans—Social life and customs—Fiction.   4. New York (N.Y.)—History—1898–1951—Fiction.
I. Belluscio, Steven J.   II. Title.
  PS3523.A659G73 2009
  813 .52—dc22

                                                                                    2008048063

A British Cataloging-in-Publication record for this book is available from the British Library.

This publication is supported in part by the Institute of Italian and Italian American Heritage Studies.

The Grand Gennaro was first published by Vanguard Press in 1935. All rights to the novel remain with
Paul M. Lapolla.

Introduction and scholarly apparatus copyright © 2009 by Steven J. Belluscio

Text design by Adam B. Bohannon
Visit our Web site: http://rutgerspress.rutgers.edu
Manufactured in the United States of America

**Frontispiece: Portrait of Garibaldi M. Lapolla courtesy of The Historical Society of
Pennsylvania (HSP), Garibaldi M. Lapolla Collection.**

CONTENTS

ACKNOWLEDGMENTS

I would like to thank the following for their contributions toward the completion of this reprint: Paul M. Lapolla for the permission to complete this project and for the hours he spent enthusiastically telling me about his father; Fred L. Gardaphé for making me aware of the Multi-Ethnic Literatures of the Americas series; Leslie Mitchner, Amritjit Singh, Carla Peterson, C. Lok Chua, and Rutgers University Press for giving me the opportunity to resurrect this classic and for guiding me every step of the way; Anthony J. Tamburri and the John D. Calandra Institute of Italian American Studies for allowing me the services of Angelo Zeolla, who scanned and performed the first edit of the text; President Antonio Perez, Vice President Sadie Bragg, Dean Michael Gillespie, and the Media Center of Borough of Manhattan Community College/CUNY for institutional and technological support; the CUNY Research Foundation for financial support; R. A. Friedman and the Historical Society of Pennsylvania for assistance with Garibaldi M. Lapolla's archives; Professor George Grella of the University of Rochester English Department for supervising my first reading of this novel in 1996; Chair Phil Eggers, Chair Joyce Harte, Francis Elmi, Maria Enrico, and Robert Zweig of Borough of Manhattan Community College for their collegiality and encouragement; my wife Vanessa, daughters Sophia and Annalina, brother Chris, and parents John and Marilyn for everything else.

1888   Garibaldi Mario Lapolla is born April 5 in Rapolla, Basilicata, province of Potenza, Italy, to Biagio Oreste Lapolla and Marie Nicola Buonvicino. In honor of his grandfather's Italian nationalism, he is named after Giuseppe Garibaldi (1807–1882), the George Washington of the modern Italian nation.

1890   Immigrates to New York City with his parents. Over the next decade, over 650,000 of his fellow Italians would follow suit.

1891   Eleven Italians are lynched in New Orleans in connection with the unsolved murder of Police Chief David Hennessy.

1898   Spanish-American War.

1910   Earns A.B. at Columbia University. Begins his public school career teaching English at DeWitt Clinton High School, Manhattan, New York, where he remains for more than a decade, with an interruption for World War I military service.

1912   Earns A.M. at Columbia University after writing a thesis on British romanticist Percy Bysshe Shelley (1792–1822) entitled "Shelley and the Political Parties of His Day."

1914–1918   World War I. Italian immigration stopped.

1917–1918   Enlists in the U.S. Army and is stationed at Fort Ontario, Oswego, New York. Mess sergeant for the hospital. Meets Nurse Margaret McCormick, whom he marries soon after. Signs a letter published in the *New Republic* on May 26, 1917, arguing that conscientious objectors be allowed to serve non-combat roles in the military. Is transferred to Washington, D.C. Promoted to sergeant first class.

1919   Son Paul McCormick is born February 11.

1921   Emergency Quota Act severely limits immigration from southern and eastern European countries.

1922   Summoned by the Advisory Council on the Qualification of Teachers, formed by Frank Graves, state commissioner of education, to determine the patriotism of teachers in New York State. Lapolla is questioned about the 1917 *New Republic* letter he signed. Son Mark Orestes is born February 17.

1924   Immigration Act of 1924 enacted, an even harsher version of the 1921 law. It prohibits Asian immigration entirely.

1925   Publication of F. Scott Fitzgerald novel, *The Great Gatsby*.

1926–1930   Chairman of Thomas Jefferson High School English Department.

1927   On August 23, Ferdinando Nicola Sacco (b. 1891) and Bartolomeo Vanzetti (b. 1888), two Italian anarchists, are executed for the 1920 murder of two pay clerks in South Braintree, Massachusetts. Given the antiradical sentiment of the court, many argue they did not receive a fair trial.

1927–1932   Principal of Thomas Jefferson Summer High School.

1928   Serves as judge in a Brooklyn Borough high school finals for the National Oratorical Contest on the Constitution.

1929   Publishes *Better High School English through Tests and Drills* with Kenneth W. Wright at Noble & Noble. Edits with poet and literary critic Mark Van Doren *A Junior Anthology of World Poetry*, published by Albert & Charles Boni, and praised highly in the *New York Times*. Divorces Margaret McCormick.

1930–1934   Principal of New York Public School 112.

1930   Exchanges letters with famed teacher and educational theorist Leonard Covello, refusing to allow the latter to use the as yet unpublished *The Fire and the Flesh* (then with the working title "La Dantone") as a sociological document for a study of Italian Americans because "it ain't no such beast."

1931   Publishes *The Fire in the Flesh* at the Vanguard Press to generally positive reviews in *Books* and the *New York Times*.

1932   Publishes *Miss Rollins in Love* at the Vanguard Press. Receives lukewarm review from the *New York Times*.

1934   Marries Priscilla Sherman. Is featured (with other Italian American authors) in *Gazzetta del Popolo*.

1935–1953   Principal of New York Public School 174.

1935   Publishes *The Grand Gennaro* at the Vanguard Press to acclaim in the *New Republic*, the *New York Times*, *Books*, the *Boston Transcript*, *Review of Reviews*, and the *Saturday Review of Literature*.

1937	Publishes *Required Grammar in the New York City Public School* at Noble & Noble. Interviewed on WEVD New York for a radio program about overcrowding in city schools.
1938	Speaks on June 29 at the conference of the National Council of Teachers of English and criticizes tendency to insist upon a "puritanical type of speech" no one actually uses and to reinforce it through teaching of grammar and usage.
1939	Publication of Pietro di Donato novel *Christ in Concrete*.
1939–1945	World War II. Over one million Italian Americans serve in the armed forces. About 250 Italian Americans, 11,000 German Americans, and 100,000 Japanese Americans are interned for reasons of "national security."
1945	In February, son Mark Orestes, trained as an Army Air Corps flight officer reported missing in action over Brod, Yugoslavia, after completing eighteen missions and receiving the Air Medal. His death was confirmed eleven months later.
1946	Serves on a Teacher-Author Committee of New York City school and college instructors to protest board of education bylaw requiring textbook authors to turn over royalties.
1950	Unsuccessfully brings action against the New York City Board of Education in favor of uniform pay for principals of all city schools, elementary, junior, and senior.
1953	Publishes and illustrates *Italian Cooking for the American Kitchen* and *The Mushroom Cookbook* at W. Funk. The former is praised and widely publicized by reviews and interviews in publications such as the *New York Times*, the *San Francisco News*, *Il Progresso Italo-Americano*, the *Chicago American*, and the *Sunday Herald*.
1954	Dies in his sixty-fifth year on January 13 at Mount Sinai Hospital after a massive stroke. His death is mourned and career celebrated by colleagues, administrators, students, and parents. The Parent Teacher Association donates to Public School 174 a plaque lauding Lapolla as "Educator, Leader, and Friend."
1965	Immigration Act of 1965 overturns Immigration Act of 1924.

INTRODUCTION: MAKING AMERICA IN GARIBALDI M. LAPOLLA'S *THE GRAND GENNARO*

When Thomas J. Ferraro declared Italian American writing "one of the better kept literary secrets of [the twentieth] century," he had in mind Garibaldi M. Lapolla, among other authors.[1] In their detailed and sensitive treatment of everyday life in turn-of-the-century Italian Harlem, Lapolla's three published novels—*The Fire in the Flesh* (1931), *Miss Rollins in Love* (1932), and *The Grand Gennaro* (1935)—form a cornerstone of early Italian American fiction for readers familiar with the works of Silvio Villa, Giuseppe Cautela, Louis Forgione, Frances Winwar, John Fante, Mari Tomasi, Pietro di Donato, Guido d'Agostino, and Jerre Mangione. However, Garibaldi M. Lapolla's writing has not garnered nearly the attention it deserves despite his renown among scholars of Italian American literature, the similarity of his fiction to that of canonical ethnic writers such as Abraham Cahan and Anzia Yezierska, and the recent entry into the canon of other Italian American fiction writers (such as Pietro di Donato and John Fante). To be sure, one obvious reason is unavailability. While Lapolla's novels were generally well reviewed—especially *The Grand Gennaro*, considered to be his best work—they soon went out of print. And despite an Arno Press resurrection of his first and final novels in 1975, Garibaldi M. Lapolla's name continues to remain in underserved obscurity; he could very well be the *best* kept secret of Italian American literature.

Teacher, Soldier, Writer

Born April 5, 1888, in Rapolla, Basilicata, province of Potenza, Italy, to Biagio Oreste Lapolla and Marie Nicola Lapolla (née Buonvicino), Garibaldi Mario Lapolla (his given name reflecting the Italian patriotism of his paternal grandfather) left Italy and immigrated to New York City with his parents in 1890 before age two. He would lose his mother at age nine.[2] An exceptional student in public school as a child, Lapolla attended Columbia University, earning a B.A. in 1910 and an M.A. in 1912, after completing a thesis on British romantic poet Percy Bysshe Shelley.[3] In 1910, Lapolla began teaching English at DeWitt Clinton High School, then located in Manhattan, where he left a great impression on his students, including Mortimer Adler, who would become one of America's most celebrated philosophers and public intellectuals of the twentieth century.[4] Thus began Lapolla's rich, productive, and lifelong career as an educator and educational theorist—a career interrupted only by military service during World War I in which he "held every position from buck private to cook to lecturer on personal phophylaxis to sergeant to lieutenant of artillery."[5]

From 1917 to 1918, Lapolla was stationed at Fort Ontario, Oswego, New York, where, after an "early . . . career . . . underscored by black marks" in which "he seemed temperamentally incapable of complying with regulations," "he disciplined himself to become a good soldier."[6] As mess sergeant, he nurtured what would become a lifelong passion and what had been a family tradition of sorts: his father had owned restaurants in Montreal, Quebec, and New York, and was known to claim descent from "a long line of cooks" dating back to ancient Rome.[7] While a soldier in Flower Unit N, Post Hospital No. 5, Fort Ontario, Lapolla met his future wife, Nurse Margaret McCormick, with whom he conceived two sons: Paul McCormick (born February 11, 1919) and Mark Oreste (born Feburary 17, 1922).[8] Lapolla also served on the associate board of the *Ontario Post* newspaper and wrote for it, taught in the fort's school, played guard and tackle for its football team, and worked as a chaplain's assistant before he was transferred to Washington and eventually promoted to sergeant first class.[9]

After his successful tenure at DeWitt Clinton High School, where he taught on the faculty alongside famed educational theorist and Italian American activist Leonard Covello, Lapolla served as chairman of the Thomas Jefferson High School English Department from 1926 to 1930 and principal of the Thomas Jefferson Summer High School from 1927 to 1932. In 1929, Lapolla's first marriage ended in divorce; in 1934, he married Priscilla Sherman, a fellow faculty member. From 1930 to 1934, Lapolla was principal of Public School 112, and from 1934 to his death in 1954, principal of Public School 174.[10]

Lapolla fought for social justice throughout his life, even running "for every office from Alderman to Congressman on the Socialist ticket" before World War I.[11] Unwilling to sell short immigrant students, he campaigned endlessly for more intelligent, student-centered pedagogical practices in the tradition of John Dewey and a more pragmatic approach to teaching English grammar, rankling school administrators but advocating what would eventually become educational orthodoxy. In keeping with his democratic educational vision, Lapolla also challenged board of education bylaws requiring textbook authors to turn over royalties to the school district and fought for uniform pay for principals of all city schools.[12] This fighting spirit often got him into trouble. For example, in 1922, he was interrogated by the Advisory Council on the Qualification of Teachers—a byproduct of the 1919 Joint Legislative Committee to Investigate Seditious Activities (also known as the Lusk Committee)—about his co-signed letter printed in the May 26, 1917, issue of the *New Republic*, which argued that conscientious objectors ought to be allowed to serve non-combat roles in the military during World War I and, more broadly, that there ought to be "a social setting within America sufficiently hospitable to all conscientious objectors."[13] Upton Sinclair would later relish the irony of Lapolla, "an artillery officer" during the war, "now . . . sitting on the bench, humbly waiting his turn to be browbeaten."[14] While Lapolla escaped the investigation unscathed, he would be unable to avoid similar controversy in the future. As principal of Public School 174 in Brooklyn in the early 1950s, Lapolla vigorously defended teachers persecuted by the House Un-American Activities Committee, arguing that they should be judged not for their beliefs but, rather, their ability in the classroom. "Aren't we, in fact," Lapolla wrote, "chasing a phantom that, in a more reasonable period, we would recognize and admit as such?"[15] Throughout his educational career, Lapolla remained aggressively committed to winning justice for students, teachers, and administrators and maintaining quality in education.

As an English specialist, Lapolla taught "grammar, American literature, English literature, poetry, Shakespeare, and remedial English."[16] Frequently dissatisfied with the status quo of English pedagogy, Lapolla published textbooks designed to teach English grammar more practically and to deliver an appreciation of literature to young students. During his career, he penned *Better High School English* (1929) and *Required Grammar in the New York Public Schools* (1937) to serve the former purpose and co-edited with Mark Van Doren The *Junior Anthology of World Poetry* (1929) to serve the latter. Lapolla was also interested in educating the general public about the delights of the Italian cuisine he had grown up enjoying and masterfully learning to prepare. In 1953, he published *Italian Cooking for the American Kitchen*, designed to help Americans learn the variety of Italian cooking; that same year, he also published *The Mushroom Cookbook*. Lapolla also left behind a wealth of unpublished writings—essays, poems, plays, short stories, a novel titled "Jerry," and other unfinished manuscripts.

The unifying thread of most of Lapolla's written work—his text-books, his cookbooks, and his novels—is the continuous negotiation between Italian and American cultures. His textbooks were designed with the Italian immigrant student in mind and the concern of how best to serve them in the American public school system. His cookbooks attempted to teach an American audience about Italian food and thereby provide an entrée into Italian history, culture, and geography: as Americans learned to prepare and appreciate Italian cuisine, these so-called foreigners in their midst would come to seem less foreign. Finally, his novels used turn-of-the-century East Harlem as a fictional staging ground for the oft-troubled coexistence of Italian ancestry and American dreams. All the while, *Professore* Lapolla is the patient and compassionate pedagogue, challenging his student—the reader—to grow beyond the limitations of prior experience.

Lapolla traveled widely during his lifetime throughout North America, South America, and Europe, including his native Italy. Lapolla was an avid artist; many of his pencil sketches, pen and ink drawings, and water colors—mostly urban scenes, rural pastorals, portraits, and still lifes—serve as a record of the people and places he encountered at home and abroad. Lapolla even supplied the pen and ink drawings of various foods for *Italian Cooking for the American Kitchen*. An expert letter writer, Lapolla infused his correspondence with wry humor and keen wit, both high- and lowbrow. He would regale his reader with evocative accounts of his New York surroundings before matter-of-factly addressing the main subject matter of the letter. His letters to younger son Mark Oreste Lapolla while the latter served in Foggia, Italy, as an Army Air Forces flight officer during World War II are ample evidence of this. In these letters to "Oreste," Lapolla discourses about Italian language, geography, and culture; the progress of the war; and the mood of Americans back on the homefront. Of themselves, these letters are little gems of geopolitics, cultural criticism, and homespun wisdom.[17] Some of the best of these letters were returned, for Mark Lapolla went missing in action over Brod, Yugoslavia, while flying a mission during February 1945. On January 5, 1946, he was reported to have been killed there.[18] An emotional man, Lapolla took his son's death very hard, and during his 1953 trip to Italy, he visited Oreste's gravesite with his wife Priscilla, writing in his trip diary, "I couldn't have come here and not done it."[19]

When Garibaldi M. Lapolla died of a massive stroke on January 13, 1954, at the age of sixty-five, Priscilla received an outpouring of condolences for "Gari," as he was affectionately known, from colleagues and friends throughout his life and career praising his qualities as an educator, intellectual, artist, and fellow human. The Parent Teacher Association donated a plaque to New York Public School 174 lauding Lapolla as an "Educator, Leader, and Friend." Although he died much too young, he had the great fortune of being remembered, and celebrated, by friends and acquaintances for all the many things he had accomplished.

"Method Realistic, But Intent Romantic"

Garibaldi M. Lapolla's reputation as a novelist, however, would be neglected until the 1980s, when scholarship began to recognize his talent and importance as "East Harlem's novelist"—or, at least, Italian Harlem's novelist.[20] Critics have rightly attributed Lapolla's obscurity in part to his refusal to accede to the aesthetic trends of the 1930s: high modernism and proletarian literature.[21] In course lecture notes, it is clear that while Lapolla was by no means opposed to the literary experimentation of the early twentieth century, he disliked the use of "pyrotechnical coloring and devices" for their own sake; and while Lapolla was himself a socialist, he dismissively refers to proletarian literature as "propaganda" "mainly concerned with revealing the life of worker-classes as they are allegedly developing a historic class-consciousness."[22] Furthermore, Lapolla celebrated what he called the "newer romanticis[m]" of contemporary authors who "have held to the notion that the novel was made to please, that factual scenes immediate to the readers' experience are not the inevitable material of the novel, that readers are still interested in the carefully organized plot, in remote peoples and times, in themes that have no bearing on modern conditions save in a large way, that propaganda for any cause is not the purpose of fiction." Lapolla admired Pearl Buck's writing for providing "pictures which please by their combination of the familiar in human nature against a background of the unfamiliar," her "method realistic, but intent romantic."[23]

This description goes a long way toward explaining Lapolla's own aesthetic approach. While his fictions are rich with the realistic specifics of place and people—East Harlem and the Italians who once lived there—the pastness of these very specifics lends them, even from the perspective of the 1930s, the luster of historical romance. Furthermore, Lapolla frequently imbues his settings with firelight, moonlight, shadowplay, and religious iconography, elements more typical of Nathaniel Hawthorne or Edgar Allan Poe than William Dean Howells or Henry

James. The traditional Southern Italian folk beliefs fictionalized by Lapolla—with their fascinating interplay of Christian providence, saint worship, Marianism, and occult mysticism—further add to the other-worldly romanticism of the novels. Finally, Lapolla's novels feature characters who attempt to rise above their sordid urban surroundings toward a transcendental plane of spiritual and—given the recurrence of the artist figure in all three of his works—artistic fulfillment.[24]

The First Two Novels

The Fire in the Flesh, Lapolla's first published novel, certainly fits this description. Set in turn-of-the-century Italian Harlem, the novel puts into motion both a business plot and an occasionally intersecting love plot that ensnare its principal characters as they make their uneasy adjustments to the ways of urban America. In the love plot, which begins in Villetto, Italy, protagonist Agnese Filoppina bears the child of priest Gelsomino Merlino and, while bearing the brunt of the village's scorn, marries simpleton Michele Dantone and leaves with son Giovanni for Italian Harlem. Never truly loving her husband, Agnese saves her affection for her business rival Antonio Farinella and Padre Gelsomino, who flees Villetto for America soon after Agnese leaves. Meanwhile, in the business plot, Agnese builds, from humble beginnings and through often-dubious means, a real-estate empire that dazzles her fellow Italian immigrants and shames her do-nothing husband. While these characters endlessly pursue love and money—"the fire in the flesh" that motivates them—one character, the young painter Giovanni Dantone, seeks transcendence from his prosaic surroundings through art.

In Lapolla's second published novel, *Miss Rollins in Love*, also set in Italian Harlem, orphaned and intellectually gifted protagonist Donato Contini and thirty-year-old classics teacher Amy Rollins are at the center of both the business and love plots. In the former, Donato and Amy must cope with a cold, rigid, and often hostile school system ill-equipped to nurture the talents of Donato. In the latter, Donato and Amy engage in a torrid sexual affair that, while in some ways symbolic of the proper loving relationship between student and teacher, is both flawed and short lived. Still, Donato is able to rise above the hurtful circumstances of his life: his gangster brother is executed; his mother dies of a broken heart; and his father, an accomplished but financially unsuccessful puppeteer, dies soon after his wife. Donato's success in his father's profession blossoms into a life-long passion for sculpture, which provides him with transcendental and, then, when he encounters fame and fortune, physical escape from his harsh surroundings.

The Grand Gennaro

Its first chapters set during the late-nineteenth-century flood of Italian immigration to the United States, Lapolla's third and final published novel, *The Grand Gennaro*, tells the story of Gennaro Accuci, a Calabrian immigrant to Italian Harlem who rises from a small-time laborer to owner of a junk business, and then "minor dictator" of the local Italian American community.[25] By pluck, luck, and unscrupulous business practices, Gennaro is able to "make America" and become "The Grand Gennaro," in effect an Italian American "Great Gatsby." In imitation of the most aggressive of Gilded Age industrialists, Gennaro, who at the beginning of the narrative is a penniless laborer, violently wrests control of his friend Rocco Pagliamini's junk business. Gennaro's assimilative program of hyper-masculine greed and brute force is ironically underscored by the series of women he beds (consensually or not), molests, or otherwise abuses—before and after he finally sends for his wife Rosaria and his children Domenico, Emilio, and Elena. The fortunes of the once *contadino* (peasant) Accuci family from Capomonte invite comparison to those of the Dauri and Monterano families, who were *galantuomini* (gentry) in Italy—the Dauris having been minor landowners from Villetto and the Monteranos full-blown aristocrats from Castello-a-Mare. When the three families move into an ostentatious brownstone Gennaro purchases called Parterre, the Accuci occupy the first floor, the Dauri the second, and the Monterani the third, an ironic, if archetypically New World, reversal of Old World status.[26] As Rosaria remains hopelessly Old World in her thought, ways, and appearance, Gennaro falls for a younger, more Americanized, second-generation Italian American woman, Carmela Dauri, who, unlike Rosaria, exhibits all the benefits of an American education. Meanwhile, Rosaria, driven mad by her strange American environment, stung by Gennaro's infidelity, wounded by her eldest son's death in Cuba during the Spanish-American War, and unmoved by her husband's too-late attention to her, falls seriously ill. Her only hope of survival is thought to be a temporary return to Italy, but she dies before her arrival, freeing Gennaro and Carmela to marry.

Toward the end of the narrative, however, Gennaro grows increasingly uneasy with his aggressive Americanism. He humanizes his business practices and, remorseful for having robbed Rocco Pagliamini of a livelihood, makes his old friend the manager of his rag business. Gennaro also sees the fruition of a long-term project: the construction of Saint Elena the Blessed, a Catholic church for local Italian Americans. Initially a monument of self-serving hubris, the church, in Gennaro's state of moral reformation, becomes a kind of penance. Rocco, however, has never forgiven Gennaro and even stirs up discontent among Gennaro's workers, who threaten to strike for better wages. When Gennaro manages to settle the labor dispute peacefully and beneficially for the workers, Rocco, enraged from another defeat by his former friend, murders Gennaro. Like so many other European immigrant protagonists—Abraham Cahan's Yekl and David Levinsky, Guido d'Agostino's Emilio Gardella, and Samuel Ornitz's Meyer Hirsch, to name just a few—Gennaro is made to pay for his hyper-assimilative indiscretion.

Like Lapolla's first two novels, *The Grand Gennaro* is written for a readership for whom the matter of Italian immigration, having all but ended with the immigration restriction laws of the 1920s, was settled. However, the matter of Italian American fitness for citizenship was anything but—a fact clearly evidenced by Italian American writers' continued tendency throughout the 1930s and 1940s to explore the troubled relationship between Italian cultural baggage and American ideals. While Lapolla was suspicious of literature as propaganda, his topical and thematic choices were no accident. Given his ethnic background and socialist orientation, it is unsurprising that he chose to write about those most vulnerable of citizens he knew so well, Italian Americans. And given his role as an educator, one could view Lapolla's literary oeuvre as a lesson to his fellow citizen-students on the full range of Italian American humanity in all its contradictory complexity, which—better than any polemical statement—served to counteract stereotypes that continued to plague them.[27] Reviews of and scholarship about Lapolla's works seem to indicate that his lesson found some sympathetic ears.

While Lapolla's first two novels earned mixed praise from the *New York Herald Tribune*, the *New York Times*, and *Gazzetta del Popolo*, neither was as well received as *The Grand Gennaro*, which earned effusive praise from most reviewers when it was published in 1935.[28] Since then, scholars of Italian American literature have noted the novel's importance in the tradition: first Olga Peragallo in *Italian American Authors and Their Contribution to American Literature* (1949) and Rose Basile Green in *The Italian American Novel: A Document of the Interaction of Two Cultures* (1974), and then, from the 1980s until the present, critics such as Thomas J. Ferraro, Robert Viscusi, Martino Marazzi, Lawrence J.

Oliver, Robert A. Orsi, Richard A. Meckel, Fred L. Gardaphé, and Neil Larry Shumsky.[29] In a statement indicative of the critical consensus, Thomas J. Ferraro considers The Grand Gennaro to be one of the most "sadly forgotten" Italian American novels.[30]

This neglect is puzzling, for the novel fits comfortably within a strong tradition of European immigrant fiction from the 1890s through the 1930s dramatizing the collision of Old and New World cultures and the struggle to establish an identity that brings the two into a viable, if uneasy, equilibrium—neither destroying the other. Scholars have documented *The Grand Gennaro*'s impact as an acculturation novel that fictionalizes the process by which an immigrant becomes American while it warns of the sacrifices demanded of the overly aggressive assimilator.[31] An important sacrifice for Gennaro is his friendship with Rocco Pagliamini. When Gennaro steals his friend's business, Rocco, aghast, marvels at how Gennaro has rapidly acculturated to the worst attributes of American capitalism: "The touch of gold in your hands has been too much. We peasants are not used to it. It does queer things to us—the good it makes mean, the mean it makes brutal."[32] Indeed, throughout the novel, Gennaro's wild assimilative drive is often figured in terms of violence and brutality.

To be sure, no discussion of this novel is complete *without* reference to its fictionalization of the Italian immigrant's acculturative process whose goal is to be taken or mistaken for a native-born American. However, while *The Grand Gennaro* shares many characteristics with narratives of passing,[33] including the protagonist's assimilative strategies, his professional success, and his adoption of American ideals, at no point does Gennaro attempt to blend completely into white middle-class culture. Although acculturated to American ways, Gennaro's manner and appearance are still decidedly ethnic, and he never leaves the locale of Italian Harlem to seek his fortune in the American mainstream. Gennaro's difference is perhaps best symbolized by the tell-tale earrings he wears, which once belonged to his grandfather and then his father. Taking great pride in having become a success as an Italian immigrant, he boasts early in the narrative, "I made America single-handed, and wearing earrings. I'll keep on making America and wearing earrings" (*GG* 1.3.7). Thus, Gennaro conjoins his assimilation with his proud maintenance of visible ethnic difference—and does so proudly and defiantly. At his colossal funeral, one attendant quips that had Gennaro been able to witness the event, he would have proclaimed, "I made America" (*GG* 1.3.12).

"Making America," that curious and outlandish locution with many "subtle and all-absorbing demands" to use Robert Orsi's wording, states the novel's theme early, recurs often, and motivates its every action.[34] Literally, the phrase refers to Gennaro's and, contextually, Italian immigrants' participation in the building of America's infrastructure.[35] In his rise from junk laborer to builder and proprietor, Gennaro is shown to "make America" as if from scratch. As Gennaro anticipates the arrival of his family from Calabria, he has his new house Italianized as if to boast the immigrants' ability to re-create America with a distinctly Italian presence: "Painters. . . worked night and day. When they were through the walls had become dazzling displays of Italian landscape. Stromboli on the ground floor puffed out lazy clouds of smoke . . . Aetna on the next floor belched black horror . . . And on the walls along the staircases the conical Vesuvius smoked incessantly . . . over the Bay of Naples" (*GG* 1.4.6). As Robert Viscusi has observed, Gennaro is attempting "to make a *new Italy* in America."[36] Then later, as the Church of Saint Elena is built, Gennaro surveys the superstructure and tells Carmela, "Real American stuff . . . Steel beams . . . not your old wooden frames . . . this is a building, I tell you" (*GG* 3.1.8). Lapolla is careful to exemplify "making America" in the most concrete terms possible.

Nearly all reviewers and critics of the novel point out the centrality of "making America" to *The Grand Gennaro* and how, for Gennaro Accuci, it becomes not only a *raison d'être* but a monomaniacal obsession to be pursued at any ethical cost. However, a more thorough examination of the phrase's figurative possibilities is necessary to appreciate fully the richness of *The Grand Gennaro*. Rose Feld first acknowledged the "many sided implications" of the expression.[37] Some sixty years later, Robert Viscusi explored its Italian origins, which, due to the double meaning of the verb *fare*, provide insight into the phrase's figurative play: "*Fare l'America*. Make America. Do America. This phrase . . . names the enterprise of many an emigrant from Italy. *Fare l'America* means not only *to go elsewhere than in Italy*."[38] Figuratively, the phrase means "making it" in America or "making good," which the narrator offers as an admittedly inadequate "approximation" (*GG* 1.1.2). In the novel, "making America" involves all the characteristics of a male-centered American success story and bears special significance for the lowly immigrant:

> it means that a nobody, a mere clodhopper, a good-for-nothing on the other side, had contrived by hook or crook in this new,

strange country, with its queer ways and its lack of distinctions, to amass enough money to strut about and proclaim himself the equal of those who had been his superiors in the old country . . . Gennaro Accuci had made America, and he was not the type to soft-pedal the expression. He pounded his sturdy small chest with his rough-knuckled small hand . . . and declared mightily . . . , "I, I made America, and made it quick." (*GG* 1.1.2)

However, Gennaro intends to sidestep all the Franklinian grunt work that is part and parcel of the myth of success. When Rocco Pagliamini first hires Gennaro as a laborer in his junk business, he tells his friend with the knowing sincerity of someone who has done it himself, "You got to sweat, my son; you got to starve; you got to turn your own relatives away starving." Still, Gennaro boastfully asserts, "I'm going to make America, and make it quick" (*GG* 1.1.3). And make it quick he does. Gennaro quickly recognizes the reality of Rocco's narrative of labor and comes to resent it. He begins pocketing a small portion of each junk sale he makes. Before long, through physical prowess and sheer cunning, Gennaro demands half and then all of Rocco's business before unethically conquering the local "old-rag-and-metal industry" (*GG* 1.1.5). "The King of Harlem" is Martino Marazzi's epithet for Gennaro with his parades, his celebrations, and ultimately, his construction for the Italian community of the Church of Saint Elena the Blessed. This pinnacle of his achievement, along with the other concrete images of his industry, vividly symbolizes Gennaro's success in making America.[39] Even the aftermath of his murder at the hands of Rocco, who shoves Gennaro's lifeless corpse into a bale, then raises with a crane, and swings it over the East River, becomes a "blood-soaked symbol of Gennaro's success and failure in making America."[40] Supplied with a healthy dose of Dantean poetic justice, the scene connects Gennaro's punishment with his sin and renders him as solitary as his reckless individualism has ultimately left him.

Another figurative connotation is the assimilative impulse foregrounded in the bulk of ethnic literature. As Robert Viscusi points out, "To make America means to construct oneself," and indeed another meaning of the phrase that suggests itself, keeping in mind *fare*'s semantic double-duty, is the immigrant's imperative to *make* himself or herself American and *do* as the Americans do.[41] *The Grand Gennaro* abundantly records its protagonist's insatiable hunger to act American, consume all things American, indeed, to *become* American so that when he says he has "made America," he is clearly describing not only what he has done but also who he is. Upon losing sole control of his junk business, Rocco can only observe as he signs over half of his enterprise to Gennaro, "Well, you have made America, and made it quick. You were born an American" (*GG* 1.1.4). When he is forced out completely, Rocco accuses Gennaro of having "the American fever," a tendency among upwardly mobile immigrants unaccustomed to wealth and prestige to embody the most destructive attributes of capitalism (*GG* 1.1.5).

In the fictional world of *The Grand Gennaro*, becoming American necessitates cultivating a lust for moneymaking. When Gennaro helps create a new millinery business for Davido Monterano, the dandified don exclaims, more than a little ridiculously, that his "whole being is being remade in the furnace of American ideals" and that the "business acumen" demonstrated by Gennaro "moves the stars . . . and all the other worlds, for it is greater than all things, . . . even love" (*GG* 2.5.3). However, Davido Monterano is at best a figurehead of a business owner who contributes little to the day-to-day affairs of the millinery center and, foiled by Gennaro in his pursuit of Carmela Dauri and mystified by his New World subservience to the former contadino, "collapse[s] into a self-pitying, helpless old man sustained only by his passionate adherence to Old World conceptions of greatness" (*GG* 3.1.2). When he dies crazed and destitute, Gennaro knows exactly why: "He could never be an American. He could never make America. His life was in Italy, and to that could he go back?" (*GG* 3.1.7).

None of this is to suggest that Gennaro's success comes entirely at the cost of his Italian past. Immigrant texts often privilege a fluid negotiation of Old and New World influences (by which, for example, Gennaro's earrings may appear "bright and shining" "not" as "incongruous ornaments" of the Old World worn by a man with New World aspirations but truly "part of the man") that ruptures the traditional dichotomization of the two (*GG* 2.5.6).[42] As Thomas Ferraro has demonstrated in his readings of Anzia Yezeierska's *Bread Givers* (1925) and Mario Puzo's *The Godfather* (1969), American immigrant literature often puts Old World folkways in the very service of accruing New World wealth.[43] Gennaro continues to identify as a once lowly Calabrian immigrant. His "unabashed and unembarrassed" wearing of his father's earrings as "the signs of [his] origins," his sponsoring of many ethnic festivals, his service to his fellow Italian immigrants, his establishment of an Italian millinery business, and his construction of an

Italian church—all serve to further his wealth and prestige, and assist in his self-fashioning as an American, his making himself American and doing as the Americans do (*GG* 2.5.3).

Gennaro's socioeconomic transformation into an American, his Columbian "discovery" and "conquest" of America, has a symbolic analogue in the series of women he attempts to claim as the spoils of his imperial victory. Indeed, the suggestive phrase "making America" cleverly conjoins Gennaro's assimilative drive with its sexual underbelly, and Lapolla is careful to lend cultural valence to the protagonist's love interests and victims. In doing so, Lapolla extends a historiographic trope that has long captivated Americans, for there is a long tradition of representing the subjugation of North America in frankly sexual terms. To begin with, in his evocatively titled classic *Virgin Land: The American West as Symbol and Myth* (1950), Henry Nash Smith argues that "one of the most persistent generalizations concerning American life and character is the notion that our society has been shaped by the pull of a vacant continent drawing population westward through the passes of the Alleghenies, across the Mississippi Valley, over the high plains and mountains of the Far West to the Pacific Coast."[44] In the imagination of European Americans of the Early Republic, the unsettled wilderness "is presented as a new and enchanting region of inexpressible beauty and fertility"—feminine qualities beckoning the male conqueror.[45] Thus, the exploration and settling of the continent—"the conquest of America" as Tzvetan Todorov describes it in his historical and theoretical study of the same name—seems almost inevitably to coincide with the subjugation and exploitation of its native women.[46] The female American continent awaits, indeed requires, the rule of the male conqueror.

The literary symbolism of this mythology is perhaps best explored by Annette Kolodny in *The Lay of the Land* (1975), in which she argues that "America's oldest and most cherished fantasy" is "a daily reality of harmony between man and nature based on the experience of the land as essentially feminine . . . enclosing the individual in an environment of receptivity, repose, and painless and integral satisfaction."[47] From the perspective of such an integrative mythology, John Rolfe's 1614 marriage to Pocahontas takes on great significance, and much of America's literary tradition, from its pastoral beginnings—in which the New World significantly was personified as "Columbia"—through to modern times, would symbolically figure the "virgin land" and its inevitable male conquest.[48] The implications of this transaction become obvious and familiar in its connection to the American myth of progress; its service, once the frontier was considered closed in 1893, of the Gospel of Wealth; and, as always, its invitation to violence.[49]

Mary V. Dearborn has identified a tradition in American literary history of encounters between symbolic European male John Rolfes and ethnically Other female Pocahontases—particularly in literature that foregrounds questions of national and/or ethnic identity.[50] It would seem, however, that when the John Rolfe figure is himself ethnic, then the Pocahontas figure, in order to be more "native" by contemporary standards, moves closer to the white American ideal. Just as Annette Kolodny views ethnically suspect Jay Gatsby's pursuit of the unquestionably American Daisy Buchanan as a modern recurrence of Virgin Land mythology, so may we view Gennaro Accuci's pursuit of American(ized) women.[51] Indeed, in his sexual exploits, Gennaro proves he has the "aggressive temperament" thought necessary of an immigrant male on the make, particularly as was understood by Italian American men, who drew upon centuries-old traditions of masculine decorum in order to define their relation to the public and private spheres.[52]

When Gennaro brutishly claims Italian American housekeeper Zia Nuora as his own, it becomes difficult for him to imagine sending for Rosaria and his family in Italy. Unlike Gennaro's hopelessly untutored, Old World wife, Nuora is smarter and prettier, and exhibits the cosmopolitan, more easily Americanized manner of a Northern Italian. Gennaro views her as more than a lover: "To lie in her arms at night, the men sleeping in the other rooms, not daring to whisper what they knew, fed his ego, proved his vast success in America!" (*GG* 1.1.7). As the arrival of Gennaro's family nears, the reader is told that thoughts of his wife "disturbed him. They did more than disturb him. They angered him. She seemed the living proof of another life from which he had fled. He had come into new ways and into new thoughts, and she would be filled with the old notions" (*GG* 1.5.1). Indeed, her Old World otherness is rendered physically in her lack of sexual desirability. When she arrives, Gennaro "found it impossible to say a word to her. She seemed so different with her Italian shoes, her laced bodice, her swinging skirts, her hair, braided and wound around her head, her skin burned with sun despite the long voyage" (*GG* 1.5.2).

As Werner Sollors has demonstrated, American literature of consent (one's willed actions) and descent (one's ancestral culture) frequently associates Old and New World experience with love interests who come to embody one or the other.[53] *The Grand Gennaro* is no exception: while Rosaria conjures up images of the protagonist's Old World, hardship-filled past of descent, Nuora reminds him of the freedom and success he has found in his New World life of consent. Gennaro himself makes the connection for Nuora: "'I was not like this, ever,' he said. 'Only my wife before this. No other woman. There's something grown up in me, a madness, I don't know, ever since . . . I picked up without saying good-bye, owing everybody money . . . I found this thing growing in me. . . It's a strength but a bad strength. That's why when you laughed and you made jokes and you stood up with your fine body tall and strong, your hair like my wife's, the strength came" (*GG* 1.1.6). Thus, Gennaro's sexual prowess increases as he comes closer to living the New World life he seeks, and, time and time again, money and sex are textually conjoined to help drive home the point. When explaining to his peers why he chooses to stay in America, Gennaro says that it is not simply because "the women here are easy to get and the money is easy to make" (*GG* 1.2.2).

More than notches on the proverbial bedpost, the women he so easily gets come closer to embodying the polar opposite of Rosaria, who, not being "a prize he had wrested . . . out of the air of a new environment," simply does not fit into his New World narrative (*GG* 1.5.3). After Zia Nuora, Gennaro takes a liking to Dora Levin, the native-born second-generation American daughter of a Jewish push-cart salesman. When he brings her back to his house, unashamed of the scandal this undoubtedly will cause, the narrator tells us: "And here he was now, head of a holy society, house-owner, a big business in hands, commanding the women he wanted when he wanted, and no one saying him 'nay'" (*GG* 1.3.4). Next, he pursues and brings home a dancer named Miss Waterson. Much to the chagrin of community moralists like Zia Anna and Don Anselmo, this sets off a string of orgiastic house parties fit for a Roman conqueror. But Lapolla's depictions of Gennaro's sexual exploits veer toward the ironic when he is shown to be ultimately fallible.[54] Dora Levin sees other men, Miss Waterson calls Gennaro "an Eyetalian," and another dancer temporarily steals his earrings. All three women provoke him to animalistic violence (*GG* 1.3.7, 1.4.1, 1.4.5). As if to underscore the point, Lapolla later has Don Tomaso tearfully tell his wife Donna Sofia, "We've made America at last" when his daughter Carmela is raped by Gennaro's son Domenico, forcing the two into a temporary honor marriage that would have made the Dauri family "rich" (*GG* 2.5.3).

Significantly, Gennaro is not allowed true happiness in love until he revises his stance toward assimilation, humanizes his business practices, and ceases to see women as material prizes to accumulate. After her marriage is annulled at the suggestion of Protestant social workers and she is sent to boarding school, Carmela becomes a perfectly integrated second-generation Italian American character, living and working among Italians but exhibiting all the qualities of the professionally and intellectually well-adjusted "new woman" described in works by Henry James, Kate Chopin, and Sarah Orne Jewett: "She spoke English so fluently, she went about with so much assurance and poise, she must certainly understand a good deal. She had been educated in the American way, dressed in the American way, held herself up in an unmistakable American way, easy, self-contained, always unembarrassed" (*GG* 2.4.5). "*Quella buona buona*"[55] and "*l'Americana*," Carmela is transformed into the perfect mate—neither too Italian nor too American—for Gennaro, who is by then neither a *contadino* nor a conqueror (*GG* 3.1.1).

Ethnic and National Literary Traditions

"Making America" also refers to Gennaro and immigrants of all varieties making and remaking the cultural and social fabric of America, participating in the building of that storied "nation of nations" Walt Whitman celebrates in *Leaves of Grass* (1855). Italians were the largest national group of the so-called New Immigration—the wave of southern and eastern European migrants who arrived in the United States between 1880 and 1924—who conservative commentators believed were waging a genetic war on an Anglo-Teutonic America peopled by earlier, purportedly superior migrants from northern and western Europe. The new immigration had its share of sympathizers in socially liberal, if Eurocentric, melting pot theorists and cultural pluralists—the former believing that distinct immigrant groups would seamlessly intermix and the latter believing that they would, and should, remain at least somewhat culturally distinct. But it had far more detractors among Anglo-conformists, who believed that immigrants should acculturate wholeheartedly to the dominant culture, and immigration restrictionists who advocated their outright exclusion from the body politic. However, if they all agreed about one thing, it was about the immigrant's power to reenact the *Mayflower* voyage and remake America anew. Lapolla helps the reader visualize this process by describing the succession of ethnic groups inhabiting the neighborhood in which *The Grand*

Gennaro is set and does so in a historical narrative discourse that gives the immigrants' cultural footprints the fixity of a *fait accompli*:

> In the decade beginning with 1880 the East River front in Harlem was a quiet near-suburban locality, prized for residences by German and Irish immigrants long enough in the country to have established prosperous businesses . . . They are all gone, these houses, now—all but a few . . . Into them rushed the peasants that had left their impoverished farms in Calabria or Sicily, in the Apuglie, or in Basilicata. (*GG* 1.1.1)

Indeed, as Robert Viscusi notes, *The Grand Gennaro* "shows Italianization and Americanization as parallel processes in the Italian Harlem of the 1890s."[56] Lapolla's Harlem was a microcosm of a broader national trend well documented in early twentieth-century American literature of immigration—the symbiotic relationship between the immigrant and the United States, one continually remaking the other with the tools of history, culture, and tradition.

Finally, "making America" reminds us of Garibaldi M. Lapolla's authorial gesture in all his novels. Having undergone the "ethnic passage" of all writers who wish to move "out of immigrant confines into the larger world of letters," as Thomas J. Ferraro phrases it, Lapolla was free to participate in the creation of a national literature as it debated, figured, and refigured just what it means to be an American.[57] The titling of the *The Grand Gennaro* is clearly a revisiting of F. Scott Fitzgerald's *The Great Gatsby* (1925), a more canonically credentialed text, much as its plot less directly rehearses that of *The Great Gatsby*. Like *The Great Gatsby*, The Grand Gennaro features a main character who escapes humble outsider origins, establishes himself as an all-American man on the make, consummates his self-transformation by bedding an all-American woman, becomes a business giant by a combination of honest and not-so-honest means, holds lavish celebrations as a testament to his greatness, and meets an unfortunate end that nonetheless feels to reader like a kind of punishment for his excesses. *The Grand Gennaro*, then, can be viewed as an Italian American revisioning of that classic work. In effect, Lapolla was pioneering an ethnically specific canon, the emerging tradition of Italian American literature comprising writers such as Antonio Arrighi (1837–1920), Constantine Panunzio (1884–1964), and Silvio Villa (1882–1927), at the very same time that he was contributing to the enrichment of the American literary tradition.

Those interested in learning about the contributions of Italian Americans to this American literary tradition would do well to begin with *The Grand Gennaro*, for it embodies many thematic and aesthetic characteristics central to Italian American literature in its infancy. The novel captures Italian immigrants immediately after the jarring experience of transatlantic migration and thereby gives the reader access to the intense feelings of dislocation and alienation that resulted from this journey. The novel also depicts the material and cultural sacrifices many Italian immigrants thought necessary for survival in the strange new world in which they found themselves. *The Grand Gennaro* colorfully describes the life, customs, and folkways of Italian Harlem, providing the reader with a rich survey of how its inhabitants worked, played, ate, celebrated, sang, worshipped, lived, and loved. Additionally, Lapolla strikes a fascinating balance—one that is common to early Italian American literature—between detail-driven realism and emotion-driven romanticism. Finally, Lapolla accomplishes all of the above through that most American of forms, the success story.

However, as he infuses an American success story with literary *italianità*—an expression proposed by Anthony Julian Tamburri as a means to read Italian American literary difference—Lapolla does more than build up an ethnic and national literature.[58] In his Italian-tinged signification, he also challenges readers' understanding of America itself. And if we accept, as does Robert Anthony Orsi, that symbolism interacts with individuals to create community, we must recognize the role of works like *The Grand Gennaro* in the construction of not only Italian American, but also American, community.[59] As he "invents Italian America" through his writing, as Fred L. Gardaphé would word it, or as he "writes Italy across America,"[60] as Robert Viscusi would, Lapolla reminds readers of the immigrants' transformative effect upon American history and culture and, indeed, participates in this very process himself.

Notes

1. Thomas J. Ferraro, "Ethnicity in the Marketplace," in *The Columbia History of the American Novel*, ed. Emory Elliott (New York: Columbia University Press, 1991), 398.
2. Maria Luisa, "Conversazioni del Giovedì," *Il Progresso Italo-Americano*, April 2, 1953, 1; Olga Peragallo, *Italian-American Authors and Their Contribution to American Literature*, ed. Anita Peragallo (New York: S. F. Vanni, 1949), 138; Martino Marazzi, "King of Harlem: Garibaldi Lapolla and Gennaro Accuci 'Il Grande,'" in

'Merica: A Conference on the Culture and Literature of Italians in North America, ed. Aldo Bove and Giuseppe Massara (Stony Brook, N.Y.: Forum Italicum, 2005), 190, 207.

3. Lawrence J. Oliver, "'Beyond Ethnicity': Portraits of the Italian-American Artist in Garibaldi Lapolla's Novels," *American Studies* 28, no. 2 (1987): 6; Robert Hornsby, e-mail message to Belluscio, October 2, 2007. Lapolla's degrees were granted by Columbia College, not Columbia Teachers College, as has been erroneously assumed.

4. Mortimer J. Adler, *Philosopher at Large: An Intellectual Biography* (New York: Macmillan, 1977), 2; *New York Times,* January 14, 1954, 29.

5. From the book jacket of the Vanguard Press edition of *The Fire in the Flesh* (1931), oversized folder 1, MSS 64, Garibaldi M. Lapolla Papers, Historical Society of Pennsylvania, Philadelphia (these papers are hereafter cited as GMLP).

6. "Editor's Notebook," *Sunday Herald,* June 21, 1953, newspaper clipping, box 4, folder 12, GMLP.

7. Garibaldi M. Lapolla, *Italian Food for the American Kitchen* (New York: Wilfred Funk, 1953), ix.

8. Paul Lear, e-mail message to Belluscio, October 1, 2007; Paul Lapolla, telephone interview by Belluscio, June 25, 2007.

9. *Ontario Post,* September 22, 1917; September 29, 1917; December 8, 1917; April 20, 1918; May 25, 1918; June 1, 1918.

10. Marc K. Blackburn, "Register of the Garibaldi M. Lapolla Papers," GMLP, 1–2; *New York Times,* January 14, 1954, 29.

11. This quotation, taken from the book jacket of *The Fire in the Flesh* (1931), is qtd. in Blackburn, "Register," 2.

12. "Teachers Oppose Loss of Royalties," *New York Times,* September 17, 1946, 7; "Principals Lose Pay Case," *New York Times,* June 2, 1950, 12.

13. "Teachers Secretly Quizzed on Loyalty," *New York Times,* May 17, 1922, 18; Norman Thomas et al., "The Religion of Free Men," letter to the editor, *New Republic,* May 26, 1917, 109.

14. Upton Sinclair, *The Goslings: A Study of the American Schools* (Pasadena, Calif.: Upton Sinclair, 1924), 84.

15. Garibaldi M. Lapolla, "Letter in Answer to Dr. Lefkowitz about So-Called Communist Teachers," box 1, folder 2, 3–5, GMLP.

16. Blackburn, "Register," 2.

17. Garibaldi Lapolla to Mark O. Lapolla, returned letters, December 25, 1944; January 7, 1945; January 15, 1945; January 31, 1945; February 6, 1945, box 1, folder 3, GMLP.

18. "Missing Flight Officer Now Is Reported Killed," *New York Times,* January 6, 1946, 30.

19. Paul Lapolla, telephone interview by Belluscio, November 11, 2007. Lapolla, European trip diary, 1953, box 1, folder 9, GMLP.

20. Robert Anthony Orsi, *The Madonna of 115th Street: Faith and Community in Italian Harlem, 1880–1950* (New Haven, Conn.: Yale University Press, 1985), 22. Richard A. Meckel considers Lapolla to be "as good as many of the better known ethnic/immigrant social realists of the 1930s and 1940s" ("A Reconsideration: The Not So Fundamental Ideology of Garibaldi Marto Lapolla," MELUS 14, nos. 3/4 [1987]: 127); and Lawrence J. Oliver claims, "outside of Puzo and Pietro di Donato, no writer has so skillfully portrayed the marble beneath the mud, to use Nathaniel Hawthorne's expression, of the Italian-American immigrant experience" ("'Great Equalizer' or 'Cruel Stepmother'?: Image of the School in Italian-American Literature," *The Journal of Ethnic Studies* 15, no. 2 [1987]: 116).

21. Marazzi, "King of Harlem," 191; Meckel, "A Reconsideration," 128.

22. Garibaldi Lapolla, "The American Novel," box 2, folder 3, GMLP.

23. Ibid.

24. As Lawrence J. Oliver writes, "Lapolla's novels display the ethical idealism—the belief that the people can rise above corrupting and degrading influences to a higher moral plane—that marks . . . romantic literature in general. Indeed, if a label must be applied to Lapolla's novels, the most appropriate would be that coined by Frank Norris, 'romances of the commonplace'" ("Beyond Ethnicity," 18–19).

25. Rose Basile Green, *The Italian-American Novel: A Document of the Interaction of Two Cultures* (Rutherford, N.J.: Farleigh Dickinson University Press, 1974), 74.

26. Robert Viscusi, *Buried Caesars and Other Secrets of Italian American Writing* (Albany: State University of New York Press, 2006), 65.

27. Meckel, "A Reconsideration," 129. Many thanks to Carla Peterson, Amritjit Singh, and C. Lok Chua for their assistance with this portion of the essay.

28. "'The Blind Man' and Other Recent Works of Fiction," *New York Times*, April 12, 1931, BR4; Harriet Sampson, "Winy Folks," review of *The Fire in the Flesh*, by Garibaldi M. Lapolla, *New York Herald Tribune Books*, April 5, 1931, 16; review of *Miss Rollins in Love*, by Garibaldi M. Lapolla, *New York Times*, February 28, 1932, BR7; Giuseppe Prezzolini, "*Stati Uniti: autobiografia e romanzo*," *Gazzetta del Popolo*, December 19, 1934; Fred T. Marsh, "'The Grand Gennaro' and Some Other Recent Works of Fiction," *New York Times*, September 1, 1935, BR6; Rose Feld, "'Making America' in Little Italy," review of *The Grand Gennaro*, by Garibaldi M. Lapolla, *New York Herald Tribune Books*, September 1, 1935, 4; review of *The Grand Gennaro*, *Saturday Review of Literature*, October 26, 1935, 28, 30; review of *The Grand Gennaro*, *Boston Transcript*, December 18, 1935, 3; Jerre Mangione, review of *The Grand Gennaro*, *New Republic*, October 23, 1935, 313; "Extracts from Reviews of *The Grand Gennaro*," box 3, folder 1, GMLP.

29. Ferraro, "Ethnicity and the Marketplace," 380–406; Viscusi, *Buried Caesars*; Robert Viscusi, "Italian American Literary History from the Discovery of America," in *The Italian American Heritage: A Companion to Literature and Arts*, ed. Pellegrino d'Acierno (New York: Garland, 1999), 151–164; Robert Viscusi, "Making Italy Little," in *Social Pluralism and Literary History: The Literature of Italian Emigration*, ed. Francesco Loriggio (Toronto: Guernica, 1966), 61–90; Marazzi, "King of Harlem," 190–210; Oliver, "Beyond Ethnicity," 5–21; Oliver, "'Great Equalizer' or 'Cruel Stepmother'?" 113–130; Lawrence J. Oliver, "The Re-Visioning of New York's Little Italies: From Howells to Puzo," *MELUS* 14, nos. 3/4 (Autumn–Winter 1987): 5–22; Orsi, *The Madonna of 115th Street*; Meckel, "A Reconsideration," 127–139; Fred L. Gardaphé, *Italian Signs, American Streets: The Evolution of Italian American Narrative* (Durham, N.C.: Duke University Press, 1996); Neil Larry Shumsky, "Return Migration in Modern Novels of the 1920s and 1930s," in *Writing Across Worlds: Literature and Migration* (New York: Routledge, 1995), 198–215.

30. Thomas J. Ferraro, *Feeling Italian: The Art of Ethnicity in America* (New York: New York University Press, 2005), 240.

31. To name a few, Orsi, *The Madonna of 115th Street*, 157; Carol Bonomo Albright, "Literature," in *The Italian American Experience: An Encyclopedia*, ed. Salvatore J. LaGumina, Frank J. Cavaioli, Salvatore Primeggia, and Joseph A. Varacalli (New York: Garland, 2000), 343; Green, *The Italian-American Novel*, 79. See also Meckel, "A Reconsideration," 128; Oliver, "Beyond Ethnicity," 6–7; Gardaphé, *Italian Signs, American Streets*, 184; and Fred L. Gardaphé, *Leaving Little Italy: Essaying Italian American Culture* (Albany: State University of New York Press, 2004), 6.

32. Garibaldi M. Lapolla, *The Grand Gennaro*, part 1, chapter 1, subchapter 5; Hereafter, this novel will be cited parenthetically in text as *GG*.

33. Famous American narratives of passing that feature African American characters who attempt to be taken for white include James Weldon Johnson's *The Autobiography of an Ex-Colored Man* (1912), Jessie Fauset's *Plum Bun* (1929), and Nella Larsen's *Passing* (1929).

34. Orsi, *The Madonna of 115th Street*, 155.

35. Oliver, "The Re-Visioning of New York's Little Italies," 15.

36. Viscusi, "Making Italy Little," 61.

37. Feld, "Making America," 4.

38. Viscusi, "Making Italy Little," 61.

39. Viscusi, *Buried Caesars*, 148.

40. Meckel, "A Reconsideration," 137.

41. Viscusi, "Making Italy Little," 61.

42. Robert A. Orsi, "The Fault of Memory: 'Southern Italy' in the Imagination of Immigrants and the Lives of Their Children in Italian Harlem, 1920–1945," *Journal of Family History* 15, no. 2 (1990): 138.

43. See chapters 1 and 2 of Thomas Ferraro, *Ethnic Passages: Literary Immigrants in Twentieth-Century America* (Chicago: University of Chicago Press, 1993).

44. Henry Nash Smith, *Virgin Land: The American West as Symbol and Myth* (Cambridge, Mass.: Harvard University Press, 1950), 3.

45. Ibid., 11.

46. Tzetvan Todorov, *The Conquest of America: The Question of the Other*, trans. Richard Howard (Norman: University of Oklahoma Press, 1999), 48–49, 58, 246.

47. Annette Kolodny, *The Lay of the Land: Metaphor as Experience and History in American Life and Letters* (Chapel Hill: University of North Carolina Press, 1975).

48. Ibid., 5, 6, 30; for a more detailed exploration of "Columbia" and early American literature, see Frank J. Cavaioli, "Columbus and the Rise of American Literature," in *New Explorations in Italian American Studies*, ed. Richard N. Juliani and Sandra P. Juliani (Staten Island, N.Y.: American Italian Historical Association, 1994), 3–17.

49. Kolodny, *The Lay of the Land*, 67, 133, 22.

50. Mary V. Dearborn, *Pocahontas's Daughters: Gender and Ethnicity in American Culture* (New York: Oxford University Press, 1986), 3–11.

51. Kolodny, *The Lay of the Land*, 138.

52. Shumsky, "Return Migration in American Novels of the 1920s and 1930s," 206; Fred L. Gardaphé, *From Wiseguys to Wisemen: The Gangster and Italian American Masculinities* (New York: Routledge, 2006), 15–20.

53. Werner Sollors, *Beyond Ethnicity: Consent and Descent in American Culture* (New York: Oxford University Press, 1986), 149–173.

54. Marazzi, "King of Harlem," 202–203.

55. That very good one.

56. Viscusi, "Italian American Literary History from the Discovery of America," 158.

57. Ferraro, *Ethnic Passages*, 8.

58. Anthony Julian Tamburri, *A Semiotic of Ethnicity: In (Re)cognition of the Italian/American Writer* (Albany: State University of New York Press, 1998), 14.

59. Orsi, *The Madonna of 115th Street*, 188.

60. Gardaphé, *Leaving Little Italy*, 13–35; Viscusi, *Buried Caesars*, 86–90.

THE GRAND *Gennaro*

To Priscilla

PART ONE

Gennaro

CHAPTER ONE

1

$\mathcal{T}$he singularly narrow house, three stories high, in which the destinies of the Accuci, the Dauri, and the Monterano families became hopelessly entangled, still throws its late afternoon shadow into the East River. The red bricks are dirtier, the fire-escapes rustier, the narrow stoop is worn down, the narrow glass-plots are bare. It wears the bitter, humorous air of an old relation, once rich, now fallen in with the indigent members of the family assembled at a reunion in which beer and pretzels have taken the place of champagne and fancy sandwiches. All about it dingy tenement houses, tumble-down frame houses, loft-buildings with broken window-panes, long rows of shacks that house the accumulations of hundreds of rag-pickers combine in a dismal demonstration of poverty. Only when the moonlight is clear and widespread, but not intense enough to reveal the numerous details of degradation, does a varnish fall upon the scene, and then the East River becomes a charmed expanse, its islands gem-like intaglios, and all the houses on the street that fronts it subdued into an intricate maze of phantoms. Guitar players are moved to strum sentimental Old World airs, and the children dance on the sidewalks.

In the decade beginning with 1880 the East River front in Harlem[1] was a quiet near-suburban locality, prized for residences by German and Irish immigrants long enough in the country to have established prosperous businesses. A solid German butcher with dubious notions of architecture had bought himself a plot not too far from the river to afford himself the luxury of a view and had erected upon it an odd oblong of a house, and just below the cornice had had the name PARTERRE inscribed in huge brownstone letters.

In it three Italian families, all from different sections of Italy, were to meet, mingle, and separate, each bearing in charred burdens of memory the shock of their encounter.

The depression that really had its beginnings in 1890 but delayed the full force of its fury until 1893,[2] had registered in Europe before it had become fully admitted into the United States. A stream of immigration began to pour into New York City. Especially from the southern portions of Italy great masses of people, for all the world like an ancient migration, braved the terrors of slow, weather-beaten steamers, and, once landed in New York, pooled into scattered communities throughout Manhattan. They accepted any place for a dwelling.

Harlem had already begun to show signs of a too great mellowness. The families that had built themselves rows upon rows of brownstones or spacious frame dwellings set far back from the street behind bush-shaded lawns had already raised their children to manhood. The children had gone off to the modernized apartments of gray stone overlooking the Hudson. The old people found themselves in possession of homes which had achieved through the years only the sadness of places that had once rung with numerous activities. Cherry wood interiors fell into disrepair, mahogany-banistered stairways creaked and lost newel or spindle, and the black-and-white mantelpieces gaped open where they had once been rigidly cemented.

They are all gone, these houses, now—all but a few which some of the second generation Italians, following obscure artistic impulses, have attempted to restore. Into them rushed the peasants that had left their impoverished farms in Calabria or Sicily, in the Apuglie, or in Basilicata. Where one family had lived, now five or six struggled for a bit of space for a bed and a chance at the only sink or water-closet.

In the back-yards, goats disported; in the front-yards, shacks mushroomed—old boards covered with rusty tin, plastered with Sunday supplements. In the streets swarmed tribes of children, bare-footed and scantily clad, forever unwashed but always screeching with glee.

2

Gennaro Accuci actually found a place in this confusion, and sent for his family. But he did not send for his family before he had succeeded in what he called, and all his fellow immigrants called, "making America." "Making good" is an approximation, but without body and associations. Something both finer and coarser clings to the expression. There is a suggestion of envy on the part of the user and also of contempt. For it means that a nobody, a mere clodhopper, a good-for-nothing on the other side, had contrived by hook or crook in this new, strange country, with its queer ways and its lack of distinctions, to amass enough money to strut about and proclaim himself the equal of those who had been his superiors in the old country. And if one said of himself that he had made America, he said it with an air of rough boasting, implying "I told you so" or "Look at me." Although he knew that his spectators would be inclined to despise him for the word, he threw out his chest. And yet there were comfort and solidity, the double fruit of egotism, in its use, and he used it, even roared it out, and laughed.

Gennaro Accuci had made America, and he was not the type to soft-pedal the expression. He pounded his sturdy small chest with his rough-knuckled small hand, having first thrust his heavy short-stemmed pipe between his teeth, and declared mightily, as best he could between closed lips, "I, I made America, and made it quick." And then, removing his pipe and allowing a slight interval to elapse, he would laugh and exclaim with a toss of the head that made his matted black curls move perceptibly, "And what's more, without kow-towing to anybody, see, no, by Saint Jerome, not a bit. I kept my earrings in my ears where my father pierced them through and I'll keep them unless the President in Washington sends me a telegram."

Seven years before, without so much as a by-your-leave to priest or mayor, to both of whom he owed money, he had slipped out of his mountain village and taken ship at Reggio for New York. He had not even told his plans to his wife. She was left with two boys, ten and two years old, and a girl of three weeks—others had mercifully died in between. She would manage somehow to keep up the farm, already overburdened with mortgages and taxes, and stave off starvation from herself and the children. The night before he had boarded *La Sicilia* he had gone to confession. But before going to confession he had knelt at the feet of Sant' Elena[3] in the old church near the docks and, pounding his breast very hard, but only once, he cried in prayer:

"I am leaving behind those I love, especially my oldest Domenico who should grow up and clear the farm of taxes and what I owe on it. It's the wars that eat up our substance. And I am leaving behind those to whom I owe money, but they shall never get it back from me. They take advantage of the poor, and they have the soldiers now everywhere and we cannot run off into the mountains with our women and raid the towns and hold the big folk for ransom and so regain what they steal from us.[4] I shall keep it all even when I make it to pay back, for such a day will come in America where I shall pray to you and keep your statue in a niche day and night with a lamp beneath. And especially I pray you, now that you know, to keep my son Domenico and make him strong and capable with his hands to be a help and an honor to me, and to be good to my wife and the other two children, Emilio the black-haired one, and Elena, named after you. And I promise you now to go to confession and lay bare my heart and do proper penance for my misdeeds, but do you speak for me before the Most High, our God and our Savior, and I shall be good in your eyes and pray to you and keep a lamp burning night and day under your statue, Sant' Elena, the blessed one."

Then he rose and looked about the church for the confessional. He had a mind to pull his pipe out of his pocket but contented himself with stroking his mustache with the back of his hand and stumping determinedly into the booth. He smiled as he came out, looked about him with the air of one who has completed a given task to his satisfaction, and thrusting his pipe into his mouth hurried out of the church.

Gennaro had never gone to school—in the village of Capomonte there were no schools—and the village priest had never got round to instructing him either in the writing of his name or the doing of simple sums on paper. Don Vito was much too old and there were so many children and the farms were none too close, and besides, what did it matter? One need not write his name before entering heaven. So Gennaro at the age of thirty-two had not learned to write or read, but he knew what was what and he made sure that his passport was in good order.[5]

He took out the complicated folds of paper on five portions of which was his photograph, and he knew where to look for the x's that marked his name, and he recognized also the picture of the new king, Humbert,[6] and the seal of the Italian realm. He had paid enough for the wax that went to affix the green ribbon on to the paper. Thankful that all was in order, he kissed the booklet fervently before returning it to his pocket, removed his hat as he passed the church, and hurried to the steamer.

3

Once in New York, he had found his way among the Calabresi already settled in Harlem. Most of them had gone into the small business of pushing a cart with an assortment of bells strung aloft and obtaining for nothing or a few pennies old clothes and rags. They lived like gypsies—in the basements of tenement houses disgracefully overcrowded, in old stores, in shacks in the backyards, some in improvised shanties knocked together out of old lumber and tar-paper and erected against the walls of houses adjacent to empty lots. Their dirty, bare-legged children overran the cobbled streets like the goats their families kept; the older ones made a business of petty thieving from the nearby wholesale markets, or collected, like their fathers but in less formal ways, old tins and coppers and lengths of lead-pipes, all of which they sold to junk-shops that lined the avenue.

Gennaro saw his chance at once. Rocco Pagliamini had been a child-hood friend. But in his youth, not being like Gennaro the youngest son, he went off to do his stint in the army and, leaving the army, had come right on to New York. He already had a flourishing junk business. The store stood on the corner where the horse cars went by and the wagons passed on their way to the markets and the ferry to Long Island. It was not an uncommon sight to see a huge flat-bottomed van with slats for sides back up against Rocco's store and take on dozens and dozens of bales of rags, all laboriously packed tight and neatly roped in rectangu-lar nets.

Pagliamini was big-chested, and swelling biceps made his arms look gigantic for a short man, especially with his thin, almost girlish, legs. For years now he had packed the bales himself, shoving them about, turning them upside down, stamping them down in the home-made bins with his heavy-weighted tamping irons, and the muscles of his upper structures had bulged and hardened and grown taut. His face alone, above his short sinewy neck, remained soft and laughing. He laughed frequently, for everything was funny to him, even when he managed to allow the tamping-iron to glance off his toes. He laughed if the horses pulled away just after the man had succeeded in lifting a troublesome bale on to the very top of the load and had not tied it down and the bale came tumbling back on them. He laughed in a thin girlish voice and called on the saints to witness how merry it all was. And he laughed when he saw Gennaro Accuci standing in front of his store, big as life.

"*Gennaru bellu, figliu du sacramentu di Gesu!*[7] In America! Why didn't you send us that much of a line (he showed a width of finger) to let us know, hey, you old shaved-off goat?"

They kissed on both cheeks, and since they had been childhood friends they laughed together and then they wept.

"And my mother?"

"Ah, the old thing," answered Gennaro, "still hobbles to church. The priest still lords it over the village."

"And how is he, the old . . . ?"

"Nothing against the old fellow, Rocco, by your leave," and putting his mouth to his friend's ear he whispered roguishly, "I owe him a thou-sand scuti[8]—that's why I'm here."

Rocco laughed. "We've got to have a feast and talk over old times. And what will you be doing here in America?"

"Making America."

"Hear that? Hear that?" Rocco cried to all his workmen who, bare-footed, shirtless, stood around enjoying the meeting between the old friends. "Going to make America at once! You got to sweat, my son; you got to starve; you got to turn your own relatives away starving. For instance, will you take off your coat now and pitch in among those filthy, dusty, worm-eaten rags and let the dirt get mixed up with your spittle and your sweat and laugh anyhow?

"I'm ready."

"Not like picking the big fat grapes off the vines."

The workmen laughed.

"Not like packing down the figs."

More laughter.

"Not like sticking the old pig after the harvest and salting down the hams and having a great feast to celebrate it all."

"I'm ready."

He was as good as his word and began at once. And that night Rocco invited all the *paesani*[9] that could be mustered together and, clearing away one of the back-yards, put up improvised tables on barrel ends and set up a keg of beer in a corner of it, and the beer flowed, and the talk flowed, and when Gennaro had drunk enough beer he got up and said boastfully, pounding his chest once with his closed fist, "I'm going to make America, and make it quick."

He worked hard in the rag-and-junk shop. The store was in reality a huge, spacious one, but the bins all along the walls and the piles of old lead and copper, pewter cans and spoons, the bales of rags, cluttered it all up, shut out the light and filled it with clouds of lint and flecks of metal small enough to float in the heavy air. The men coughed constantly between shouts and oaths and laughter at coarse jokes.

4

Gennaro watched his chance. He saw boys bringing in copper bottoms, lead-pipes, old pewter pots. He saw boys bringing in old pieces of plate, scraps of gold—tiny scraps, but gold—copper nails, zinc tubs battered down into lumps. He saw that these things brought in most money. He saw, too, that there were rags *and* rags. He learned soon to pick out the silks and grade them, pick out the linens and grade them, the percales, the cambrics, the broadcloths. He did it so well, Rocco made him chief-assorter and raised his pay. He put the money he got into an old earthen pot, and he buried the pot, peasant-like, in a corner of the backyard and dug it up only at night. He got permission to make a bunk for himself in the junk-shop and sleep there. Rocco told him he was crazy. It was hell to sleep in that place, hot and crawly with bugs, and the air was filled with lint and dust of the metals. But Gennaro knew his own mind.

He was thinking of Domenico, his oldest son almost going on eleven now, and Emilio the curly-haired one, the little girl, and of his wife, too, with her heavy bosoms and her big eyes that just looked at one wonderingly but filled with trust and affection. This was a dog's life, working for Rocco, working for anybody, fumbling through old rags, cutting one's fingers on tin and scraps of iron. What could he do on a dollar a day? He ate twenty cents of it and saved the eighty. What was that? That wouldn't make America. So he watched the boys coming in with old copper bottoms and pieces of lead-pipe. He took one aside, a slinking, thin lad with slit-like eyes that always looked frightened.

"One cent more a pound for the copper—half of the copper; the other half, the old price. But don't tell nobody."

Gennaro handled the pushcart ragmen the same way. He found ways ways of hiding the half he bought for himself. He succeeded in getting most of the boys to come after hours, late in the evening. It was then he sorted out his own purchases. He was honest enough in this for a while.

But it was slow work "making America," even in this way. So he threw one rag in every hundred into a pile meant for himself. These he bundled up into bags, but he soon found himself with too many bags, and so he built himself a shed in an empty lot and stored them there. The slit-eyed lad assisting, he carted over the stuff in the dead of night. One night in the week the boy piled up the stuff in an old push-cart and pushed it down to an appointed street far away from Rocco. There Gennaro met the youngster and they pushed the cart all the way down to Allen Street and sold the junk to the big Jewish dealers, and then pushed the empty cart all the way back, returning in the small hours of the morning, dead tired.

Rocco found out, and confronted Gennaro. They were alone in the store. The men had left for the day. It was the summer after the one when Gennaro had arrived, and extremely hot. The lint, the flying dirt, the close-packed bales, the piles of metal made the heat into a glue-like cloud that smelled throughout the store, stuck to the eyes of the men, gummed up their bare, sweated biceps, pasted strings of dirt along the neck-muscles.

"What's this I hear, *porcu diavolu?*"[10] Rocco began without preliminaries.

"You hear right."

That was all he said. Gennaro had struck Rocco over the jaw with the back of his fist, swinging his right arm from the left shoulder with terrific speed. Then he calmly stuck his pipe into his mouth and lit it, confident that he had knocked his man unconscious. He had. He waited for Rocco to come to, mopping his face, pulling up his trousers and tightening his belt. When he felt Rocco make the first stir, he planted his foot upon the man's chest and held the body down.

"Let me breathe."

After an interval Gennaro removed his foot, watching warily for the next move. But he knew that Rocco was too good-natured and trusting to carry a knife and must be much too weak to offer further resistance.

"Not a word, Rocco," he said curtly, puffing calmly on his pipe. "I'll give you up all I made, but I want half a share in the business."

"I should have known," Rocco mumbled. "You did the same when we were kids."

At this point the slit-eyed partner of Gennaro's schemes appeared out of a pile of rags.

"One more word, Rocco, and if that ain't yes. . . . What's the use? I'm telling you, you can't make America just working. It's too long to wait. Only bosses get along, like you, like Struzzo round the block owns all those houses. I'm not going to keep on working for others all my life. I got enough now to start my own business, but I'll join up with you and we'll go halves."

The slit-eyed boy gasped and then laughed. Gennaro struck him a blow with the flat of his hand and the boy fell down whimpering.

"All right," said Rocco.

"We go and sign. Come on."

They signed up in the café on the corner opposite, a big barn of a store with sawdust over the floor and three-legged tables smeared with the remains of spilled coffee, sugar and syrups. Cakes dipped in colored sugars, gummed together by the heat, were piled up in the windows. The place was hung with thick, acrid smoke. Gennaro and Rocco, looking groggy and uncertain on his feet, took seats at a table.

"Two coffees and some rum," Gennaro ordered.

In a minute a thin dapper young man in a double-breasted coat, with pants fitting close over his ankles, swung into the door behind a light bamboo cane that seemed to be pulling him along. Bronzed, with a sharp aquiline nose and thick eyebrows set in a narrow forehead, he looked Arabian.

"You're both here, then?" he asked jauntily of Gennaro and Rocco. "That's fine. I have the papers and we shall lose no time."

Salvatore Cicco passed for a lawyer, although he was employed only as a runner for a firm of lawyers. He plied a brisk business in Harlem, drawing contracts, business arrangements, leases, getting the ignorant out of jail for a consideration, fixing up trials even for the guilty, with such a string of successes to his credit that the community looked upon him as having some intimate connection with the law-making powers of the country.

He spread out the papers and they all signed, Gennaro with a cross, Rocco laboriously tracing huge letters across the page. He had learned to spell out his name in the army. After he had completed his difficult task, he looked up, and for the first time since the encounter in his junk-shop he could look Gennaro squarely in the face and laugh.

"Well, you have made America, and made it quick. You were born an American."

Salvatore Cicco extended a bony hand to both.

"Luck."

"Drinks to everybody," shouted Gennaro.

Everybody got a drink, and everybody drank, and that's how Gennaro made America, or really just began to make it. Gennaro did not sleep in the shop that night but insisted without hesitation or fear of contradiction that he would share Rocco's room. It was merely a matter of picking up an old cot at another of the junkies, throwing a mattress on it and placing the thing in any available space in Rocco's hired room.

5

Zia Nuora did not consider the arrangement at all unusual. In fact, it had seemed unnatural to her that Rocco had persisted in having his room all to himself. It overlooked a jumble of backyards which once had been miniature gardens and had contained shade trees. They were now neglected, and the inevitable old-lumber shacks with their tar-paper roofs dotted the yards. But because of the expanse of space behind it the room did have more than just a breath of air.

On hot nights Rocco delighted in pulling down his mandolin from where it hung on the wall near the picture of the Holy Virgin with a cresset under it and, sitting on the edge of his cot, bang away on his instrument the plaintive tunes of his native Calabria. He sang to himself in quiet tones, almost whispers, until, lost in the charm of the melody, he would forget himself, and his thin girlish voice would rise into clear tenor and hang poised on a melancholy "a" far above the surrounding noises. Zia Nuora would shake her head at such times in a slow process of memory, and with hands knuckled from hard work would press her breasts close to her and listen. When the song concluded, she would say to herself if necessary, or to anyone who was around, "Say, a man that can sing like that shouldn't waste his energy alone on a cot."

Gennaro spied the mandolin the first glance, and gave his chest a blow.

"By Saint Jerome and the Holy Calendar, you still have the old mandolin! Oohey there, Zia Nuora, fetch us a pitcher of wine and get another chair for your worthy self and we'll have a real *festa*.[11] We have made America tonight and we're celebrating. We'll stick the *don*[12] to our names yet, hey, Rocco?"

The celebration, however, fizzled out after three glasses of wine and a song.

Rocco did not respond to Gennaro's gay mood. When Zia Nuora had made up Gennaro's cot, without a word both men slipped off their outer garments and with no further preliminaries threw themselves on their cots and went off to sleep. Gennaro possessed enough self-confidence to be sure that his business with Rocco had been terminated to the satisfaction of both and that all that remained was to arrange some method of working together as bosses. So, grunting good-night, he shut his eyes and fell fast asleep at once.

There were no shades to the windows. The moonlight streamed in and etched the cots and the forms of the men sleeping on them. Except for a table against the wall between the two windows and a chair thrust under the table, there was no furniture. Some shelves on the wall on which were the few shirts and pieces of underlinen belonging to Rocco relieved the stark barrenness of the room. Between the windows hung a picture of the Virgin, with a red lamp burning under it.[13]

Quiet came in with the moonlight. An elevated locomotive on Second Avenue whistled shrilly and, as if in sympathy, a tug on the river wailed. Rocco kept looking at the ceiling. His eyes remained immobile, patient, watching. There was but one thought in his mind. After a while, gently, without the slightest sound, he reached under his mattress, lifting his body slowly, and pulled out a large jack-knife. He let some seconds elapse and turned his eyeballs in the direction of Gennaro on the other side of the room.

He turned on his right side with his back to Gennaro and opened the knife. He ran the blade between his thumb and index finger slowly. Satisfied with its sharpness, he hid it in his right hand, turned on his back and kept looking at the ceiling. After an interval, he slipped one foot off the bed, followed it with the other, and sat up. He saw an earring in Gennaro's ear dance with the moonlight.

Rocco was given to laughter and cheer and taking things as they came. He would rather be friends than drive a bargain; he would rather remain friendly than gain an advantage. He found it paid just as well. This man in the room with him, who had come from the old country with the determination to pile up a stack in a short time no matter how he did it, was outside the scope of his understanding. He had seen men like him and dealt with them in his business as best he could, and found that by holding to his own and giving way only under compulsion he could play an even game with them. But this man, sleeping so quietly at his side, with whom he had been comrades as a lad when they both looked after their fathers' sheep and goats on the mountains behind Reggio, was made of meaner stuff.

This man had stolen from him half of his business—a business that was making him wealthy, that would enable him to return to Italy and go back to the village in the Piedmont where he had soldiered and where he had met Elvira whom he was going to marry, Elvira with silk black hair, thin as cobwebs, and blue eyes that were like the morning light, who laughed so good-humoredly at his queer Calabrian accent and liked to pull at his short flat chin just because she couldn't get a good hold of it. She was waiting for him and he was intending to go back, in a year or two, no longer, and take over her father's holding. It was only a little cup of a farm in a mountain hollow but free of the dry winds that poured in from Africa despite the mountains, and rich in green grass, with luscious grapes big as plums on the slopes, a cow, and sheep, and real horses, not the small starved asses in his part of the world.

A tear fell down his cheek and he sucked it in with his lips. Would he kill now and ruin his entire future? But he would do it neatly—start right under where that earring gleamed and danced in the moonlight and slit his neck open the way they did pigs after the harvest. There would be no outcry. Like the rest of the men who were making America in those early immigrant days he kept his money with him: gold pieces, silver dollars, the big rag-like bills, suitable symbols of the work he did. It would be a minute's time to stuff them into his bag. He would be gone a moment after—the thieving swine would not wake up to give the alarm. Elvira would be horrified and would not join him in South America beyond the Andes where his brother had gone and was making his fortune. But he would give her a chance to choose. As he thought, he let the thin blade of the knife slip between his fingers. Finally he cut a hair off his head with it, and holding it in the moonlight with two fingers slit it easily with the blade.

He rose quietly. Gennaro still slept, his head on his pillow, his toes up under the blankets quiet as little knobs of stone, his small mouth open, breathing gently. The train rumbled by in the near distance. It covered whatever shuffle his feet made. The swine, look how he sleeps; the bastard wolf out of the mountains; the starved dog with his mad tongue lolling. *Madonna santissima,*[14] full of mercy, you understand. God give me the strength. You will forgive. Mam-ma, over there in Capomonte, you would be the first to put the knife in my mind. This will mean that I shall not see you again. I was coming, *mam-ma mia,*[15] coming soon, and was going to put a chain of gold about your neck, money in your hands, how hard now from working in the stone-patch of a farm you have, and tell you to sit down and look out over the hills and have a glass of wine now and then with something to dip into it. This sneaking bastard of a mountain wolf, he comes along, mother mine, and I befriend him, and he bites the kind hand I extend him. You understand, dear Virgin, my mother, and you will all pray God to forgive a man whose anger is poison in him now, forgive him for what he does.

He approached the figure of the Madonna with the wick still burning though the oil was close down to the bottom of the lamp. He lifted a muscle-drawn face to it, a tense visage without a smile, and eyes that had filled with tears and gleamed. His lips trembled and he kept beseeching without words: Forgive me what I do. I could not live alongside of him, the world is too small for both of us, it would be no use, no matter where I turned I should see him now, all men would be like him, and I should hate them, what's the use, mother of God, you are understanding and kind to mortal sinners, can I go on this way, giving this whelp of a mountain boar what I piled up with my sweat and my agony, being good to everybody and playing the game fair? I could not, could I, sweet Holy Virgin who begot the good God himself and loves all men? You know I could not. Give me a sign that you understand.

He turned abruptly, evidently without waiting for a sign. Gennaro had turned on his side, and the noise of it had frightened Rocco. The impulses of anger in him had rigidified to the point where they could not relax. He dragged his bare feet cautiously across the uncarpeted floor, he felt a splinter enter one, but he went on, incapable of stemming the energy of revenge that was sweeping through him. He knelt down softly by Gennaro's bed. He would seize him quickly by the hair, the way they held a pig's head back in the old country, and, digging the knife right there under the earring alive with moonlight, run the blade quickly, quickly down the side of the neck and leave the knife stuck in it. He seized Gennaro's short curly hair, raised the knife and plunged it down, but it missed, and stuck in the pillow. Gennaro jumped up. So did Rocco.

They looked at each other, Gennaro with interrogation in his eyes, Rocco alert, resisting.

"Well, what is it?" Gennaro asked.

Rocco sprang on him and clutched him by the throat. But Rocco had failed to reckon with the strength of his opponent. Gennaro threw him off with the ease of a mastiff shaking off a little dog.

"By Saint Jerome and the Holy Calendar,[16] so, you want to continue the fight," and he kicked Rocco where he lay sprawling, attempting to get up. At the same time he reached quickly for his shoe and before Rocco had a chance to rise began pounding him on the head with the heel of it, and then, not satisfied with that, hurled himself upon the man on the floor and dug his teeth into Rocco's cheek, bit furiously and pulled open the flesh. The wounded man gave out a cry that rose like a thin stream of horror into the moonlit silence, hung poised in the night and mingled with the lugubrious wail of a tug on the nearby river. Zia Nuora came rushing to the doorway.

Gennaro thrust his hand over the wounded man's mouth, and looked up.

"Don't stand there like a she-ass braying," he exclaimed. "Throw a dress over yourself and run out for the doctor."

"What's all this? What's all this? In my house?"

"It's nothing. See that knife stuck in the bed. That was meant for me. But nothing happened. Don't stand there like that, woman, undressed."

Zia Nuora escaped as from a madman. Gennaro lifted Rocco on the bed, a limp, unconscious mass.

The next morning he insisted that Rocco stay in bed, and he went to the junk-shop and assumed control. It was the beginning of his dominance not only of Rocco's thriving business, but gradually of the whole junk business in Harlem. Methods not quite so direct and ruthless as he had applied to Rocco, but violent and effective in subtler ways, put him finally at the head of a huge old-rag-and-metal industry.

Rocco was compelled not only by the wound in his cheek but by a foot festering at the point where the splinter had entered it, to remain at home for many days. Before going to the junk-shop one morning, Gennaro sat on Rocco's couch and talked.

"You're a fool. But we'll forget. I want you to get well now. We'll build up the business together. Not just to make a few dollars out of it and go back to the old country with a feather stuck in our hats and a few gold chains hanging across our bellies. You see I have slept in the same room with you even after that night, and slept soundly. We're going to let bygones be bygones, you and I, and work together, and pile it up big. I'll send for my family, and you, you send for your mother—she'd rather be here with you than slaving away on the hillside. Send for the girl you've talked about. We have had blood of each other, we can now be friends."

Rocco's soft face with its lights of laughter looked blankly at the strange man on the cot, sitting with all the case and assurance of friendship, making plans for a common future. He tightened his hands under his covers and stretched out his arms taut, trying to keep back the hatred in him.

"I say it again, Gennaro. The American fever is in you. The touch of gold in your hands has been too much. We peasants are not used to it. It does queer things to us—the good it makes mean, the mean it makes brutal. Give me the money that's mine, and you can have the business. You stay here, I'll go back to the old country."

Gennaro stuck his pipe into his mouth and thrust it upward with his lips.

"You'd be crazy. And I'd be crazy to let you go. You have a good thing going, you know all about it. I'd be lost without you. You'll stay."

And then, cutting short the conversation, he called out, "Hey, there, Zia Nuora."

6

Zia Nuora was a person of considerable height, with a large bosom and slender legs. Possibly because of her size, she had obtained the title of Zia,[17] or possibly because her rooming house was a haven for lonely men and her manner put them at their ease. The five rooms that ran the length of the old tenement were always crowded, three, four men to a room. They came and went, but the place was always filled. The rooms were furnished no better than Rocco's and Gennaro's—several cots, crude chairs or stools, the image of the Virgin or San Rocco, San Biagio or San Antonio[18] with a lamp burning under it, the trunks with the men's clothing and effects, and nothing else. The floors were old and the boards gaped but they were always scrubbed clean.

The room overlooking the street was a large one and afforded Zia Nuora some opportunity for artistic effects. An old white mantelpiece held a wooden clock that could be heard over the talk and the noise of forks and spoons when the men crowded around the huge table in the center of the room for their one meal of the day. There were half curtains at the windows, and on the walls lithographs of King Humbert and his father, Garibaldi, and an immense one of the battle of Solferino.[19] In the corners stood earthenware spittoons.

She made the beds for all the men, she saw to their simple washing, cooked the meals, swept up, even wrote the letters, for she was one of the few women who had gone to school in the old country. She presided alone at the table, filling up the plates of the hungry boarders without any reservation, expressed genuine offense if they failed to come back for more, joked with them, gave them nicknames and joined even in the coarse fun that went about the table. Her husband worked out of town and came on a visit once a month or sometimes at rarer intervals. The men joked about it with her.

"What an arrangement! If my wife was within reach. . . ."

"Come, there, Luigi the boaster, what would you do? You're here to make money and you'd make it anywhere."

"Hey, man does not live for money alone, not a woman for that matter."

Beyond such bantering they never got. It was left to Gennaro to attempt more.

When she entered the room where Rocco lay on his cot, she was surprised to see Gennaro.

"You here?"

"I came to see how you were treating my Rocco. No soup for a sick man, not a nice chunk of chicken—beans and pasta like the rest of us! You're making America faster than all of us. Go to the market today and get a fowl or two."

"I'm all right. I don't need . . ." Rocco was about to protest.

"You know nothing. You lived like a creature of the fields ever since you got to this country. So have I. It's going to be different from now. Hear that, Nuora *bella*?[20] A fowl and some pastina,[21] very fine, for an invalid."

"You'll go marketing yourself, my grand signore. You get here what you get."

She flung out. Gennaro winked at Rocco, raising his pipe into the air with his lower lip, and then laughed.

"I'm all right," whispered Rocco, wincing with the pain in his foot. "The doctor squeezed all the pus out this morning, said I would be better."

Gennaro walked out slowly without paying any attention, chuckling to himself. Zia Nuora had gone to her own rooms, immediately across the hall. Her kitchen was there, and the two rooms she and her husband occupied. The living room facing the street made a pretense of lavish elegance. There was her portrait as a bride done in flat watery oils on a large canvas, her broad face with its high cheekbones looking gloomy rather than hopeful, in the center of a group of other photographs of her husband, herself, her family in Italy, some of the boarders who had gone and left mementoes of themselves. There were heavy plush chairs, vivid green, with lugubrious Cupids in crude relief on the woodwork, and a cumbersome plush sofa with a red fringe. A three-legged table with a round top stood in the center of the room and upon that a statuette of a half-draped woman holding aloft a clock that would have weighed another woman to the ground. The white marble mantelpiece, relic of a bygone finery, disported an array of figurines of shepherds carved in wood, a cocoanut husk with a waterscape painted in red, and a crystal cordial set. The shades were always drawn, and the curtains, of heavy crochet, made by Zia Nuora herself, were pulled across, so that the room was invariably dim. The consequence was that to the simple peasant immigrants, to step into the room was to reduce them to awed silence, especially as the thing that first struck them was the figure of Christ hanging from the cross above a red lamp between the two windows.

Gennaro opened the door unceremoniously and saw Nuora standing at the window, the shade drawn back, peering out into the street. He shuffled slowly to her and put an arm about her waist.

"*Lazzarone,*"[22] she cried, turning round and so forcing his hand off her body.

"*Sei bella.*"[23]

"I don't need you to tell me."

He placed his pipe in his pocket.

"I want you," he said simply, his eyes suffused with red, his breath slow and heavy.

"You have a wife, I have a husband. I don't do things like that."

"My wife's a million miles away. So's your husband."

"Leave me at once."

"My wife combs her hair like that," he answered, smiling, "a part in the middle and flat over the head, shining black like yours, the braids on the neck. It's a good way."

She placed her hand on his chest and pushed him. Gennaro laughed, put his hands into his pocket and eyed her up and down.

"My wife's smaller, but stronger," he continued. "But she has thick lips, not red like yours, and her eyes are brown, not blue. I haven't seen her for two years now. I've been with no other woman. I like you."

"Insolent poltroon."

She put up her two hands to push him. It was the signal for him to clasp her with both arms about the waist and lift her off the floor.

"Be good. Do not fight," he pleaded with her.

He threw her on the couch with overpowering strength.

"There, my sweet one, you see who's stronger."

He had his way with her. She lay panting and exhausted on the couch, weeping gently. He arranged her clothes about her and pinched her cheek.

"There now, quiet, now, by Saint Jerome, quiet."

He slapped her affectionately on both cheeks, laughing nervously.

"I was not like this, ever," he said. "Only my wife before this. No other woman. There's something grown up in me, a madness, I don't know, ever since I saw the farm in the old country going for taxes and falling always deeper in debt and no hope ahead, and I picked up without saying good-bye, owing everybody money. I felt alone like I was in the fields, alone, and the hail coming down and no place for shelter. You understand, Nuora. You, too, have come here leaving your own behind you. Is there anybody wants to leave what he has been with all his life? You know. You are good to all the men—that's why. We're alone without mothers and without wives, working, some with the pick, others on the rags, and we're miserable and you smile with us, and you arouse us, too. But the other men are good. I found this thing growing in me ever since my farm kept going from me for the taxes and the mortgages, see. It's a strength but a bad strength. That's why when you laughed and you made jokes and you stood up with your fine body tall and strong, and your hair like my wife's, the strength came."

She sat up, staring at him wildly.

"Now there," he said gently. "You go and get the fowl for Rocco, and we'll have a fine meal—the three of us."

He was kneeling at her side and looked up at her like a boy petulantly dictating to his mother. He rose and sat down beside her and stroked her hair, passing the rough flat of his hand from her forehead to the nape of the neck. There was something brutally conquering in the gesture that seemed to justify the preceding violence and to mollify her. She looked at him sideways with a soft glance that made him smile and rise from the couch at the same time so that he might take his pipe from his pocket and as usual thrust it into his mouth, if rather awkwardly on this occasion. He patted her familiarly on the face.

"Go," he said, "and get the fowl. Let's have a feast. You and me and Rocco. I'll bring in some wine."

He breathed deeply as he watched her go, and smiled.

"They'll take off their hats to me yet," he thought, pulling hard on his pipe. "I'll be boss here . . . peasant once, but no more . . . I know now . . . take what you want when you want it. That's the trick!"

He strode back to Rocco, shoulders high, pipe out stiff, earrings all agleam.

7

His conquest of Nuora solved for the present the problem of his family. The absence of her husband for long periods made it easy to accept his role of lover without fixed possession. Bartolomeo and Nuora had vowed to amass as much money as possible in as short a time as possible and return to their meadow home in Lombardy. The money he earned bossing railway gangs was all saved. The boarding-house yielded even more. From Barto's point of view the arrangement was ideal.

It was even more so for Gennaro.

"Good for you, Nuora," Gennaro exclaimed, "and for me this way." He slapped her cheek affectionately to emphasize his approval.

"We're going back to Italy the first chance," she told him.

"Well, until then," was his reply.

"And if your wife desires to come when she hears how well you are doing?"

"Well, until then. But she will stay until I call for her."

"You have a son, he ought to be learning English now he is still young."

The mention of Domenico was like a prod to an old memory of affection. The wavy-haired boy with his square shoulders and dark smiling eyes came back many times to chide him. The rag business was prospering. His methods had already succeeded in gaining the bulk of the trade in Harlem. He wheedled better prices from the paper manufacturers the more he extended his hold on the rag-pickers. Money was coming in fast. He was a power in the community. They had elected him president of the society of Saint Jerome. He walked at the head of processions on feast days and paid for having the lamps of red and green and white strung across the streets and for huge detonators that climaxed the march of the bands and the society on the day of the feast of Saint Elena. Padre[24] Anselmo consulted him and had even broached to him the problem of building a church for the Italians themselves instead of continuing hiring the basement of the church belonging to the "*Inglesi.*"[25] There was no reason why he should not have sent for Rosaria and the youngsters. But Nuora wrote his letters for him, and, by the holy calendar, could he have her send off the letter that would end their intimacy?

Their intimacy had a charmed quality. To lie in her arms at night, the men sleeping in the other rooms, not daring to whisper what they knew, fed his ego, proved his vast success in America! End it all! No, by the saints. And yet in some obscure animal way he knew he should love the woman at whose side he had slept from the day he was eighteen, whose children he had seen born under his very eyes, while the pain of their birthing filled the highland valley in which they lived, who had risen from the bed of her agony and gone into the fields with him under the sun and in the face of the hot winds—a patient obedient soul, if not with the fine broad face of Nuora, nor the upstanding figure, nor the sweet Northern speech. In some deep gloom of memory he felt her move about close to him, and saw her with the child Domenico in her arms, and then Emilio, the curly-haired one, and Elena named after his own patron saint whose scapular he wore.

The heavy hours of toil with her, followed by the dark drowsy nights when they sought the soft of their bodies for easement and the sleep that would not flow into their exhausted work-drawn muscles—these hours came back in his scattered broodings about her. They seemed in a far-back time before the man he really was had emerged out of his strength, the new strength that cut down the halters that bound him to the life of a peasant-slave. Sometimes they became vivid, flared up in a light that might have been remorse as he fell away out the tense arms of Nuora and the soft heaviness of her breasts recalled by their occasional touch of his body the soft, heavy body of Rosaria. He heard the goats bleat and the grunting of the pigs, and in the quiet lights of the dawn he followed his own form to where old Don Paolo, his faithful donkey, waited for him, and in his mind he went through the whole farm routine of the morning and then the tousle with Domenico. It was sweet, but the sweetness was a snatched thing, a matter of a few moments now and then. For his thoughts filled with the anger that his work was for the taxes alone, and the burdensome mortgage. The best of the figs he picked went to pay the government, the choice pressings of his grapes.

He remembered the week before he had decided to tell them all to go to the devil. Don Erminio, the lawyer, had come up to his stucco house with its green doors and the stable adjoining—a sleek fat fellow with a comfortable paunch that he thrust forward with pride ahead of his cane.

"A fine evening to you, Gennaro," he had bassoed with plump assurance.

How Gennaro hated the round full voice with its accents of command!

"And to you, signore,"[26] he had replied stiffly, rising as was necessary in the presence of an important gentleman.

"You have some fine kids, and I see your sow has had a fine litter, too."

"Saint Elena be praised."

"Yes, of course."

He sat down on a stool and looked up at the rafters where still hung the salami Rosaria had put up, the remainder two of the hams he had salted, and three very fine pieces of *cacciocavallo*—the excellent sharp cheese for which he was well known, made according to his own father's recipe—the best in those parts.

"You want for little, if you have all this. And I can feel certain you must have some top-notch wine in your butt."

Rosaria had come forward with the tiny Elena in her arms.

"Will it please your good sir to have a nibble of these things?"

How he had hated the sight of the huge dish with slices of ham and cheese and the large glass of wine she placed before Don Erminio! The rotund little lawyer had fallen to at once and between mouthfuls praised food, children, and farm. At the same time he kept repeating: "You know, Gennaro, you ought to find a way to pay off some of the mortgage and maybe a trifling sum to Don Vito, the priest. It's all for the good of your family, Gennaro, to pay off a bit now and then."

He had wanted at that moment to do the same thing he had done to Rocco, Rocco who had befriended him and never had nagged at him, boss though he was. But these strange impulses of self-assertion had not yet channeled in him, and he had not had the strength nor the courage to raise his fist and come down on the flabby jowls of the pompous fool.

Anger swelled in him, however, and shook him inwardly. Rosaria saw it and came close to where he was and placed the baby Elena in his arms. He felt the little cheek against his, and so he said nothing. That night Rosaria spoke no word to him, but pressed against him, and it was like the baby's cheek, and that, too, was sweet, and he tried to forget.

Such scenes came back as he rolled away from the arms of Nuora and the kisses of her full mouth. And the christening scenes, too, at which they had all danced while the bag-pipers played, at which Don Vito, the priest, had drunk a bit more than he should and pinched the cheeks of the girls, and sometimes without knowing better the cheek of old Zia Chele with her thousand wrinkles. How they all laughed on those occasions!

What was it that kept him from sending for Rosaria and Domenico? The boy was fourteen now, and should be getting along, and he should learn this new business of rags he himself had learned. Something made it impossible. Was it Nuora, with her broad face and full lips, and her soft speech and her passion? Was it that in spite of his money, his position among the paesani, he had not yet struck roots in the country to which he had come?

And so he kept sending money to Rosaria, his wife, and she wrote back what was money? He sent enough just to keep them going. Could he not send enough so she might save over and above what they needed and so take passage to New York and rejoin him? But, of course, if he was minded to remain in New York without them, he must have a good reason. Was he not making enough to pay off all the arrears on the farm and let her sell out?

Don Erminio interposed in the letter remarks of which Rosaria knew nothing—lectures on his remissness both to those whom he owed money and to his family. Gennaro heard Nuora read them and his fists clenched. But he did nothing. And so three years went by.

8

Between him and Rocco the broken friendship had been cemented. They contrived to conduct their business without friction. And though Rocco was aware of the relation between Gennaro and Nuora, he kept his tongue.

One evening, one of the wandering rag-pickers pushed into the yard his cart filled to the top with rags, old bottles, pieces of old metal. Gennaro examined it and discovered that it was an unusually good buy. He offered a trifling sum.

The old rag-picker tightened up his belt with an angry pull and looked up smiling. He had a little face with a pucker of wrinkles at both corners of his mouth, a mustache that bushed up into his nostrils, and wore an old hat cocked jauntily over his forehead.

"Five dollars! I paid out that much, Gennaro *bello*. What will you be doing, having the blood of us all?"

"Well, and what have you got there? At the best, some pewter. The rest is trash."

"You do well on trash, my grand signore. You do very well on trash. You buy houses."

Gennaro walked away. He had seen his good friend, the undertaker Francesco Struzzo, pass by, and called out to him. They sauntered up the street. The old man took off his hat wearily and scratched the bald area on the top of his head.

"The big stink," he said to himself. "Somebody will get him yet."

Rocco at that moment happened along and saw the cart.

"Nobody taken care of you yet?"

"What a rushing business you must be doing," cried the old fellow sarcastically. "Here you let a man with a prize load hang around for a half hour before paying attention to him. I'll go down the street where they won't keep me waiting and give me a good sum, too."

Rocco looked over the contents of the cart.

"How much do you want?"

"That's for you to say. I wouldn't give it up for less than ten."

"I'll give you nine. But let me look again. Ha, you have a couple of good pieces of pewter here."

"No less than ten."

The old man glanced around to make sure that Gennaro was not in sight. Evening was falling rapidly. The noises of the street had changed from rumbling carts on the cobbles to the sound of infinite voices.

"All right, ten," said Rocco and, pulling a roll of bills out of his pocket, counted out the ten into the old man's hand. The rag-picker rushed immediately to the back of the yard, dumped the load on the ground, and threw the rags into their proper place, the scraps of iron in theirs, the old coppers in their bins.

"I'll take the pewter," Rocco said.

The pieces consisted of an old battered tray, a coffee pot with the spout off and the top hanging loosely from the hinge, several cups, and a creamer. The old fellow had contrived to hold them together by an old cord he had run through holes which he had pierced into the various items. Rocco took hold of the cord and was about to go into the sheds with his purchase when Gennaro appeared on the scene with Mr. Struzzo the undertaker.

"Oh, I see, you gave them up for five dollars."

"Why, I gave him ten," answered Rocco. "The lot's easily worth it."

"By Saint Jerome and the Holy Calendar, I offered him only five, all the cheap junk ought to fetch."

The rag-picker smiled with his funny wrinkles puckering closer at the corners of his mouth.

"So, you put one over on me."

Struzzo, an angular tall man who towered over the other three, burst into laughter.

"That's a good one, beating you at your own game."

"You're a fool, Rocco."

"It's worth all of ten."

"Let it be worth a hundred. You're a she-ass."

Struzzo had a high wheezy laugh and a way of putting his hat back on his head at the least bit of excitement. He wheezed now with merriment, and shoved his hat farther back. He had no notion how he was angering Gennaro who never could take the slightest belittlement. But had he had any idea of it, he would have laughed even louder.

"Let me hear, Gennaro, by Saint Jerome and the Holy Calendar," and he thrust his hat still farther back.

"There's no use getting hot over it, Gennaro," said Rocco quietly. "I know my business as well as you."

"I wouldn't have you around long enough to puff a candle out if you didn't."

"And you ought to be in there with the men sorting the junk, sitting on your hams and glad of the job."

"You weren't good enough to keep me there."

"Somebody will yet show you your place."

"It won't be you."

"I'll do it yet maybe, who knows."

Gennaro's anger was up. He shambled slowly toward Rocco, allowing his pipe to take a sharp upward angle. Rocco had a vivid memory of the meaning of the gesture, and, though he kept his ground, watched steadily the movements of his partner, the laughing mocking eyes, the shoulders alternately thrust forward as Gennaro advanced.

Struzzo had stopped laughing. Everyone was well aware of the temper that Gennaro could display, its quick rise, his loss of all caution, the sudden blow that followed. He himself was a man of easy good-will and found it simple to dissolve all states of mind in the ripples of his laughter. He had never been face to face with Gennaro's anger. They had entered into several deals together—the purchase of a number of houses—engaged in participating mortgages on others, and gone on common bail for a number of men. He realized the value of Gennaro's directness and forcefulness in their mutual undertakings and was not going to permit a momentary flash of temper to undo—as well it might, should he inflict a real injury on Rocco in the presence of the rag-picker—the success of their enterprises.

"Better close up shop," he suddenly exclaimed, "and get home to your dinner. I hear her husband is back."

Gennaro heard and understood. It meant nothing to him. Bartolomeo Todaro was in the habit of returning periodically.

"Rocco Pagliamini," he said slowly. "Saint Elena forgive me, but you anger me. You make me want to spit in your face. You so much as tell these ragmen that I am cheating them, that you're good and I'm stingy. I ought to put an end to it, all right, now, and the best way would be to bash your jaws in once and for all, you little scared rat."

"You'd better do that to Bartolomeo."

Rocco spoke deliberately and without the fear that Gennaro had designed to arouse in him. Gennaro had known Rocco as a child. He had bullied him then. He had already assumed a new mastery over the laughing, timid man by punching himself into a partnership with him. He had disarmed the fool the same night and beaten him into submission. He was surprised now not to see any signs of cowering in Rocco, and he sensed at once after the remark about Bartolomeo that something actually was up, something of which Rocco knew more than he had revealed.

"I'll bash in his jaws, too," he answered quickly.

Struzzo caught him by the shoulder before he had a chance to raise his fists.

"Don't be a damn fool. It's late; close up your place and go home."

"You'd better," Rocco continued. "You'd better settle your affairs there."

Gennaro laughed quietly, if nervously, deep in his throat, and moved off the scene.

"You close up, Rocco."

Without another word, he took his way home.

CHAPTER TWO

1

Bartolomeo Todaro, a northern Italian,[1] shorter than the average of those Germanic-looking men, had an oblong head with a stocky neck to hold it up, and a face prematurely cut by deep wrinkles that ran longitudinally across his cheeks. Sparse sandy hair, which he rarely combed, clung about his head as if he still retained the fluffy gossamer of his baby days. That and the small blue eyes in deep sockets gave him, by contrast with his old-looking cheeks, the incongruous expression of having remained a boy despite the fact that he had grown to be a full-bodied man. One might have thought, too, that because of his work with a gang of men engaged in repair labor on the railroads, his hands would be hard and rough. As a matter of fact, they were soft and unwrinkled, with slender fingers and nails that he kept long and shining.

He had had several years of schooling, but whether it was that or some natural tendency to resist the advances of years his voice was gentle and soft, perfectly modulated to be the vehicle of his sweetly rhythmical Northern speech. He had three passions: a violin, which he carried with him back and forth no matter where he went; Nuora, his wife, whom he loved with the fervor of an adolescent; and his old homestead in the Lombardian plains to which he was resolved to return at the first opportunity.

His wife's boarders knew of his return by hearing the strains of Rossini and Donizetti[2] floating sentimentally above the cries of the street, sounds that filled them with a revived sense of their exile and yet plunged them at once into a new serenity of resignation. And they knew as soon as they heard them that that evening they would be alone, lost without the presence of Nuora—despite the fact that since Gennaro's coming she stayed up with them only short whiles. They always looked forward to the meal with Bartolomeo present for it turned into a festal repast, macaroni with the Bolognese sauce[3] that was so different from what they knew, roast chicken, plenty of wine, and the good cheese that Nuora was always at great pains to buy. Nuora presided with a sense of her being the wife, as it were, of each and all of them,

31

keeping the talk going, prodding each one to express himself, and not ever once stinting on the food which she piled up on their dishes. She had worked hard to prepare it and was glad to see it go.

When Gennaro arrived, the table had already been set. That much allayed whatever fears Struzzo and Rocco had imparted to him. Not all the men had yet returned from work. Carmine Zingaro, the gigantic red-head who claimed that he was supporting nine nephews in the Argentine[4] by the money he was making as a brass-worker, was sitting at the window, his long clay pipe hanging down below his knees, looking as he always did, as if he were searching the opposite wall for deep secrets. He saw Gennaro and turned away immediately.

Seated on the sofa, his legs spread out, his hands clasped in front of him, his head down, was Salvatore Danni who had just found work again but in spite of it had failed to come out of a kind of half-melancholy, half-rebellion, which had the effect of increasing the sadness of the other men. He heard Gennaro come in, lifted his head, gazed at him for what seemed a longer interval than necessary, made a noise deep in his throat, and resumed his position.

Giovanni Sardi was busy with his accordion. He was a young man who slaved as a barber, as he put it, whenever he could find a day's work. He preferred to labor only on Saturdays and Sundays, for then the tips would be numerous and bountiful, and the remainder of the week he spent making chance acquaintances with the nurse-maids in the parks in the better sections of the city, or attempting to discover all the gamut of emotions in the soul of an accordion, mandolin, guitar, Jew's harp, or any other instrument he could borrow or purchase. Always elegantly dressed in the one suit he kept for the time he was not employed, he prided himself particularly on his hair-dress—thick, stiff hair which waved at the least combing and which he wore in two pompadour-like mounds, each off a straight glaring part in the middle of his head. He, too, stopped playing, and, Gennaro thought, showed somewhat more effrontery than usual by staring at him with a glint of laughter in his eyes.

"Well," said Gennaro to himself, "so we're in for it tonight."

Aloud he cried, "Good evening, my fine gentlemen, and a hearty appetite."

He strode across the room, stopping first to throw an olive into his mouth. He crossed the hallway between the living-room where they ate and the rooms occupied by Nuora and her husband and rapped vigorously on the door.

The door was opened by Bartolomeo, holding the violin at his side.

"If one wants to wash, then what?" asked Gennaro in a loud voice, conscious that all the men were now glaring at him through the open door. At least, Giovanni Sardi had ceased playing on his accordion.

"If one wants to wash, one washes," answered Bartolomeo in his quiet voice.

"Well, then, with your permission," and he advanced a step.

"Your place, sir," replied Bartolomeo, "is down the hall there, where all the men go."

"I pay a bit extra for using the other. That one's filthy."

"That is just it, sir. We want no filth in our own quarters."

His voice remained at its quiet low pitch, and his blue eyes were so devoid of anger that Gennaro was at a loss what to do or say. After all, this fair-skinned man with his wrinkles and his expression of a schoolboy worrying about his examinations offered him no point of attack. If he knew, he was displaying no indignation, and certainly no disposition to quarrel. If he didn't know, it would be just as well not to arouse his suspicions.

So he said simply, "You'll return then the little extra I have been paying."

"With much pleasure, sir."

"And I give you notice that I shall leave."

That, thought Gennaro, ought to settle it. He paid well, on time, got Nuora cheaper prices at the markets, threw in her way opportunities of lending out money at high rates. Bartolomeo was intent on returning to Italy as soon as he had laid a sufficient sum aside. Leaving him, thought Gennaro, would be the surest way to strike at him.

In reality he did want to give Bartolomeo a blow with the flat of his hand and laugh as the baby-face fell to the floor.

Instead, however, he stuck his pipe into his mouth and went down the hallway. Carmine saw him cross the street and enter the barbershop opposite.

2

When he returned, the eight boarders, including Rocco, Nuora and her husband were all at the table. In the center was a great platter piled with spaghetti steaming under delicate light carroty-red Bolognese sauce, and the men's plates were filled with it. A jug of red wine and enormous slices of bread on another platter completed the course. The men ate heartily, noisily, smacking their lips, talking between mouthfuls. Carmine had just finished off a second helping of macaroni when Gennaro entered. He drew the bandana-like napkin across his heavy lips and bushy red mustache and rubbed energetically. Then he seized a glass of wine, and, holding it high, cried:

"To Gennaro Accuci, the rag-man, who made America, and made it quick."

Gennaro saw Nuora bend her head over her plate as if she were expecting a storm to burst over her head. The sarcasm implied in Carmine's toast, with its not too subtle reference to rag-man, had not passed unobserved. Gennaro knew it, but stomached his anger.

"Fine words, those," he replied, "and I thank you."

"And, ho, there," continued the big brass-worker, who to all appearances had already drunk too much, "ho, there, you little whippersnapper of a barber, make way for the most successful rag-man in all Little Italy."

"*Evviva*,"[5] several shouted and began shuffling their chairs to make room for Gennaro.

A pause intervened as Gennaro seated himself opposite Nuora.

"Well," he said, rubbing his hands and then seizing a napkin, "this has been a welcome indeed, and you certainly have prepared a feast for a king."

"The rag-men's king . . . a toast!" cried Carmine, lifting his glass.

"And I am, I am the rag-men's king," answered Gennaro, "hey, there, Rocco, what do you say? And what are you all?"

"Honest workmen who mind their business and are content," replied Carmine.

"Content with what? With a crumb, the third pressing of the wine— peasants still in this country, afraid to open your mouths—"

"Afraid?"

Carmine had risen to his feet. The huge head teetered slightly. His neck bulged with anger.

Nuora kept herself busy lifting forkfuls of macaroni to her mouth, making a pretense of ignoring the men, smiling occasionally to cover up her fears. Bartolomeo had acted queerly the whole afternoon, questioning the men, sitting around in a gloomy silence unlike him. How much had he learned?

Once she had tiptoed behind him, put her arms around him and was about to draw his head back so she might kiss him. But he had gently removed her arms from his chest, turned about and looked into her eyes quietly and steadily. She had blushed to the roots of her hair and laughed uneasily, but recovered herself sufficiently to kiss him full on the lips and then shout half-hysterically, "My baby straw-head."

He had laughed, too, then, and returned the kiss. But it was a timid, hesitant gesture, troubled and unassured.

Now she was even more uncertain. For the most part, the men had minded their own affairs, had kept their silence and tolerated Gennaro. But they did not love him. They would be only too glad to witness his downfall, or at least such a discomfiture that would cut across the fibres of his pride and leave him halt and limp. Was Carmine starting something now?

In an attempt to postpone the storm, she cried across the table, "Hey, there, *mangionaccio*—big-eater—pass that plate of yours and fill it up again. I don't want a string of the macaroni left. And you, Gennaro, you have hardly begun."

Bartolomeo rose up, too.

"As long as you understand, Gennaro Accuci, that there is nobody here that is afraid."

"Of what? A cafone,[6] a clod-hopping lout, a dunghill rat, that puts on airs because he is not opposed to taking what is not his?"

Carmine's words fell from him deliberately. He faced Gennaro and accused him directly.

"We'll call no names," Bartolomeo interposed.

"No names is right," flashed up Gennaro. "If you mean me."

"He means you, me, anybody."

Gennaro was amazed. He was convinced that Bartolomeo knew. What did this all mean?

"I thought he meant me," Gennaro said, resuming his seat.

"After all, Gennaro *bello*," resumed Bartolomeo, "it could mean anyone in this country. Why does anybody want to leave the people he loves and the things that were his if what he gets is no more than a few *soldi*[7] to buy a crust of bread? Everybody here wants to make all he can. There is hardly anyone who won't go a little beyond what he ought if he can pack up and go back and have something to show for the long trip he took and the tears he shed when he left. That's all we mean, Gennaro—we can't make America any other way."

Gennaro kept swallowing his macaroni without once raising his head. The speech interested him profoundly. It sounded like a sermon Don Vito might preach. His thoughts became extraordinarily mingled with memories of his children and his wife getting all dressed up for the mass, he with his sash of red around his waist and Rosaria with her yellow kerchief with its pink fringe over her head. He resolved that he would send for them at once, quit this stupid life with another man's wife, stop bullying Rocco, put an end to some of the shady transactions in real estate that he was engaged in with Struzzo, the undertaker.

"I am no better than anyone else," continued Bartolomeo. "Here I have a lovely wife, capable, willing, and very dear to me. What have I done for her? Kept her bottled up here in these smelly streets, working like a beast of the field, while I went off somewhere else, driving men to work, mean rotten work under the sun and in the rain, digging and hammering, and sleeping in kennels like dogs. What for? We had a little villa in the country and a farm on it. It lies out under the skies like a bit of a jewel and it has mulberry trees and vines on the hillsides that bear grapes that are gold and firm and make wine fit for the table of King Humbert himself. We had pleasant days on it and in the evening when I had time for my violin,—Gentlemen," Bartolomeo rose to his feet, "you all have similar places and your wives and mothers are there and children waiting for you. It's where we belong."

Gennaro was moved. He wanted to beat his breast the way he did in church. Giovanni, the barber, kept pressing the mounds of his pompadours with nervous fingers. Carmine grunted his approval. The others listened in a spiritual calm. Nuora alone appeared nervous, running her knife across the plate and gazing up fitfully at her husband.

"What's more," he announced, "it's where I am going, and going right away, Nuora and I. I hate this country. It turns us all into different sorts from what we are. The clodhopper apes the man of education and good family; the man of good family and education becomes timid, or he's too well brought up to break the law and he loses out. The last are first and the first are last and the whole world seems upside down and crazy. I'm going back where everyone knows his place and things are orderly and decent. I've made a bit of money. So, we're on our way, hey, Nuora, on our way back. Right here in the back pocket of my pants is my ticket across. Fill up your glasses, my good friends, and drink to those who have the good sense to return."

They drank despite their consternation. The talk became general. Cheese was brought out and more wine. Each one boasted of his own native section of Italy. Wines were compared, and feast days, and the ways of their mothers. They decided upon going back as soon as possible, all but Gennaro and the young barber.

"This city's where I am going to die," Giovanni Sardi declared. "The life here, the freedom, always somewhere to go by day, by night! You slave a little, that's true, but you can go places and meet people. And the girls . . ."

"That's it, you renegade. The English girls—they're better than those of Palermo, are they?"

"They ain't stiff like the images of the good saints."

"Only painted up."

Everyone laughed.

Gennaro had become heated. He leaned all the way across the table and slammed his fist down so that the plates shook and wine spilled out of the glasses.

"*Diavulu santissimu,*"[8] he cried in his own dialect with its cluttered sounds and interminable u's and eerie sing-song. "I ain't one to be afraid of anything, and so I am going to stay right here, and not because the women here are easy to get and the money is easy to make. You have got to be quick and shrewd and have no fear—that's all, and the strong man is bound to win. What was I out home? A nobody, dirt off the sidewalks, a *cafone!* There were those that were my betters."

He jumped to his feet, cleared a space for himself and dramatized his statements, bowing low in servile pantomime, looking appropriately abashed, scraping his feet, humbly rubbing his hands together.

"Sure . . . when the lawyer passed I had to bow; and when the baron rode by in his carriage I had to breathe in the dust his horses kicked up; when the captain of the troops stamped by, what did I have to do? Jump out of his way like a jack-rabbit, and whine beg your pardon, beg your pardon. Bah, that's ended here."

He pounded his fist on his chest.

"Here I am Gennaro Accuci and proud of it. I bow to no one, and though I wear earrings in my ears there are those that know they cannot pull my nose and they dare not tell me to get out of their way. Go back, all of you, where they know you're ninnies and fools and the stuff of the dunghills. Grovel at the feet of your betters!"

He turned suddenly on Nuora.

"You going, too?"

"Yes, with my husband."

She looked him square in the eyes without blush or quiver.

"When?"

"We go in ten days."

"You like it?"

She felt the full force of his eyes upon her, the same evil strength which overpowered her once and continued to hold him to her against her will, though all her emotions galloped out to meet the onrush of his. She could not understand what his questioning implied. Inwardly she trembled, but she exerted every effort to appear self-possessed and natural.

"Why, Gennaro, I go where my husband goes."

"Where he commands?"

"That's a wife's duty."

"But what business is all this of yours?"

Bartolomeo had found his tongue and lashed out his question.

"What I have seized and made my own I hate to give up."

Carmine strode heavily across the room and laid a strong hand on Gennaro.

"You—you low-down idiot—shut that mouth of yours. Things have gone well thus far. Let the fine feast we all had with the good cooking and the cheese and the excellent wine end right. Sit down."

Gennaro did sit down, stupefied for the moment. The noises of the street mingled with the sputter and the hum of the gas-jets, and above them all he heard the whirring of voices. He had a fantastic desire to shout to everyone that he had been lovers with Nuora. Why not? That would clinch the matter. The world would know how mighty he was, how he strode to success in this country. Making America wasn't all money-grubbing. There was mixed up with it a bit of romance. Damn it, by the thousand miracles, they could make a ballad of his career and sing it at the crossroads.

But he thought better of his wild egotism.

"I'm a thick old country lout," he managed to blurt out, keeping Carmine to one side. "But by Saint Jerome I got feelings like the rest."

"Who the hell cares?" demanded Carmine.

"I hate to see Nuora going. You all hate it. She made it pleasant for you here."

3

"Too damn pleasant for you," piped up Rocco.

This was the first word he had spoken all evening. At the best, Rocco spoke but little. Ever since Gennaro had taken to bossing him around, he spoke even less. Everyone was conscious, however, that deep-burning masses of hatred were preparing to explode out of him like the lava in the heart of a volcano. They were horrified to hear him blurt out the remark. It could have only one meaning.

Bartolomeo, like Gennaro, had drunk a trifle more than was good for anyone. Their faces were flushed, and the hostility between them had not been disguised by the speeches they had made. It had been kept in a precise balance, on the part of one from fear of getting to learn too much, on the part of the other from fear of being pushed too far into action that must result in violence.

Rocco had evidently been biding his time, in some fashion curiously anxious for the outburst, as if he had had a hand in bringing it about. His words now seemed to confirm the vague belief. They awaited with dread the reactions of both Gennaro and Bartolomeo. Nuora, once always the central spark of all merriment and gayety, had been uncommonly quiet.

Rocco spoke again. "I repeat, too damn pleasant for you."

Carmine burst into a roar. One knew not whether it was laughter or anger, or just merely a command. They all turned their eyes to him.

"And too damn pleasant for me, too," Carmine was saying. "Too damn pleasant for all of us. Why do we keep on living here? I got a girl I could marry. You all have wives you could call from Italy. Rocco has a sweetheart in the Piedmont, a fine strapping girl, he tells me, would be a fine companion for a man. Why don't we break away from here? You know why, Bartolomeo, you know why? Because you have an angel for a wife. She has been kind to all of us—*una simpaticona.*[9] She has made it too damn pleasant for us all and it's a good thing you're taking her away . . . we should never let her go in a month from now."

Everyone laughed. Gennaro glared quizzically at Rocco. Rocco lowered his head and smiled.

"Where's my mandolin?" shouted Giovanni.

He seized it.

"You there, Mastro[10] Bartolomeo, out with your violin."

"By the Virgin, yes, let's have some music."

The men tuned up. They played. The others listened.

Gennaro broke up the party, however, by rising and saying, "I'm going for a walk. How about a walk, Rocco?"

The men stared at them, but they went out for their walk. It proved to be the end of their partnership in business.

As soon as they had reached the street, Gennaro turned to his friend quietly and said:

"I think I know what you were up to. But we'll forget it. I want to say something—you and I can't keep on together. How much do you want for your share?"

The evening was hot, the street filled with crowds. All the stores were opened, the bakeries with their multitudinous forms of loaves, the groceries with their strings of garlic and salami hanging outside and their windows crowded with boxes of macaroni of various shapes and color. The cafés were doing a thriving business. Men sat out on the sidewalks playing cards, and the white-aproned owners stood up at their freezers crying out in gay sing-song, "Have your gelati,[11] have your ices . . ."

Rocco was silent, Gennaro patient, waiting for his answer. They were jostled and shoved. They merely pushed on, keeping as close together as possible.

"Well?" inquired Gennaro.

"I'm thinking."

"Let's sit down and have coffee."

They sat at a round table on the sidewalk, the elevated locomotives rumbling by, sparks flying from their stacks whirling about for a second and then going out into the darkness.

"We can't make a go of it any longer, Rocco. I don't want anything worse to happen between us. You are set on things a bit underhand. We have had bad moments. There's no need of them, is there now? You break away, get another place, you know the business well, it wouldn't take you long."

Rocco looked up at him, his small blue eyes flashing with anger.

"You want me to get out."

"It's the best way."

"Why not you?"

Gennaro shrugged his shoulders and then gulped the remainder of his coffee, making a slow sucking noise.

"I say you," he announced.

Rocco stared in amazement.

Since Gennaro said nothing, Rocco at length spoke again.

"How much will you give me?"

"Half."

"Who'll say how much it's worth?"

"Name your price. If it's right I'll say yes at once. Otherwise, I'll name mine."

"Five thousand."

"I'll give you four and pay the rent of your new place for six months. I have a good place in mind for you."

"You own it?"

"Yes . . . but what's that? You can have four stores."

They walked home in silence. But just as they got to the door of their boarding-house, Rocco stopped and seized Gennaro by the arm.

"This is to say good-bye. You have been an evil in my life. We'll pass it over. See that the money you make don't sour in your stomach and you puke it up like a sick baby."

And he hurried upstairs. Gennaro followed, shrugging his shoulders and laughing to himself as he stroked his mustache. He had every intention of speaking to Nuora that night before he went to bed. But she and her husband had already cleared the dishes and were asleep as well as the rest of the men. Carmine alone was sitting by the window.

"Come here," he called to Gennaro.

When Gennaro came up, Carmine said, "See here, you fool, you escaped tonight. Go slow. You're in for something yet. Go to bed now and leave me alone."

Again Gennaro shrugged his shoulders. Walking slowly to his room, noticing that Rocco was already asleep, he threw off his clothes, got on his cot, and with his hands behind his head he fell off into a deep sleep at once.

4

Gennaro never got to see Nuora alone during the ten days before her departure for Italy. It was not because he was busy with Rocco. He spent considerable time helping his partner getting established in the four stores he owned about ten blocks south. Nor was Nuora unwilling to see him. She was busy, too, but she could have found the time were it not for Bartolomeo and Carmine. If it was not Bartolomeo, then it was Carmine who was with her. The red-headed giant greeted Gennaro with effusive roars every time they met, shaking the smaller fellow's hand, pouring him out a glass of wine, shoving a plate with cheese in front of him, offering him fruit, and even going to the extent of insisting upon his eating.

"What, a bull like you not eat! Gennaro *bello,* you're losing your manhood."

On the date set for the sailing, the men who had boarded with Nuora took the day off from their employment. Giovanni had spent half the morning on his hair-dress. Carmine had donned a heavy black broadcloth he had brought over from Italy several years back, greening now around the edges of the lapels and sleeves. He had outdone himself to the extent of purchasing a celluloid collar and a tie that was redder than his beard. Salvatore Danni, the homesick one, had come all shine and polish, thin as a willow twig whittled of its bark. He stood by erect and lonely, his sharp sallow face pensive and sad.

"Yours is a blessed fortune, Nuora, to be going away. Maybe you'll find time for a bit of prayer for me and my dear wife and the little ones. You live to the north and they to the south, or I should ask you to kiss them for me. But we must each one bear his own cross like the good Lord. May he keep my dear Rosina."

They made a sort of wedding procession as they left the house. Bartolomeo and Nuora, like the rest, clad in their finest, led the crowd. She had refused to purchase herself any new clothes, and had spent a good portion of the ten days feverishly recasting her wedding dress which she had worn not only to the church but to the steamer and then from the steamer to the apartment which she had occupied since her arrival. The cream satin, with shining small diamond patterns all over, brushed down to the sidewalk, flouncing out from her knees in a saucy whorl. It clung tight about her torso, establishing definite outlines for her large frame and full breasts, and separated into two distinct areas at the waist where a broad blue ribbon made a commanding belt and ran around to the rear to become involved in a huge double bow. Her hat, too, she had bought in Italy eight years previously, a huge Leghorn that flopped about her head. She had sewn into it a whole garden of forget-me-nots, violets and wild pinks of a glossy thready velvet that took the afternoon sun and bounced it from one bunch of petals to another.

Bartolomeo had insisted on going back to Italy in an American suit of blue serge with a ribbon about the edges of the coat. The high collar effectively hid the green cravat he had bought in a moment of dazzlement. The trousers fitted tight and clung about his ankles in multiple parallel wrinkles. His boyish blue eyes sparkled, and he held tight under his arm the violin from which he never parted.

The men followed, each one carrying a suitcase or a small trunk. Gennaro had said his good-byes at the door, shaking hands stiffly.

"By Saint Jerome, you look like a duke and a duchess!"

He had made up his mind not to accompany them to the boat. When he saw them board the horse-car, he made an about-face and hurried to his rags and old metals.

There was something of the serenity of sadness about him that communicated itself to the men at work in the rag bins and the metal stalls. Their voices became subdued. They sang now in a hum instead of in the lusty loudness to which they were accustomed. They worked faster, and as Gennaro passed by them they looked up furtively.

There never had been a time when Gennaro wanted so much to stop all labor and to sit around with the men and talk about himself and them and what made them leave the old country. A persistent incapacity to open his mouth prevented him. He had a mind to send out for a whole case of wine and call in anyone from the street and drink until the dark came and they all had to return to their beds and fall asleep.

That he knew he could always do. Gennaro never carried his troubles into bed with him. But night was far off, and he hated this feeling that had come upon him—a new type of sensation, a sense of his having been roundly cuffed by someone he could not resist, a masterful overpowering person, and then left in a corner to weep out his shame by himself and wait for the departure of pain from his muscles and his heart.

The afternoon threatened to be a long, dreary drag. Gennaro looked ahead and shut his eyes. What he saw was a vacant dark, what he heard was silence. He had the desire to take something valuable in his fingers and twist and twist and twist until it broke, even something alive, something that would give a quick initial cry of pain and then become still from too great agony. That might ease his own hurt. For the first time since he had come from Capomonte, Gennaro felt that there was not much to Gennaro.

CHAPTER THREE

1

Isaac Levin's daughter took Nuora's place.

During the three years Gennaro had been amassing money and property, he continued attending church on Sunday mornings and participating in the processions in honor of the saints. He became president of the society of Saint Elena,[1] formed, as the gaudy pink banner of heavy fringed silk proclaimed to the world, for the purpose of mutual protection against disease and mishaps. Some days after Nuora's departure he marched at the head of a noisy and flamboyant parade.

The feast of Saint Elena had already achieved the distinction of outvying that of the Madonna of Mid-August,[2] and all the Italian immigrants journeyed from the four ends of the city and from outlying places in New Jersey and Long Island and even from points in Connecticut. They poured into the twenty or thirty streets bordering on the East River in Harlem with their children and their relatives, the great majority still dressed in their peasant costumes. Gypsy-like, they wandered through the streets camping on the sidewalks, crowding the stores, marching behind the procession.

Occasionally as the band passed by, fanfaring boldly into the air, a woman or a girl, overcome by the sight of the image of the saint borne by stout men in a colorful *baldacchino*,[3] raised her voice into a shout of entreaty. Dozens of others, men and women both, would then get on their knees and cry aloud or mutter wild, incoherent prayers, beating their breasts, raising their hands with fingers widespread. Or they rushed into the midst of the parade, and begged the men, carrying aloft the silk-gowned saint, to halt.

"A moment, just a moment. Here, Saint Elena, the blessed, here is a bit of money, all I can spare . . . it is for you and your good works and the glory of God and the church . . . here . . . here . . ."

With excited hands a bystander pinned a five-dollar note on the skirt of the saint.

Gennaro was sure to step out on such occasions and address all those within hearing.

"Saint Elena protect and help you. That's the man! And you, there, don't hold back—give what you can, the saint needs it all."

Candles were placed in the baldacchino, rings thrown into the box at the foot of the image or made secure to her dress by enormous safety pins. Girls threw off their shoes and joined the procession. At one point an old woman held up the parade to throw herself at the base of the wandering shrine.

"Sweet daughter of God, thou holy one," she screamed, "I cannot give you a thing . . . not even a little candle of one cent . . . only my whole heart . . . and I cry out with it . . . see to it, oh, dear one . . . you are so near to Jesus and you can talk to him . . . I cannot, being just a humble person and old and worn out . . . maybe something can be done for us . . . we are starving . . . there is no work—give my message to Jesus and His father, and may they help us."

Gennaro was moved.

"Here, old woman, take this and go home."

He put a bill into her hands.

Without hesitating she threw it at once into the box at the foot of the image.

"There, for you, dear one . . ."

"Don't be a fool," Gennaro cried, while everyone about them wept over such undoubting adoration. "Here," and he took her by the arm and led her out of the crowd, "go home," and he slipped another bill into her hand and left her weeping, to return to the procession.

Several blocks up, the parade stopped again. The sidewalks were lined with booths, each booth strung with dried nuts and laden with masses of tinted cakes and *torroni*.[4] The street was a roar of people. But the gutters had been cleared.

All along the car-tracks ran strings of huge fire-crackers—melon-shaped detonators that some successful store-keeper had donated in honor of Saint Elena. At one corner of the street the grateful worshipper stood with his family—a man of immense proportions, with a paunch that occupied half of the space that he and his family of three daughters and a wife stood on. His eyes twinkled in his heavy fat-creased face as he looked on in worldly self-pleasure. Gennaro went up to him to thank him in behalf of Saint Elena.

As if by a perverse movement of the head, he saw Isaac Levin's daughter standing on a barrel end. He had never seen such a full, ample-bosomed young woman with hair pure gold, knotted high above her head. The crash dress she wore fitted her with caressing closeness. Opened at the neck, it exposed to his dancing gaze an expanse of white skin. Gennaro stared.

Then the detonators began firing. The noise commenced with a trickle of pop shots. They increased in volume and speed by the second. The air filled with smoke. Shouts of laughter broke loose a whole pandemonium of petty hysterics. Then bomb-like reports! Windows shook, babies cried, men laughed. As the last burst of thunderous smoke filled the street, the band struck up the Italian royal march and shouts of glee rose high and clear.

Gennaro heard but paid no attention. Isaac Levin's daughter had displaced every other thought.

At the end of the day, when the complete procession filed into the church, memories of her worked in and out of his thoughts like a colored thread. The kerchiefed women kneeled, the men took off their hats and bowed one knee, the band-players laid aside their instruments and lowered their heads. From the organ rose a peal of triumphant exaltation. The priest, standing before the blaze of candles, made his voice rise in steady intoning over the uncertain confusion. Gennaro bowed his head at the altar and struck his breast.

"Don't fill my mind with such thoughts," he muttered. "Give me the strength, O Saint Elena, to send for Rosaria and Domenico and curly-haired Emilio, and the little girl named after you."

2

He hurried home.

He had bought out the furniture Nuora and her husband had used, and rented the three rooms they had occupied next to the five they rented out.

Zia Anna, not much bigger than my middle finger, as Gennaro put it in describing her, was fussing around with his meal. Her tiny body was slightly bent so that she was constrained to draw up her chin to look at one, and she never did that without patting with her thin diminutive fingers the flat wisps of gray hair she was always at great pains to comb down and back over her head. The disturbing thing about her was that she had a husky whispery voice that now and then broke into a sharp treble that failed to hold out for the full length of her word. One was not sure whether to laugh, as she might have intended one to do, or to pity her for the age that was actively transforming her from something delicately small into a figure slightly bizarre.

But she had a good heart, as she never wearied telling everybody who remained long enough to listen, or do you suppose she would have followed her shameless son-in-law to these parts of the world where one may never go to church without being in mortal danger of dying without confession, so dangerous are the crowds and the horses and the cobbles in the streets. What a creature this son-in-law of hers, who left his children to grow up as they pleased without manners and a proper respect for anyone and without learning a trade or anything while he went out after his work, and what for, just to spend money on these "English" women who had cast a spell over him and made him blind to his duties? Did she dare protest? What would happen to the little girl, Gemmina? And the other little ones? A vicious little trio—like that father, the good-for-nothing, never home, wandering the streets, learning evil. Especially that little girl—where would she end? The good God be praised, but I can never understand why he takes away the good ones like my daughter and leaves these scoundrels to ply their wicked work in the world.

Thanks to Gennaro, Zia Anna was able to earn enough money to get food for the three *birbantoni*,[5] as she called her grandchildren, and whom she loved passionately despite her tirades against them. It was her objective to save enough to gather them together one fine morning and go down to the ships and so back to Salerno where they could grow up with some thought of God in their minds. Not that she knew how she would go about it, but the good Gennaro would help her.

"Ah, Gennaro," she greeted him at the door, "you are not a minute too late nor too early. I cooked you a bit of veal with peppers, and a dish of string beans in tomato, and they're ready for you at once, and the wine you sent, it's the best ever. I could not help sipping a bit of it."

Gennaro walked past her without a word and sank in the chair in which he had been in the habit of sitting with Nuora.

"It must have been a tiresome day, what with marching in the heat at the head of the procession, and the noise and all, but the good Saint will know her duty when you go knocking at heaven's gate."

Her voice broke in the middle of "heaven," and Gennaro laughed.

"The saints themselves'll cackle when I get to paradise."

As always, Zia Anna felt ashamed of her voice, and looked embarrassed.

"But I mean it. You are good."

"You're talking nonsense, Zia Anna. You'd know the truth if you were now what you were twenty years ago . . . your breasts round and firm . . ."

"How you talk! Send for your wife, you'll soon get over what's ailing you."

"I should, and I will. . . . But you understand, Zia Anna, when the blood boils! There's a pretty Jewess . . ."

"Hush, my child . . . hush . . . God-killers[6] are not for you . . . nor them candy-lickers, the American girls! Sit down here to this glass of wine and this fine dish. You'll have to be going to the big fireworks soon . . . and you need something inside of you."

3

He ate and drank rapidly, and without another word left for the scene of the fireworks. On his way he stopped in Isaac Levin's store.

Isaac Levin had come from Russia, expecting to land in America. He had landed instead in Little Italy and had become even more Italian than his Italian customers. He spoke their language, if with his own personal touch. A thin man with a sharp noise and small oriental eyes, he had appeared on landing considerably older than his thirty-five years until he had decided on shaving off his beard and mustache. This he discovered to be a business necessity at once.

He had begun going about the streets of Little Italy with a cart that was a veritable dry-goods shop. It carried remnants of velvets, ginghams, muslins, cambrics. In a corner, handkerchiefs of diversified hues and sizes were piled up high. There were woolen drawers for men and woolen drawers for women—red and blue and ribbed. Cotton stockings and undershirts, heavy-seamed overalls, safety-pins, and whale-bone stays for corsets, and corsets . . . spools of thread and darning-needles—all of these things he had learned to call in a variety of Italian dialects, and he pushed his cart about, shouting out the names of whatever came to his head first whether he had it or not! He throve; that is, he throve when his beard and mustache did not get into his way.

They got into his way because the Italian boys had decided that it was good sport to bait all men with long beards and loose coats. Long beards and loose black coats were the sign manual of the killers of our Lord Jesus Christ, and they were to be punished until the end of all days for their infamy. Isaac Levin had his beard pulled, and while he turned to take a crack at the boy who had pulled it, his cart was overturned, and while he stooped in frantic horror to right the cart once more, his beard was pulled again, and choice pieces of linen and red flannel drawers were snatched and done off with. He had been a rabbinical student and had been taught to reverence the unshorn cheek. For months he resisted valiantly the small voice that whispered within him to shave it off.

He talked it over with his wife—this was as many years ago as when Gennaro had first landed in New York—and it had been decided between them that the best thing to do if he was not to lose his stock periodically was to remove his beard but depend on Sara's retaining her sheitel[7] in order to make it all up in the sight of heaven. So, because Sara remained within doors, she continued wearing her sheitel over her shorn head, and Isaac hurried with quick little steps into Pasquale Salerno's barber-shop, looking about him furtively and somewhat afraid, and amid the laughter and encouragement of the Italians present for the first time submitted his cheeks to the exposure of the sun and the rain.

"Sure," the men told him, "this is America. A mustache, that's all right, but a beard—by the Virgin, what could one do with a beard in America?"

Isaac emerged a handsome man despite his thin sallow cheeks and longish narrow nose, but what's more he was never again molested. And so at length his pushcart increased in size and contents until finally he parked it always in one spot and instead of his finding customers, customers came to him. Then he hired a small store, and the store was soon filled with cloths and notions, dresses and overalls, until the only available space in it was a narrow corridor between the counter and the shelves opposite. The women who crowded it had to pivot about each other like revolving spools for the farther one to get out or the newcomer to get in. But Isaac prospered, nevertheless prospered so much that he required the aid of Sara, and so Sara came into the store, and before long they both agreed that the sheitel caused too much comment and that, instead of buying, the women insisted on talking about it, and the sheitel came off and the fine-spun gold of her hair began to grow in again, and like Isaac she, too, emerged a handsome person. It was not accidental then that Gennaro should have been moved by the sight of their daughter. Dora was seventeen, and full grown.

When Gennaro entered the store, father and daughter were behind the counter. It was a maze of shelves, boxes, bolts of cloth—hot from the narrowness that channeled and retained the heat. From the ceiling hung a huge white globe with gas jets in mantles humming within and casting a glare that threw fantastic shadows of everything over the floors and walls.

"New pair of overalls."

Gennaro asked it boisterously as if it were going to be refused, but without looking at anyone or anything in particular. He was fearful of coming face to face with the young girl. He already had had a glimpse of her full body, the towering white neck, the heavy pompadour over her forehead and the hair pulled up neatly off her neck to join the mass in front. It unnerved him. He thrust his pipe into his mouth, and then with trembling, unhappy gestures sought the scapular of Saint Elena under his shirt, touched it, rapidly kissed his fingers, and made the sign of the cross.

"What kind?"

Gennaro heard Isaac's laughing voice, a voice like Rocco's, pleased at everything that went on, especially his success. He looked at the two of them, father and daughter, and mumbled his reply uncertainly.

"Blue . . . not too big . . ."

He was conscious of the girl staring at him. He felt his face flame, and then slowly he turned to her. Isaac had gone back to fetch a box of overalls.

She was smiling, amused at something she evidently considered comic. As she smiled her whole clear-white face, with plump cheeks and large blue eyes, danced before Gennaro's eyes. Then, as if miracles were happening, it retreated into sudden darkness but flashed out again like a distant light and came closer and closer to him and began to take on the appearance of a madonna, the madonna of many pictures he had seen, similar to the images in the church in Capomonte cut out of wood, girlish, innocent faces. He was unable to withdraw his eyes from her, and the more he looked at her the more she seemed the living presence of the madonna.

"You like Saint Elena," is what he finally blurted out to her.

"You're funny," she replied, "with the earrings."

"You no like?"

"Sure . . . let me see."

She leaned over the counter and touched them with her hand.

"Gold?"

"Sure, gold."

"Why do you wear them?"

"My father in old country, he put them on."

"You ought to take them off."

He shook his head, and then leaned over the counter and patted her cheek.

"You're nice—like Saint Elena."

She withdrew, frightened, as her father came up with the boxes of overalls. Gennaro did not need them, but he bought two pairs.

"You go see the fireworks?"

"Let's all go," the girl cried.

"Yes—we go," assented Gennaro.

"Dora—you go inside," her father shouted, shocked and angry.

"Oh, I'm going."

Isaac addressed Gennaro.

"See, I'm Italian, too. I speak Italian. I live here with Italians—the only Jew here, see. I cut off my beard, but I'm a Jew, and I stay home when fireworks for the Saint get shot off, see. You go inside, Dora, with your mama and the boys."

Dora went inside reluctantly and Gennaro hurried out.

Bands filled the night. The streets were noisy with crowds. Booth owners yelled. Tinted kerosene lamps blinked and shook in the dark.

"Hey, there, make room!"

They recognized him.

"Make room for Gennaro."

"Never a feast like this . . ."

Caesar never swelled with greater pride. Thoughts of Rosaria threaded through his mind. If she were present to enjoy all this! He would send for her. Put out of your mind these images of that madonna-like Jewess! The full firm breasts, the towering neck! *Diavulu santissimu,* forget it, Gennaro. You came here to make America. Hear the bands, see the crowds. The priest will be in the grandstand, too, and he will bless you and all this. A Jewish face . . . but her body! Saint Elena protect me! Am I become like a rain on the hillside?

"This is a great day," he heard Don Peppino, the café-owner.

"If the rain don't come down."

"Rain, on Gennaro's holiday. God would not dare."

"You said it," replied Gennaro.

Nevertheless, he hastened to give the signal for the fireworks to begin.

As he rushed up the platform, waving his pipe, the bands struck up *The Star Spangled Banner* and followed it with the *Royal March.* Under the twinkling lights festooned over the stand his earrings flashed like fireflies. He rubbed his hands. What a scene! He heaved with satisfaction. There was the East River at the end of the lots, black and motionless, like heavy oil, with only the lights of the barges on it answering the lights of his own festivity. Whew! The thousand poles sticking into the sky with candle-studded arms and pinwheels filled with color that would flame and sputter against the sky! Was ever such a thing Capomonte? And he, he, Gennaro, the farm-yokel, had assembled it all!

"Let's go," he shouted.

Pinwheels sputtered, crimson, yellow, green. Sky-rockets blazed, dozens and dozens, pouring continuous hoses of fire into the central sky. A whole area of fence burst into flame, noisy, eerie. Heads and hands were lighted up, the whole mass of spectators revealed singly in the expanding illumination.

"Strike up the music," Gennaro yelled, "and always more music! Nothing soft. Make it like thunder."

He became suddenly still, transfixed as with adoration. He seized Struzzo by the arm.

"Look, the Jewess . . . like Saint Elena herself."

He stopped short. His breath came and went. Before Struzzo, puzzled and amused, had a chance to say a word, Gennaro had made his way through the men busy setting the fuses. Dora was standing by herself in the front line of spectators. He seized her hand.

"Come with me," he said simply, smiling.

She recognized his earrings and followed.

"You see better . . . look," he whispered in her ear as he placed her in front of him against the railing.

"More music," he shouted. "Don't ever stop playing."

Struzzo leaned over him, but Gennaro threw him off.

"You're crazy," Struzzo told him.

But Gennaro yelled to the foreman of the workers below.

"Come on, hurry it up, hurry it up. Do you want rain?"

Lightning zigzagged in and out of the artificial fire thrown into the night. The crowds began to seethe and stir. Too fascinated by the spectacle, others refused to move. A portion pushed into the area occupied by the fireworks. Police drove them back.

"The trumpet, the trumpet," cried Gennaro.

It was the signal for the grand finale.

"Hey, there, my own little Saint," he called out to Dora. "Watch this—your face—watch."

He put an arm about her and pressed her close to him. No, those were not flares against the sky. They were fire coursing through him. The flares rose up, turned and squirmed, hurried here and there, red and blue, yellow and purple, and then with sputterings and whizzings, explosions and thunderings, a whole mass of jets spouted into the air, quieted, stopped. Against the black of the East River had risen out of the darkness, with a background of gathering clouds shot through with lightning, the form of a church. Shouts of wonder filled the air.

Gennaro bent toward Dora.

"Great, no?" he asked, and brushed his face against her cheek.

Another jet of fire, curling, rushing, rising and falling. Another vast hush. A streak of lightning, and then a whole sputter of color preceding a burst of thunder. The sputtering stopped, the smoke cleared away, and there in the midst of the church of fire stood the form of Saint Elena, her innocent face, outlined in flame, looking benignly over the hushed, adoring crowds.

"Your face, see," said Gennaro as he took Dora's cheeks between his hands. "Your face . . . you there . . . the madonna . . ."

"And now," he concluded jubilantly, "let it pour."

Whistling, shrieking, the rain tore through the night.

"I want to go home," Dora cried.

"Yes, my saint," said Gennaro.

"I don't want to get soaked."

"No, you come with me."

"Hurry."

Did she understand him?

4

Zia Anna was waiting for him. She stared at Dora, and then at Gennaro.

"Go upstairs and get some dresses . . . anything that will fit this girl."

She raised her hand slowly to her shoulders and made the sign of the cross, too dumbfounded to say a word.

"Well? Hurry," cried Gennaro.

"God help us, and all the saints," whispered the old woman. "The man's gone crazy."

She hurried out as fast as she could.

"You much wet, ha, my saint?"

Dora laughed.

"Am I?"

"You take off the dress, ha?"

"Gee, I got to. It's sopping."

"You no 'fraid strange man, ha?"

Gennaro was close to her and had lifted her chin with one hand. He breathed hard, his eyes shining.

"No 'fraid, little saint?"

She laughed again. "I'm a big girl."

And while he continued staring at her as if he did not believe what was happening, she giggled and said, "Gee, but you're funny."

"Funny? Me?"

But he said the words mechanically. His mind in actuality was leaping back across the years and fetching up out of the past the image of a young man in Sunday breeches with short coat and red sash over his waist and a little feather in his corduroy hat, diffident in spite of all his bravery of clothes, respectful of everyone, bowing to the lawyer and the notary and the big peasant proprietors as well.

It was a Thursday but he wore his Sunday outfit. He followed some feet behind his father, and he recalled how the old fellow would turn around and shout good-humoredly, "You're never afraid to chase the wolf in the mountains? Does a pretty girl frighten you? Come on, young man, be brave."

The scene in Rosaria's kitchen flashed in front of him. The girl standing by the hearth, she, too, in her Sunday best, swinging pleated skirt, tight-fitting bodice with a blue vest, a red kerchief on her head, fringed with yellow. Her father, too stout to move, his legs, or what portion could be seen under the paunch, stretched out, his long clay pipe raised in mid-air, his fat cheeks puffing with the laughter of welcome. Her mother, with a great earthen tray with earthen cups and a decanter of wine, at the door leading to the only other room. How he trembled as he approached, how ashamed he felt having his father and mother come begging a wife for him!

And here he was now, head of a holy society, house-owner, a big business in his hands, commanding the women he wanted, when he wanted them, and no one saying him nay. Dora's repeated, "Sure, you're funny," meant nothing to him. It was enough that she was there in front of him, madonna-like, her cheeks glowing from the exertion, her wet hair gleaming like straw under the sun.

"You a saint."

"And you a funny man. Sure. With those earrings. You give them to me."

He slapped her playfully on both cheeks.

"You never get those earrings."

And then he caught her in his arms, wet though they both were, held her close to him, took her damp hair into his mouth, bit her on the ears.

Zia Anna entered without knocking.

"Shame on you," she cried to him. "Shame . . . a man with a wife and children . . . shame . . . what's happening to us all in this devil country? The saints forgive you your sins . . . you're a wicked man."

Gennaro snatched the clothes out of her arms, took her by the elbow and pushed her out of the room. He turned to face Dora. They looked at each other for a second, and then burst into laughter.

5

After several weeks, everyone in Little Italy had heard some version of Gennaro's affair with a Jewess.

"Such a good family she comes from, so hard-working, they mind their own business. For shame on the man."

Such were the comments of the Italians. Struzzo, one morning, walked into Gennaro's shop. As usual there was barely enough room for a man to find a place for his feet, and Struzzo told Gennaro so.

"Stand on your head," was the answer.

"You're doing that yourself."

The women sorting rags, sitting on their haunches in the yard outside, had raised a song. The men engaged in tamping down the rags in the bins took it up.

"What's that?" asked Gennaro calmly.

"I'll come to the point, Gennaro. I'm not afraid, see."

He thrust his hat behind his head and laughed.

"Well, well, come on."

"You're making a fool of yourself with that Jew girl."

Gennaro said nothing. He would have been the first to level that accusation at himself. He was stubborn enough, however, never to budge once he had taken a position.

"Gennaro, reason the damn thing out. You're thirty-six, got a fine business, the people, they respect you, see what I mean."

Gennaro gazed up at the tall angular man with a kind of boy-like interest. He began to feel that possibly he ought to pay attention to a man like Struzzo who had, like himself, made America, commanded the admiration of hundreds of people, had a fine growing family, the older boy already marked out as an outstanding youth, studying to be a doctor, one of the girls beautiful and of fine manners, of marriageable age, sought after by splendid young men. He himself could have just such a family—Domenico full-grown and an aid to his business, Emilio going to the schools and studying to be a doctor, too, and the little girl, Elena, becoming a lady like Teresina Struzzo.

"Don't you see, everybody talking about you? Isn't right. It makes an impression. . . ."

Perversely Gennaro answered. "That's my business. We'll drop it now. How about that house, the Parterre?"

Struzzo sat on an upturned copper boiler.

"All right. Your business . . . not another word from me. The Parterre? The old Dutchman wants too much for it. Let's wait. When all the other houses around him are bought up by the Italians, he'll sell, and damn cheap, too."

That same day the priest of the church which Gennaro attended passed by. Gennaro had seen him and had begun to fear that he would be in for another scolding. Don Anselmo, however, had not even looked in. He had made sure that he would be seen, and that was sufficient.

A young man in a difficult parish, he had made it a practice to think thoroughly before he acted. Uprooted from their original soil, where each one measured by a kind of social instinct the distance he could go in assertion or rebellion, bravado or effrontery, these men here in America, tasting a freedom they had never before had, could not be handled as they had been in Italy.

There it would have been sufficient to storm into their homes and lay down the law in no uncertain terms. Even that would have been too much. Some words spoken in the mass would have been enough for even so audacious a person as Gennaro. But here in New York even the priest had better go slowly.

He had not gone more than several paces when Don Anselmo turned back and stuck his head into the door.

"I did not see you. Good morning, my dear Gennaro."

"Don Anselmo *bello,* I kiss your hand."

"A beautiful morning this October day."

"You're on your way somewhere? If not, I have a bit of wine here from the old homestead. A sip?"

Don Anselmo entered.

"There was a baby born up the street—they'll be giving me a drop of cordial."

"Ah, but you are a young man and Calabrese. Whenever did a Calabrese refuse a bit of real wine?"

Don Anselmo moved among the bales of rags, drawing his cassock up close about him.

"No place here for those long skirts of yours. See what the women do . . . tie them up behind them. You ought to try—you'd be a picture."

"You'll pardon me, Gennaro," said the young priest. "It is warm in here and there is not much space. I'll take off my hat so I can find room for my head."

"Ah," replied Gennaro at once, "America gives everybody a chance to find room for his head. Especially for a fine aristocratic head like yours."

Don Anselmo took the wine without answering and held it up between himself and the doorway. He raised and tilted the glass—a heavy cheap one—and seemed to be trying to find the most effective angle of refraction.

"Gennaro," he finally answered, "this is a silly thing to do, but I have just noticed that I can hold this glass in this fashion—watch—and observe the objects through it, and they look reddish and far away. But if I hold the glass this way—see what I mean—this way—why then everything I observe seems closer, bigger, and not at all red, but a washed-out stupid sort of pink. We never really know what we see, what we do."

"I always know."

Don Anselmo was not aware that they had an audience. But at Gennaro's remarks the women working outside made deprecatory noises with their mouths at his boldness in standing up to the fine young priest.

"You have many working here?" he asked.

"Getting bigger by the day. Nobody else is so big."

"You have become an important person."

Gennaro slapped his chest.

"With my own hands—you know it."

"Possibly some help from God and the good saints."

"Well, why not, I prayed enough, and gave them enough."

The women had moved nearer to the door.

"What has been given can be taken away."

Shadows flitted across the wall. Gennaro knew that the women had crossed themselves. He listened closely and discovered that they were repeating "God be praised" in quiet voices. So they were glad to hear him raked over the coals by this young priest with his fine manners and nice way of talking? They would find out, and he would find out, too, his holiness notwithstanding, that there was no fooling with Gennaro. What Gennaro wanted, he did, and there was to be no one interfering.

"I'll take my chances on that," he declared.

"I admire you, Gennaro," the priest said quietly, putting his hand on the rag-man's knee. "You have confidence, you have a daring soul."

This line Gennaro did not like. He realized what was coming next.

"But there's no measure to your boldness. But, but—what am I doing? Preaching to you . . . I make it a practice never, never to preach to one person alone. It never does much good. What I stopped in to say—"

"So you did come on purpose?"

"Well, in a way. I should not have come in if I thought you were too busy. I stopped in to say that I have just heard from one of the parish priests near Capomonte that he has been transferred here to New York and is about to come."

Gennaro whitened.

"He could accompany my family? You mean that?"

"It would be advantageous, would it not?"

"I'll think it over."

"Very soon. I must write."

"Another glass?"

The priest drank his other glass, but left immediately after.

Gennaro jumped to his feet and rushed into the yard.

"What are you all doing out here?" he shouted. "What am I paying you for? Keep working, come on, keep working!"

The women bent their heads and the rags slipped rapidly through their fingers. Silk pieces they threw in one bag, wool in another.

Gennaro dug his hand into the wool bag and pulled out a dozen strips.

"I thought so. Wool and silk mixed," he bellowed. "You good-for-nothings. May you have the rabies and the saints forget you."

"We all will if you keep biting at us."

"You shut up, Filomena Cantinello. You do too much talking as it is. You have a family . . . don't forget."

He stormed out as fast as he had stormed in among them, and spent the rest of the morning in a furious survey of his establishment. No one escaped his anger. He became particularly enraged with the men tamping down the rags in one of the bins.

"You're not packing figs, you rotten sons of she-asses."

He jumped into the bin himself and ordered all the men out.

"Watch," he shouted, "all of you."

The men crowded around, climbing on boxes to look in. Gennaro kept stamping with his feet, sometimes with one, sometimes with two. Then he would seize the tamping iron and with vigorous movements bang down on the rags.

"This way, you loons. Keep them even, work fast. It's the way to make America, work fast, fast."

He piled out, sweating and glaring.

"And you might do a little cleaning up. Look at those pictures on the wall—naked women—for shame—alongside of the good saints, too! Tear them down, tear them down."

He hurried into the street. As usual it was jammed with pushcarts. On the curbs squatted rows of old women, selling stale rolls from the American bakeries. Bags bulging with them stood up on end. As purchasers came, the old women dug their hands into the bags and filled the aprons of the buyers or bundled the rolls into old newspapers. They shouted as they carried on their business. Gennaro leaned back against the jamb of his doorway, his hat thrust back, his pipe in his mouth, uneasy in mind.

"My wife won't do that," he thought. "She'll be a lady and wear a hat."

But he was not yet certain that he would send for her. Maybe he had better sell out and return to Capomonte. With his money, he could lord it over the countryside, be the grand signor himself. No interfering little pope of the aristocracy even, like Don Anselmo, would stick his twitching snout into Gennaro's affairs. But it took a year and a quarrel with Dora, and drunken sorties into the "English" places.

6

Isaac Levin was aware of what had happened to his daughter. But with her he confessed he was powerless. She was one of those sweet-looking girls with a waspish tongue and an unbridled manner. Unlike her brothers she had found few things to interest her in the life of her father and mother. She had left school, but though she remained at home she refused to help in the store or with the family chores except under the greatest compulsion. Gifted with an unusual type of beauty, she discovered soon that she was particularly attractive to the Italian men of the neighborhood. Blond women with fair skin like hers were uncommon.

And how she managed to swing provokingly her full, rotund body, fitting closely in her clothes.

The young men of the vicinity made it a practice to loiter around the store. The older men, in passing, never failed to stop and watch the younger ones. The women disapproved of her and made no effort to conceal their feelings. For their pains they gained only catcalls from the young men and sharp words from the girl. She was in awe only of her younger brother—a quiet, morose-looking lad with preternaturally intense eyes who spent most of his time studying.

He spoke to her but rarely, and certainly never allowed himself the privilege that was his mother's and father's only, of scolding his sister the way he had a mind to do. She had brought him up during those early days when her mother and father were so busy in the store that they had practically thrown Moses aside and permitted him to grow up as best he could. Dora had washed and fed him, clothed him, put him to sleep, and all this despite the fact that she was only four years older. She loved him and was happy to see how bright he was and how much he was liked by his teachers. But he was soon immersed in his books to the exclusion of her, and she merely looked on as he grew.

He put up his own lunch in the morning before starting for school and when he returned he found something to eat, did his lessons, and then went to the library. It had just been opened. And although it was more distant from his home than his school—in fact, twice as far—he rarely missed a day. He always returned with books, read through the evening and went to sleep. Neither with his father nor mother did he exchange many words—they were always busy in their store—and soon he found it useless to talk with Dora.

Nevertheless, Dora stood in fear of him. Simple-minded, pagan to her every pore, she admired this silent, studious boy whose mind seemed bent on things far removed from the ordinary.

"More books?" she asked one night as he returned fairly late.

"Yes," he answered, and pushed her aside.

She followed him into the rear rooms where they lived. There were three rooms all cluttered with boxes containing extras of the goods sold outside. Even the bedrooms were filled with them. The kitchen alone, containing a stove, several wooden chairs, a large sofa to one side and a broad table in the center, had been left unencumbered. Moses threw his books on the table, went to the closet close to the stove, cut himself a slice of bread and a chunk of salami, poured out a glass of tea and sat down to read.

"What's the matter, Moses?" asked Dora as she leaned over him, one arm around his neck.

He quietly removed it and told her to leave him alone.

"You're always reading, you never want to talk to me no more."

"Go and talk to the *goyim*,"[8] he answered.

Her father might threaten to beat her. Her mother might yell at her, "May you break a leg, the way you treat me." It would not affect her. These simple words of Moses were another thing. They stung her at once.

"There ain't no one else."

"Leave me alone."

"You hate me."

"Yes."

She went to the sofa and buried her head in her hands.

"Why do you want to cry?" Moses shrieked the words at her. "You make mother unhappy, and you cry yet."

"You'll see," she said, sitting up. "You'll see. You'll all be sorry."

7

That night she went to see Gennaro. Zia Anna had never been won over to approve of the arrangement. She needed the few dollars she earned taking care of Gennaro's apartment and so she kept her tongue, especially in his presence. With Dora it was another matter. There were times, like the present, when she felt the impulse to blame the whole thing on the girl, and she believed that lashing at her with words and gestures was the perfect way to bring the child to her senses.

"So," she said, half in Italian, half in the few broken English phrases she had acquired, "so, again! *Che vergogna . . .* what a shame. You ain't shame?"

"Leave me alone," Dora yelled at her. "Leave me alone."

"You cry? I see you cry. Get the nice man . . . and leave Gennaro . . . he got the wife, he got the children . . . shame . . ."

Gennaro had been having a similar scene with Struzzo. Struzzo never lost an opportunity to bring Gennaro to his senses too.

"This is the last time I speak of it," he said. "But it's hurting your business, my business. We got money invested together. What hurts me, hurts you."

"We just sold a house and made money; we just bought a lot and that'll make money. My rag business . . . it's going stronger . . . bah!"

"Well, then," cried Struzzo, taking a stand in front of his seated partner. "Well, then, here goes for the truth. You might as well know it."

He towered over Gennaro and seemed momentarily to overpower him.

"You're getting old . . . see, there's white in your hair, and look at the wrinkles."

Gennaro laughed.

"Who's going to give a damn for you very soon, ha? Do you think a young girl is going to stick to you? You got a wife, you can't marry her. She knows that."

"So? What you driving at?"

"Haven't you heard? You are a worse fool than I thought. The big shot—and he knows nothing."

Gennaro was not going to reveal that he was alarmed.

"So they'll not elect me president of the society. Well, the church won't get much after that."

"It's not that, either."

"I had a good mind once to help Don Anselmo build his new church. Let him try to take a hand in the society . . . and . . ."

"It's not that, I'm telling you. It's Dora—"

"What do you mean, Dora?"

"All the young fellows are crazy about her."

"Well . . ."

"Put two and two together. You're getting older. How long do you think you can keep it up with a young one, hey?"

"Let anyone interfere—"

"One! Two, three . . . they buzz around her like flies around sugar. And with earrings, too."

Gennaro slapped his chest.

"Say, Struzzo. I made America single-handed, and wearing earrings. I'll keep on making America and wearing earrings. I'll take my chances with them all, old, young, middle-aged. There ain't no one good enough to take what's mine."

"And what if somebody with black hair and a handsome face, who can sing sweet songs under her window and take her to the dances, ha, what if he comes around and he does take her away from you?"

"There's nobody dares."

"Go and ask."

He flung into his flat and brushed Zia Anna aside.

"You, get upstairs."

He watched her go.

"And you," he said to Dora, tilting his pipe, "you got to tell me something. You been seeing other men?"

She was not one to be easily intimidated. She laughed quietly and faced Gennaro with mocking lips. They were like two strange dogs looking at each other, growling softly.

"Can't you fix that jet?" she inquired sharply. "It makes a noise like a saw."

He lowered the flame.

"Now it ain't bright."

Angrily, he turned the flame up once more.

"Hoo ... listen to it now ... it's worse."

He got up on a chair.

"Got a hairpin?"

She fumbled around in the blond mists of her hair.

"Here."

He all but put out the light.

"It's too dark that way."

"Shut up," he shouted.

"I'll say what I want."

He merely took off his hat and threw it across the room on to the sofa. Then he busied himself prying into the holes in the gas-jet with the hairpin, and alternately lowering and raising the flame. He had finally cleaned out all the carbon he could and was satisfied that the light would be strong, even, and noiseless.

"Yeh, that's better," said Dora.

He got off the chair, slowly put it back under the table, and, leaning back on it, looked at her steadily and repeated, "You seeing other men?"

She laughed and nodded her head up and down.

"You been?"

"You ain't married to me."

From the same position, he demanded again, "You been?"

"You make me laugh. Sure. What do you think? Who are you?"

The direct attack that he was in the habit of adopting evidently was instinctive with Dora. He had encountered the method before, but he had never been thoroughly stirred with anger.

"You been, then?"

"Sure."

"Who?"

"None of your business."

She weaved her way to the couch, her arms akimbo, never once taking from him her laughing, mocking stare. In the second that it took her to sit down, he ran his eye over her body, the soft contours, the filled-out bosom, the long white neck. It was as a ripe fig to a green pear, he thought, as the image of Rosaria at eighteen came back to him. It is like fresh milk to curds, he thought, as he recalled the ample figure of Nuora. It had been his—he, peasant-born, a yokel, rind of the fields.

He flushed, his breath came and went. But it was not passion. It was the sudden realization that he was not so big a person after all. This flesh-stirring body before him, full of youth and the unflagging energy of young muscles, gave a snap-o'-the fingers and no more for him, for him, Gennaro Accuci, who had made America, and made it single-handed, yes, sir, and without removing his earrings. She could sit there with laughter about her lips making fun of him.

"So . . . they tell me truth."

He lunged forward and was about to seize her by the wrist. She knew her man well enough to have foreseen what he might do. As he moved she quickly jumped erect on the couch and with a flash removed the long hatpin from her hat.

"You touch me, I dare you," she smiled as she spoke. "You put your hand on me and I'll—"

He heard her light laughter lose itself in her throat. If only she would cease her smiling, stop her laughing, give up her mocking of him! The anger in him would subside. But she laughed again, merrily. Not only did she laugh but she made fun of him.

"You look too funny when you're angry."

He seized her about the knees and was about to fling her on her back on the sofa. Again she was too quick for him. She threw herself head first with all her strength, and so she hung over his head and shoulders. With every move he made to shake her off and throw her on the sofa, she plunged the hatpin without mercy into the soft flesh of his buttocks. He screamed, and she laughed. He turned ferociously on his heels in an attempt to set her on the floor, but she clung to him with one arm and stuck the pin into him again.

"*Putana!*"[9] he yelled in Italian.

With one frantic movement he swung around and let go of her. She tumbled to the floor, but with miraculous suddenness found her feet and ran for the door.

"Look what you done—spoiled my hat—look, my dress, too . . . you old fool!"

The hatpin had penetrated deep into his flesh and he was too much in agony to attempt to retaliate either by word or by deed. He merely crunched his teeth with the pain of his mortal as well as his spiritual wound and gazed at her.

"What do you think I was going to do? Waste my life with an old man? Sure I got other fellows. Sure, young ones without no earrings. So you wanted to beat me up, hey, you old cheap fool? You got another try coming to you—but not with me. I came to say good-bye to you and I wanted it to be nice, see, with wine and sitting around the way we used to, see. But you got fresh, you old—"

"*Putana santissima,*[10] get out of here," he shouted.

"Yeh, but I put it over on you, you old toad."

She slammed the door in his face and was gone.

8

Gennaro stood in the center of a vast desolation. All around him ran the circle of hills that enclosed Capomonte and out of the depths of the woods on each of them came voices that blared, "Old fool." He stood still, listened, shook his head slowly.

"Sure, I am the old fool," he said to himself.

During the excitement, the pain had gone out of his flesh. But now in the great silence and the never-ending loneliness it returned to mock him all the more. He saw how funny it was, too, but at the same time realized the tragedy he was undergoing. His massive pride had been given one little shove and failed to stand up.

"Old? You think I'm old, Struzzo, do you? I'll show you."

He lay down on the sofa, clenching his fist.

"Sure, I better send for Rosaria, and Domenico. He must be a big boy now. And I wonder, how does she look, my baby Elena! Six years old now, and there's Emilio, too, the curly one."

Like everything else he did, his next move was sheerly impulsive. He put on his hat and rushed to Dr. Giovanelli's office. Dr. Giovanelli was the only Italian doctor to have come to America in the wake of the first immigration. He had need to. His age had begun to tell against him in the town of Reggio, and people had begun to weary not so much of his failure to help anybody as of his failure to stop repeating, "Ha, I, I staunched Garibaldi's wounds at Aspromonte.[11] Into my arms he fell, and quickly I stopped the blood, or that big heart would have ceased to beat." But his self-proclaimed saviorship of the great general was not a sufficient substitute for medical skill, and with the dwindling populace his practice had fallen off more and more. So he decided to follow it to America.

With him he carried his story. Nothing elated him as much as to tell it anew to his patients, but nothing exalted him to feverish heights of reminiscent glory as much as telling it to fresh ears. With the story, he had carried with him his old frock coat, much too long for his short stocky body, his high hat with its trimming of braid already aged enough to be showing light tints of green, the enormous walking stick with the gold ring about its handle, the gift of the famous patriot, and the red sash he wore across his shoulders and around his belt—the same sash he had worn as the chief marcher in the parade in honor of Italian unity at Reggio at least fifteen years back.

These were the signs manual of his importance as a physician and surgeon. For a few years his stout little person was seen proudly erect behind his stick and under the greening high hat, making its way in self-sustained glory through the congested immigrant sections. If the occasion seemed propitious, he unbuttoned his frock coat and stuck one hand into his trousers pocket. Then, despite his long white beard, like his hat also slightly tinged with green, the red sash across his chest would flash out like an abrupt trumpet call and everybody knew that the physician who had staunched the wounds of Garibaldi at the famous battle of Aspromonte was alive and in their very midst.

His office was like himself—nothing new and clean in it, piled with ancient medical works, the mohair couch threadbare and greening, too, the walls hung with portraits of his revered general in various poses, and with an enormous lithograph of the battle of Aspromonte at the exact moment when the red-shirted general was reposing in the arms of Dr. Giovanelli himself. He had had the lithographs made at his own expense, and after sending a copy to Garibaldi, one to King Victor Emanuel, he had given them out freely to the citizens of Reggio and to each of his patients. It is said that the cost of this generous outlay had depleted his treasury and that he had never since been able to refill it. It was evident that he would therefore have a great contempt for the *cafonacci*[12]—the clodhoppers—that had succeeded, in their own phrase, at "making America." And particularly did he despise Gennaro, but not to his face.

He was seated at his enormous second-hand desk with its cracked roller-top, peering through his square glasses at the Italian papers that had just arrived in the mail. The gas above his head emitted a whistling bluish flame that had for many months now been covering both the ceiling and the wall with a fine layer of soot.

"Don Pasquale, Don Pasquale...," cried Gennaro.

The doctor turned about slowly.

"You bellow like a stuck pig, my man."

"And stuck I've been ... a nail ... in my flesh here ... at the shop ... an accident ..."

"Well, well, I've attended worse wounds than that ... there was the wound of Garibaldi ..."

"The devil with Garibaldi."

"My dear sir ..."

"By Saint Jerome, do something."

The doctor was peering helplessly at the expanse of flesh that Gennaro had exposed.

"Where? I see nothing. No blood, no wound ..."

"Here," he placed a finger on the spot.

The doctor pressed, and Gennaro shrieked.

"Hush, hush, my man, Garibaldi with a worse wound—"

"By all the crazy saints, to hell with Garibaldi—do something."

"There's nothing much to do, my man, nothing much ..."

He washed the flesh with alcohol, pressed it once or twice, especially because it made Gennaro shriek, and then applied a wet dressing.

"What!" cried Gennaro. "Am I going around with a diaper?"

"You'll have to wear it, Gennaro *bello,* or do you want an infection?"

The humiliation he had experienced at being stabbed with a hatpin in the rump was as nothing to the degradation he felt at having to wear a wet dressing over it. He picked his way cautiously through the crowded streets. But everybody recognized him. Though he tried not to limp they saw that something was wrong.

"No broken bones, Gennaro?"

"No, it's nothing."

"What's wrong?" Mastro Donato, the baker, was solicitous. He put his stout arm about Gennaro's waist. Gennaro winced and withdrew. "Have you seen the doctor?"

"Oh, it's a bit of nothing—just a bit of nothing."

9

He escaped and reached the doorway to his home. Leaning against the jamb, a mandolin under his arm, was Giovanni Sardi, the young barber with whom he had boarded.

"Whey, Gennaro *bello!*"

Gennaro drew up and winced.

"Something hurt you?"

"Yes, you fool, something hurts me."

"I'm sorry."

"By Saint Jerome, who cares?"

"I've been waiting an hour for you, sir," pleaded Giovanni.

"What for?"

"I come to ask a favor."

"Me? Why me? Tonight?"

"I see . . . it's a bad time . . ."

Giovanni looked the incarnation of youth, slim, immaculate, his suit carefully pressed, his straw hat set jauntily to one side over his massed hair, his eyes alive with energy. Gennaro eyed him with envy.

"Still strumming away on your old instruments, hey?"

"It's a pastime . . ."

"Nothing else to do?"

"I'm working. But it's not so nice, working for yourself . . . you know . . . I have an idea . . ."

"Got ambition, now, hey?"

"Yes . . . that's why I came here."

Hesitatingly Giovanni outlined his scheme. He desired to establish himself in a barber shop among the English, as he put it, on the other side of the town. There was a good chance there to make money. He had in mind marrying a beautiful girl, but a very beautiful girl. No, she was not an Italian girl, but what did that matter? She would make him a good wife. He had been out with many girls not Italian, and he had found that they were nice girls, very nice girls . . .

"But, you, you understand?"

"Well, naturally." Gennaro's face lighted up. "You still see some, hey?" he added, his eyes dancing.

"Sure . . . why not?"

"Take me."

"What?"

"Take me . . . you want money for your store. You will have the best barber shop . . ."

"But, you can't . . . you know, just like that . . . besides . . ."

"I'm old, hey, and wear earrings? Hey? You mean that? But I'm not too old to make America with all my earrings! By Saint Jerome and the Holy Calendar I could cut open that young throat of yours!"

Giovanni drew back into the shadow of the doorway, holding his mandolin in front of him for protection.

"Oh, I'm not going to touch you," shouted Gennaro, laughing at the same time. The sensation of being able to bait someone had restored his self-confidence. "But, the devil, let's go out, not to-night, but soon, hey, . . . you and me. We have the good time. You got the girls, I got the money."

Giovanni pleaded, "I'm going to be married."

"A few more nights . . . that's all . . . and don't forget, the barber shop."

CHAPTER FOUR

1

One night soon after, Giovanni escorted Gennaro to a music hall. It overlooked the Harlem River. It was an enormous, barn-like structure. The lighted windows rose like walls of garish tinsel above the elevated railway terminals that it paralleled. The gas-jets flared and blew to one side and the other, and so with each wind the whole exposed surface of the building seemed to pulse with alternate dark and glow.

Inside, the floor was strewn with sawdust where the tables were set under a balcony that ran the length of the hall on both sides. A stage at the front, without a curtain, was a sputtering mass of lights. As the men entered, the whole hall had burst into wild singing. The occupants of each table banged their glasses, stamped their feet, clapped their hands, in rollicking accompaniment to the shouted song. On the stage, several women in tights, holding canes with both hands in front of them, side-stepped and bounced first to the right and then to the left, jerking out the tune in shrieky, scratchy voices. At the piano sat a big-bosomed woman with shoulders exposed and skirts that were not intended to conceal the rotund masses on which she reposed.

Gennaro did not hear the song. His eyes had lighted on the girl singing the stanzas before each of the prolonged choruses. She was a blond, thick-set hoyden, so corsetted that her breasts in parted firmness stood out boldly above her bodice. She swung her black-silk skirt—she was the only one so dressed—with heavy abandon, ogling and smirking archly while on her head glittered a polished silk topper.

> "I'm not too young, I'm not too old,
>   Not too timid, not too bold,
>   Just the kind you'd like to hold,
>   Just the kind of sport I'm told . . .
>
> "Tarara boom de ray
>   Tarara boom de ray
>   Tarara boom de ray . . ."

The crowd took up the chorus interminably while the young woman jounced her hour-glass figure back and forth across the stage.

"You know that one?" Gennaro inquired of Giovanni.

Giovanni claimed only a casual intimacy with the blond singer. He promised to effect an introduction. Giovanni knew the ropes sufficiently to call for the manager. Mr. Fitzgibbons shuffled his way through the maze of tables and dancers and stood overlooking Gennaro and Giovanni.

Mr. Fitzgibbons seemed to walk on towers—his legs were so long and vast. But he needed to walk on towers, for his abdomen expanded into a huge conical mass with the apex at the neck. The neck itself proceeded from the abdomen by smooth natural stages, escaping an ample region of shirt-front bestudded with sparklers and topped with a collar with enormous flaps on each side and a huge black bow tie in front. The neck became chin at once and after chin narrow walls of smooth-shaven jaws that moved with great slowness whether Mr. Fitzgibbons talked, chewed or smoked. He was now smoking, and he held the cigar—like himself built on unrestricted lines—at a sharp elevation to his chin so that its shadow fell easily across a massive nose. Neither Giovanni nor Gennaro could see his eyes, for they were as effectively shaded by the eyelashes, heavy, black, and long, as if his eyes had been windows over which the curtains were drawn. Someone had said "How do you, Mr. Fitzgibbons?" in passing, and Mr. Fitzgibbons had raised a ring-covered hand and murmured in a deep basso, "How do you do?"

He now stood in front of Gennaro's table. His presence must have bestowed upon their sitting-place a special dignity, for everyone stared in their direction, waiters, dancers, singers, piano-player. They looked up at him sheepishly.

"Who's Mr. Accuci?" he bassoed, pronouncing the name in his own fashion.

"That's me," answered Gennaro, awed.

"It is, hey? For God's sake . . . ," he drawled the imprecation out in thorough-going disgust.

"Sure, Mr. Fitzgibbons," piped up Giovanni. "That's Mr. Accuci. He has a big business and . . ." He slipped several fingers over each other to indicate possession of considerable money.

"Yea, what of it? How about them fool things?" And without any hesitation, he gave Gennaro's earrings a fillip with his enormous fingers. As he did so, he laughed deep down in his throat.

"The Goddammest things . . ."

Gennaro sprang to his feet, his eyes flashing.

"Sit down," laughed Mr. Fitzgibbons, not really alarmed at Gennaro's gesture but mindful rather of the decorum of his place. The only fights allowed were those the bouncers engaged in, and they always won. And as he said "Sit down," he pressed his hand on Gennaro's shoulder and forced him into his seat.

"I hear you want to talk to Miss Waterson."

Giovanni explained that he meant the small chunky young woman at that moment kicking up her legs under her silk-spangled skirts.

"Yea—that one," Gennaro pointed to her, so that the people about the table giggled.

"We'll see about it," Fitzgibbons bassoed, "that is, if it can be arranged."

It was arranged. Miss Waterson hurried to Gennaro's table not long after the conclusion of her act.

"Mr. Accuci?"

She asked it with professional brightness, but of Giovanni, who, despite the fact that he was intending marriage, gazed at her wide-eyed and more than superficially interested.

"No . . . I'm Sardi."

"Oh, how do you do, Mr. Sardi, pleased to meet you, I'm sure. What'll we drink? I'll have a fizz, gin . . . sure . . . Here, waiter, three gin-fizzes . . . that's right, hey, Mr. Accuci."

She had drawn up her own chair, crossed her legs, made a pretense of gathering her skirts about her, but not without first raising them with an innocent-seeming flirt high above her knees, and then leaned back and surveyed the men. Gennaro was dazed, and looked it.

"Hey, what you so crabby about, Mr. Accuci? You need a drink."

"No, I need you."

"Oh me, oh me, oh my," she cried coquettishly, "say, but you think you're a knockout."

"Sure," he replied, putting out his hand and placing it on her knee. "You swell gal . . ."

She giggled.

"Me like . . ."

"You're an Eyetalian."

"American gals—they nice," he said, gazing intensely at his companion as he leaned over once more and put his hand again on her knees.

"He's funny, ain't he?" she inquired of Giovanni. Giovanni sat embarrassed and uneasy, somewhat ashamed of his companion but

anxious to prove that Gennaro, in spite of his awkwardness and blunt-
ness, was the right sort.

"He got the big business, and . . ." He winked and repeated his gesture of one finger slipped over the other to indicate that Gennaro had
plenty to spend.

Miss Waterson developed a new interest.

"I like you, too," she said, and slapped Gennaro on the cheek with
two fingers. "You're funny though—sure—with them earrings. Maybe,
see, cause we ain't used to them on men in this here country."

"My father, he gave me . . . " answered Gennaro proudly.

"Let me try them on."

"They no come off." He put down her hand forcefully.

The waiter had put the gin-fizzes on the table.

"Have a drink," she cried, handing Gennaro a glass.

As she did so, she sat on his knees and made him sip it with her.

"They're gold, ain't they?"

"Sure."

Giovanni was slowly drinking his gin, making faces at it—he would
rather have had wine—but furtively glancing at Gennaro and the girl.
She had placed a hand around Gennaro's shoulders, and with the other
was examining the earrings closely. Gennaro sat still, as if overpowered,
his eyes blood-shot, the muscles of his face tense, his breath slow and
uneven.

"You got holes in your ears, ha? Funny . . ."

She ran one hand over his cheeks. He reddened and stared into
vacancy.

"Say something, old boy. You like me?"

He put his arms about her and clasped her hard, sunk his face into
her breasts, and seized the flesh of them between his teeth.

"Hey, what the hell!" She laughed.

He pressed harder.

"Stop it," she cried.

"Gennaro, Gennaro," whispered Giovanni, "*per l'amore di Dio, che
fai?*"[1]

Miss Waterson slapped him hard over his ears, and he gave way. She
jumped off his knees and slapped him again on the other cheek. Gennaro rose, too, sheepish, trembling, aware that everybody was looking
and that the huge bulk of Mr. Fitzgibbons was slowly clouding out the
view ahead of him. The piano was strumming faster, the singers on the
stage singing louder, the gas-jets flaring more wheezily, the dancers on

the floor shuffling noisily, the voices of the crowd raised to higher pitches, Giovanni red as a beet and shrieking at him.

Mr. Fitzgibbons finally stood in front of him, gigantic, a menacing smile slipping across his smooth features like a film of water.

"*Che buole chisto?*" Gennaro asked Giovanni in his own dialect. "What's he after?"

"*Non fa niente, santissima madonna,* Gennaro,"[2] pleaded Giovanni.

Miss Waterson looked frightened, and stared from one of the men to the other.

"Oh, it was nothing, Mr. Fitzgibbons," she said.

"Say, bo," that worthy addressed Gennaro, "this is a respectable place and we don't want no dagoes cutting up around here, understand, or by hell you'll get out of here double quick."

"What I do?" Gennaro tried to defend himself, and then he noticed that Miss Waterson was actually smiling in sympathy with him, and so he continued. "Me like her, see, and I give her the one kiss, and she get the excite . . . and dat's all . . ."

"Put a bill on the table for the waiter," Giovanni whispered in Italian.

Gennaro went into his pockets calmly.

"We just want to have the good time, dat's all. You no want, all right. I pay . . . we go."

He stripped a five-dollar bill off a roll and laid it on the table.

"Oh, we didn't mean nothing, Mr. Accuci, only you see, we don't want no trouble."

He took the five-dollar bill, pocketed it, placed some silver on the table to pay for the fizzes, and an extra quarter for the waiter.

"Go ahead," he continued, "have a good time . . . And you, Miss Waterson, what the hell do you want to be yelling for anyhow?"

2

Giovanni's trick had worked. At the end of the show, Gennaro, somewhat tipsy, was strolling down the avenue with Miss Waterson on his arm. It was the beginning of a long string of parties in his apartment. Zia Anna was more than ever scandalized. She went to Don Anselmo and pleaded with the priest to put an end to them.

"*E'nna vergogna, Don Anselmo . . .'nna vita stupida*[3] . . . You got to do something. What they do! It's filthy . . ."

"Ah, you are a good woman to come and tell me all this," said the priest, stroking her hand benignantly.

"Here's what they do . . . you listen, and you'll understand."

"I do understand. You go now and offer a prayer for him."

"A hundred he needs, if you'll let me contradict you," she whispered, her voice cracking on the word. "But you ought to hear . . ."

"I can very well imagine."

"How can you? You have had no experience of such things."

He smiled at her persistence, realizing that some obscure impulse at vicarious self-gratification lay at the bottom of it, and decided that he would allow her to talk.

"Well," he said, "tell me."

Zia Anna drew up her chair closer. Her thin face broadened out with anticipated horror at her revelations. She assumed an attitude of utter seriousness, almost as if she had been called in by the conclave of holy angels themselves to talk over the matter of an erring soul's regeneration.

"Well, first, he orders all kinds of food . . . it's a disgrace the amount, with people starving."

"You get a share?" asked the priest, shocked.

"When they've had their fill, they leave lots, so I take it," she confessed.

"That's nice."

"What we would do without it, I don't know."

"But if I put a stop to it all?"

That puzzled her for the moment.

"We'll find a way," she decided. "But it's his wife, he here with so much money, she on the other side, waiting to be called. It's a shame . . . But it's not the food only . . . Then they drink."

She said this last with an air of finality, and punctuated it with a profound silence, her lips pursed, her eyes wide, her hands raised.

"How many?"

"Two or three girls, other men . . ."

"Yes?"

For a second she looked closely at the priest. Was he becoming too interested? She was sorry she had begun her story.

"I should not be telling you these things." She stopped and looked alarmed. He waved his hand. "But it's for his good . . ." Seeing that he nodded assent, she resumed. "So they drink . . . wine, cordials, these strong American drinks too . . . and then they sing . . . they sit on each other's laps . . . the men and the women . . . and they take off their clothes. . . . It's filthy, Don Anselmo, *'nna vergogna . . . schifosa*⁴ . . . way into the night . . . they lie sprawled everywhere . . . naked."

Don Anselmo rose and took Zia Anna by the shoulders.

"Go down, my dear, and go kneel before the image of the good Saint Elena, and you pray for him."

She rose, shaking her head slowly, her eyes filled with tears.

"It is a shame . . . that I should live to be so old and see these things go on. What a country this is, Don Anselmo! We should all have stayed on our own vineyards and suffered a little poverty. What of it? To come here for a living and to become beasts . . . *'nna vergogna* . . ."

Gennaro had compelled Giovanni to attend several of his parties. The young fellow had protested.

"I don't want to. I want to get married. If she finds out . . ."

"Do you want your money?"

"You promised . . . it's a loan only . . ."

But Gennaro had felt from the beginning a need of some sort of moral support for his orgiac doings. It was a necessity with him that he be accompanied in them by others who, by accepting them, did by some subtle means make them appear less undesirable. After Giovanni had appeared at several, Gennaro decided that he must have other companions. He invited the café-keeper, and then Salvatore Cicco, the Arabian-looking lawyer's runner, and finally he even inveigled Struzzo.

3

"You never told me who you going to marry," Gennaro informed Giovanni one of the mornings after. His face was swollen, his eyes shot with red, and he felt all but steady on his legs.

"You are not going to marry Zia Anna's granddaughter?"

"I'm not marrying an Italian girl."

"Ah, you do well," and he slapped Giovanni forcefully on the shoulder. "You do well . . . they're too quiet . . . like dead rabbits."

He laughed.

"Well, who . . . who? How much money you want? Five hundred? Sure . . . you can have it . . . right away . . . you're no good any more anyhow . . . you sit around moping all night . . . who you going to marry?"

Giovanni pleaded that Gennaro would meet her eventually. What was the reason he had to know?

"It's got to be a secret, Gennaro. If the parents learn, they'll stop it— that's why."

"Hey, I'm your friend."

"Not here anyhow."

They were in the rag-shop. The men working in the bins, those sorting the metals, moved about slowly, coming closer and closer as they changed from one heap of articles to another. Giovanni knew they were all ears and attempting to learn what it was all about.

"Let's go upstairs."

They went upstairs. The large dark room was a haphazard collection of old scraps of iron, pots, pans, stoves, pipe, piles of old rugs, brass fenders, copper boilers. It reeked with the odor of discarded things, and the air danced with motes of lint. Where the sun penetrated, numerous sunbeams swung debonairly across the dark spaces. Gennaro stood in the path of one of them, and his small round face with its dark mustache and deep-set eyes ravaged by memories of debauchery became a gargoyle-ish center of radiation for a thousand strands of light. Giovanni recoiled at the sight and sat down on a mound of old rugs.

"So, out with your secret," Gennaro demanded.

"You'll keep it?"

"Sure."

"You see, she's a Jewess ... and beautiful ..."

Gennaro stared at the boy with horrifying penetration. Slowly he took his pipe out of his pocket, thrust it into his mouth, lighted it with great attention, blew out the match, put it under his foot and stamped on it.

"A Jewess, ah?" he asked in a steady, quiet voice.

Giovanni was frightened and stirred uneasily on the rugs. But he could not stop now. He leaned over eagerly and broke out into nervous speech.

"Very beautiful.... I love her ... *La voglio tanto bene.*"[5]

"Who, tell me."

"The drygoods-keeper's daughter."

"Dora?" Gennaro queried with raised intonation slowly, his eyes going up, his lips closing tightly over his teeth.

"Yes ... Dora."

"So? And you ask me for money?"

"Why not? You lend money."

"Me ... you rat, you rind of the garbage pails ... you do!"

Giovanni withdrew as far as he could on the mounded rugs. Gennaro kept staring at him. But the tension broke as suddenly as it had developed. Gennaro began to smile, and then, taking the pipe out of his mouth, he laughed.

"Well, why not, why not? Five hundred? Sure, and may you prosper, may you have a fine business. I'll come sometime and get shaved and then you'll see something . . . sure. . . . Come with me."

Giovanni had no idea what this was all about, but he did as he was told and got his money.

"Where's the barber shop going to be?"

"Where the Americans live over there by the other river."

"Well, you'll see me anyhow."

"But you won't tell . . . not for a long time—will you? You promise?"

"Sure."

4

He was as good as his word. Isaac Levin rushed into his rag-shop some mornings after and demanded to know the whereabouts of Dora. Gennaro put a chair in front of him.

"Sit down, Mr. Levin. How should I know?"

"You know—you know—you. . . ." He was inarticulate with rage.

"Why, has anything happened?"

"She ain't home. She left last night, without no hat, without nothing like, and not a word to nobody, and she ain't home yet this morning."

The men looked at each other in silence.

"Ah, Mr. Levin," Gennaro said finally, "you should be happy. You have a fine business . . ."

"You, too . . . but what's a fine business? It's nothing—bah," he spat on the floor. "It's dirt when your daughter, your very bones, she go, she ain't like us."

The man burst into tears, his face lifted shamelessly to Gennaro's, his hands raised pleadingly.

Gennaro felt tears in his eyes, too, and rose and walked about the small unencumbered space in his shop.

Sympathetically, he slapped Mr. Levin on the shoulder.

"She'll come back."

"And if she comes, so what? More trouble . . . always trouble."

Gennaro let it go at that, but after Isaac had left, he stuck his pipe ferociously into his mouth, stamped around his place shouting orders to the men, and finally rushed out and ran into Struzzo's undertaker's establishment. That long-legged angular gentleman was on his knees in the display window arranging the placing of a new coffin, a flashy affair of purple velvet with an interior of snow-white pleated cushions.

"Hey, Gennaro," he called, "Come and see this one. It's a beauty . . . a prince could lie in this."

"Well, it wouldn't be long enough for your stringbean legs."

"Ah, I'd have to have a special one."

"It is a beauty," admitted Gennaro, studying the coffin with some care. "Got time?"

"Sure. What's up?"

"You know that lot?"

Struzzo had crawled out of the window and sat himself down at his desk. The office, like Gennaro's rag-shop, in an old two-story brick building, had not been built for light. It was dark and even less acceptable to the nose than Gennaro's establishment.

"Well, what about the lot?" asked Struzzo.

"It'd be a good place for the church Don Anselmo wants."

"Why, you want to give it up?"

"Maybe we could give it to him."

"My God, man . . . that lot's going to bring in a fortune someday."

"It's a damn good spot for the church."

"Whew!" Struzzo whistled, picked up his hat from the table and thrust it far back over his head. Then he laughed. "You're either being funny or you're crazy."

"All right, then, I'll pay you for your half."

They argued at length, but in the end Struzzo took his share and Gennaro called on Don Anselmo. The young priest's office was on the first floor of an old brownstone that had been converted into a rectory. The large front room, as it was called, was stripped of everything. The broad flooring had been painted a terra-cotta red, the walls a dark brown. There were some ordinary deal wood chairs, unpainted, against the wall, a cheap flat-topped desk between the high windows, an image of the Madonna in glazed colors in one corner, and toward the back a small chapel with a white-and-gold cloth and some candles.

Gennaro took off his hat and stood dumbly like a boy who is about to be punished. He crossed himself and then said, "A good morning to you, Don Anselmo, and I hope I find you in good health."

"Oh, good morning, yes, indeed, perfect."

"That's fine. I'm in good health, too."

"Splendid, splendid."

"I come like a surprise to you?"

"Very . . . here, take a chair."

Gennaro sat down, twirling his hat between his knees.

"It's always so quiet here, Don Anselmo. It reminds me of the underground cellar in my home town where we kept the wines and the cheese."

"Yes, it is cool . . . very nice . . ."

"You know, I always think did I have an education I might be a priest, too."

Don Anselmo repressed a smile, in fact, made himself look very serious. "That might have been a good calling for you. It might have kept you out of mischief."

Gennaro squinted up at the priest, afraid that he was being made fun of. He smiled, nevertheless, and countered, "Maybe . . ."

"Of course." Don Anselmo smiled too. "Have a bit of wine."

"No . . . no." Gennaro was emphatic.

Don Anselmo suspected that something had happened. Was his blustering parishioner having a revulsion to what Zia Anna called his stupid, smart-kid ways? Had he come this morning penitent and ashamed? He was astounded at Gennaro's next words.

"Remember that lot Struzzo and I bought? It's yours—yours for the church. It's a beginning. We got to buy some houses next to it. Got to make it a big church . . . The biggest in Harlem. Cicco'll bring you the deed."

5

Don Anselmo's hopes, however, were soon dispelled. Gennaro evidently had no idea of giving up his disgraceful rounds of pleasure, settling down to a model business life, sending for his family, and becoming a force for good in the community. He did not give up his orgies. He did not send for his family. He did both in his own good time, but not from any pious motives of contrition. The thing happened because of the fantastic symbolism Gennaro attached to the golden hoops dangling proudly at the sides of his head.

His parties became more frequent, but also more intimate. Rarer and rarer were the occasions now when he entertained groups of men and women. For the most part he preferred to shuffle into the music hall, cast around the expert glance of the jaded founder, make a new selection, and march off with her to his apartment.

There was a new dancer one night who seemed almost too easy for Gennaro. She had consented much too quickly. The next morning she was gone, and what was more, his earrings were gone, too. He jumped up at once and looked into the mirror. He saw in front of him the unwonted sight of his head minus the gleaming jewels. Nothing had ever frightened Gennaro before. This was the first time. He seemed now stripped, his clothes torn from him by ghoulish hands, made a fool and a mockery. How would he dare go into the street and be seen without his earrings?

He rushed to the window and looked upon backyards with their trees and their clothes-lines lashed by rain. The rain swept like sheets recurrently shaken by almost humorous hands across and across the expanse of yards among the small brick houses that squared-in the block where Gennaro lived. It whistled, and it fell off into a momentary silence, tattooed immediately after on the fences and the tar-papered sheds, and in a second was off again wailing, shrieking, whistling once more. He pressed his face against the window and peered into the dark turmoil of noisy water and for a minute he seemed to have forgotten what had happened to him. Zia Anna's knock at the door shook him back into consciousness.

"I got your coffee," he heard her whispery voice.

"Get out of here with your damn coffee," he shouted at her, and at once began dressing.

Few people would be out, and he would run to the elevated station, put his collar up about his neck, and make immediately for Fitzgibbons. The girls working for that full-bellied worthy lived for the most part in the hotel opposite—a flashing red-brick affair that had been put up in anticipation of the crowds destined to attend the World's Fair, but glad to second-fiddle Fitzgibbons' emporium of the dance and music, now that somebody or other in Washington had decreed that the fair was to go to Chicago. It was a mecca for couples from Westchester and the downtown sections. Rooms were easy to get, and the accommodations were almost as good as could be had on lower Broadway. Fitzgibbons had a share in it, lived in it, and hired the rooms to the girls he employed, for sleeping purposes, for living purposes, or for business of whatever sort they were pleased to conduct. It was constantly filled. Gennaro had eaten and drunk with the rest of them in the rooms set just one block off the Harlem River, in view of the bridge over which the elevated locomotive thundered, and affording a sight of the slow waters of the Harlem muddying their way into the East River.

The rain was so heavy that before he had reached the station he was mercilessly soaked. His coat clung to him as if it had been glued by the water instead of merely drenched. He sloshed into the half-empty car and huddled in a corner for the few stations' ride north. He had another block to walk on the other side. If anything, the rain was greater when he got off. He plunged into it and despite puddles in the cobbled gutters he dashed madly across and into the large receiving room of the hotel.

The red-faced clerk behind the counter yelled at him, "Hey, there, what do you want to do, flood the place?"

From his body coursed rivulets that snaked their way into pools all about him over the black-and-white marble floor, under the black leather chairs and divans, and around the shining brass spittoons. His hesitation was of only a moment's length. He heard screaming laughter in the dining room. He forced open the doors and looked in.

Fitzgibbons, standing with his back to Gennaro, was at the head of a long table. Several of the dancing girls were ranged along the sides. No one was eating, but everybody was looking up at Fitzgibbons in various attitudes of laughter.

"Nobody he getta deesa eerings from me—me the big dago what no give the damn for Presidenta, Kinga, or big business man. . . . See . . ."

In some fashion or another the enormous Irishman had attached the pendants to his ears and was entertaining the young women with imitations of Gennaro, At the other end of the table Gennaro saw the girl who had stolen them—a bright-eyed blond with puffed-out cheeks and the tiniest mouth over a fat neck and a high-corseted bosom. Gennaro walked up to the table.

The open door had changed the temperature of the room to such effect that everyone looked around. They screamed. The smooth fat jowls of Fitzgibbons topped by the shining earrings at each side fell, into ridiculous repose.

Gennaro thrust out his hand. He was too anxious to recover his crescents to do anything else.

"It was just a joke," Fitzgibbons smiled as soothingly as his hard-boiled expression would allow.

"Honest," the girls cried.

"Give me," Gennaro demanded.

Awkwardly and constantly smiling Fitzgibbons removed the earrings.

"Only a bet—a little bet. I bet Margie a five-spot she couldn't steal them, see . . . that's all, see . . ."

Gennaro took the earrings, fastened them into his ears, and then quietly strode over to the blond Margie.

"And this for you," and he slapped her first on one cheek and then on the other.

6

Pursued by a series of curses in the choicest diatribe of the streets he stalked out and once more dashed through the rain. As he sat in the elevated car he realized by what a narrow margin he had escaped a serious struggle with Fitzgibbons, possibly a fight that would have ended in disaster. The chill of the rain was in him and he shivered. As he did so he seemed to shake from sight the multitudinous windows glinting opposite him, the rain-washed roofs. Out of his ears went all noise. His body felt light, his dank clothes fallen from him, a helpless creature in the center of unending space. Voices called, but they were not of the people about him.

"Yes, Rosaria," he answered, "yes, Domenico, and you Emilio with the curly hair, and my baby Elena, yes."

He failed to get off at his own station, was taken far down town, and woke up days after in a hospital. His round of debauches had finally taken its toll. He had been chilled to the bone, developed a high fever in the train, and begun shrieking and crying out with delirium. It was Father Anselmo who discovered him. The first words he said to the priest were, "Padre Anselmo, you better arrange for my family to come."

Considerably thinner, quieted and rested-looking, he turned up in his shop and called all the men and women together.

"You been very good to me," he said, "while I suffered. You worked hard. This is for you share and share alike. . . . You, Tomasiello, you take this money, see," and he put a large roll into the frightened old man's hand, "because you are the oldest, you count it out . . . one for you, and one for you, see . . ."

Tomasiello had lost the lashes from his eyes and every hair from his head and face. He was thin, scrawny, and all atremble, an indefatigable worker who never said a word nor sang a note, but patiently, with wide-open eyes and wide-open mouth, selected one rag from another and carefully laid it in its proper pile. He was so overcome at being singled out by Gennaro that his head trembled violently on its thin neck and the pupils of his eyes wandered about disconsolately.

"Well, get started, get started," shouted Gennaro.

And the old man began.

"One for you, Carminuccia, and one for you, Totonno, and one for you . . ."

His voice quavered and shook like the sounds out of a wheezy accordion. Everybody smiled at him, and the more they smiled the more uneasy he became.

"Come on, Tomasiello, they're only rags like the ones you handle every day."

"Yes, Gennaro *bello,* only rags"—and he continued counting. "They're the rags that come out of those rags like maggots out of old cheese."

The counting stopped.

"Now for a keg of beer," cried Gennaro, "and some *pizze*[6] with tomatoes. My wife is coming."

After this party he met Don Anselmo and together they went to call on Mr. Muller in the narrow house on Pleasant Avenue. In the spick and span front room with its heavy-tapestried upholstery of a dozen colors, under the watchful eyes of a bronze giant that held aloft a noisily ticking clock, Gennaro counted out the cash that was to make him owner of the house. Mr. Muller's little eyes in their deep beds of fatty tissue twinkled as each twenty-dollar bill was placed before him.

"These bills," said Gennaro, "see, I found them in the garbage and the yards. I found them on the streets, rags that were once fine dresses on the backs of American ladies. . . . I piled them up, I tied them up, I put them on my back. I carried them like a donkey way downtown. I sold them. . . . See, there they are, two thousand rags, each one a *scuto.*"

His teeth flashed, his earrings gleamed.

Mr. Muller blinked.

"I move out right away . . . next week."

Painters rushed in as Mr. Muller moved out. They worked night and day. When they were through the walls had become dazzling displays of Italian landscape. Stromboli on the ground floor puffed out lazy clouds of smoke into a sky that was too blue for credence. Aetna on the next floor belched black horror, but all down its sides and for miles about, running with quiet romantic leisure, highly colored hamlets made their way to a cerulean sea. And on the walls along the staircases the conical Vesuvius smoked incessantly while huge sombrero-like poplars began to sway in the wake of the clouds over the Bay of Naples.[7] And wherever there was no picture, there were clusters of elephant roses, fantastic gargantuas of reds and pinks. So was the house of Gennaro Accuci made ready for the home-coming of Rosaria and her three children.

CHAPTER FIVE

1

Gennaro had not allowed himself to think what his wife would look like nor what her reactions would be to him and to her new surroundings. No sooner did images of her shape themselves in his memory than he made some movement of the hand, some change of position, because in that way he found he could drive them out of mind. They disturbed him. They did more than disturb him. They angered him. She seemed the living proof of another life from which he had fled. He had come into new ways and into new thoughts, and she would be filled with the old notions.

Of course, in the last years, with his fast-made money, he had gone off half-cocked, made a splutter of sound and thorough fool of himself. The things he did were not the things that he should have done. Power he had of a sort and a business that he had built up to a real height. In the days at the hospital with nothing else to do and all his energies relaxed he wondered whether what he had done with his money would have been what Don Erminio the lawyer would have done, or Don Biagio the mayor, or the baron who had come once or twice a year to look over his holdings in Capomonte. He had decided in the quiet of his bed that those were not the things those important gentlemen would have done.

Don Anselmo probably was right. And yet at the time, though he would send for his family, he trembled to think that between them and him was now a great gap. The ocean that separated them was as nothing to the change that had come about in their outlooks. Even their bodies must have been transformed. Vivid blotches in his thinking were all that was left now of the debaucheries he had practiced. But he was intelligent enough and honest enough withal to understand that he could not have led the sort of life he did unless something deep in himself had demanded it. And this was the fear that beset him most. What would Rosaria be like, with her heavy body, her large hanging breasts, her slow shamble of a walk? Would she be able to replace all those laughing young girls with their shameless tricks?

He shuddered. But he had laid it upon his soul that he must send for his wife. She had it coming to her. She had been patient for seven years. She had taken the money he had sent to her, but had written back that it was not the money she wanted but him, and to have her children and her under one roof with him, wherever he was. She had heard, too, of some of his doings, and had mentioned them, but not in a storm of complaint. She was ashamed, as she said, to have to talk to another all the things that were in her heart. If she could write it would not be so bad. Then she might be able to let him know in truth how much her loneliness and the news of what he was up to had hurt her. Domenico was getting out of hand, too. He was growing up fast and knew more than was good for him. He was learning no trade and since she could have help on the farm he had refused to do any work. She had wanted him to learn a bit of reading and writing and he had for a while gone to school to Don Vito, but he was not much interested in it and he could not even now write her letters for her. He liked to dress up and go to the piazza and stand around and have the crazy young girls look at him. He needed a strong hand to set him right. Elena was so pretty, too, with her black hair, and she was seven now and she had learned to read better than Domenico. Emilio, too, Gennaro would love him. He kept asking about his father and America and when would we all go . . .

And yet he shuddered. Gennaro frankly did not know what he would do with them. He spoke his mind out in the confessional one night and felt the better for it.

"It is no sin," the priest behind the partition had told him, "that you are thinking of the difficulties that will be in your way. First of all, you must put aside all thoughts of the sins you have committed. A penitent heart is the first step. Then prayer, and more prayer, and faithful atten-dance at mass—every Sunday without fail. Then the will to do right, to see eye to eye with God and the saints and the Holy Spirit. . . . Jesus is at your side, and especially do I charge you to beseech the intercession of the Blessed Mary, mother of God, and do you walk with a humble heart, and with the thought of the good Saint Elena, your patron saint, ever in your heart, for I who speak these things to you am man, but also God, and his Son, and the Holy Ghost, and so I say rise and be going again among men but with a contrite heart and the spirit of Our Lord to be doing good and not seeking in mind or in the depths of your memory for evil that may be or was . . ."

He continued at some length, repeating and restating the same thought, while Gennaro on his knees chafed and became increasingly impatient and finally wondered "What does he know of it all?" And then he wondered that he should have thought that and knew at once that he must, must without question, accept the words of the priest and follow them.

2

The Parterre was, at length, ready. Struzzo and Gennaro and Don Anselmo surveyed it from the vantage point of the sidewalk opposite it.

"A mansion, I tell you," declared the priest.

"Yes, sir," assented Struzzo, "and I advise you hold on to it. . . . God, that's going to be worth money some day . . . you got it dirt cheap."

But it was the next night that it was lighted up in all its glory. The first electric lights were coming in, and Gennaro, vowing that a person who had made America must have the best, insisted upon them. The floor flush with the sidewalk, and the one immediately level with the stoop, blazed with the red and green globes Gennaro had installed. Crowds filled the two floors. Above, the rooms were dark. They were to be rented out—in fact, one floor already had been rented. The milliner, La Monterano,[1] who had been making her little pile, too, in a shop downtown, was to occupy the second floor.

"A good family of some class," Gennaro assured his friends. "They had money once and education in their *paese.*[2] It was Don Anselmo recommended them."

Rosaria had landed. Gennaro saw her first through a grilled fence in the new immigrant station at Ellis Island.

"She's grown big, like as if with child," was his first thought.

She called out to him, and fell to weeping at once. The child Elena, whom she held in her arms so that she might obtain the first view of Gennaro, wept with her mother. At her side, Domenico, cockily dressed in an outfit he had purchased in Naples, kept scolding her.

"Do you have to, here, in public? Oh, stop bawling."

Emilio stuck his curly head against the railing and peered out in great amazement. He had recognized his father at once but kept the fact to himself. He had never been told of his father still wearing rings in his ears and he had no recollection of them when his father had been home. The sight astounded him. So many young men had returned to Capomonte from America and mocked the old men who still clung to the ancient custom that Emilio could not help but be astounded. But that, too, he kept to himself.

"I don't know them, I don't know them," Gennaro repeated to himself interminably. "Are they mine? Those four mine?"

He shrugged his shoulders, thrust his pipe into his mouth and advanced. His wife flung herself into his arms at once, weeping loudly. But he found it impossible to say a word to her. She seemed so different with her Italian shoes, her laced bodice, her swinging skirts, her hair, braided and wound around her head, her skin burned with sun despite the long voyage. And why did she have to weep so? He put her gently aside without a word and stooped to pick up Elena.

"You're a chunk of a doll," he said to her, and then, holding her close to him, he took her cheek in his mouth and made believe to bite it. "A doll, and solid, but alive, alive!"

He put her down to glance at Emilio.

"Hey, there, curly," Gennaro cried.

"Hey, there, yourself," the young boy answered, looking up.

"They say you're smart."

"Sure, I'm smart."

"That's the only kind we want in America."

"And I'll make America," he said, pounding his chest the way his father did. Don Anselmo, Struzzo, all the crowd laughed.

"And so you are Domenico?" Gennaro asked of his handsome son, a stocky, big-shouldered youth, who already at eighteen sported a firm mustache, turned at the ends and thinning to a shadow.

Gennaro rapped him on the chest with his knuckles.

"This is a workers' land, young fellow. What do you want with those mouse-tails?"

At the party the liveliest person was Domenico. He mingled with the men and expressed himself freely, boldly. He danced with the women and talked to them from a height. The house his father had provided for the family seemed to have gone to his head. All about him he heard praises of how his father had "made America."

"A country yokel, all right. But he has a head on his shoulders."

"Owns half the houses on this block."

"They all respect him—the President even. . . . By the Virgin."

Domenico arrogated the glory of it all to himself. Gennaro watched him closely.

"No son of mine except in evil," he mumbled to himself on several occasions.

"Can he do anything?" he asked Rosaria.

Bewildered, the fatigue of the voyage still showing in the drawn features, her eyes excessively bright from excitement, her face flushed and damp from the confusion, the noise, the unusualness of her new place, the crowds of people, poor Rosaria sat holding her hands in her lap, smiling nervously at everybody, jumping up, sitting down again, shrieking to Elena, nodding at this one and the other one, happy and unhappy at the same time.

She gazed at her husband without understanding.

"Can he do anything, that big son of yours?"

"Oh, Domenico?" she replied, frightened, trying to steady herself by taking one of her husband's hands. "Not much. I told you, he learned nothing . . . no trade."

She talked quietly, in a low voice, apologetically. He walked away muttering something she could not understand. Zia Anna was nearby and drew nearer, dragging her chair. She patted Rosaria's hand as if dispensing a healing sympathy.

"He's a good man . . . believe me . . . when he wants to, nobody can be so kind. . . . Don't open your ears to what everyone says. Men are men. They don't change in America or anywhere. We women have to understand that, and forgive them. He's a good, good man with a big heart. . . . He has, of course, what man hasn't, done—well, now, you have no more than placed your foot in New York, as I might say, and you have much yet to learn . . ."

Mandolins cling-clunged and feet shuffled, and there was the rise and the fall of laughter and the lulls in the talk in between. Rosaria seemed to be constantly gulping something, her mouth opening in amazement and shutting again over and over.

She neither heard nor cared what Zia Anna said. She neither saw the men who were introduced to her nor did she pay much attention to them. The women meant even less to her. Domenico appeared effectively to have floated away into the great roar about her, and Emilio and little Elena, though they kept returning to kiss and pat her hand as if to renew their own as well as her energies, likewise seemed to have slipped, slipped into a far distance where there was only blazing light, the shuffle of feet dancing, the cling-clung of mandolins, and the laughter and the talk of men and women forever and forever. But she, she sat completely alone, having gained nothing for her losses, not understanding why she had come, for Gennaro, smile as she would, touch him gently as she would, look up to him beseechingly as she would, seemed to pull away, to shake her off, to recede farther and farther into the unknown into which he had departed years back. She wanted to weep and could not, so she kept holding her hands in her lap, looking to the right and left, smiling with swift nervous jerks of her lips and opening her mouth wide in amazement and shutting it again.

3

That night she lay at the side of her husband, sobbing. She had attempted to throw her arms about him and to pull his face to hers that she might kiss it. Very slowly he had extricated himself from her embrace and gently pushed her to the other side of the bed. He said nothing. He did just that—took her arms off his body and with his hands quietly pushed her to one side.

He lay on his back, his hands behind his head, saying to himself over and over again, "What could I do, what could I do, that's how I feel?"

He heard her crying, and once or twice reached for her body and patted her on the thighs. He withdrew his hand at once. Something had been changed in him in the seven years of their separation. Rosaria was not a prize he had wrested, as it were, out of the air of a new environment, by the use of elements within his own personality, by dint of his new-found soaring ruthless egotism. She had been allotted to him in a pattern of life where each person knew what to expect. She had been in due course selected by his parents as a suitable bride among the maidens of Capomonte. She had been offered to him by her parents. Attractive, certainly, she had been, a buxom young woman with a mass of hair and strong arms, fit for the farm and the vineyard and the cheese-yards. The men outside of her circle would not have sought her out. Peasant she was and peasant she would remain.

But he, he, the grand Gennaro, he had become a somebody. He could now take his place with those who had position and responsibility. The money that bulged out his pockets, that had bought him the Parterre, and had made him the owner of so much property in America, he had amassed by himself by force, by trickery, by superior strength. But he, *he* had done it . . . that was the point. And now that he had as his own such an accumulation that would put to shame the holdings of the baron of his Calabrian countryside, he, Gennaro Accuci, by his own right, was not Gennaro Accuci who had the farm at the foot of the hillslope but just plainly Gennaro Accuci, a man.

So he thought, in a fumbling incoherent dream-state, lying next to Rosaria. Out of him had gone the adolescent animal passion he had had for her in his youth. It had been exactly that. They had loved because all things with life must some day love. No more. He knew now why he had hesitated so long in calling for her. And as for the children, it was only Elena and possibly Emilio who stirred him at all. Domenico sickened him with his gay mustaches, his foppish dress, his handsome, cheap little face. It was Domenico of whom he had thought most, Domenico his first born. But Domenico now was a dandified fool, too much unlike what he had expected, who gave every indication of enjoying himself instead of working, putting on airs because he, Gennaro, had made America. Well, he would give the popinjay a chance, try him out, see what might be done with him.

Some blocks down from the Parterre were the gas-houses. The great chimneys rose into the air, solid, unlovely, sooty. Some distance away a series of gas-tanks, like huge stationary bugs, blew themselves up into the landscape and then after some hours slowly lowered themselves into the ground, leaving only the skeletons of their supports visible to the eye. By day, they were ugly and grimy. The brick walls around them were scrawled with adolescent conceptions of the forbidden parts of men and women, splotched with daubs of paint, plastered with bill-boards announcing the performances of the burlesque on One hundred and twenty-fifth Street or the melodramas in the Opera House. The sidewalks in front of them were the crackly dirty cinders of the coke used in the furnaces, dumped there periodically and flattened out.

The buildings rose out of mounds of bituminous dust and even huger hillocks of coke. The windows were perfect targets for boys, and so always gaped with broken panes. Empty lots stretched on each side piled with the refuse of kitchens and factories. Tin cans and old lumber, slag from the wire-works further down, rusty iron, newspapers and rags caked with mud and dirt and worked into the ground, and in and around all these articles weeds shot up, occasionally a bush of wild aster, and along the edges even scraps of golden-rod.

The windows of the Parterre overlooked both this sight, and the broad expanse of the East River as it eddied around the islands and lost itself in the turmoil of Hell's Gate. By day the view was both ugly and beautiful—ugly if you looked out of the bedroom window and saw the haphazard mass of coal and stacks that formed the gas yards; beautiful if you looked out on the quiet areas of water, dotted with green-covered islands, whirlpooling here and there as a lazy tug chugged by with its tow of barges. At night all was beautiful with a quality of strangeness that sometimes brought terror in its wake. For when the furnaces had reached the full height of their heat the valves were opened and the stacks belched forth columns of smoke in a roar of power that was like the prelude to an eruption of greater force. A minute after, the smoke disappeared and in its place, to the accompaniment of a rocket-like explosion and enormous puffings and wheezing, flames appeared, reaching and reaching into the silence overhead. The darkness gave way and for the period of a second the quiet black river became lurid and noisy, the buildings all about grotesque silhouettes.

Gennaro was accustomed to the noisy flare of the flame. It burst without warning but those who had lived in the neighborhood were aware of it and paid no heed to it. During the evening, when the party had been gay and there had been the sound of laughter and the music and the dancing, the huge jet of fire noised out into the darkness and as quickly withdrew. Rosaria had not noticed it. But now as she lay sobbing at the side of Gennaro every sound took on a special distinctness, and since they were strange sounds they became fraught with significance, mystery, even horror.

The thick braids of her hair lay the length of her breast. With each sob they moved. She clutched them within her hands and now and then pulled at them as if she were in some fashion to find solace in the movement.

"The good God help me," she said aloud, "and forgive you, Gennaro. In a strange land, how horrible, to be alone with your husband . . . oh, so much alone."

She sat up. The braids fell down her back and she thrust her hands out for Gennaro. She shook him by the shoulders.

"Gennaro," she called.

"What is it?" he asked quietly.

"Why did you call for me?"

"You wanted to come."

"Why should not a wife want to be with her husband?"

Gennaro did not answer. He had no answer for it. He just kept lying there with his hands behind his head.

"I gave you my youth, I dug at your side in the soil, I bore you five children—the Lord be thanked that two are dead."

He stroked her hand gently.

"Do be quiet, Rosaria. You are tired. . . . Sleep . . ."

"Seven years I waited. . . . Seven years . . ."

He thought he saw her thick lips trembling with fresh weeping. He did not want to hear her tears again. He, too, sat up.

"Rosaria . . . *ti voglio bene* . . . I do like you . . . but what, what do you want?"

She stared at him, her eyes opened wide with incredulous agony. She brought her heavy hands to her face and buried her face in them. Her whole body shook.

Out in the darkness there was a violent blast. Rosaria jumped up with fright and screamed. The heavens were lighted far and wide with the crimson glare of the gas-house stacks. Her whole body quivered with fright.

"Gennaro, Gennaro ... all the saints help us ..."

She fell to the floor. He rose up immediately, at first ready to smile at her foolish fears. But when he saw her body heaped at the side of the bed he became alarmed. He lifted her in his arms and for the first time since she had returned, some of the old tenderness of their first contacts came back to him. He kissed her on the eyes, on the cheeks, and called her name.

"Rosaria, *bella mia.*"[3]

She stared at him with her great eyes filled with fright.

"It's nothing ... nothing ... only a factory where they make the gas ... come to the window ... let us look out ... see the river there ... how it moves so slowly. ... Hear now? What a sharp whistle that was! That was the boat, there, see, with the two red lights strung up like peppers ..."

She smiled like a pleased child.

"And over there, far off, see, little islands ... see, the house there like a church with the round roof ... they have insane people there ... but sh ... sh ... don't be frightened ..."

She pressed against him with a new assurance.

"And now the other side. See those black shadows ... and the others like big trees ... that's the gas factory ... see ... now watch ... don't be frightened ... there ... whew ... there it goes ..."

Out shot the billows of smoke and immediately after the great soaring pillars of flame. Rosaria drew back into her husband's arms, and clung to him, smiling and happy.

Until morning they lay drugged with the memories of old passions. ...

4

After a swallow of black coffee Gennaro shouted to his son Domenico to hurry with his coat and hat. It was an early day of the fall, and unnaturally cold and gray, rain threatening from the East River.

"Not like the weather in Capomonte, hey, Rosaria?"

In her own unexacting fashion Rosaria had been happy for the several weeks that had already passed. She had been particularly made glad, almost excited into gayety, by the numerous callers. She lost no opportunity to display what she had brought with her from Italy.

"What could I do during the long evenings but crochet and embroider?"

Her beds were spread with elaborately crocheted covers. Whole areas of the finest white thread meshed and remeshed into patterns of kids that seemed always to be revolving about rosettes and then ambling away into borders of cherry leaves. Her petticoats were trimmed with delicate lace of her own making and she had had time in the long evenings of her seven lonely years to embroider in charming flower patterns numerous pillow cases and to have edges for them of lace even more exquisite than for her petticoats.

On the wall of the front room, fitted out by Gennaro in the heavy plush furniture of the day—green, glistening between yellow trimmings of braids studded with brass knobs—she had hung a quilted cloth into which she had embroidered with infinite detail and in vivid coloring the image of Saint Elena. In front of the cloth she had erected a shelf, and on the shelf she had placed a wooden effigy of the same saint. Her child-like face was an innocent, staring one, with glowing red cheeks and dark heavy lashed eyes. Her black hair fell down her shoulders loosely. A tight bodice laced across with ribbons, fitted her frame, and from her hips fell the folds of a silk dress, pure red bordered with yellow. At her feet stood a small pottery lamp with oil and a wick, burning.

As the neighbors were ushered into the room each one made the sign of the cross and knelt before the blessed lady.

"The sweet saint bring you prosperity, Rosaria *bella*."

"May you make America, she willing, the blessed one."

"Ah, with so pretty a saint, you will be happy."

And for a while, Rosaria was happy. But she had misgivings, and especially about Domenico. Gennaro and he did not get along very well. They were always at each other, arguing back and forth. Domenico had no business to talk back to his father as he did, but neither had Gennaro the right to keep baiting him, berating him for getting home late, for failing to report to the shop early, for staying away from the rags as if they were filthy and would soil his hands, mocking him for his pretensions at being a lady-killer, for Domenico had already found his way in the remote sections of Harlem where he had been seen walking arm in arm with girls.

"Let him alone," Rosaria kept warning Gennaro, "it's so new, this country, he is lost, just as I was."

"Sure ... let him alone ... is he like Emilio? He comes to the rag place after school. You should see . . . he works. He pitches in to everything. . . . The other . . . a lady's man he thinks himself . . . always barbering himself . . . stinking with perfume."

On this particular morning he shouted, "Hey, there, *lazzarone*,[4] put a move on."

Domenico came down. He had dressed himself in the first new suit he had bought in America and was the picture of supreme self-confidence. His striped brown trousers fitted him close about the buttoned shoes. His coat was buttoned close to his collar in which reposed the knot of a yellow-banded tie. His hair was slicked down flat, parted in the middle and finger-waved at the edges over the temples. His mustache, waxed to a shine, at each end left the horizontal for a perpendicular twist upward.

Gennaro eyed him up and down contemptuously.

"Well, you little prize lamb, paying a visit to the queen?"

Domenico smiled as much in self-appreciation as in embarrassment.

"Do you mean to say you're coming to the rag-shop dolled up like that?"

"Let him alone," Rosaria called. "He'll change at the shop."

"By Saint Jerome, he'll get into work clothes right here."

"But, *ta, ta* ..." pleaded Domenico, frightened at the prospect.

"Yes, yes, my dear, do as your father says ... do it for mother."

"He'll do it for me."

"I'll change at the shop," Domenico consented.

"And I say here. Got a girl down the block to parade in front of, that's the idea, hey?"

"Damn it, why did we ever come here?" shouted Domenico.

"Yes, damn it, why?" Gennaro repeated.

"*Madonna mia bella e santa*,"[5] interposed Rosaria, making the sign of the cross.

Elena, in a little petticoat, had run in from the kitchen, her pig-tails, tied with a piece of muslin, hanging down her naked back.

"And why isn't she dressed and ready for school, hey?" shouted Gennaro.

Rosaria was thoroughly scared. She looked up at her husband with trembling lips. "I'm here alone all day . . ."

"So. And you'll keep the little one home from school? Why? Emilio is already off."

Rosaria seized Elena and ran upstairs with her.

"See that she is dressed at once," shouted Gennaro, and, then, turning to Domenico, "and you, too, poltroon, get up and change your clothes."

He stamped out of the house, slamming doors. But when Domenico had not turned up at the shop after several hours he dashed back.

Rosaria was frightened more than ever. Not, however, at the sight of her husband livid with rage, as at the disappearance of Domenico.

"That's the way you brought him up . . ."

"He's a good boy," she retorted.

"A good for nothing . . . a doll-face, a whore-chaser!"

"And whose fault is it, whose fault? I had the care of the three of them alone."

She sat in a chair and wept, beseeching him with red eyes to sympathize with her.

"I'm like in a nightmare, Gennaro, in this strange land. . . . So much noise, so much hurry, cooped up in this house . . . scrubbing . . . washing . . . I don't mind . . . but you hate me and mine . . ."

He left.

That night when Domenico returned long after dark, Gennaro followed him into the room that had been assigned to the young man and Emilio.

"Where have you been all day, my saint's child?"

"Seeing the sights."

"Who gave you the money?"

"I had it."

"From whom?"

"My mother."

"Yes . . ."

In a flash, Gennaro had pulled the belt out of his pants and before Domenico was aware what was happening, Gennaro had begun lashing the boy. Emilio heard the screams and jumped out of bed, screaming with fright. Gennaro forced Domenico into a corner of the narrow room, between a chest of drawers and the wall. Methodically, persistently, as if he had been an official whipper of men in prisons, he plied his belt over Domenico's body. Rosaria rushed in and stood in the doorway, too overcome to offer resistance. Emilio ran up to her and clung to her waist.

"Gennaro," she cried, "Gennaro . . . don't . . . no more . . . you are killing him . . . what are you doing?"

All of Domenico's cries had ceased. Only a whimpering, dog-like whine came from him now and then. Gennaro was satisfied. He pushed aside his wife and youngster and went into his own room. Elena, her pig-tails about her neck, was sleeping in her cot at the foot of the bed he and Rosaria occupied. Her legs were out of the covers and her feet off the bed. Gennaro, panting heavily, looked at the girl for a second and then stooped over and covered her completely. The next minute he was on his knees, his head in the crook of his elbow, praying,

"*Madre santa,*[6] and you, too, Saint Elena, be good to me, be good to me . . ."

For months after that there was peace in the family. Contrition had fallen on the soul of Gennaro, and he showed it in the thoughtless indulgences he allowed not only Domenico but everyone else in the family. He gave the older boy money to buy himself more clothes. He insisted upon Rosaria going to the American shopping districts and getting transformed into a semblance of an American woman.

"That kind of skirt they wear only in Capomonte," he exclaimed humorously, "and my wife must never go out with a shawl over her head, but with a hat and plenty of flowers on it . . ."

PART TWO

Rosaria

CHAPTER ONE

1

Some weeks after Rosaria had come from Italy, another family had moved into the Parterre. The family of Davido Monterano consisted of himself, his wife, and four children. In Italy Davido Monterano had been an army engineer who had been court-martialled because of inefficiency. He had been discharged from the army, had refused to return to his native town of Castello-a-Mare, had met his family in Naples secretly and embarked for New York. After all, what would have been the fate of an ex-captain in the small town, cashiered out of the army and thrown back into the civilian population in disgrace? His father would have suffered even more than he, and his children would have grown up in an atmosphere of contempt. It was too horrible a prospect for Captain Davido Monterano to face. He claimed what little patrimony was coming to him and decided on the chances of a career in business in New York.

Davido Monterano was never known to stir out into the street without a cane. He owned a variety of them. In fact, it might have been said that the man was making a collection of canes. He possessed a large assortment, ranging in thickness and structure from stout and knotted to slim and smooth. A mountain-ash twig he himself had whittled into a favorite walking stick. One, he claimed to be a gift from his colonel for a suggestion he had made. The suggestion had resulted in a pontoon bridge for which the Italian army had become distinguished. It was a thin ebony cane with a handle rich in inlays of precious stones and a ferule of gold. This he invariably sported on Sundays and on such evenings when he and his wife went downtown to the opera, of which he was inordinately fond. Now, without the canes *Il Signor Capitano*[1] Davido Monterano would have felt himself insignificant, completely and irretrievably sunk into the morass of common *contadini*[2] and *cafoni*[3] among whom he was compelled to live in New York. His family was one with a past in Castello-a-Mare. Among its members it boasted a bishop who had received several votes in the selection for the new pope. It boasted a general in the Thousand of Garibaldi. One had occupied a chair in literature in the University of Naples until an unfortunate secret affair with the daughter of a countess had leaked out and he had been shot by her father in a duel. His father was an outstanding chemist, and many of his researches had enriched Italian industry if not himself. And his mother had been the niece of a Cardinal. Oh, yes, Davido Monterano, forced to make his living in New York among a pack of low-born peasants, could not have sortied out of his home or work-place without a cane. A cane set him apart.

But he took pains to set himself apart in other ways. He wore nothing less than a frock-coat or a cutaway no matter where he went. As a matter of fact, he persisted in sending his dimensions to his tailor in Naples and importing the fabric cut according to them out of real fine old Italian broadcloth or heavy twilled serge. The tailors here in New York had then merely to assemble the garments. That also set him apart. He seemed just then to have emerged from his balconied-mansion in Castello-a-Mare, ready to step into his carriage and be whisked off for a call on the Conte di San Rocco, his dearest friend.

Besides these sartorial distinctions, Davido Monterano had other marks of the high-born family *per bene.*[4] His hair he wore *all'Umberto,*[5] cut short and then made to stand on end like a brush but in such fashion that the outline of his aristocratic head would not be in any way diminished. Huge mustaches, full over the lips and falling in ample bushiness to each side, gave his broad face, with its thick heavy nose, an air. Taller than the average, with a substantial torso, swinging his cane in leisurely rhythms, he was a figure to make even Gennaro feel that he had been transported back to Capomonte where he would have to lift his hat and bow to the important gentleman. And he spoke massively in a measured basso, quoting at the slightest suggestion whole passages from Giusti, Manzoni, Dante, Petrarch. He rendered them as if these poets had written expressly for him.[6]

2

La Signora Monterano was a small woman, all bosom and hairdress. Her quiet face had a finely chiseled little nose between small apologetic eyes, all surmounted by a mass of brilliant auburn hair. It was so long it had to be braided dozens of times and then the braids had to be piled up in a gigantic mound on her head. The hat sitting on top made it seem all the more mountainous.

Like her husband she, too, refused to throw off her continental styles in dress. Hanging on her husband's arm with one of her own, she held up the train of her Italian silk gown with the other, wrapped it partly about her knees and then trusted to the superior strength of her husband's locomotion to make progress. But though, like her husband, she maintained the fiction of their superiority over the common crowds among whom they lived, she had long ago lost her illusions.

She had worked from the first day of her arrival. By sheer accident the sort of work she found to do was the making of women's hats. She had been trained like all Italian girls of whatever station in life to a skillful acquaintance with the needle and cloth. Intelligent, eager to learn, she had soon mastered the millinery art and had even reached the point where she made successful suggestions and had been promoted to forelady. She was given charge of employing and discharging the girls who worked in the shop. It was not very long before she had surrounded herself with young Italian women passionately devoted to her. She taught them to make flowers, to stitch in such ways that the threads were ingeniously secreted among the ribbons and the flowers—short ways of achieving the best results, all the tricks that she herself had picked up without much instruction from anybody. The money that she earned had kept the family together.

The captain had of course made it clear from the beginning that he was not to be compelled to demean himself by accepting a mere manual occupation. At first he attempted to become a writer for the newly organized Italian newspapers. They soon found that the inefficiency that had earned him his discharge from the army was a deep-seated element of his character. He decided upon opening a school for the children of the better Italians who desired not to allow their offspring to forget the beautiful language of Italian poetry. That enterprise lasted several months. For a year he drifted. He accepted a bookkeeper's position with a firm of salami and cheese importers. But he was compelled to give it up.

"*Maria, mia buona,*"[7] he pleaded with his wife, "honestly, have you ever sat among mountains of salami, loose and strewn about like a lot of dead arms, packed into canisters, hanging from the ceiling by the hundreds, filling the whole place with their stench? And then they have decided now to import cheese too. . . . *Dio santo, cara, non ne posso piu*[8] . . . I can't sit among all those smells. It's like being a fisherman on the docks at Naples. . . . I must leave, I simply must . . . I'll find something."

They had brought with them her old mother who had looked after the children while the parents went out to work. She had been permitted to come into the country despite her almost total deafness, but had they known how crushed her heart was the authorities would have decided upon sending her back. From the day she arrived she complained about everything. She withered into half of her size before three months had elapsed. But despite the fact that she herself needed more attention than the youngsters, she looked after their wants, cooked for the family, even attempted to wash and iron. But she, too, like Mr. Monterano, had come from a family *per bene*—a very good family, if you please—and was overcome by the calamity that had befallen her son-in-law and had compelled their removal to such alien shores where one lived in the same house with rag-pickers and where one was constrained to be on terms of intimacy with storekeepers and peddlers.

More so than her son-in-law, La Signora Alba Morellini made sure that those about her recognized the fact that she and hers were of superior origin to the peasant and mountaineer population that crowded into Harlem with every incoming steamship. She kept her gowns in repair or had copies of them made according to their original patterns. Unlike every other older woman of the neighborhood she insisted upon a tiny ribboned hat to surmount her gray hair. One piece of jewelry she would not part with when the family needs had required the pawning of them—a jet necklace with huge stones terminating in a jet cross upon which hung the figure of Christ in pure green jade. With that unusual ornament about her neck and down her bosom, hat aristocratically centered upon her hair and made secure with a black bow under her chin, she pattered after her family, keeping the four children together, admonishing them how to walk in the public streets, considering from what sort of family they were. She believed she was talking in reserved modest tones. Actually she shrieked. When she was fairly certain that the proper gait and the proper posture had been attained from the cane-swinging father to the toddling Ervi, youngest of the four, then she felt free to look around belligerently and haughtily, daring any one to declare that the family pretensions were not being maintained.

Indoors she worked as if she had been born a slavey. She cooked and marketed, she scrubbed the floors, she laundered the children's clothes—they were conspicuous in school for their neatness—she starched her daughter's petticoats—let it not be said, when Maria raised her dresses, that she wore unstiffened garments beneath. And she insisted upon carrying out all these duties with the shades down. For, if by chance she were drawn into conversation about her household, she gave it out that they employed domestic help as they always had done in Italy.

3

Ervi, the three-year-old boy, took sick. Dr. Giovanelli unbuttoned his frock-coat and showed the gleaming expanse of red sash over his shirt-front. More than that he found it impossible to do.

"An obscure affection of the alimentary tract, Signor Monterano," the bearded patriot exclaimed, sitting with his hands over his cane. "We shall recommend clear soups, the windows shut, quiet, and these drops."

Mr. Monterano spent the whole of his days and nights, without much sleep, at the bedside of the boy. The child had been a chubby youngster.

For some months after he had been dressed in the morning, he would return to the bed of his own accord and sleep. La Signora Morellini thought nothing of it until the boy complained of the severest pains in the stomach, refused all food, and vomited what he was urged to eat.

The old lady wore herself even thinner than she was by constant attention to him, and Mr. Monterano discovered in the illness another reason for hating the work he had found as a presser in a skirt-manufacturing place. He stayed home and held Ervi's hand, singing to him softly, making paper models of boats, houses, goats, butterflies, and dozens of other animals and insects. La Signora Maria returned worn out from her day at the millinery shop and remained awake half the night with the child. But not all of their care and love could overcome the lack of knowledge of the Garibaldinian physician, and Ervi with his straight black hair, his white face now small and hollow, a perfect foil for his enormous brown eyes, smiled at his father and mother and then stopped breathing.

They were living at this time in another of the houses owned by Gennaro, considerably further south than the Parterre. Gennaro was all sympathy. He kept visiting the family, offering aid and advice, and even money. His earrings invariably caused them all to shudder, all except Ervi who found them interesting enough to look at and even to touch. The day when they were to bury the boy, Gennaro ordered out the society of

Saint Elena with a band to accompany the family to the cemetery. But they were required to postpone the ceremony to the following day. The old grandmother had worked too hard; the death of her grandson proved too much for her. She was sitting in a straight-backed chair at the side of the small coffin. The room had been darkened. At one end Struzzo had erected a small wooden chapel covered with black and gold cloth, a candelabrum at each end, in the center a crucifix. The coffin, a white shirred-silk covered box, on trestles draped in purple material, was perpendicular to it. The grandmother insisted on sitting at the head of it. Occasionally she lay her elbow on it and put her face in the crook of her elbow and wept softly.

"That you should die in a foreign land, my little one. The good saints take you to them and love you as we loved you. My bit of a butterfly— to think that we made fun of your pot-belly and that was the cause of your death. I tried hard, Ervi, *caro,*[9] to keep you well, worked hard and made you the nicest things I knew, and kept you dressed the way it became one of your good family to be seen . . ."

Mr. Monterano lifted her up and begged her to lie on the bed.

She turned against him, sharply. "This is where I belong—with him. I saw him born—with my own hands I helped him into the world. I consented to dragging him, a little baby, a tiny thing, across the wide ocean, and gave him with my own hands the awful food of the ship. . . . I should have said no to all this crazy ambition to move into a strange land. . . . I should have said no, no, no . . ."

She wept with her head on the little coffin. In the morning when they were preparing to go to the burial ground, Mr. Monterano gently took her by the shoulder to escort her into the bedroom. But the small exhausted shoulders were heavy and stiff. The withered body refused to move.

La Signora Maria had wept at her son's death at the beginning, but mindful of her mother's condition she had controlled herself as the day wore on. It was enough that the shawled neighbors with their children pressing against their knees should raise loud lamentations, a fitful unrestrained wailing that in the end became a chorus of subdued prayer as if they were in church, responding to the Kyrie Eleison.[10] She herself would set an example. So she dressed in dark clothes and sat very quietly, saying nothing. At the proper time she rose to feed the three others. She had instructed them to keep out of the death room and play downstairs or in the backyard. When her husband went to her and, laying a gentle hand on her shoulder, said, "Maria, your mother—

she doesn't breathe," she rose to her feet, looked about her as if stunned, and then with quivering lips but not a single tear she went up to her mother and asked her, "Mother, are you listening to me? Can you hear? It will soon be time to bury Ervi." No answer coming, she turned to her husband,

"We shall have to bury her, too. How much she wanted to go back to Castello-a-Mare, Davido, and be buried under the oak trees in the Campo Santo."

She consented to having Gennaro, their landlord, order a band and the society to march behind the coffins. Gennaro had never lost the peasant's admiration for "better families." To do them a good turn whipped up his ego to a coursing speed.

Her husband took her aside.

"We can't permit this . . ."

"Why not?" Maria asked, sharply.

"Not even she would have liked it. It's a custom of the *contadini*, a barbarous custom. Shall a family like ours . . ."

"I have had enough of your family and my family. We are here, in America."

And so the procession of two hearses, one white, one black, preceded by a carriage with flowers and followed by a slow band, blaring out funeral march after funeral march, wound itself down the avenue. All the pushcart vendors stopped their screams, took off their hats, and lowered their eyes. The women on the sidewalks laid aside their shopping baskets, kneeled, struck their chests with their fists, and prayed. An old woman was crossing the street as the hearse neared. On her head she carried, ingeniously balanced, a huge loaf of bread, as large as a cart wheel and brown as a nut. As she moved, the skirts hanging loosely from her hips swung to the easy rhythm of her gait. She hurried to the curb and, still with her burden on her head, she kneeled, facing the funeral cortège, clasped her hands and prayed.

"The good God take them both to Him. The Holy Virgin be praised for her kindness to us on earth. Hail Mary, full of grace . . ."

Everybody heard, and everybody joined in, "Hail Mary, full of grace . . ."

And so in the clear autumn light the Monterano family buried their own.

Gennaro had ordered a sumptuous meal when the family returned from the cemetery. Rosaria had spent the whole morning, assisted by several of the neighbors and Zia Anna. There was soup with pastina, roast chicken, macaroni with heavy tomato sauce and cheese, peas cooked in a small quantity of oil with onions and no water, whole dishes of fruit, and small cakes. Roberto, Saverio, and Gilda, the three Monterano children, discovered a real use for death. They were not alone. Around the table were gathered Gennaro and his wife, Dr. Giovanelli, Struzzo and his wife, a stiff buxom woman with a hairdress so hard and shining that it seemed a brocaded helmet, the Monterano seniors, Zia Anna, and Don Anselmo the priest. They ate abundantly, the wine flowed, and laughter rang where before there had been the cries of grief.

Gennaro rose toward the conclusion of the meal. He struck his chest with his hand and said in a loud voice:

"America ain't all rich pasture. There's sour soil here, too."

Don Anselmo had drunk possibly a trifle more than a person of his calling might be expected to, and he leaned over to Signora Maria and whispered in her ear, "*Un mascalzone quello, sa, ma ha del cuore* . . . a son-of-a-gun, that fellow, but kind-hearted . . ."

Mrs. Struzzo had stuck one of the huge napkins under her neck and allowed it to drape her ample bosom. She thought she had heard the good priest say something holy, and she crossed herself. Then she raised the napkin from her chest and covered her eyes and face with it and began to weep. It was a signal for all the women to do likewise. In a few minutes the gayety had changed. Sobs and prayers filled the air. The children, too, began to weep. The men were touched, but they thought it necessary to move about the room quieting everyone. Finally Don Anselmo clapped his hands for silence and said, "Let us all kneel."

"Merciful God," he prayed, "thou hast taken our loved ones, and may they repose in peace and be of the company of the angels. We shall ever pray for the repose of their souls. Give us the strength to go on and to do our share."

Gennaro jumped to his feet.

"That's what I was going to say. There's sour soil here, too, and we got to work hard. I want this good family to move out of these rooms and come to the Parterre. I have a fine place with pictures and sunlight . . ."

4

La Signora Maria consented to move into Gennaro's new house. The walls were garishly painted. She threw up her hands in horror at the narrowness of the rooms, at the gaudy splashes of landscape painted on them, at the long climb of three steep flights, at the possibilities of the children falling out of the windows. With the death of her mother she assumed full command of the family. She had come to the inevitable conclusion that there was no use looking to her husband to repair the family fortunes. At the best, they were going to consider themselves fortunate indeed were they able to keep clothes on their backs. There would be the added problem of who was to look after the children and do the housework while she was away at work.

Roberto, about seven, was a quiet boy, strong, with square shoulders, large serious eyes, a delicately pointed chin, and at his early years, possessed of an ability to comprehend the situation of the family that astounded his mother.

"You will have to get Gilda and Ernestino to school, Roberto, see that they dress and are neat, and when they come out for the noon hour you must see that they eat. I shall leave the key with you, and there will be bread and something on the table all ready. . . . You can, can't you?"

As usual his reply was in one word, "Yes."

He had learned English with astonishing rapidity and prided himself on it. When his mother spoke to him in Italian, he invariably answered in English.

"Why in English, Roberto?" his father would exclaim. "You wish to forget your own sweet language?"

The younger ones took their cue from Roberto. The consequence was that Il Signor Monterano provided himself with an English and Italian grammar and taught both himself and his wife. They spoke the language with an accent that made the youngsters laugh, but was in reality filled with exquisite cadences and soft sibilant sounds.

La Signora Maria's plan was to take her husband into the millinery shop, teach him the business, and then start a small one of her own in her own rooms with him in charge while she continued her work downtown. In less than six months Mr. Monterano felt himself capable of his new enterprise. The death of Ervi had sobered him, and the sight of his wife, rising early in the morning to help with the children, returning fatigued at night to prepare the family meal, laboring hard in the shop and maintaining throughout a calm even spirit, shamed him into application. He never abandoned his canes nor for that matter his astounding suits, but he managed to overcome his aversion to work, or at least to suppress it. He became ambitious for his children and was excited at the way in which Roberto distinguished himself at school.

The only vacation he permitted himself was to call on his children's teachers once a month.

At such times he would dress himself in absolute military precision, comb out his mustaches, brush back his hair with considerable pains, and swing ahead of him the ebony cane he had received as a gift from his colonel. He attended the school performances in which Roberto participated, and spent much of the evening conning the same books as his son. He had mentioned over and over again that his father had been a great chemist, and Roberto, knowing all too little what it might mean, announced that he was going to be a chemist too. Davido Monterano was agitated. He wept to himself with the joy of the prospect. On his way to work in the mornings he passed a toy shop, and found it displaying a chemical play set. He brought it home and Roberto had his first try at litmus paper and boiling one liquid from one color into another.

The four rooms became transformed in time into a small millinery workshop. The one overlooking the street was fitted out with benches and forms. Four girls were employed, two of them girls who had worked with Maria. The room was flooded with sunlight. Through the windows one saw the river stirring lazily under quiet skies.

CHAPTER TWO

1

After the wars with Menelik,[1] the Villetto branch of the great bank of Naples in Basilicata failed and the whole countryside became for the time being still more impoverished than ever. The responsible officials had fled the province. Some were known to be in hiding in Italy. Several had made their way to the seaports and embarked for America. It was the first marked exodus of the Villettani, the beginning of the emasculation of the town—a veritable emasculation, for the young men unceremoniously pulled up their stakes and moved off in the wake of the escaped officials. The church crowd on Sunday was only a mass of shawls and skirts which, in the words of Don Pietro, the parish priest, was not a wholesome sight to show to heaven. The fever to be off to the far lands had come like a blight in the turmoil of those days and had done its deadly work.

Tomaso Dauri, inheritor of the *don* from a long line of landowners, small as his lands were in extent and poor as they were in yield, had lost a considerable sum in the collapse of the bank. He had voiced a deep-seated opposition to investing when first the establishment of the bank had been broached. But Don Tomaso had the fatal inability of not being able to withstand the persuasions of friends, and further he prided himself on being an apostle of progress. One had only to mention the word progress and Don Tomaso became an enthusiast. Trivial matters like the economic difficulties which followed the loss of a good deal of his ready money did not alarm him. Time moved, and as it moved changes came about, and with each change one adopted new ways. That was the sum and total of life.

"Well, we all have suffered," he announced to the first assemblage of townsfolk gathered in his spacious house overlooking the piazza to consider ways and means to recover their losses. "Surely we have suffered. The floods of progress sweep all things before—some to better things, and some to worse."

He flattened down with his fingers the bushy halves of his mustaches, and poured more wine for his friends.

"And besides," he exclaimed, "it is in our youth that we must have trust. Come here, Carmela. This is the world's gold," he cried, and placed his hand on his daughter's head.

Carmela, twelve years old, his oldest child, blushed violently, her golden-brown skin transformed into the glowing texture of a reddened pear.

"You are now one of us," her father continued, "and when we too go to America we shall look to you to help restore your family to its real eminence...."

These were grandiose words, and they alarmed his wife. The assembled friends, however, were impressed, and showed it. Donna Sofia knew that the germ of his purpose to go to America had sprung into being only at that moment. It was just like him. He felt the flush of a thought and expressed it in grand language, especially in the presence of an audience. Then he felt too much pride in the poetic quality of his statement for him to consider its practical elements. From that moment on he became the slave of his own casual eloquence and moved heaven and earth to put it into effect. No one had discovered any other reason—certainly not Don Pietro—why with seven children he had decided one fine day to take passage for New York. No matter how violent was the opposition of his wife, Donna Sofia, she could not alter his purpose. She accepted the inevitable like a bad destiny and prepared to dismantle her home and make whatever plans for the future in America it was possible to draw from the distance of Villetto.

Carmela, although only twelve, like so many southern girls was already grown into the promise of womanhood. Her mother had put up her hair and lengthened her dresses.

"What a shame to lose these great long braids."

"Could we not keep them," Carmela asked, her arms about her mother's neck, "and just wind them about my head?"

"But you would look so monstrously old, my darling."

"Yes, but if I am to go to work in America, then?"

Donna Sofia embraced her daughter.

"Oh, what a terrible thing, my own, what a terrible thing!"

Don Tomaso stood in the doorway in his stocking feet.

"Why terrible?" he laughed. "You are always making the worst of things. When you see a shadow it's a ghost, and when you see a donkey in the woods it's a wolf."

"And it's just the opposite with you. Everything is going to turn out just fine. The sun's coming right after the rain, and after the earthquake there is always a chance to build new houses. That's all right with things, but not with human beings. What'll happen if we all get sick on shipboard?"

Donna Sofia might just as well have been blowing on a pair of bellows. The more she objected, the more Don Tomaso's plans flared up. He would never face the facts nor would he become angry at anyone for calling him a fool because of his blindness. He ran into difficult situations with a gayety that would have been charming were it not invariably foolish. He refused to see the danger signals ahead, and the more danger was pointed out to him the more obstinate he became. But always he laughed about it. He laughed beforehand. He laughed afterward. If what he undertook succeeded, he would face you with laughing eyes, without taking offensive credit to himself, and say, "Well, now, what's become of all your prophecies?" If he failed, he would shrug his shoulders and laugh it off. "Well, we failed! What of it? There's tomorrow again."

Don Tomaso sold all the lands he had inherited except a section of hill-ledge, forest-covered, in which his father, an inveterate hunter, had been found dead. He had let go old pieces of furniture, dating back many years, to a family in Melfina who seemed foolish enough to want to purchase them. He had put on the block the splendid house on the rise off the piazza—a house that had always held one of the Dauri family as far back as memory could go. The villagers shook their heads for the shame of these ill-considered doings. Don Tomaso merely laughed.

"We're approaching a new century. Let the old things go."

They came to his going-away party. Everyone tried to be merry. Considerable wine was drunk in the attempt.

"Hey there, Don Tomas', you won't get this stuff in America."

"Why, I'll send my agents to buy it all up and leave you dry as the dust on the roads."

They all patted Carmela on the head and embraced her affectionately.

"It's like uprooting the loveliest plant in the garden, taking her from Villetto."

Donna Sofia wiped the tears from her eyes with stealthy backhand movements.

"She'll be your mainstay, Donna Sofia. I'll bet all the doctors and the other great ones will stampede you for her hand."

"You bet, she's the one will make America for you."

Don Pietro, his uncle, the parish priest, alone persisted in clucking his tongue.

"It's a crime—a crime to steal off with our best blood. The Lord Jesus and our Holy Mother protect you all."

Don Tomaso went about from person to person, pooh-poohing this remark and the other, joyous, child-like.

"Why stick in Villetto? It's a pretty enough pot on a mountain shelf. But one needs space to expand in. Whoa, there, make room for progress!"

In New York he discovered very soon that the several thousand scuti he had realized on the sale of his possessions were not going to last any length of time.

"Dio Santo, everything costs so much here."

His wife crossed herself and looked beseechingly at her husband.

"All right, I know. We'll buy less."

2

They had taken rooms close to the East River in Harlem, in a building bought up by Gennaro and Struzzo on inside information that the houses in that vicinity were to be condemned to make room for a park. The park did not get under way for years, but that it was contemplated, that the plans were drawn, that a park would eventually displace the ramshackle dingy houses, dirty and infested with vermin, everybody knew and everybody believed. Especially the owners. And so it was thought bad business to keep the stairs, the plaster, the water-closets— one to several families—in repair. There were four apartments to a floor. The stairs led to landings that ran the whole length of the tenement. Upon these landings opened the doors of the apartments. The boards creaked, the banisters creaked, the gas-light sputtered and wheezed, on the walls ran streaks of moisture, here and there were patches of mildew. The plaster was broken everywhere, and slats, like skeleton ribs, showed in the open holes. For water-closet the four families on each floor had the use of a single bowl in a coffin-like room—it was no larger—wainscoted in tin to the height of a man and painted a vile green where it was not rusted. A small dirt-encrusted window with broken panes right under the flushing-box provided the only ventilation. The families were responsible for keeping it clean and arranging for the prevention of embarrassments. The consequences were that the place became fouler and fouler, until one or the other of the women, unable to bear it any longer, corralled the others and with mop and water set about washing it down.

Donna Sofia had thrown up her hands in horror no sooner had she been taken to her new home, procured hastily for her by friends. They had heard of her coming only a few days before the family arrived in the city and secured the only rooms available in an already crowded section.

Don Tomaso laughed despite the fact that the children crowded about him, bewildered and unhappy.

"What holes! But it's only for a few days. It's like getting caught in the dark out hunting and you take the best shelter around. Only a few days."

That he was shocked goes without saying. But he was not going to reveal his feelings. In his own mind he had already foreseen himself— what with his fine family traditions, his education, his personality, his willingness—mastering all the difficulties ahead of him, amassing an immediate fortune and moving out to places he was sure existed where there would be all the evidences and appurtenances of progress.

"We'll make headway, hey, my chicks, and then—a house on Fifth Avenue for us. You have not heard of Fifth Avenue? Shame on your ignorance. The place where only millionaires may live."

He confided some of his misgivings to his wife as they lay in their bed, both miserable, both uncertain of the future, both regretful of their trek across the ocean. It was fortunate that he obtained work in a piano factory on the other side of the Harlem, and that Carmela found employment in a button-manufacturing place near the river further south. Donna Sofia resolved to keep the money they brought with them intact, and to live only on the wages Tomaso and Carmela earned. The two left early in the morning, long before the crowds poured into the streets, when the lights on the river were gray and long and the mists became slowly suffused with the rising sun. She stood at the window watching them go down the street to the avenue where they parted, he to walk alone in one direction, and she to join other girls who were employed in the same factory. Then she hurried back to take a look at the big-boned Gianni with his high cheekbones and sunken eyes, Giovanni the next in years but always pale and thin, Immanuele, her fourth-born, a mischievous lad who looked like an angel when he slept—the three of them in one bed, their legs hopelessly entangled. She straightened them out, brushed back the hair from their foreheads, kissed them and made the sign of the cross over each of them.

In the next bed, a foot apart from the large one, slept her other two boys, Carlino who had inherited his fair skin and pale-brown eyes from her own family but who was the perfect replica of his father, and the baby, two, Modesto, a chunk of a boy who thrived on the villainous fare of the steerage, walked the boat like a sailor, enjoyed the jostle in the streets, made friends by poking his fingers into everyone's hand and looking up with a huge smile of recognition. He had cried when he was not going to be permitted to sleep with his brothers. Carlino had to be severely admonished that he was not to toss wildly while he slept, for fear of kicking Modesto. He had promised, and the two slept together as if they were peas in a pod, subtly tied to separate spots.

Over them Donna Sofia also made the sign of the cross, but she ended by kneeling at the foot of the bed and, pounding her breast gently with her fist, offered untold sacrifices of her time, her heart, her worldly goods first to one saint and then to another for the continued good health and good behavior of her children. She had religiously kept the old calendar she possessed in Villetto with the saints' days and their names blazoned in red, and the title of the appropriate prayer to offer to each one, with the whole prayer stamped in black if it was not too long. Before going to bed the night before, she made sure to have the name of the saint in mind and to con the inscribed prayer for use the next morning. She was assured by this means that she would omit no heavenly power that might intercede for her in behalf of her family. She had thought of the plan before leaving for America and had asked Don Pietro's advice about it.

"It can do no harm, and may do considerable good," he had told her, patting her on the head and calling her a good soul.

For three months her devotion to the saints had resulted in a substantial modicum of peace and happiness and even such well-being as was possible under the circumstances. In a little brown earthen jar—she kept it in the wall behind one of her saint's pictures where the plaster had given way—she put the money that they had brought with them from Italy. Into it she added whatever Carmela and Don Tomaso brought home on Saturday nights.[2] She had discovered that it was possible to cook with pork-lard instead of olive oil, that the hard stale bread sold on the sidewalks by the old women was good eating especially if covered over with steaming bean soup mixed with a little celery, that the family was content to have meat at the most twice a week, and that fruit, if not cheese, was plentiful and cheap. At the end of three months she had saved a third of all the money that came into the family as wages. Don Tomaso made eight dollars a week and Carmela four. In fact, she felt herself rich enough to permit Don Tomaso to purchase a guitar for himself, a mandolin for Gianni, and a flute—but much later—for Immanuele.

At night Don Tomaso gave them all instructions in music. Before long they strummed away on their instruments and the nights passed, as Donna Sofia put it, without confusion. She sat at the table with Carmela and remade and remade their clothes to keep pace with the constant change in girth and height of all of them. Donna Sofia, without much talk, had made it clear that the family was going to make America.

In her heart, however, deep as the assurance was that came from her prayers, she had one misgiving. She was happy that Carmela was a quiet self-contained girl. Naturally she had become an outstanding figure in the family, young as she was. The Dauri family in themselves had achieved an early distinction for minding their own business and conducting themselves as a well-mannered family *per bene*, without putting on airs and demanding that they be accorded privileges which they had necessarily lost on coming to America. Don Tomaso in his breezy easygoing fashion made friends with everyone without slipping into any kind of intimacy with people. There was a family under them who must have lived, as he phrased it, in close communion with their pigs and jack-asses in their mountain home in Italy. They could neither read nor write their names, and they allowed the children to run wild instead of sending them to school.

"They're a good crowd, though," he said one night. "Offer you anything they have. . . . They work as rag-pickers for Gennaro Accuci, the landlord, but they're good, very good. . . ."

Carmela had made friends with one of the girls of this family, a child somewhat older than she who made up for whatever lack of schooling and careful home-bringing by shrewd common sense, a good portion of effrontery, and a marked ability to look after herself. Concetta ran the family, and as befitting one of that eminence she mounded her black hair high over her forehead, wore her skirts close down to her ankles, and swung her body with considerable self-possession. Her sharp nose made her look older than her fifteen years and the way she crowded her breasts in her tight-fitting blouse gave her the appearance of a matronly maturity not at all belied by her knowledge of the world.

It was she who first awakened in Donna Sofia the fear at the center of all the even-tempered ways she had evolved with her family.

Concetta had come upstairs before the children had risen.

"Donna Sofia," she had called out, "I want a word with you this morning. How about it?"

She had run up without being particularly invited and, taking a backless chair, sat leaning forward confidentially, one arm akimbo and one resting on her thigh.

"It's this, Donna Sofia," she whispered, tossing her head for the older woman to come closer. "Carmela. She's damned pretty—'*nna ma-doncinella . . . sa*[3] . . . and I advise you. There's a crowd of he-devils in this damned city, you understand, got noses they poke under every skirt they get wind of, see, and they hang around the factories all hours . . . well, all I say," and she held her torso erect and pressed down with her arms as if straightening it up, "always keep a bitch tied and don't have the strap too long. . . ."

Donna Sofia was thoroughly alarmed but kept a calm face.

"Carmela is well-mannered and reserved. She'll give nobody any cause. . . ."

"Sure, she won't. Of course she won't. But a grown pup'll smell bitch . . ."

"Listen here, young woman . . ."

Concetta was not one to listen to any one.

"Just a bit of advice, that's all."

She got up, flounced about, shouted out "Good morning to you, Donna Sofia *bella,*" and thumped down the hollow stairs.

Donna Sofia's alarm was increased by Carmela herself that evening.

"Don't be frightened, Ma, but I do wish Papa would come with me to the button-factory."

"Why, child, is anyone bothering you?"

"No, but he could get work there."

"Who's bothering you, *cara?*"

He was a smart-looking young man, with a mustache turned up at the ends, dark-skinned, and ever so nicely dressed. He was downstairs when she went out with the girls to eat their lunches. In the evening he was again downstairs waiting, and now he had taken to waiting for her in the morning on her way to work. He followed her everywhere.

"Only now, he stopped me, took his hat off very nicely, and said something . . . I ran. . . ."

Donna Sofia obtained the promise of the other girls that they would always accompany Carmela to and from the factory. One evening she stood waiting for her daughter in front of the house. The winter darkness was already heavy, the mud-caked street was deserted, a quick noisy wind blew toward the river, and Donna Sofia huddled all the closer in her shawl. She crossed herself. Carmela was alone, walking rapidly, the young man behind her.

"Mother of Jesus, keep her."

Carmela ran up and clung to her arm.

"There," she said, "there he is."

Donna Sofia stopped the young man. It was Domenico Accuci, debonair in a flashy overcoat and slouch hat.

"You stop following my daughter."

"I am sorry, signora. I—I just want to know her like a friend."

"Move off and let her alone."

"No offense, no offense."

He pulled the lapels of his tight-fitting coat, lifted his hat, smiled to Carmela, and moved off.

"Bold fool," Donna Sofia called after him.

"Oh, it's nothing," Don Tomaso declared that evening. "It's the custom of the country, my darling—that's all. Boys and girls play here together, not like in the old country. You make a fuss over nothing. . . . It's a form of progress, woman. Let's eat. This is good pasta with beans. I really think they have better beans here, and their pork is leaner . . . much."

"We ought to get out of this hole anyhow," Donna Sofia kept saying.

"Oh, it's a vile enough place," her husband agreed. "Let's make our pile first, and then . . ."

3

The winter was on in dead earnest. Cold raw days set in and the stove in the kitchen was kept filled with wood. It blazed and roared perpetually. The children crowded around it, playing their games or banging away on the mandolin. Donna Sofia had just added more wood. There was to be macaroni with sauce and cheese, and meat. In the dusk the stove shone like a crimson-topped table, its cover glowing with heat, its numerous pots and pans steaming into the cold air. In the red light it emitted, the miniature porcelain niche with its blue-gowned Madonna within gleamed bright and radiant. The huge brewery display calendar beside it seemed to have blazed up, the red factory windows lighted quite mysteriously. Outside was only the far-away calling of the wind. Occasionally into the silence the gas-house stacks roared, flared red, and disappeared into the darkness.

"Well, well," cried Don Tomaso, "but it's cold. Never such cold in Villetto, hey, boys? It may snow—who knows—and oh, the fun that will be."

"Fun for sure," cried his wife busy at the stove. "It will get into everyone's clothes and who knows who'll be sick."

"What a way to talk! Have you ever seen snow? Have you ever felt snow? Have you, you monkeys?"

The boys shouted no in chorus.

"Tell us, tell us."

Don Tomaso made them take seats at the table.

"Now . . ."

There was no need. Down from the sky the flakes had already begun. They flung themselves almost gaily against the window panes and melted at once.

"They're like butterflies that die," shouted Gianni.

The others put their noses against the glass and peered out.

"It's everywhere."

"It's quiet . . . oh, so quiet."

"Let's open the windows."

"No, Tomaso, don't do that. They will catch their deaths of cold."

"Go on, spoil everything. But try to stop us, hey what?"

The windows were flung open. Already little drifts had gathered on the sills. The children scooped them up with their hands.

"How cold, Ma . . . it's melted already . . ."

"It's white velvet, Ma . . ."

"Oh, shut the windows, shut them, I say."

There was laughing and shouting. They rubbed snow on each other's noses. They wanted to go out into the street and stand under the falling flakes.

"I'll come up all covered—like the flour man in Villetto."

No one could hear the others. Donna Sofia joined the chorus.

"Carmela will be caught in it," she said, but smiled with pleasure at the delight it would be to the girl. For she, too, now saw the snow for the first time remaking the night as if by a kindly magic. She was not old enough to remember the only snowfall that Villetto had ever known, and the spectacle in front of her was as new and as startling as it was to the children.

"Funny how that chimney looks now," she said with as much animation as her youngsters. "Like a queer man . . ."

The windows were shut soon, and they all crowded about the table.

Don Tomaso began a story of a whole battalion that had been lost in a whirlwind of snow, and of how a regiment of huge dogs, without human escort, had been sent out to find them.

A slamming of a door—the water-closet door, Donna Sofia cried—brought an end to the tale. The door rarely slammed that way.

"Quiet," Donna Sofia whispered.

It was unmistakable. There were the sounds of smothered outcries. There was the noise of a neighbor's door opening, then of steps coming up the stairs, a tattoo of knuckles on their own door, and a low voice, "Quick, open, quick . . ."

"*Dio mio,*[4] what is it?" Donna Sofia opened.

Two or three other doors had been opened on the landing. Heads were thrust out in the squares of light. There was the sound of the knob in the water-closet door turning. Concetta stood outside the door.

"Hurry, Don Tomaso . . . I'm afraid . . . terrible . . ."

4

Don Tomaso hurried out, other men following him. In the damp half-lit hallway a huddle of people had collected. A low painful cry from the water-closet caused the women to shudder and cross themselves. Don Tomaso pulled at the knob. The door was latched from the inside. He pulled again. Dead silence. The men looked at each other.

"But why call me?" Don Tomaso finally asked. "Why me?"

Concetta had made her way to the front group of men.

"I'll tell you why . . . Carmela is in there and a young pup that's been after her for weeks . . ."

Donna Sofia shouted, "*Madonna mia,*[5] *madonna mia,* what is it?"

"*Dio santo!*"[6] another woman whispered.

"A filthy country—no law—no decency . . ."

Don Tomaso had given the door a desperate jerk. It blew open as if a strong wind had pushed from behind. Domenico Accuci had evidently thought it out. If he unlatched the door exactly at the time they pulled from without, the men would be thrown back against the wall, held there momentarily by the door, and he would have a clear passageway to the stairs, and freedom. Like an alley-cat fleeing from pursuers, he dashed out and made a leap for the stairs. But one of the men had been as quick as he. The two of them were heard tumbling down the steps.

Donna Sofia had got one view of the toilet and shrieked. Carmela lay crouched in a heap near the bowl, her long hair, loose and disheveled, hanging in the water, an arm thrown back as if it had been wrenched out of its socket, her dresses torn and cluttered about her. She tried to cry out when she saw her mother, but her lips moved only into the pattern of a slow smile, and her eyes danced with feverish light. Then she started to lift the arm that had been thrown over the basin. A thin clear shriek, sharper than the sound of a nail drawn over steel. Her whole body lifted off the floor, her white thighs showing. A thud like a padded mallet, as her body fell swiftly. Then silence, and her young face turned into a white daub with red eyes.

Don Tomaso had understood enough in one glance.

"Leave him to me," he shouted.

The men let go. Before Domenico had a chance to rise, Don Tomaso had sprung upon him. A cry, like that of a dog suddenly run over by wheels, leaped into the air, shutting out everything else. Don Tomaso had dug his teeth into the young man's cheek and bitten into the flesh.

Concetta had enough presence of mind to gather up the children and take them to her own flat. She came up again for the cooked meal on the stove and reported later that the youngsters had been fed and were fast asleep.

Donna Sofia sat next to her daughter in bed, quiet now, gazing dumbly into her mother's eyes. Occasionally she managed to mumble,

"I ran the whole way. Tried to hide . . ."

The mother kept bathing her cheeks, stroking her hair, praying silently.

"What did he do, Carmè, what did he do?"

"I ran the whole way . . . through the snow . . . it moved all about me like spots in front of my eyes . . . I ran the whole way . . . how a dog runs . . . the whole way . . . I tried to hide . . ."

Don Tomaso came in and stood by his wife.

"You're like a trembling animal," she said to him as he pressed disconsolately against her. He was worse than that to himself. As if the objections that his wife and Don Pietro had raised against his coming to America had postponed their full weight in order that he might feel it in a moment of torment and desolation, he stood aghast at what had happened, feeling that it was at bottom his fault. His body hung not like a trembling animal but rather like a poorly filled sack that cannot stand erect. His hands had lost their usual gestures. They drooped limp at his side just as his face sagged, his strong military torso bent over, the lighted black eyes looked blank and lustreless.

"We must find him. He must marry her . . ."

Donna Sofia broached the subject in a horrified whisper.

"God help the poor child," is all he could answer.

"You hear?" she questioned. "It must take place . . . at once . . . at once."

Don Tomaso shrugged his shoulders and fell into a deep silence.

"We must lose no time. . . . You said you bit him . . . you'll be able to find him . . . he could not go far."

Carmela raised her face piteously.

"What is it, Ma, what is it?"

Donna Sofia leaned over and put her arm around the girl's head. "Sleep, baby."

"What is it you are talking about?"

"No . . . no . . . my baby . . . do be quiet . . . you must sleep . . ."

"It's my arm, Ma . . . only my arm . . ."

5

The bedroom, unlike the kitchen, was small, had no gas, no window. The only air came from the adjoining room, where the boys slept, through a diminutive aperture with several panes of glass, eight by eight, opening into an airyway. In a corner right above the bed Don Tomaso had built a little shelf, and on it there stood a kerosene lamp with a red base and a small globe without a shade. It threw a steady glare on the bed, a soft quiet light, unagitated by the wind. Carmela saw it as something to which she was not accustomed, and turned her head to look at it.

"It's the madonna, Ma, looking down on me and smiling."

"Hush, my dear, hush . . . it's only the lamp."

"But it is . . . she is coming down the sky."

Don Tomaso clutched his fist and bit his lip.

"You'll see, it's only the lamp," Donna Sofia said, and she reached up for it and placed it on a chair at the foot of the bed.

Carmela followed it with her eyes and kept looking at it.

"There, you see," her mother assured her. "You are here with me and your father . . ."

The light fascinated Carmela. She kept staring at it. Ease seemed to come to her with the faint flicker of the wick. She shut her eyes and breathed quietly.

Donna Sofia turned at once to her husband.

"You hear, Tomà, no matter if nothing happened . . . the scoundrel must marry her."

"She's but a baby," Don Tomaso whispered desperately, clasping his hands and holding them above his head.

"Not enough of a baby for the brute to tear her apart.... The villainy of it ..."

"We'll go back to Italy."

"Back to Italy!" She laughed. "You fool ... always escaping your trouble. You and your mighty plans. ..."

"*Per l'amor di Dio, Sofi'* [7] ... be charitable ..."

"Why? Why? You got us into this mess ..."

"It was for the best, I thought."

He spoke in low tones, pleading, attempting to still the wild voices that were shouting at him in his own heart.

"The best ... well, we'll make the best of it now. If you won't go out and find the wretch, I will, and I'll drag him here and keep him here. He'll marry the girl or I'll have his stones out."

Don Tomaso was not familiar with this side of his wife. He thought of her as a mild-mannered person like himself, one who minded her affairs, knew her place as a wife and mother, and never, like so many others, lost control over herself and became hysterical, frantic, unappeasable. True, nothing really had ever happened in their lives to unnerve them. The loss of their money in the bank was in all truth a thing of nothing. Although she had opposed the move to America, he knew her well enough to realize that she was glad of it and had looked forward to the day of their departure with as much excitement and gayety as he himself. She had entered into the spirit of the children who saw in their migration a sort of vaster summer picnic. She had never ceased railing at what she called a fit of idiocy—this going-off debonairly to America. But had she been more fundamentally opposed, it would never have taken place. She had stilled her own doubts in a ferment of hopeful anticipation. In some vague, prayer-like attitude, they had both thought of their journey as a pilgrimage of happy travelers who would find new security, new significance, new days.

Everything had gone well until this.

"Pietro, Pietro, you must pray for us, you there in your chapel, so near to God, and so sure.... Mercy on our souls!"

"Tomaso." Donna Sofia was standing up. She was satisfied that Carmela was asleep and would not hear. "You will go at once and fetch the boy."

He placed his hands upon her shoulders and held her gently against her will.

"I don't even know where he lives."

"It's the landlord's son."

Don Tomaso had only met Gennaro when that earringed gentleman had come to collect the rent. Tomaso's impression of him had been one of amusement at the haughty disdain of the world with which Gennaro appeared to be wearing the golden ornaments in his ears.

"A true peasant if ever there was one, obstinate and proud. He'd snap his fingers in the face of the devil himself and for that matter the Lord God."

To think of the chunky impertinence, as Gennaro got phrased in Don Tomaso's mind, as the father-in-law of his daughter—the thing seemed preposterous. A thorough boor lifted to prominence by the crazy customs of America! At the same time, torn as his heart was with grief, he could not repress a smile as he said to his wife,

"Indeed! Well, we shall be marrying our daughter into the best of American families."

"Let it be a family of wild pigs, she'll marry him."

Suddenly Carmela sat up.

"No, no," she shrieked, "not him, not him!"

Donna Sofia seemed to have forgotten Carmela's condition.

"Quiet," she commanded. "You will marry him. We shall have no open shame in our family."

"Not him . . . not him . . ."

She fell back into her pillow, sobbing.

"Hurry, Tomaso."

6

They were too engrossed in their thoughts to hear the heavy footsteps in the hallway. But they did hear the loud knock on the door. When Tomaso opened, the visitor proved to be no other than Gennaro, his short pipe stuck into his mouth at a challenging angle, a smile curled around it, his heavy plush hat pulled well down over his forehead. He shouldered himself in without much ceremony.

"Shut the door," he commanded.

He drew a chair from the table and sat down, his legs spread out.

"You're Don Tomaso, and you're Donna Sofia," he pointed with his pipe.

They nodded, and stood by helplessly.

"Where's this pretty daughter of yours?"

"The insolent jack-ass," thought Don Tomaso, "behaving like a military commander."

"You have heard?" asked Donna Sofia.

Gennaro nodded without looking at her. He addressed his next remark to Don Tomaso.

"By rights," he said, "I ought to slit your bowels open."

"I hope," replied Don Tomaso at once, "I do not have the occasion ever to say a similar thing to you. For I should do it without thinking about it."

Donna Sofia pressed closer to her husband and held his arm.

Gennaro stood up, but immediately sat down again.

"I have a sort of temper," he explained. "Words like yours, Don Tomaso, provoke a man. But I'll keep quiet. I came here really to put things to rights."

Donna Sofia and her husband looked at each other. Don Tomaso merely stroked his mustaches, gently put his wife aside, got a chair and sat down.

"You sit there," he said to his wife.

They waited for Gennaro's next words.

"My son, Domenico, is a lazy, good-for-nothing poltroon, not worth a cent in the shop and less outside. Not like me. You see, I wear my earrings like an old-fashioned yokel. I care that much for people," and he snapped his fingers by way of illustration, "and for what they say. I do things."

He pounded his chest.

"I have made America. Hard work, not being afraid, going after things . . ."

His hand traced a generous semi-circle in the air.

"I own all this property, I have a big business, even the politicians, the priests, the police—they all know me and come to me. I know a thing or two about America. . . . I could put you out of these rooms . . . why not?"

"That might be a blessing," Don Tomaso interrupted, with a smile.

"Ha, you joke, do you?" Gennaro retorted. "It's no joke, though. Gennaro Accuci owned a fistful of dirt in Italy—Capomonte, Provincia di Calabria, Città Communale, Reggio—to be exact, and he was nobody. But here, I own lots and houses, and businesses."

"You are fortunate," Donna Sofia assured him.

"In everything except my son. He's a do-nothing and he puts on airs. He thinks of women only . . . and now he does this thing—chases a little girl into a hole like an animal. Bah! I spit on him."

He got up and stamped to the other side of the room. There he stopped suddenly.

"I beat him to a pulp when he came home. I knew what that hanging cheek meant. It's sewed up now, but he'll have it as a reminder the rest of his life. You did right, Don Tomaso . . . and what's more . . ."

He sat down again, and this time removed his hat and placed it over his knee. Donna Sofia made a gesture to take it from him.

"No, Donna Sofia," he said deprecatingly. "Never let it be said that Gennaro Accuci does not know what to do. He understands as well as others. Domenico shall marry your daughter, and at once."

Now that what Donna Sofia wanted was practically a settled matter, she burst into tears.

"My poor child, my poor child."

Don Tomaso said nothing. The tears ran down his cheeks and he let them slip into his mouth.

"Doesn't it suit you?" asked Gennaro angrily.

"Yes," said Don Tomaso, nodding his head. "Yes, it suits. Of course, she is young . . ."

"A baby," interposed Donna Sofia.

"But a big girl, they say," argued Don Gennaro, "and very pretty. How long before she would marry anyhow?"

"It's the will of heaven," Donna Sofia assented.

"Let's put it that way," was Gennaro's answer. "Tomorrow, Friday, I shall see Don Anselmo, and the thing will be done Sunday. This maybe will put some manhood into that dolled-up poltroon of mine. And of course, my good people, you will not live here any longer. You will come to the Parterre."

When they were alone, Don Tomaso and Donna Sofia looked at each other without saying a word.

"We've made America at last," he said after some seconds. "We're rich," and he sat down at the table, buried his head in his arm and wept like a child.

Donna Sofia hurried to Carmela, who was sobbing wildly.

"Not him, Ma, not him . . ."

"The good God will make it right."

The young girl sat up.

"The pain's here, Ma, in my arm. Help me, help me, Sweet Mary."

7

The nuptials of Carmela Dauri and Domenico Accuci were duly solemnized by Don Anselmo. At first he had protested against the event on the natural ground that there was no definite proof of a child. It was

Gennaro who brushed aside the objection. The young ram had run the child into a corner and the whole world had heard. It would not be fair to her. Imagine the tittering among her friends, the way the young boys of the neighborhood as well as the men would look upon her, fair game now that the initial step had been taken. She would be followed and her life would be made miserable.

Such, too, were Donna Sofia's thoughts, and it was such arguments that she employed to quiet her husband's fears. He was glad that Don Anselmo had taken such a positive stand against the wedding. Like himself, the priest looked upon the marriage as a blasting of promising youth far worse than the mere disgrace of her rape, brutal and vicious as it had been. He thought of the young man, too. A slouching, work-shirking adolescent, unused to ready money and the freedom it brought, unused to a commanding place in a compact community such as Little Italy was, he had not risen in character, in ability. Don Anselmo spoke his mind to Don Tomaso as a man who could understand.

"It is fundamental sociology," the priest maintained, rather proud of the opportunity to employ long technical terms. "In a small group, without the restraints of an orderly upper class with power and position, the tendency is for the men and women who achieve a place of wealth and command to follow the lowest, and not the highest, instincts. The highest instincts are not so much basic—like fear, for instance, or sex—as they are superinduced by culture, the training at the mother's knee, the dictates of the church. The worst characters tend to be imitated, not the best. The vicious assume control. It becomes smart and swaggering to be bad. That's what happened to our Italian peasants—a good lot, a thrifty hardworking group, but for so many years restrained by poverty, by lack of education, by customs that had the virtue of sanctity. But give them freedom, and see what happens. . . ."

Don Tomaso, like the priest, was happy that he finally had a chance to talk of the higher things in a higher way, eschewing the homely dialect entirely and fumbling for the grandiose words of the standard language, words that in themselves were an event to employ, a self-sustaining pleasure to discover still residing in one's memory.[8]

"Far be it from me to find any flaws in your reasoning, Don Anselmo," he added. "Culture is a slow process. Of course, it changes its character gradually, as the whole of life moves onward. I have always been proud to look upon myself as a believer in progress, and so I subscribe to ideas which—I do not say it slightingly, you understand, for I do have a real veneration for the church—may not seem quite the right thing to a member of the cloth. I mean, that I do not look altogether with horror upon the rise of our peasantry in this country to positions of power and trust. I must confess it goes against my grain to be compelled to be respectful to a flock of *cafonacci,* clodhoppers, and cabbage-pullers with no manners. It does, but I see the justice of a society that allows them the right to advance. And so I say freedom may be bad for them momentarily, but give them time . . ."

"That is the essence of it," the priest admitted. "And that is why I say it would be a shame to compel Domenico—and Carmela—to be married. They would have no opportunity . . ."

They decided, in a bravura of a splendid *non-sequitur,* to do what they could to prevent the marriage. But Gennaro and Donna Sofia were stronger than they. Domenico was far too cowed by his father's treatment of him, and Carmela too sick to do more than weep. In Gennaro's case there was more than the mere desire to see justice done. It was his hope that the marriage might result in improving Domenico, although in his own heart he failed to see actually how anything could improve him. And furthermore—and this was the true motive—here was an opportunity to ally himself with a family that had been of some consequence not only in its own town but in the whole province from which it came. The Accuci family would be connected with the best of Italian families. He would have disdained to admit the thought. Yet despite the fanfare of boasting about his prowess and his ability Gennaro retained much of the admiration of the European peasant for the classes superior to his own. He had made up his mind that Domenico would marry Carmela, and the marriage took place.

He broached the subject of a real festal day. They would have a whole series of carriages to take the guests and the couple to the church. On their return there would be a big dinner at his home, and Don Felippo, the café-keeper, would provide confetti for the crowds outside, cakes for the crowds inside, Giovanni Sardi would have a real orchestra—the young barber had added a sideline to his business—and there would be dancing.

Donna Sofia had refused.

"I want it quiet, very quiet. Right here at home. Don Anselmo will consent."

"He'll consent or I'll know why," shouted Gennaro.

Don Anselmo performed the ceremony at home. The boys looked on with amazing patience, unable to understand just what was happening to their sister. Carmela, because of the dislocation of her shoulder-blade—

attended to only the day before—and her state of shock, was forbidden to leave her bed. Dr. Giovanelli would not have allowed his chief Garibaldi to leave the hospital under similar circumstances. Domenico proved even a greater source of wonder to the boys. First of all they thought he looked slightly queer with a cross of adhesive tape over his cheek. But what they could not fathom was why he looked so pale and trembling, and so sick, like a ghost. He had such wonderful clothes on, too—a suit that was very blue and fitted him tight around the waist, and a big white cravat that pushed up his chin, and he had his hair plastered down with shining oil and finger-waved at the edges, and a white carnation, ever so huge, in his lapel, and shoes that caught all the illumination from the candles they had set up in Carmela's bedroom.

Gennaro himself was even funnier. The boys restrained themselves from laughter—all but Immanuele who had to keep his hand over his mouth and content himself with sneaking a laughing glance out of his eyes first at one brother and then at another. Gennaro's earrings stood out more than anything else, more than his curly hair brushed up into a mat, more than his bright green tie, more than his black coat with braid all around it, and his glaring russet shoes. Evidently he must have polished the earrings. There was not a wink of light in the room that did not find them and ricochet away. Immanuele went so far once as to point at them, his whole face prepared to burst into titters. After the ceremony Don Tomaso took him by the ears and shook his head. "For being an unmannerly rogue," Immanuele heard, remembered, and wanted to laugh outright.

When it was over they all went into the kitchen. Don Anselmo removed his surplice and rubbed his hands. Donna Sofia had in the meantime poured the wine into the huge red glasses that Gennaro had sent over on purpose. In the center of the table was an immense tray with an enormous pyramid of small cakes, a confectionery series of Babylonian towers. On each step, as the circular layers mounted, were candies in glossy, colored papers. On the extreme peak stood a bride and groom in black and white paper clothing, arm in arm, and looking foolishly radiant. Don Tomaso brought out the white-covered box with the images of the madonna on top used in the bedroom for a chapel. This he placed on the table with the candles still lighted. As the candies flared up, the snow drifts against the windows quivered with color and the tumblers with wine blinked in mocking replica.

"Looks nice," Gennaro declared as he seated himself.

Donna Sofia offered him the first glass of wine.

"True *Gragnano*,"[9] he said, lifting it, "and I am glad to drink your health, Donna Sofia. . . ."

"Not mine," she retorted, "but the health and the happiness . . ."

"Ah, for sure, for sure," Gennaro cried. "Here there, dollface," he called out to his son, while the Dauri boys almost forgot their manners, "what are you doing here? Take yourself a glass of wine, and one for the bride, and go in there where you belong . . ."

Don Anselmo in a gentle voice and with a helpful gesture assisted the boy. With the priest's arm about his shoulder, Domenico, looking not so much sheepish as crushed, went into Carmela's room. Urged on by Don Anselmo, with a wry painful smile, he held the glass out for Carmela to take, and said, "You'll have some wine . . ."

Don Anselmo nodded to her to accept it. Carmela, however, could only stare and stare at Domenico, her pale face set as in a plaster mold. There was neither smile nor twist of pain in the tender soft muscles. Her eyes, ordinarily alive with their bright brown pupils, were cold and faraway and yet uncomfortably nearing and nearing, as if she were about to rise and come close to them. Yet she lay still in her bed, the crocheted cover close under her chin, with the corn-silk red of her braids drawn across it. The priest was touched and looked about for a place to rest his glass.

Domenico gazed back at his girl-bride without knowing what to do. All the weeks he had been pursuing her, dog-like as Carmela had described it to her mother, she had filled his imagination with strange visions. There had been a real point in possessing her, and he had been foolish enough to believe that all he had need to do was to seize her forcibly, and the animation in her eyes, the promise of beauty in her rounding body, would respond without reserve to his wild caresses. There she lay now like a beaten animal, frightened and frightening, his by the law of God, but never his by the wish of her heart. He realized it all in a stupid, unhappy way. The braggadocio of his spirit was crushed and the brute force of his desires tempered to the sight of the pain in Carmela's whole attitude. More so than even she, he stood stiff and still, not knowing exactly what to do.

"Say something to her," the priest whispered into his ear. "You love her . . . something."

As if he had been pushed, he fell to his knees at Carmela's side, the wine spilling over the floor and the cover of the bed. He lowered his head and whispered hoarsely, "*Ti voglio bene . . . ma davvero, davvero*[10] . . . I love you."

Carmela turned her face away, while he strangely sobbed.

"Got to move right away out of here," Gennaro's voice was booming inside. "There's the second floor in the Parterre. Narrow rooms they are, for certain, but painted up grand. Sure, you got a big family, what of that? And there'll be my wife to help out, and upstairs there's a splendid family, well-connected in Italy, ah, you'll like them."

8

It was decided that night that Domenico and Carmela would live with their respective families until the Dauris moved into the Parterre. Gennaro assumed charge of the whole affair, almost as if it had been his wedding. Not a day passed before the moving that he did not put in an appearance at the Dauri home and stalk boldly into Carmela's room.

She possessed too vigorous a body and too buoyant a spirit to be completely overwhelmed by her experience. As the days passed, life flushed back into her cheeks, her eyes resumed their usual liveliness, and to a certain extent she fell into the spirit of the whole arrangement. It fascinated her despite the dread she felt about it. She refused to allow Domenico to come to see her, but she realized that it was more from shame than from hatred of him. But she would permit her mother to mention the details of the moving—something which at first caused her to shrink back as if she had been struck sharp sudden blows. In a week or two she either had forgotten the full horror of her marriage or the forces of life were too powerful. She recovered her animation and her beauty. Gennaro was the first to notice it.

"She's like our mountain-flowers back home," he confided to Don Tomaso. "The rains can't kill them and not even the sand storms . . . A lusty little beast, and a sight for the eyes. . . . A lucky brute, my son."

Don Tomaso shuddered inwardly, and later confessed to his wife that he did not approve of the unabashed admiration Gennaro evinced.

"It's just the peasant in him. How else can he express himself?"

The shoulder had set, Carmela's appetite had returned, and she was up and about the house. A few days now and the moving would take place. Gennaro came to announce it. As usual he went to see Carmela.

"Ah, but you're a handsome wench, my darling," he shouted at her. "And you put on flesh and look like twenty. . . . You could get away with it even in the municipal office."

He stroked her lovingly on the cheek.

"And now, Donna Sofia, I've permitted myself a privilege," he said, taking his pipe out of his mouth and replacing it immediately after with some vigor. "I have ordered the tailor on Second Avenue, where the new electric trains are running overhead, you know . . . well, I have ordered him to give you, for your five boys, one suit apiece . . . no, no . . . no fuss about it, no no's and no thank you's . . . this is a free offering from a man that's made America to one that's going to . . ."

He snatched his pipe out of his mouth, and glared. There was no answer.

"As for Carmela, the dressmaker will come right here, and she'll have the dresses half-ready like. Two stitches here, two stitches there, and you'll see, she'll be the belle of all Harlem. And for you, too, there's a dress—ah, yes, you, too." He raised his hand deprecatingly. "You must not spoil my pleasure. My wife will have a new dress and then you can meet and talk things over."

The moving was a gala day for Gennaro. His own wagons with four horses each, which he used to cart his bales to the jobbers and the mills, he had cleaned out thoroughly and backed against the tenement house where the Dauris lived. Not that it was a strange sight for a family to be moving and for vans to be against the curb loading on the furniture. But it was rare to have horses with plumes in their harnesses and jingle bells appended. The word went round that the young bride was to come out, and a crowd collected. Concetta, despite her own curiosity and the exasperating fact that she had not been allowed to see Carmela, attempted to drive the loiterers away.

"What do you think, there's a Punch and Judy show? Get out."

Don Tomaso had gone off to work early that morning. He for one was not going to assist. It was enough that he had been either cajoled, compelled or persuaded—he did not care which—into the plan. Donna Sofia might argue for all she wished that under the circumstances what could they do? As long as they were confronted with the situation, was there anything else? Gennaro was well off. There were girls married as young as Carmela. She would adjust herself, and with the help of Gennaro every one would gain. They would be in for some money. He might go into a business of some sort.

"When I do, Sofi," he told her, "it will be with money I have saved penny by penny with my own hands, which I have earned penny by penny with my own sweat."

"Don't put on the airs of an orator, my good man, little it becomes you these days. You've got us into this mess, and now you want to fly away from it with a clean shirt-tail."

Don Tomaso had said not another word. He had put on his hat and bolted out for his walk to the river. Gianni, the oldest son, followed him. The boy put a hand into his father's and walked rapidly.

"I'm going to get a new suit," Gianni informed Don Tomaso.

The father squeezed the child's hand and hurried even more. Several men who had evidently heard of the marriage of his daughter to Gennaro, the property owner and big shot of the community, lifted their hats to Don Tomaso. He glanced at them and hastened his steps.

"I can't go so fast," Gianni exclaimed. "Stop a minute." He pulled at his father and caused him to stop. Gianni had seen something on the sidewalk. He stooped rapidly, and like a bird he clawed at it, then straightened up in a second. The father jerked him forward.

"Look, papa, look!"

Don Tomaso was compelled to halt and ask, "What, what now?"

"Look!"

Gianni had picked up a bill. His father took it, opened it out and discovered it to be a five-dollar note.

"It's money—a good deal of money."

Gianni stared.

"Listen, Gianni. We'll tell nobody of this. Understand me, nobody. It will be yours and mine—we found it together. We'll save it, and add to it."

"But I don't work."

"In a year or two you will. You will leave school and work. I'll add to it myself, and then you; and together we'll build a big business of our own, pianos, or houses, or laying sidewalks . . . selling pickles, picking up rags . . . something will make big shots of us in this country . . . and gain us honor . . . honor because we have money in our pockets . . ."

Gianni looked up at his father in consternation. He was not sure whether the words were meant seriously or in jest. He did sense an undercurrent of laughter in the speech, however, and he felt he ought to laugh, and he did. His father seized him lovingly about the shoulders and wept. Gianni did not see the tears, but realized something was wrong and tried to extricate himself from his father's embrace.

"You promise, Gianni?"

"What, papa?"

"You and I will save, and make America together?"

"Yes, yes."

Then the whole matter struck Don Tomaso as ridiculous, and he laughed aloud. The boy laughed, too.

"Come," said his father, "we'll have a good time."

They entered one of the innumerable cafés that blazed in the winter twilight. The one into which they went was small. Sawdust covered the floor. Three-legged tables with marble tops stood everywhere. The gas-jets were like huge fans, blue at the base and pronged at the edges, making more noise than they were emitting light. Behind the marble-topped counter the owner, a scared little fellow with more hair on his eyebrows than he had on his head and a sallow face sunken in at the cheeks, cried out, "A hearty good evening to you, Don Tomaso, and congratulations. A fine match. . . . What will it be?"

Don Tomaso's spirits drooped.

"What, Gianni?"

"Let's have *sfogliate*,[11] and *taralli*,[12] and *boccotoni*,[13] and . . ."

The boy gorged himself, as his father described it, like one of the fat roosters in their country place at home, and they started back home. Don Tomaso put the remainder of the five-dollar bill into his wife's hands.

9

Rosaria was not on the stoop, as Gennaro had commanded, on the arrival of the Dauris at the Parterre. Nor was Domenico. But there was no collusion in the double absence. Domenico sat by the roaring fire in the rear kitchen, his hands in his pockets, his small pointed shoes as far out as they could reach, his head thrown back on the chair in a pose of utter unconcern with himself, with what was going on in the cold sunny day outside, with what was happening upstairs, with the changed ways of his life. Drifting through his thoughts were scenes of the nights now gone when he paraded with the other young men along the avenues of the "English" further west and made delightful feminine hauls, as he expressed it, from whose limbs would come the rags that would enrich his father. As for him, they offered . . . he shut his eyes, he dozed, he held them in his arms, he laughed with them in the ice-cream shops, in the rear of trolley-cars, especially the new ones they had installed on Third Avenue that took one away up north where the trees were and grass and sky overhead. The nights in the bars near the Harlem River, Fitzgibbon's Emporium of Music and the Dance, with the events ensuing, the whiskey gulped down with valorous anticipation, the stumbling up dark steps into small bedrooms, the quick undressing, the naked girl in front of him, the fingers moving maddeningly over her body, the smell of the air as it flowed over him from her body, the cool touch of the flesh that turned to flame. . . . The day dream intensified as the fire blazed and its warmth enveloped him . . . but it burst and shattered into a quick explosion of fear.

He trembled inwardly but did not once change his pose. He had been ordered to be on the stoop, dressed in his bridegroom outfit. He hated it. He was going to stay where he was. That passion-flower had bewitched him once. How did he know she was so young? How did he know that she swung her body to stir one's very depths without malice, with no understanding of anything? Besides, he had meant nothing really. He wanted merely to become friends, as he had told her mother, just to know. He was willing to court her in the Italian fashion, wait for years until he was old enough. He would have sat in one corner of the room and she in the other. He would have been happy to know that she was in the room with him, and maybe once in a while when no one was looking he would steal a kiss, a mere kiss, a brush of the lips, a nibble at the neck. No more. Honest. It had all turned out so funny.

He wept, the tears rolling down his cheeks. But he did not move. In the long narrow kitchen with no windows open, the stove going full blast, he was overcome with the heat and his own languor. He would willingly have kept the position throughout the day and the night save when he must of necessity have drink and food, or when the overstimulated senses of his youthful body poured a molten lava through him and he would shamble down the street all dressed-up fine, and sneak up later into hall bedrooms and have his moment's wildness. His father had money. Why should he have to work? What was money for? The lieutenant of the garrison in Capomonte had money and could sport around. The baron's son, it had been reported, was having a gay old time in Naples. Why? They had money. That is what money is for. Domenico envisaged no other life. That was the sum total of his thoughts, experiences, dreams.

His mother had gone out shopping deliberately. She had for the first time summoned enough courage to offer some kind of opposition to the dictation of her husband. She had spoken against the enforced marriage. Let women keep their daughters home. It was, after all, the mother's fault. Oh, Domenico had really done no harm. Surely, it might have been a vicious attack. He had intended all the harm there could be, of course, of course. They were both young, however, babies both. To pummel the lad, beat him into a whimpering pitiful animal crying out for mercy—what for?

"You yourself, Gennaro, haven't been so good, from what I hear."

"That's my business," he had told her, "my business, not yours."

"That's why you kept me slaving on the farm. . . ."

"And I say it's my business. You're here now under my roof. Who put the dresses on your back? Who feeds you?"

"*Scellerato!*"[14] she screamed at him, herself like a wounded animal showing her fangs. "Good-for-nothing! Root-scavenging pig, dirt-eater! Talk that way to me. I slaved for you, saved you the land, brought up your children . . ."

"And now look at one of them—a runt of a ram with just one idea in his head . . ."

"He got it from you . . ."

They had fought it out a hundred times since Domenico had crept home with the flesh hanging from his cheek, to be beaten despite his sufferings until he could cry no more. She had persisted in her objections to the wedding, had refused to attend the ceremony, to help with the fitting out of the rooms upstairs, and she intended carrying her rebellion to the point of not being seen on the porch ready to receive the family of Carmela. But Gennaro, on the morning when Carmela was to come to her rooms with her entourage of father, mother, children—Gennaro looked upon the girl as the center of the group, the reason for all the changes and the new arrangements—he had made peremptory demands upon his wife.

"You will put on your new dress, and you will be on the stoop, mind you now, and greet them all. Lord God Almighty, don't let's make matters a thousand times worse, you hear, you hear!"

He stuck his pipe into his mouth and glared. She had said nothing. Instead, she busied herself with getting Elena and Emilio off to school, and when Gennaro left took up her shopping basket with the aim of making a day of it. She would go eventually to Zia Anna, or drop into the parish house and have a talk with Don Anselmo. She might take him a chicken and some greens, and possibly spend an hour or so making some noodles for him. Anything would do, so long as she could occupy her mind and still remain off the stoop of the Parterre.

She was home in time for Emilio and Elena's lunch. The Dauris had been installed in their new apartment. Of that much she was sure. Five shouting boys had rushed like little madmen up the steps, slid down the railing, stood on the top step and progressed downward by rabbit leaps of two and three stairs at a time and gone back the same way, screamed in the hall to discover how far their voices would carry, stood on the opposite sidewalk and yelled up to their mother, and their mother had come out on the fire escape and shouted back at them, all in great glee. Rosaria had a good mind to go out and slap them.

"Well-behaved, of a good family—bah!" she said to herself. "So, we're just yokels, and they're a good family, educated, well-connected in Potenza, Rionero, everywhere—bah!"

The heavy Rosaria sank disconsolately into a chair, hands in lap, her children away, alone. Domenico had determined, like her, not to be on the stoop. He had gone out, where, she did not know. She was glad he had braved his father. There would be a scene in the evening. Let it come. Her eyes wandered about the narrow kitchen, along the oilcloth pattern on the floor, scrubbed to a shining finish, a square at a time, until her eyes danced, up the oak-strip wainscoating and around it, as if she had a mind to count every slab laid so tight into the wall, so close to each other. On and on her eyes wandered—up the green painted wall, the calendars she had tacked up, one with a girl in green skirt at a well, happy-looking and buxom, as she herself must have been when a child, and finally her eyes rested on the majolica niche at one end of the room with its image of the Madonna and child, bright in their yellow and blue enamel, serene-looking and offering help. Rosaria made the sign of the cross, and she fumbled in her skirts for the deep pocket where she kept her change and her keys, and, along with them, her beads. She took them out and ran them through her fingers.

"Fifty Aves a day, sweet mother of Jesus, will I repeat, half seated and half on my knees, but a favor, a favor, sweet one, a tiny favor for one who has come to a strange land and is unhappy. Let me, dear mother of God, always be brave for my children's sake, and be able to stand up against the man, their father, whom I don't seem to know now after the long separation. You promise, Madonna mia, you promise?"

She went up to the image, her eyes raised to it, her hands clasped in supplication.

"It is not much . . . and this, make my Domenico happy . . . if needs be with her, the girl he has been forced to marry . . . or without her . . . but if one is to suffer let it be her . . . if one is to have an illness let it be her . . . if one is to die let it be her . . ."

At this point Domenico returned. She heard the front grade-door slam heavily.

"Well," she inquired of him, as he shambled across the room, hands in his pockets, fully dressed.

"I walked out when they came, that's all,"' and he fell into a chair.

"What will you do?"

"Do?" he shrieked at her. "I married her. She married me."

A fierce tumult of feelings flashed in his eyes as he stared at her. She turned her head away from the shame of the passion they held. "I'll show them all," he shouted. "My father, her mother . . . all of them!"

Rosaria drew her shoulders together as if she were escaping blows of the fists. She shuddered through her whole frame to hear him talk as he did. When he was through, she went up to him and kneeled at his chair.

"My baby," she called to him.

"Stop it, ma," he cried out brutally to her. "Stop it . . . why will you torture me, too?"

She learned that it was no use. She had hoped to win Domenico over to a firm stand against continuing with the marriage in actuality. The fact of it was there and there was no denying it. But need one be perpetually bound to a mistake like that forever and ever? If this is a new country, then we'll try out new ways. Gennaro will see that more than one can play a few mean games.

There was no doubt of it—it was hatred for her husband that put the new thoughts into her head—hatred not for him personally, but for his high-handed attitude toward her, his persistent contempt for what he was pleased to call her backwoods manners, his foul characterization of their son Domenico, their first-born, whom they had both nurtured with such love and such care as at first seemed eventually would break their hearts, it was so intense, so fervent. Anything now to thwart Gennaro's will, to wring the frozen fibers of his being until some of the warm blood of love flowed into them again. She had thought it out, and decided upon a long series of struggles with him until she should finally emerge if not complete victor at least possessed once more of his admiration, his respect.

Around this insane marriage the fight would wage, she hoped. But now, as she heard her son, her spirits fell away, her purposes became feeble, and once more she realized that she must be resigned to the cruel twistings of a fate which she had never once foreseen. The life on the hard farm in Capomonte, the care of their goats and their pigs, the work on the vines growing so riotously on the hillsides, the stamping out of the oil from the olives they grew, putting up their salamis and their cheese—that is what she had looked forward to until the end of their days. Not this: the life of a rich man's wife who was no longer able even to arouse his passions nor to retain his love. In a strange land, too, where things were topsy-turvy, where there was not a bit of green, and no rest, and the lowly were high and mighty and those who could command respect at home were mere nobodies, so that men like her husband could strut around and play the big fool.

"The good Mary befriend you," she said to her son, taking his face between her hands, "befriend you ever and ever. Amen."

10

It was Donna Sofia who had enough sense to understand that the mothers of the bride and of the groom should become acquainted as soon as possible and arrive at some idea of how they were to conduct themselves. It was only a minute after Rosaria had gone to the stove and said, "I'll just fix up a bit of pasta with eggs and cheese," that the doorbell rang and Domenico went to open it.

"Donna Sofia," he called out, trying to make his tone cheerful.

"Oh, come in, come in, you won't mind being received in the kitchen like this fixing up a bit of something to eat for the boy—your boy, too, now . . ." Rosaria laughed nervously.

"It's just as it should be, one home almost."

Donna Sofia spoke in her most correct Italian, suggesting a little too obviously that she had been trained to speak in school as a lady should. Rosaria knew only the dialect, was not ashamed of it nor of herself, and spoke in the rough burring and sing-song effect of her native Calabrian.

"The apartment's all so marvelous—I mean ours, Carmela's, upstairs. And this kitchen, how fine. You have everything, even copper kettles as in the old country. Imagine . . . how lovely for you . . ."

"Yes, we manage with what we have."

"But you know I came down purposely . . . of course, we are all upset but you will excuse us . . . my husband and I and Carmela . . . she's tired, poor thing, still lying abed, you know . . . we want you all to come upstairs tonight. . . . I'm preparing a chicken . . . oh, nothing . . . and a dish famous in our hometown, a sprig of this you know, and that, and a dash of the other and you have it, tasty . . . very nice. You must all come."

Rosaria consented, why, she could not tell except possibly to avoid quarreling with Gennaro.

"It goes without saying, Domenico, that you'll be there, too. It is, after all, your home."

Sofia had acted without Don Tomaso. On his return from work, he was astounded at the preparations going on. It seemed that the Accucis were not to be the only guests, but the Monteranos as well. La Signora Monterano had left a note for the newcomers, welcoming them in a language that she considered culled from the flower of Italian poetry, at least such of it as she knew from her husband's interminable quotations. To the note the captain had appended a line quoted, as he was at pains to notify Don Tomaso, from the finest translation into Italian of the great poet Shakespeare. Donna Sofia had run up at once to the top-floor. But it was too good of them to write such a note, and was she in the way? There was so much going on in the small rooms, five girls all busy sewing in chairs, two making flowers, a woman bigger than three of the girls together at a pressing table heaving and panting with the weight of the iron, head-forms of wood and wire everywhere, and the floor littered with ribbon-ends, and canvas-shreds, and threads, and a thousand pins. And then do those grand hats come out of all this? And you do all this, Signor Monterano?

The captain bowed and worked his way out to the door.

"Surely we are busy . . . *or per dilletanze ovver per doglie,*"[15] he smiled as he misquoted the famous exile. "Like Dante, whether it be pleasure or pain, we work in bitterness who tread a foreign shore. . . ."

He accepted for himself and his wife.

Don Tomaso listened to the explanations. He was at the sink washing the piano stains from his hands and arms.

"So," he exclaimed, "Gennaro got the house together for you—the furniture, everything. It's better than being a landowner, isn't it, having a good-looking daughter one sells to the first bidder? Well, well—that's progress, that's America."

Donna Sofia ignored him. "You'll speak more quietly if it's going to be that tune," she advised him. "Carmela is inside—lying down on the sofa."

Lather an inch thick covered his arms. "Things have been put in place . . . even the madonna over the stove, and what a bright new stove this is—gas, no less, as befits the in-laws of the grand Gennaro . . . and pots filled with good things. . . . When do we eat?"

"The children are eating upstairs—one of Signor Monterano's girls is staying over, looking after them. We'll all eat here."

Donna Sofia had begun to speak in tones that had an intent of mollifying her husband. She divined accurately the tragedy that had occurred within him, the loss of a self-respect which he had taken for granted all his life with a buoyant ease without ego. She tried to help him adjust himself to the changed conditions without arousing the bitterness of his feelings.

"Yes," she repeated, "we'll all eat here. Notice this table—"

He had finished sloshing the last of the cold water over his arms.

"I have noticed it. Opens up, I suppose—a new-fangled American contrivance. It would have meant years of sweat-pouring for us before we got this, hey, all by our own efforts? We are beholden to the great man."

"It's making the best of the worst," she said quietly. "Do you think I am enjoying all this? Please be good, Tomaso . . . for Carmela's sake."

They looked at each other with renewed understanding. After all, there had been a time when they had seen eye to eye on most things. She always had been ready to fall in with his plans, he to listen to her suggestions. He shrugged his shoulders in a gesture of resignation.

"You know me, Sofia, there's nothing I like better than a banquet. As long as Gennaro doesn't make a speech, pounding his chest." So, he changed his tack. "The Monteranos, too, will be here? Well, what a party! He's a great talker, I hear, and she's a great eater. That ought to make it perfect. And I do want to meet Rosaria . . . a stout peasant wench she is from all reports."

He held up Donna Sofia's chin. "Don't be angry with me," he pleaded, his eyes betraying the emotions in him. "You know what grand hopes I had when we left Villetto—what a future was going to be ours. Well, as you say, let's make the best of the worst."

He kissed her, and walked through the railroad flat to the front room overlooking the street. Carmela, her knees drawn up close to her chin, evidently in a new dress, with her hair braided about her head, lay asleep on the sofa. How pale she looked! Don Tomaso thought of that first, and had no eyes for the green-plush sofa, the green plush chairs all cheaply stained, nor for the brass clock ticking like a miniature sledge hammer on the mantelpiece, nor for the big looking-glass that fantastically distorted Carmela's girlish figure. He saw them, but they angered him.

11

Carmela opened her eyes, and smiled.

"Sleep," Don Tomaso said.

"No, come here."

There was something incongruous about her long dresses and adult hair arrangement, and her young face, her young figure, her girl's voice.

She had grown older within. In a week the girl had been transformed into a woman. Don Tomaso took her hand and patted it.

"Sit here," she said, making believe she was bossing him. "You see, I'm all grown up—see my long dresses? Domenico bought them, and all this, too. Grand, isn't it, all the furniture? Mama says that is the way to begin keeping house—having everything. She's going to let me have all the linens she saved up from when she was a girl, all hand-embroidered and everything. I haven't done much, you know that, no sewing, or anything. We're going to have the cloth on the table tonight you used at your wedding in Villetto. Won't that be grand? Mama says that you had the same thing we're going to have for dinner, too. It'll be just like when she was married."

She had drawn close to him and put her head in the bend of his neck. As she talked she stroked his cheek, and pulled baby-like at his mustaches. And he held her around the waist, pressing her nearer and nearer to him.

"Domenico will be good to me...," she whispered.

He patted her.

"Mama said so. He's to come up tonight and bring all his things. Did you see the other room with the big brass bed? That's to be ours. . . . Mama says that's to be ours . . . and she told me I must tell you . . ."

She wept softly, and he drew her closer without saying a word.

"But . . . papa . . ."

Her body shook against his, and he became frightened.

"Tell me, darling, tell me . . ."

"I don't want to . . . I don't want to . . ."

Despite her feelings, Carmela contrived to look steadily at her father, her eyes wide open, lips trembling, face pale and weary. The first few days after her shoulder had set and the state of shock diminished, she had appeared cheerful enough. Don Tomaso could not believe it, but it was so. Carmela had always been a serious child. They never dared raise their voices to her, much less administer chastisement even of the slightest sort. It meant wounding her to the heart.

Because of her sensitiveness and her loveliness a whole attitude had been allowed to grow up around her. She was a king's daughter sojourning by a happy chance in the mountains of Villetto. At the least, she had all the qualities of a duchess, awaiting her marriage to a distinguished personage of the realm. She was the hillside Cinderella biding her time until the prince of Rome journeyed to the southlands.

On the great feast days she was first in the processions, her long hair with its reddish gold flowing like a veil over her shoulders, bearing the candle for the shrine. Don Pietro, her uncle-priest, had objected to the way she was praised to her face, but he was guilty himself, and would not have allowed a procession to set out from the Cathedral unless Carmela led it. When the bank had failed and the family made plans to migrate to America, it was Don Tomaso himself who had placed his hand on the girl's head and declared that the world's gold was in her.

Under all these praises she had learned to think of herself as charged with a real destiny. She was to enrich the family. She believed it all with a sweet faith and a premature solemnity. At twelve she was thinking like a girl of eighteen. Don Tomaso recalled how he had surprised her the night when the bank collapse had been announced. He himself had been deeply troubled. But he had made every attempt to give the appearance of cheerfulness and not seem to have lost a jot of his buoyancy and laughter.

He had risen from his sleep and was roaming about the huge house set on the rise off the piazza. The windows opening on the second floor balcony and the smell of their jasmines and acacia had been like a soothing hand over his face. In the moonlight the hilltops stood out like the knuckles of a half-closed fist. Their shadows fell long and quiet across the vast landscape. On the piazza itself the cathedral had preempted the available spaces for its own shadow, and the smaller ones of the houses about either were lost within it or not visible at all. Evidently, thought Tomaso, there is no one so disturbed by the fool disaster as to be prowling about like himself. There should really have been a revolution. Men should have taken up arms, around the culprit officials, shot them dead like dogs, or at least pummeled them into contrition.

He tiptoed to the balcony. A shadow from Carmela's room fell across his path. He looked up. There was Carmela, her nightdress hanging in still folds from her shoulders, standing in front of the mirror. She had heard some talk of the great loss the family had sustained. There had been words more or less in jest about how much she was being counted upon to rebuild the family fortunes. And there she was before the mirror trying to put up her hair in the manner her mother had indicated if she was to be considered grown-up and eligible and not a mere strip of a girl.

He recalled the talk that had gone before.

"She'll marry soon," her friends had assured the family.

"Oh, yes, indeed, such a serious young woman already."

"Your beautiful daughter will be much sought after, as the Virgin willing, why not?"

Carmela's imagination soared. She dreamed and hoped. On the trip across the ocean, Don Tomaso had overheard his wife say to Carmela, "It won't be long, sweet. You're getting on to a big girl—for your age almost grown. We must find an important person for you."

These memories were in his eyes as he looked at Carmela now. They were in hers, too, as she returned her father's look and cried, "I don't want to, I don't want to . . ."

What had been painted as an experience of beauty and peace had turned out beastly and ugly. The future that had not been so many years off had become immediate and weighed upon her like a horror. America, the far-off land of wonder and glitter and happy ways, was a place of ill-smelling streets, whirring noises, frightful men who pursued one.

Even here in the Parterre it was stupid and unlovely. What was all this show of furniture and mirrors and oil-cloth covered kitchen? She sensed how much it hurt her father and yet realized that Donna Sofia was doing her best to snatch the greatest possible good out of an unhappy situation. Deep in her heart was the desire to be of some account in her parents' life, to fulfill for them in some patched-up fashion now some of the hopes they had entertained of her.

But deeper than that was the stronger need to feel that she had come into her own by her own efforts. She knew nothing of this young man with his dandified dress, his sallow checks, his debonair mustaches, who had followed her day after day and frightened her. Sheltered always as she had been in Villetto, to her the freedom to be about on the streets of the great city had appeared at first as an exciting adventure. And then she had wanted never to leave the house again. She had been terrified by the young man who kept raising his hat to her, brushing up against her, and whispering stupidly, "How do you do, *bellezza?*[16] Come on, smile, you charmer." What did all these things mean to her? They pleased her in a way, for her friends laughed about them, and told her not to be worried, and seemed to look upon her with a certain envy. But she hated it all and had wanted to stay home and not go to work any longer, except that she knew her few dollars were needed.

And so here she was on the night when there was to be a celebration of her wedding, pleading with her father. He seized her face in both his hands and kissed it over and over again.

"We'll stop all this," he exclaimed.

"No, no," she cried. "Mama ... what would she do?"

She ended the sudden silence that had fallen upon them by drying her tears and saying brightly, "Mama says he really is nice, and you see, his family has money."

But she could not maintain her pose. She shuddered and covered her eyes with her hands. "He followed me, papa, I tried to hide, I tried to hide ... oh, he held my arm ... it's my arm, papa ..."

The father took her into his embrace and patted her affectionately, gently. "My little one ... sh ... sh ... it will be all right."

But just as quickly as she had fallen into her paroxysm of weeping, she came out of it, dashed the tears off her face with the back of her fists, sat up on the couch, put her hands to her hair to feel the braids, smiled, laughed, and then clapped her hands on her father's.

"I know. It will be all right. Mama says so, too. . . . You know, I think, though, I am not going to stay around here. . . . I'm going upstairs with the Monterano family ... sure ... Guess what for? Learn how to make hats ... yes, papa ... Oh, what would I do around here all day? To make hats will be fun."

Gennaro's voice, high-pitched and assertive, filled the rooms.

"What now, hey, Donna Sofia, and doesn't this show we've made America? Everything smells fine. . . . There's wine on the way. . . . And where's the lovely daughter?"

He stalked into the front room.

"Well, well, Don Tomaso *bello,* and how are you this bright winter day? How do you like the snow? Lasts and lasts like the sirocco.[17] And what about it, hey, Carmela? Nice stuff, hey, nice stuff—nothing like this in the old country," and he slapped the plush velvet, the marble-topped table, and looked around pleased, pipe stuck out, hands in his pocket.

Assent was inevitable.

Then he put his arm around Carmela's shoulders.

"Hey, there, I see you've put on the nice new dress. Green—a good color, green ... with your red hair, hey, Don Tomaso? How many of those green dresses and red ones and yellow ones and purple ones, more colors than in a church window, just become rags and come into my bins and get packed up to make money for my pockets ..."

Don Tomaso wanted to laugh outright in his face, but decided on banter instead.

"Well, you're the man to collect the rags, all right. I hear you're a very king of rags."

"Call it king, or boss, what you please, Don Tomaso—each rag turns to gold in my hands."

He stooped to whisper into Carmela's ear, "And, my darling, put energy into that fool kid of mine and it'll be yours—yours!"

Carmela looked up at her father, smiled, and said, "Maybe the dinner is ready. I hear the Monteranos."

12

Rosaria had come up even earlier than her husband to help Donna Sofia. At their first meeting there had been some constraint. Now in the presence of food and in an atmosphere of welcome they were drawn to each other.

"Ah, Rosaria," Donna Sofia said at once. "You're on time to help . . ."

"I'll be only too glad."

"Here is the cloth, and the dishes, see, they're up there. Careful, though, climbing up."

They spoke of nothing but the needs of the moment.

"Everything smells so good . . ."

"You are sweet to help."

Then the Monteranos came. Davido Monterano wore his best frock coat, a huge black cravat full under his chin, and he looked about him for a place to deposit his hat and cane. Donna Sofia was too busy to take them from him, and Rosaria much too overcome by his height, his grand mustache, his pompadour, his important military air. So he stood, hat in one hand, cane in the other, while La Signora Monterano held up the train of her mauve taffeta dress around her knees, her beruffled bosom splendid with a coral necklace and lavalière pinned quite decorously over her heart. They smiled and bowed in unison.

"An honor to have been invited."

"Ours," pleaded Donna Sofia, stirring the sauce with a wooden spoon.

Gennaro put them all at ease at once.

"I'll take your hat . . . ah, Signora, you sit here in the big chair . . . ah, you'll need it . . ."

Finally Domenico arrived.

"And so this is the groom?" asked Monterano, rising and bowing.

Domenico flushed. Carmela looked down.

"Always dolled up," cried Gennaro. "God, do you have to, I ask, do you have to comb your hair like a barber?"

Don Tomaso felt called upon to defend the young man, not for his sake so much as for Carmela's. She was trying to be brave and behave like a person of an age to have been married and assume her place among her elders. She sat up brightly next to La Signora Monterano, smiling and talking.

"It's the style of the country, Gennaro," he said. "Styles are for the young."

"Surely," added Davido Monterano, throwing an olive into his mouth, "we are young but once . . ."

La Signora Monterano was an efficient person, and as forelady in a big millinery shop had drawn a big salary. But she was never so efficient as she was at the table. She ate with the appetite of a trooper and drank wine with gusto.

Rosaria commented on it. "I like to see a woman eat."

"It's what she does best," her husband added.

"If we don't eat in this world," La Monterano offered by way of apology, "what else is there to do? We should take the good that's put before us."

Occasionally the children came storming down from upstairs demanding more of this and more of that or to complain that one or another of them was behaving like a pig and nobody was getting enough. Immanuele came in crying. He refused to go upstairs again until Don Tomaso promised to go up and chastise Gianni. Gennaro went into the hallway and bellowed, "Hey, you mountain goats, behave, or we'll all be up with straps."

It was a noisy disorganized affair. Gennaro insisted upon relating how he had built up his rag business. After he had drunk a full quart of the coarse red wine he preferred, he launched into a lecture aimed directly at Domenico on the necessity for minding one's business. It was the American way. Of course, he had been guilty of a little wildness himself. People talked about it yet. But first and last he had paid attention to the details of his work.

"Dolling up's no way. Parading up and down the avenue making eyes at the girls is no way. That's over now. You have a fine girl for a wife, of good family, mind you, young pup. Look at her, a real beauty! They don't come so pretty often, Don Tomaso, but then you and your wife, you're not ugly yourselves you know, hey? Think you can have children like her, Domenico—are you man enough, tell me, are you man enough?"

For the first time since she had known the boy, Carmela felt a great pity for him. She kept repeating in her mind, "Why doesn't the old boaster stop yelling at him?" But never once could she raise her eyes to Domenico's, though steadily aware that he kept looking at her no matter how he fidgeted in his chair.

"Sit still, you big baby," his father had shouted at him. "You'll be shaking the food off the table. Always been the same," he explained to the guests.

Her mind seethed with images of him pursuing her along the streets, leering, raising his hat, showing his teeth in a frank attempt at winning her by smiles, jostling her as she pushed her way into the hallway of the factory. Her friends' voices rang in her ears. "Sure, talk to him. Ah, go on, walk with him. . . ." And then the evening when he had come alongside of her as she hurried alone through the snowfall. She remembered how she had run and how he quickened his step, too, and ran after her. Mrs. Monterano talked to her, but she did not hear. It was only his steps in the muffling snow, and his cries, "Don't be afraid . . . I just want to talk to you, *bellezza* . . . ." She did not feel Mrs. Monterano's hands patting her now and then. It was the pressure of his arms about her, the hot nauseating kisses on her neck, the wrenching of her arm as he held her and pressed her against the wall, his heavy breath . . . and then the hand along her thighs, and the thin quick pain like the thrust of a white-hot rod. . . . The food turned in her stomach. The warm kitchen filled with the smells of the cooking, and the stench of the wine . . . they felt like oozy cloths bound about her. She wanted to tear them off and shriek and run. Oh, the fire-escapes outside! She could climb them, climb them. Up, up, where it would be cold, lonely, away from all of them. Oh, why did her mother look so sweetly at her and her father, too, and everybody? Mrs. Monterano was a sweet lady but she ate and ate. She was a nice person and so kind, and Rosaria, Domenico's mother, how sad she looked. Unhappy like herself. Oh, why did Gennaro talk like that to his son? Couldn't he let him alone, baiting him like that?

She looked up for the first time at Domenico. Although he had heard his father badgering him perpetually he had really paid no heed. The thoughts of the morning were spinning around in his mind like huge pinwheels blurring out with their noise and color all other sensations. He moved the chicken in his plate from one place to another, turned the macaroni over and over and took a bite now and then. Only the wine could he take wholly. He sipped at first and then swallowed, and then he gulped down a whole glass like water, hoping it would slip through his body, cooling it. His eyes wandered from the dark night with its shadows of clothes lines and dim-lit windows to the clock on the wall to Mrs. Monterano's pompadour, which fascinated him, and the lavalière bobbing up and down on her big bosoms and then to Carmela, at the shining braids of her hair, her young, pale cheeks, the soft mouth, the full bodice, and he gritted his teeth and the thoughts ran wild through his head. She was his now by law, by God's law. They were man and wife. So they said to him. He remembered the wound on his cheek and the blows his father had struck him and the kicks and the sickness afterward, how his stomach had soured and he'd keeled over and lay limp. But now, now, she was his.

Carmela looked up at him. Their eyes met. They could not withdraw them. He grew red, uneasy, helpless. She just stared. Domenico's thoughts and feelings could not be subtle. His childhood had been spent in a coarse world, and his passions whirled within him like a boiling liquid. One look at the eyes of Carmela, filled with a passing pity for him, and the assurance came to him that she, too, like him, was anxious for the party to end. She had merely looked and then lowered her glance at once. It was enough. The morning's anticipations became redoubled, he sank into a still soft ooze of feeling. . . .

Carmela had merely looked up and then lowered her glance, and everyone about her had smiled. How she hated them! Winking at each other, too, and her father getting up and going inside, and Gennaro shouting, "Well, it's time for us old ones to be making off, and leaving the young. . . ." How he laughed, and then the hand of Mrs. Monterano on hers, soothingly stroking her. . . . All the old fright came back. She wanted to run out into the snow, the cold particles melting on her hot cheeks, the wind pressing against her skirts, the dark falling about her, and climb, climb, into the air, up the fire-escapes to the roof tops, shout, fight him off, kick him with her foot, stamp on him. Why did he look like that, just as he did when he raised his hat brushing past her and said syrupily *"Bellezza"*?

But they're all leaving . . . the children being put to bed . . . the house is still . . . she's alone, sitting in the kitchen watching Gianni's and Giovanni's let-down couch being made up, the children in the room inside shouting at each other as they are getting ready for sleep, Rosaria at the sink piling up dishes and talking. "Such a sauce, Donna Sofia, we don't make in our part of the country. And the chicken! Where did you get such tender chicken? You must come downstairs soon, I have a dish with ricotta you'll like." And Donna Sofia, busy with Gianni, slapping him for kicking at Immanuele. And the kitchen so hot! Why are they leaving her alone? And he with his sallow face, why, why is he leering, leering?

Her mother came to her and took her cheeks in her hands.

"Your father is ready to go to sleep, he's tired. There, my chicken," she said, kissing her. "And Domenico must be tired, too . . . hey, Domenico, tired?"

He looked up, scared and red.

The children had fallen asleep. The Monteranos' footsteps on the floor above had quieted. The stove had become black, the fire steadily getting colder. Outside, the dark night had turned into a dizzy movement of white particles dashing against the window panes.

Carmela smiled at her mother, wanly, with uneasy eyes.

"Come, we'll get the bed ready, you and I. . . ."

They walked through Donna Sofia's room, the first nearest the kitchen, small, narrow with a bit of window opening on an airway, containing, like her own, a big brass bed that took up all the room and glittered in the night from the kitchen.

"Ha, they're asleep already." The three boys lay together in another big bed in the next room, a white iron bed, with only one mattress. Carmela's and her mother's had two.

"We'll remove the spread," announced Donna Sofia.

It was a crocheted cover with rosettes in the center of large squares, each square cut by a multitude of diagonals running into the rosebud. Carmela's fingers trembled as she held the ends of it and helped with the folding.

"I think you'll be warm enough with two flannels and a nice quilt. Here," she pulled it from a box under the bed.

The red and yellow pattern glared, and the sheen of the satin glimmered. Carmela stroked it, and then stopped suddenly. At the door Domenico stood watching. She felt his eyes upon her. The room reeled. She did not dare move for fear she would fall and whirl with the bed, the walls, the crucifix, the lamp burning under it. . . .

13

And then her mother left her, and the door closed behind her. Domenico stood near it, smiling. She leaned against the bed with her back and arms, her eyes opened wide, white and cold, pleading silently with him not to come near, to let her alone.

"*Ti voglio bene, sa, davvero, ma davvero.*"

What did she care that he liked her?

"Go away," she whispered hoarsely.

He shook his head and smiled.

"Go away."

"You must undress . . . we're married . . ."

She moved slowly about the bed, still with her back against it, feeling her way with her hands.

"You got to, now . . ." He smiled at her as he said it. "I got a right."

She had got to the foot of the bed, and with surprising suddenness had dashed into the front room into which her own room opened. It was dark save for the light from the bedchamber. The green plush furniture looked like black water in the night. He pursued her. At first he ran, but stopped, and walked in cautiously as if stalking her.

"Damn," he said quietly, "*porca madonna santissima,*[18] going to fight again, now we're married . . . ?"

She could not speak. She held herself erect at the table, looking scared and unhappy, still pleading with him in every detail of her posture to get away, leave her alone.

"Listen," he cried, and yet subduing his voice as much as possible. "There ain't going to be no fight . . . the law made you mine . . . the law of God. . . . Didn't the priest hold up your right hand to God and then you kissed the cross, didn't you? Carmela . . ."

It was the first time he had used her name. She listened.

"I meant nothing the first time. . . . I didn't, really, I didn't . . . just to talk to you, honest . . . it happened . . . *ma ti voglio bene assai assai* . . ."[19]

Nothing he said could make her shut her eyes, stop staring at him in fright, as if she could not understand what he was doing there in the same room with her, her father allowing it too, not rushing in to drive him out.

"Go away," she repeated.

She moved away, near to the window. Again he followed, almost mechanically, certainly stupidly, she thought. Couldn't he see she wanted him to go away? Couldn't her father realize it out there and come in and tell him to be gone? She had pitied him for a moment that evening, but she had not seen him look the way he did now, his jaws set, his eyes bright, his breath fast and uneven, angry, determined. She heard the slight pat of the snowflakes against the panes behind her. The whole scene of the weeks before became a sudden daub before her eyes. She put her hands to her face and fell in a chair, sobbing. He ran up to her quickly and got down on his knees before her, putting his hands around her waist.

"Carmela, Carmela," he whispered to her. "No crying. Why cry? Why cry?"

He tried to remove her hands from her face and get her to look at him as he pleaded with her.

"No, no, no," she screamed. "Go away . . . go away. . . ."

She pushed him off. Before he knew what had happened she had opened the window. The snow poured in dizzily, a white flash of cold. When he looked up, she was on the fire-escape, climbing up. He ran to the window sill and jumped out. She was banging on the panes of the Monterano apartment.

CHAPTER THREE

1

*L*a Signora Maria Monterano was the kind of person who realizes her superiority to the world in general without expressing it openly to any one. Her family had been of consequence in Castello-a-Mare. They had often been entrusted by the parish with the care of the needy and the infirm. It had been a tradition with them. Even when one of her uncles, a young seminarian, had broken definitely with the Catholic church during the wave of free-thinking that had passed over Italy in the wake of the Risorgimento and had gone to the dismal extent of embracing the Baptist faith, eventually becoming the impoverished minister in charge of an Evangelical mission in the heart of a thoroughly Papist community, her family lost none of its prestige as lay people of importance. She herself continued her ministrations among the poor and added quite gratuitously to her duties the further task of admonishing the shiftless and even the sick in the proper methods of orderly and respectable existence.

Her husband's dismissal from the army failed to curtail her self-assurance as much as it aroused the efficiency at the bottom of her personality. The first thing she did when it had been decided to leave Italy and Castello-a-Mare in particular to seek a way of life in America, was to call on her evangelist uncle. The money for his work came from New York—that was an established belief in all circles. He must therefore be acquainted in that Protestant stronghold, reasoned La Monterano, and so she went to him immediately not only for advice but for letters to persons he might know in New York. One of the letters was to a certain Miss Emma Reddle who conducted a mission in the congested Italian areas of Harlem.

No sooner had Carmela flung herself in her arms—"a wet bird she was," as Donna Maria kept saying, "come in out of the rain"—than her mind was made up. When first she had heard of the marriage of the young people she had expressed the belief that it was a more immoral act indeed than the attack itself. She had rushed at once to Rosaria and forcefully revealed the full extent of her horror at the impending marriage. She realized, however, how impotent the poor woman was—in constant fear of her husband's high-handed ways, and distrustful of herself too. La Monterano, undeterred, laid down some exemplary maxims as to the relation of the wife and the mother to the household and its development.

"You must understand, in a strange land or not, that it is your place to defend your children's interests to the very last. Domenico may have done a great wrong—it will be a greater wrong to both of them to go on with this absurd wedding."

Against her husband's protests she called on Don Anselmo and spoke without reservation on the sinfulness of the marriage.

"As a priest, you should have stopped it. Why couldn't they have waited? Maybe no harm has been done . . . who knows? But for two children to be compelled . . . it's a disgrace."

"As a priest, signora," Don Anselmo answered, "I did what I thought best."

She gathered her skirts about her and left in a fit of appropriate indignation. The indignation was not altogether aimed at the priest, but at the Church itself. It had been growing ever since her arrival in New York. Its first appearance had coincided with her visit to the basement church over which Don Anselmo presided.

The Irish Catholics of the neighborhood had built themselves, several years before the great mass of Italian peasants had arrived from Southern Italy, a splendid granite edifice with an imposing steeple and an equally impressive flight of stairs leading to an elevated double-doored portal between pretentious columns—a rococo affair but solid, symbolic of their rise to a dominant place in the city. Now, like the other congregations in the section, they felt, and felt with a peculiar force, the necessity of providing a place of worship for these newcomers—Catholics like themselves if of a laxity in religious devotion quite without a parallel in their own experience.[1] Furthermore, some form of spiritual safeguards had to be set up against the disintegrating influences of their sudden uprooting from their native soil and their settlement in a community whose ways were completely new to them.

Donna Maria Monterano naturally had sought out the parish-house immediately upon her arrival. She had been shown where the Italians worshipped, and before going to see the priest she had slipped into the basement of the Church of Our Lady of Olivet. She was astounded and horrified. Above was a spacious nave beautifully decorated. Here in the basement it was mean and restricted, the air was effectively shut out, there were no windows and the ceiling was low, the benches were crude and without cushions, the altar was an improvised wooden affair, a matter of some tables and a railing. It was evident that the Italians, good Catholics though they were, had not been thought good enough to be allowed the use of the upper story of the church.[2] She reddened with the shame of it and wondered why it had to be. She spoke her mind to Don Anselmo at once, and he tried to make her understand that the time would come when they would be enabled to take over the whole church or build one of their own. In fact, Gennaro Accuci had already donated the plot. It was a disgrace nevertheless, she persisted. I for one would rather not come, she answered.

And as a matter of fact, when the first Sunday arrived, she climbed the stairs and entered the section reserved for the use of the "English." She was required to pay ten cents to enter. She merely brushed the man aside and stalked in with her husband, her mother, and her three children. It had caused a commotion of a sort, and Don Anselmo felt called upon to visit her and admonish her against a repetition of the offense. That settled Donna Maria. Armed with her letter to Miss Emma Reddle she decided to cast in her lot with the Protestants in the manner of her uncle. That evening she presented herself at the mission house over which Miss Reddle had charge.[3]

2

The Protestant churches were far more splendid than the Catholic one, and all of them stood on the street which boasted the greatest width, a macadam pavement, broad sidewalks lined with tulips, sycamores and maples, and interminable series of brownstones with ivy-colored fronts here and there, and at odd intervals more imposing gray limestone dwellings guarded in front by soft-looking lions or what passed for gargoyle-like griffes. The Episcopalian congregation had erected a slender campanile of Gothic lines in the center of wide and close-trimmed lawns. Across the street, at a respectful diagonal, a low limestone building without belfry or tower but with a massive set of quartered-oak portals behind equally massive iron railings, was the church belonging to the Congregationalists of the neighborhood. One block further west, a simple red-brick building with a number of squat gables provided a place of worship for the less flamboyant but none-the-less assertive Methodists.

On the corner of the same street, however, the veritable temple of the section stood, made to look venerable with tradition by a forced growth of ivy. The Baptists had among them the great chocolate manufacturer, Martin, a bachelor who had made so much money that as he was nearing old age he concerned himself entirely with good works. The beautiful buildings were his donation to the service of God. Feltspar steps raced up on two sides to a series of paneled bronze doors, each panel in itself a fine piece of bas-relief, and the doors separated from each other by twisted columns of a rich reddish marble. An organ and the loft in which it was housed attracted the attention of the entire city. It was no uncommon sight to see the spacious church with its fine stained windows completely filled not only for the morning and evening services but for the afternoon recitals. Mr. Martin was present on every occasion. If the wind was blowing from the right direction, the fragrances of his concoctions encircled the buildings, filtered into the church itself, and left an unmistakable impression of the origin of all this splendor.

When the Italians kept pouring in, filling up the old tenements, transforming brownstones into slum-like dwellings and finally infiltrating into the better streets, the churches were confronted with a problem. Not only was the poverty of the alien hordes a source of distress to the good ladies and charitable gentlemen of the congregations, but the need of claiming them for God became also a considerable cause of concern. Here was an opportunity for missionary work which far transcended their efforts among the heathens in distant lands. Each of the churches began to win over for the Lord the more wretched among the swarthy-faced crowds that swarmed all about them.

But to invite the Italians to sit with them in the gorgeous pews of their splendid edifices—that was another matter indeed. They were dressed outlandishly, they were unwashed, they were strange and foreign looking. It would never do. Father Cassidy felt he had done his duty in setting aside the basement for their needs. The Baptists, the Methodists, the Episcopalians, hired out empty stores, put up rude benches, had the cross painted in black on the window, splashed the word MISSION over the entrance, installed a young woman to take charge, and lo and behold they were convinced that the naked and the hungry, the homesick and the diseased of body, the unclad and the shivering would be taken care of in the eyes of Jesus and the Lord God. As a matter of fact, the work done was often the means of saving many a family from sheer wretchedness and squalor, if not from starvation. The most indefatigable as well as the most effective among the women engaged in the task was Miss Emma Reddle.

She stood almost six feet in her low sensible shoes, and she had discovered every possible way to wear her blouses, her gowns, her hair so as to reduce the attractiveness of her excellent features. There was no mistaking the sweetness of her smile despite her large mouth, nor the serene quality of her disposition as it revealed itself in her cheerful blue eyes. Her hair was so definitely piled up over her forehead that besides adding stature to her large frame it made her face, which was broad and full and evenly proportioned, seem unusually small, almost diminutive for a woman of her massiveness. Heavy-bosomed, heavy-hipped though she was, she walked with marked grace and ease, never coming down so hard on her feet as to give sound to her steps.

Mr. Martin had selected her from a multitude of applicants when he opened his mission among the Italians. She had been from the first an excellent choice. Not only did her own mission flourish, but she made converts to the big church rapidly. The method was simple. If a family seemed to be of some refinement, or at least to possess a modicum of literacy, after a preliminary series of visits to the crude meeting-place in the store, the children were clothed by Miss Reddle in brand new garments and directed to report to the Sunday School in the big church. At the same time they were enrolled in what was known in the neighborhood as the Soup School.

There, besides being instructed in the rudiments of English, the children were fed at noon, and on specified days sent home with bundles of clothing, food, and even toys. In winter, coal was supplied to the family, but to obtain it, they were required to show their children's attendance cards properly punched each Sunday. In time, the elders were invited to the church. This was, however, only in such cases where the older people were willing not only to discard their native costumes but also appeared to wear with some measure of casualness the American clothes supplied them by the mission. Another requirement was that they could carry on a short conversation in English with Miss Reddle or her assistants.

Such families achieved real prosperity. The girls were taken into the chocolate factory, the boys were enrolled in the Fife and Drum Corps, and later jobs found for them.

La Monterano's first position as milliner was Miss Reddle's contribution to the family. Il Signor Davido obtained his numerous jobs through her. Without her, the ex-engineer and the genteel lady of Castello-a-Mare would not have found it simple to disport themselves on Sunday afternoons dressed as a family of real standing should be.

Nevertheless, Miss Reddle—not that she was without knowledge of it, but she said nothing—obtained only the kind of loyalty that is the price of a gift. When Ervi, Donna Maria's youngest child had died, it was not the square-shouldered prosperous-looking minister of the Harlem Baptist Church who was called in, but the simple, even gay-mannered Don Anselmo. But toil in the vineyard of the Lord is a lengthy and an uncertain process. Miss Reddle was well aware of it. She said nothing. Even when the most devoted of her converts sneaked off to mass on Palm Sunday, and quite unabashed stuck the sprig of palm into their hats or lapels or pinned it as a foil behind their cheap laval-lières, Miss Reddle said nothing. The Lord knew she was a steadfast worker, and she culled her grapes year in, year out, with patience and forbearance. She was sure of the victory in the intervals between con-ception and birth, birth and marriage, marriage and death. On the other solemn occasions, the chances were too great. Her converts reverted to the rites of their fathers.

3

It was no surprise to her to see Donna Maria brushing off the snow from her coat and stamping with her little feet on the floor of the Bap-tist Mission.

"Ah, good Miss Reddle," she cried in her strong Neapolitan accent, "I am so glad to see you. Ah, you are much warm in here. That is good."

The closing door shut out the rush of cold and the flutter of snow. Miss Reddle cried cheerily from her desk, "Always so good to see you, too, Donna Maria. Any word from your uncle?"

"Ah, he will not come, he will not come. . . . It's an obstinate thing . . . much obstinate, no?"

Miss Reddle agreed, and asked about the millinery business.

"Very, very good. So I think. My husband, he do well. He learn, oh so rapid . . . and he have the time too for Roberto. . . . Ah, those two! Miss Reddle, you don't know. They sit up and they read, and read . . . and they learn the English together, and they make such big plans for the future."

She laughed, and struck Miss Reddle on the hand affectionately.

"You have been so good. . . . Maybe you can do something. . . ."

Miss Reddle turned on her chair, adjusted her skirts about her so no portion of her shoes might show, and sat up attentively.

"It's about a family. They have a daughter . . . charming . . ."

She narrated the whole story. Miss Reddle listened without inter-rupting. Donna Maria left out few details. Miss Reddle grew red on one occasion, and distinctly showed her shocked feelings on another.

"You see, she climb the fire-escape. She knock on the window. She wake Roberto, he scream, I get up. I scream. I see who is there. I take her in my arms, shut window—ah, terrible, terrible."

A fitting pause climaxed her rapid narrative.

"They should not be permitted to live together, no?" La Monterano asked finally, with some heat, as if she were about to grapple in argument even with Miss Reddle.

The missionary said "no" several times, but only with her lips.

"Well, what you think?" asked Donna Maria. "Something must be done, no, ah?"

"It's difficult. It will be Mr. Accuci who will put up the fight," Miss Reddle announced after some thought. "But the marriage must be annulled, will be annulled."

She looked too overcome with horror for her words not to appear decisive. Together they planned a line of action. It should be done, if possible, without calling in the official agencies, the police, the children's societies.

"Carmela should be placed in a home . . ."

"*Dio santo,* no . . . the family, they need her. . . ."

But Miss Reddle always proceeded in a steady line. She paid no heed to the difficulties except in so much as it was necessary to face them and remove them.

"Surely, I understand. We'll put away three of the boys too. That will give Mr. Dauri a chance to support the others well, and even save some money. . . . Mr. Martin needs a first-class carpenter in his shop. . . . He could hire her father at an increase over his present pay. You see, we'll have to bribe them all."

Donna Maria shrugged her shoulders skeptically.

"The girl must be taken out of the present surroundings. They're bad for her, Donna Maria, bad . . . you see that? And the other children, too . . . it's wicked, wicked . . ."

She moved fast. Before Donna Maria had had a chance to sit down to her dinner, Miss Reddle had knocked at her door.

4

Carmela, pale and bewildered from the experience of the night, looked frightened as Miss Reddle bulked her way into the kitchen. No, she did not wish to leave her mother. She wanted to live with her parents, go to work like the rest of the young girls. If only they could move away, far away from here, not see Domenico.

"Please, signora," she pleaded with Donna Maria, for Carmela could not yet talk English. "Please, do not let them put me away. I didn't do anything . . . you know that . . . please."

Donna Sofia came running upstairs. She had heard of the arrival of Miss Reddle and suspected that it must be about Carmela. Without waiting to hear what had been said or done, she shouted at the top of her voice, "What does this meddling Protestant want? Carmela, you come downstairs where you belong. You hear me . . . you come downstairs."

The whole of the Monterano family was present. Mr. Monterano stroked his mustaches seriously and laid down his napkin. Roberto, the oldest boy, a solemn-looking eager-eyed lad just turned eight felt that it was not his place to remain where he was. He devoured his pasta and peas with great speed and noise, beckoned to his black-haired sister Gilda and his younger brother Ernestino, who was all eyes and seemingly no appetite, to hurry with their food. His father kept whispering, "Quick about it. Take them inside and shut the door."

Donna Sofia kept shouting. "You hear, Carmela! No more of this. You're a married woman now, and grown up. Downstairs with you, and hurry."

Neither Donna Maria nor Miss Reddle thought it fit to interfere. Carmela stared open-eyed from one to the other, more bewildered than ever.

"Ma," she finally cried out, tears in her eyes. "I don't want to come downstairs."

"No but's, no if's . . . you come where you belong."

"But I want it to be as before. I want to go to work . . . and be as before . . . you hear, ma?"

"You will do as you are supposed."

"Never," shrieked Carmela, "never, never . . . I hate you all . . . I hate you all!"

She turned to Miss Reddle. "Take me away," she cried, "take me away . . ."

Donna Sofia turned her anger on Donna Maria.

"What right have you to interfere, tell me that? It's you, you have put notions into her head."

There was a knock at the door, and Don Tomaso entered, the stains of his work on his face and hands.

His gentleness brought a pause in the excitement.

"One can hear you all the way downstairs and into the street. It isn't right. What is it, Carmela?"

His daughter threw herself into his arms and wept.

"A shame—a pity. . . ," murmured Donna Maria.

Her husband patted her on the head admonishingly.

"Better say nothing . . . poor child."

He hurried his own brood into the outer room where his millinery shop was set up.

"What is it all about?" demanded Don Tomaso.

"I came here to talk with your daughter," Miss Reddle informed him.

"That Protestant woman," Donna Sofia told him confidentially. "Sticks her nose into everybody's business . . ."

"I don't mean to," Miss Reddle interrupted, speaking in broken Italian. "I came here to see if I could not help . . ."

Don Tomaso turned to her, Carmela pressing disconsolately against his body. "Let me speak," he said to his wife. "What can you do, signora?" he asked. "This is among us. What is there to be done? Nothing. You understand we have our burden. The good Lord had seen fit to weigh us down with our own cross. We shall bear it. It will take time. Things will get adjusted. Time is the essence of all adjustment. You have heard of the story, perhaps? Well, that is too bad, too bad. We hoped it would not spread about too much. For this young girl's sake, you understand . . ."

"Always a speech," shouted his wife in anger. "Always a speech. Why do you have to talk to anyone, explaining, apologizing, this, that, saying wise things that mean nothing? She has no business here—and Carmela belongs downstairs."

And then the door seemingly blew open, and Gennaro, pipe in mouth as usual, hat on head, shouldered his way in. With a significant toss of the head toward Miss Reddle, he inquired gruffly, "What's this woman want, Don Tomaso?"

"It's the Protestant woman," Donna Sofia hastened to inform him, convinced him that in Gennaro she had found someone who could handle the situation according to her ideas.

"I know," Gennaro answered. "You got the mission?"

"Yes." Miss Reddle was calm and quiet.

"Why you no stay there then, ah? Why you come bother the people?"

"May I ask?—"

"You ask nothing, see," was his retort. "You got no business here. Your business in your store, give the poor the coal, and steal them from the church of God, see. That's what your business is, you ask me, you go back there, and leave alone the people . . ."

"Mr. Accuci . . ." Miss Reddle was patiently attempting to be allowed to say a word.

"You no call Mr. Accuci, or mister anybody . . . you go where you was, see, and we take care of our own . . . Mr. Accuci . . . and how you know my name . . . I no come to you ever . . . Mr. Accuci . . . bah!"

"Everyone knows you . . ."

"Sure everyone know me. I know. But how you know me, you come here and say Mr. Accuci in a voice like that and tell me you got business here. You ain't, see? You leave alone the people . . ."

Miss Reddle rose. "Very well, Mr. Accuci. But you have not heard the last of this. I thought we could settle the whole business without calling the authorities . . ."

"What autorities, what autorities?" asked Gennaro contemptuously. "Me the autority here. . . . You call the police. Well? I say, you go away. The police, they listen, they smile, they go. So?"

He laughed as he held out his palms questioningly.

"Very well," answered Miss Reddle, and, bidding them all good night, she left.

5

Within the month, the hand of Miss Reddle was upon everyone. It was fortunate she had an assistant not only in Donna Maria, but in Don Tomaso as well. Carmela had, of course, returned to her family. But her mother had come to understand that the marriage had been too precipitate, and even if it had not been there was no basis in love and affection for it to be continued. Miss Reddle's suggestion that steps be taken at once to annul it legally and then find some means of building up an entirely new environment for the girl, in the end, prevailed. It was not so simple to win over the family to her plan of placing Carmela and several of the boys in the juvenile asylum which had been established in the northern outskirts of Manhattan from an endowment provided by Mr. Martin. The asylum was his pet Americanization scheme. It was to remake immigrants in their tender years. He encouraged admissions. Don Tomaso listened carefully, weighed all the arguments, and agreed to persuade Donna Sofia to consent to the arrangement.

"After all, we cannot accept all this furniture," he pleaded with his wife. "Gennaro may say that it's ours . . . it isn't really, and you know it, Sofia. We either return it to him, or we pay him for it. . . . There are no two ways."

Donna Sofia's chief argument against any new plan that involved immediate trouble was to question the wisdom of ever having come to America.

"We don't fit in, we don't fit in, and that is all there is to it. . . . This is no land for people who have always been respected, like us, and who learned no trade, no business. Here you are every night daubed up with paint, worn out with work . . . why, why did you ever say 'Let's go to America?' Why?"

The patient Don Tomaso whistled very low, and turned his eyes up as each word pierced him—for it hurt him to the quick to have what he himself knew to be a mistake harped on. He stroked his wife's hand.

"I understand," he agreed. "It was wrong. How shall I ever be able to make it up to you? I don't know. But I am thinking now of Carmela and whatever bit of self-respect we have left. Carmela will come back a different person. The boys, too. They will know English. They will have learned some trade . . . have an education . . . and it will help us, too . . . we can save a little money . . . pay for this mess of stuffed junk . . ."

Gennaro met his match in Miss Reddle. He tore into her mission again, hat on head, pipe in mouth. He burst into action at once.

"I got things to say."

Miss Reddle drew herself up closer to the desk, placed her elbows on it, folded her hands, and leaned over.

"Mr. Accuci, your hat, please! And I cannot stand the smoke from your pipe."

The ice of her tone, however, failed to freeze him in the least.

"See here, you stop putting your nose in . . ."

Since she merely listened and said nothing, he continued.

"You make more trouble. Why make more trouble? We got plenty. I marry when I was nineteen, Rosaria seventeen . . ."

Miss Reddle queried, "Well?"

"Leave alone the things—that's well."

Gennaro resorted in the end to measures of reprisal a trifle more primitive than argument and appeal. The young men who sold him old metal were of a mind to do anything within reason to earn an honest penny or two to save real work. They thought nothing of yanking lead pipes from the plumbing works in the cellars of apartment houses. That was a bit of child's' play for them. They staged petty hold-ups in the open streets. At night they often found it convenient to blackjack their victims and then drag them into the open lots near the river. There they despoiled their victims of whatever was handy—watch, cash, clothing.

Many of the boys built up a profitable trade with the pawnshops. Some of them graduated into higher types of brigandage as the years passed, and several became associated in short time with the growing political organization of the neighborhood.

Gennaro knew them well, acted as their fence, managed to get them out of scrapes with the police and even bail them out of the lock-up when they succeeded in getting that far.

Now he called upon them for assistance. The Baptist mission was wrecked one night quite mysteriously. The policeman on Gennaro's beat called with an air of casual interest the next morning. Numerous wagons were carting away the piled-up bales of rags.

"Lots of junk all right," the policeman said, taking off his high gray helmet and laying alongside of it his billy. "Good business . . ."

Gennaro laughed. "How you like it, hey, what the dago man does in America, make the money like that?" And he snapped his fingers.

"You're soaking it away, ain't no doubt of that, Accuci! . . . Slick article, I say."

"And you say right."

"When are you giving up them earrings?"

Gennaro laughed again. "That's my luck."

"Say, you better take something out of your ears, because I got to spill an earful into them right now."

Gennaro looked up, somewhat taken back, but smiling.

"What do you mean, earful?"

"Well, the Baptist mission. We know who done it, see, the captain says . . . well, he's a good friend of yours, but he can't buck Martin, see?"

As the officer walked out, Gennaro scratched his head thoughtfully. He was computing just how much more he would have to stack up to reach the extraordinary influence that Martin seemed to have with the police. But he decided generously, not coming to any satisfactory answer to his problem, to call off the young wreckers. His anger remained, however, and it became a sheer impossibility for him not to visit it upon some one. The most likely person was the inventor of all the mischief that had occurred.

6

There already had been scenes between father and son.

Domenico had fallen into a greater depression than any one of the others. He refused to do anything about Carmela. Egged on by his father to rush up to the Dauri flat and assert his rights, he merely stared and sank lower in his chair. Only to his mother he confided that he wished the whole thing were over. If he should go to prison for it, as his father had shouted on any number of occasions, it was all right with him. Prison was better than the hell of having to stand up against his father day in and day out.

"A little rooster with the pip," yelled Gennaro at him, "that's all you are. A sick pup with his tail between his legs, yelping out of fear. Bah! I spit on you. What kind of man are you anyhow? You could chase the pretty thing into a water-closet, and now what do you do? Hang out your tongue—like this—and pant—like this—bah. . . . You're a dirty little coward. You make me puke."

One day Domenico had jumped up out of his chair. He ran to where his mother was ironing, listening patiently, saying nothing. He seized the iron out of her hand, and made a gesture of throwing it.

Gennaro laughed ironically.

"Well, well . . . now he's getting brave, lifting his hand against his father. But the hero can't go up stairs to a little girl, his wife, and throw her on her back and let her have it and then make her behave. . . . You good-for-nothing little ram!"

"Come here," he yelled at Domenico, as he rushed home after the policeman's departure.

"What do you want now?" the harassed boy asked.

"Listen here, you whelp!"

"Again?" demanded Rosaria. "Let him alone."

"You keep out," shouted her husband. "Listen here, Domenico. We're being made fools of left and right. It's going to stop, and you're going to stop it, see."

Domenico stared in dismay.

"You go right upstairs now. And drag that young bitch down here where she belongs—with you."

"I can't do that."

"But you're going to."

"No, I can't."

Before he could add another word, Gennaro had struck him a vicious blow over the ear. Domenico, stunned, looked at his father with open mouth. Then he reeled slowly, pinwheeled with his hands and shoulders, and fell, a helpless lump to the floor. Rosaria threw herself upon her husband, but he seized her around the waist and sat her down on a chair.

"He's all right," he cried. He stooped over his son, shook him, and finally, by dint of cold water and wine, revived him.

"Now listen here," he said. "You've got to get out of this house. Anywhere. But you are not staying here another day. You and me can't live under one roof. Get that? I'll give you money. Go away somewhere— get a job, be a man . . . and never come back."

No amount of opposition from Rosaria availed. Domenico, in fact, averred quite resignedly that he had contemplated that very thing himself. Since he was to be given money voluntarily by his father, which of course would relieve him of the necessity of having to steal it as he had planned, Domenico considered the departure as something in the nature of a moral victory. Carmela could do as she pleased. He, for one, was through. He would go West. That word had been mentioned frequently. If his father had found it possible to make money without having anything to begin with, he would too.

"You'd better join the army," is what Gennaro said. "There's a war coming. . . ."[4]

Rosaria burst into tears, but continued preparing the dinner that Domenico liked. For the three days that he remained before leaving, he was fed on the best that Rosaria could assemble. News of the plan had got to the Dauris, and they were relieved.

They stood at the window behind the curtains to watch Domenico go down the street. If ever he had dressed with all the sumptuousness that his indolent pleasure-loving nature craved, this time he outdid himself. Suitcase in hand, he marched off. They all saw him board the street car a whole block away. Since their arrival in New York, they had seen the horse-cars replaced by trolleys and had been frightened at the noise and the speed. Domenico leaped on the moving car and everyone gave a cry of fear.

"That's over with," Don Tomaso said, and Donna Sofia crossed herself and wept. "*Gesu, Giuseppe, e Santa Maria*[5] . . . may the scoundrel be blest wherever he goes."

For no apparent reason, Carmela burst into tears and clung desperately to her father.

7

Carmela, Gianni, Giovanni and Immanuele were groomed for their admission to the Juvenile Protective Asylum. Miss Reddle insisted on Carmela's hair being let down, her dresses shortened, in short, on discarding once and for all all the accessories of an adult woman which had been forced upon the girl. The three boys and their sister were then enrolled in the Soup School, and despite Donna Sofia's protests expected to go to the mission for services. The whole process took all of three months.

The winter gave way to spring, and through the crowded streets the wind swung cheerily and warmly from the East River. The grass outside the Parterre sprang up green and sparkling. Fresher and more spring-like than the quiet waters of the river, the young green of the grass, and the tender flush of life on the trees along the avenue was Carmela. The knee skirts became her, the mass of her hair, corn-silk smooth and tinted, flowing down her back, restored her prettiness as if by magic, and the vigor of her childhood shown in the red on her cheeks and the sparkle in her eyes. She enjoyed the afternoons in the mission, follow-ing Miss Reddle about with the admiration of a lover, and took upon herself, with all the enthusiasm of her released spirits, seeing that all the children were all up in time to go to school in the mornings. She began to learn English with ease, and by the time they were ready to enter the asylum she, as well as her brothers, talked, if not fluently, the new lan-guage, certainly without fear.

"You are not sorry to leave us?" asked her father.

Carmela shook her head vigorously. "I am. But it will be better for us all. No?"

The day before the departure Donna Sofia insisted upon a secret visit to the Catholic church, she and the four children.

"We'll do the stations of the cross," she said, and they all kneeled as they moved from bas-relief to bas-relief.

"Dear Jesus, you who have suffered so much, you will understand. We are doing this for the good of us all. Be merciful. It is not as if we are forgetting you. These people are Christians, too, these Protestants with their wealth and their power. They saved us all from a horrible future. It is only for a short time. Be merciful to the children . . . look after them in the place they are going . . . they will need your protection, and do not be hard on Tomaso and me . . . we are anxious to do our best."

She hurried out for fear of encountering Don Anselmo.

That night she spent making the noodles—*lasagne*[6]—which the children loved best of all her dishes. What other way has a mother of giving supreme pleasure to her loved ones on the eve of their departure for what place the good God only knows? She had the noodles dried and ready for their ricotta filling before the morning was gray in the skies. She was up long before anyone else. Painstakingly she laid out in the pan first one layer of broad yellowish noodle and then a layer of the soft white ricotta, with a sprinkle of meat balls and sliced eggs, and over that a generous covering of the richest red tomato sauce, and so until the pan was filled. The satisfaction of her work eased her heart of the anguish that was stifling it.

Then she cleaned the three chickens she had been at pains to buy alive the night before. She stuffed them with the egg and parsley dressing for which she was famous in Villetto, trussed them, and placed them in the oven along with the *lasagne imbottite*.[7] On the stove a soup was boiling to be made from the giblets, the necks, and the feet of the chickens. Dandelions were all cleaned and in water for the salad, and the slices of *prosciutto*,[8] salami, pimento, the olives, and the celery, were all assembled in a huge dish—for the little nibble before the real meal began.

La Monterano had insisted upon supplying a basket of fruit. "Where could she get such things, and in spring too?" Donna Sofia was impressed and happy for the children's sake. Don Tomaso had been commissioned to obtain as good wine as could be procured. "It must be the finest dinner they have ever had. What will they eat in that awful place? Just those messy cereals with sugar and a lot of mushy potatoes."

The children were mercifully drugged with food and wine, so that when they reached the asylum they seemed to be unaware of what was happening. The long trolley ride in the cars, pulled by underground cables, had been interesting to Don Tomaso. Besides holding on to Carmela's hand, he merely kept staring at the motorman who pulled back a huge lever longer than himself and in that way set the car in motion or brought it to a standstill. He kept figuring out what would happen if the cables slipped? He hoped they might slip. Maybe that would be the best end for them all. When they all stood in front of the huge iron gates that opened into the asylum, he turned to his wife with trembling lips.

"Why, why didn't the cables snap?" he asked.

She did not understand to what he was referring, and looked at him blank-eyed.

"Hurry," Miss Reddle said, and they all followed her up the long gravel road leading to the main building of the asylum. The noise of the crunching pebbles pleased the boys, and they hung behind to churn their heels into them. Trees lined the walk. Through the trees they caught glimpses of wooden buildings, a row of low brick buildings, finally an open space with hundreds of boys running back and forth and shrieking.

"No girls," Carmela informed Miss Reddle.

But Miss Reddle placed her arm about Carmela and laughed. "Many. On the other side of that big building, see it? Oh, yes, many, many girls."

A woman even more enormous than Miss Reddle met them in the large barren reception room, ushered them into a smaller room occupied by benches with cane backs, and in a short time the children were taken over by a woman in an efficient blue-and-white striped uniform with a blue frilled hat towering over a huge pompadour. She seemed merely to surround them by just opening her arms, for they were at once lost to view as she sailed out of the room to the accompaniment of cries not only from the boys but from Donna Sofia as well. Don Tomaso made a brave attempt to suggest that he was above such human weakness by rising and walking up and down the room with his hands clasped behind his back. Miss Reddle held Donna Sofia's hand and rattled off something very soothing in English but without any effect upon Italian ears.

Emotions have a way of finding a natural limit of expansion and contraction, and then seeking their true outlines. Donna Sofia came to an end of her weeping and conducted an animated conversation with Miss Reddle on her goodness in saving the family from disgrace and poverty and providing an opportunity for the children to learn American ways and so preparing to assume the responsibilities that would be theirs when they grew up in this strange, strange country.

Don Tomaso made a speech without interruption from his wife. No one could ever have surmised the peculiar twisted road that they were to travel after leaving Villetto. Imagine, in not much more than a year, there had fallen from the lap of destiny nothing but bitter fruit for them, and they were good people who had always commanded admiration and respect in their own country. He, for one, had outlined to himself a course of action which would shortly restore to them the prestige they appeared to have lost. They were not *contadini*, they were not a band of *cafoni*, yokels without education and good manners. He was embarked upon a complete statement of his plans for the future—conceived as he proceeded.

The door opened and the children stood in front of them looking like extremely polished mannikins. Carmela's hair had been gathered into one pigtail and tied up with a plain muslin ribbon. She had been supplied with a frock of a cheap cotton material that made a pretense of retaining a printed pattern. She was shod in heavy soled shoes and her legs cased in black ribbed stockings. The boys had been in like manner transformed. For some institutional reason the suits they had worn, each one sufficiently individual to endow its owner with a measure of difference, had been replaced by black ribbed stockings, gray knee breeches made of material employed in cheap flannel blankets, scarecrow-like coats of the same fabric, glazed blue shirts with collars that did not fit. The blue frilled efficient person told them to curtsey. Evidently they had all practiced the bow, and they curtsied together, smiling foolishly. Don Tomaso and Donna Sofia looked at each other stupefied, but exchanged a glance of mutual assistance.

"Don't they look clean?" the blue frilled cap simpered.

"Like cracked clay saints," Don Tomaso said in Italian, and the children laughed, although it was evident they wanted to cry. They did not dare cry, for it was evident, too, that the blue frilled cap had rehearsed them in the art of keeping back their tears. They looked at her and she held her lips tight. They did likewise.

"Now go and kiss mother and daddy good-bye. Say good-bye, and don't forget . . . nobody cries in the J. P. A."

Donna Sofia did not know which one to embrace first. First she held them all, and then each singly, and began the process all over again, kissing them at any point of their bodies where she managed to find them with her tear-filled eyes. Carmela clung to her father, and he merely held his body very tall and stiff and allowed his hand to play an irregular tattoo on her arm. The big-boned Gianni, oldest of them all, was the first to break the Stoic silence. He burst into a shout of independence. He would not stay. He wanted to go back. He would show them. He would run away. Blue frilled cap caught him by the arm and gave him a severe shaking. In a maneuver executed with remarkable rapidity she had surrounded them once more, their voices raised in different keys of wailings and groanings, and without mother or father being aware of what had happened, she had billowed them out of sight. Miss Reddle had taken hold of Donna Sofia under her arms and was escorting her out, telling her it was all for the best, all for the best. Don Tomaso had put on his hat, but he took it off again to watch his wife and Miss Reddle proceed slowly out of the room. He took his handkerchief out of his pocket, shook it in the air with some vigor, and then found it necessary to mop the inside of his hat with it. Having done that several times, he followed the others. The cries of the children in the meantime had been lost in the general silence.

CHAPTER FOUR

1

At the end of two years, the three boys returned home. Carmela, however, remained a year longer. Besides their changes in stature and habits, they had mastered English and forgotten Italian. But more important than these was the transformation effected by close discipline, daily contact with masses of children, lack of variety, restricted environment, absence of opportunity for independent effort—in other words, the prison-like shelter from all the natural ways of life.

After one year in the asylum, Carmela had learned enough English to be placed in charge of a Sunday class for girls. She had gone through all the grades of the regular school with high marks. There was no high school and the child would have been a problem. But her skill with the needle was discovered early, and she was given the task of mending the sheets and the pillow-cases, the table linens, and even the clothing of the younger children. She chose her own assistants among the girls, made them into able seamstresses like herself. Many privileges were accorded her. She was allowed to stay up late to read, to crochet, to embroider. She turned out dainty doilies, artistic antimacassars, lace of a charming and delicate texture and pattern. They were gifts for the instructors and the instructors boasted of her skills and showed her off to Martin and his committees as an indigenous product of the asylum.

Before long, the sewing work in the classes took on a strictly useful character. Hours that had appalled children and supervisors became enchanted periods. The teachers had enough good sense to turn their gifted pupil into an instructor, and Carmela threw her efforts into the work with such delight and ease that the manual work of the girls from crude, knotty, unserviceable patches evolved into lovely finished articles that made them proud and happy.

She was seventeen when she came out—buxom, vigorous, beautiful. Her return to the Parterre was triumphal. Donna Sofia had talked about it to her neighbors for months. Don Tomaso, who had made many friends among the habitués of the cafés, had walked among them with an unmistakable air of exultation, and he had been no less voluble than his wife. Gennaro himself suggested to everyone that he had a kind of proprietary interest in the young woman and sang her praises without stint. Donna Maria, become even stouter than she had been and a conspicuous figure in the community because of her success in the millinery business, spoke in paeans of admiration.

It became a contagion in the Parterre. The children of the Montera-nos, Roberto in particular, listened with awe at the descriptions of this remarkable goddess that was soon to descend upon them with her charm, her beauty, her marvelous skills. Gilda, now eight, wanted to be assured that Carmela would like her. Gianni, who had gone to work with his father as a carpenter, refused to commit himself about his sister, while Immanuele and Giovanni admitted grudgingly that she was all right. Alberto and Modesto, however, could not restrain their enthusiasm at the homecoming. Every day they asked, "How long now?" Only Rosaria kept her tongue to herself, and her thoughts too. On one occasion only did she speak up, and then it was to tell Gennaro that he appeared to have nothing else to do than go gadding about shouting hallelujas about a young wench that had brought only pain in their lives.

2

During the last year of Carmela's stay in the asylum, the Spanish-American war had been fought. Dewey's return to New York City was an occasion for a furore of patriotism, pride and enthusiasm matched by no event within memory of the Italians.[1] Even more than the strictly American sections of the city, Harlem, with its settlement of Italians, celebrated the triumph of the American navy in a way they had hitherto reserved for their saints. Fifth Avenue was no match for the buntings, the lamps festooned across the streets, the archways draped in flags, the firework displays set up for the great celebration of the evening.

Gennaro was the center of all activity. He had gathered the numerous societies for mutual help, each vaunting a patron saint by whose name it was called, into a committee of welcome for the glorious admiral. Not only were they to have their local festa, but they were to march in a body, flags waving, bands blaring, as many thousands of men and women as could be persuaded to march trailing behind them, through the neighborhood, then west on One hundred and Twenty-fifth Street, to station themselves on the heights overlooking the Hudson and wait for the fleet to steam up. Gennaro had sufficient influence with the politicians and police to have a whole section of the cliffs reserved for his host of celebrants.

There was no family that had not prepared either to join in the festive march or to find its own place on Morningside Heights. Their preparation consisted not entirely of brushing down their Sunday best, and putting a knockout polish on their shoes. To it was added the assembling of huge picnic baskets. The Monteranos, as befitted a family that had once been in the military, had made a special purchase of a commodious wicker basket. They had invited the Dauris and their children. In consequence, the basket was packed with six roast chickens, a quantity of stuffed peppers, a whole *provolo*,[2] a sharp cheese shaped like a ninepin and as large as those used in bowling alleys, a whole mound of fruit, and four bottles of wine, besides a small loaf of bread per person. Dewey was going to be feasted if not with Lucullan[3] delicacy certainly with Roman abundance. That night, they would all return to view the pyrotechnical wonders that Gennaro had donated out of his own pocket. There could be no celebration for him unless it ended in bombarding the skies with sizzling streams of color.

The societies had massed in front of the Parterre, each one in a uniform more resplendent than any admiral of the American navy could ever have conceived. The streets squirmed with children. Crowds of men and women filled the stoops or thrust interested heads out of the windows. There was enough noise to gladden even Gennaro's heart. He was accoutred in a uniform of an officer of bersaglieri,[4] shining green with a red sash across the chest from shoulder to hip. The bands all struck up *The Stars and Stripes Forever.* There were all of six bands, and they had planned to start the triumphal procession with a concert of Italian and American patriotic pieces, to be played by the entire ensemble.

The huge volumes of sound billowed mightily into the skies, serene and blue that day as if in consonance with the occasion. It was deafening. Flags waved, hands clapped, shouts went up. Gennaro stood on the stoop, his earrings gleaming like jewels, his keen swarthy face rippling with smiles, raising his sword as a command for the march to begin.

A telegraph boy had worked himself through the crowd and pushed up to Gennaro. He handed the grand marshal the envelope. Gennaro, puzzled, passed it on to Struzzo, who towered beside him in an equally dashing outfit.

"Maybe they are asking us to join the downtown parade of the soldiers."

"Maybe it's from the President—his congratulations."

"Well, well, Struzzo, what the hell is it?" demanded Gennaro.

Struzzo's face had turned pale.

"Better wait until all this is over," he suggested, stuffing the telegram into his pocket.

"Is it for me?" asked Gennaro.

"Yes . . . but wait, please, tomorrow . . . not now."

Gennaro insisted.

Struzzo pleaded. About them the crowds milled and noised. The bands had swung into the hymn to Garibaldi. Everybody shouted approval.

"When do we get started?"

The subordinate leaders were becoming impatient. On the river the tugs had begun a continuous whistling and shrieking. The Admiral's fleet had been sighted out at sea and there was no doubt now but that the ships would be ready for the welcome of the city.

"Well, what?" repeated Gennaro.

"It's about Domenico . . ."

They had heard nothing about him for the past three years.

"Domenico? From him? What does he want?"

"He don't want much no more," answered Struzzo. "Just died in the hospital down in Santiago."

Gennaro whistled. He fumbled in his pockets for his pipe. Not finding it, he passed his hand over his face and then stared at Struzzo.

"By Saint Jerome and all the saints," he mumbled.

Struzzo put a hand on Gennaro's shoulder.

"What'll we do, tell Rosaria now?"

Just then a flashy young man in a blue and red creation, with a mass of yellow plumes streaming from his hat down to his shoulders, reached Gennaro.

"Say, Gennaro, they want to get started. How about it?"

Gennaro again pulled his sword out, flashed it high in the sunshine. A huge detonator on one of the roofs blazed and roared. Shouts and cries from the crowd. The bands began marching to the banging rhythms of the *Double Eagle March*. Gennaro fell into line alongside of

Struzzo. Left and right he turned, waving his hand to this person and the other. As he marched, the people in the windows called to him and waved handkerchiefs, hats, tassels of ribbons.

"Hey, Struzzo?" he asked. "We certainly made America. No?"

3

He told Rosaria the next morning, gruffly. She seized his hands, made him tell what he knew, could he find out more. He merely stroked her cheeks, stuck his pipe into his mouth, and stumped out of the house. He refused to talk about it, but he became kinder to her. She went about doing her house-work mechanically, speaking even less than usual. She had told Emilio and Elena about it, but they had already forgotten their brother, and could offer her no sympathy. She stopped talking to Don Tomaso and Donna Sofia. The rift between them had been somehow patched up, but she had never shown any real eagerness to be with her tenants. It was natural that she should be the only person missing on the steps when Carmela walked up between her father and mother. She refused to be present at the dinner in honor of the girl's return. And when Gennaro that night tumbled into bed with her, smelling of wine and mumbling drunkenly, Rosaria rose, and went downstairs into the kitchen. Gennaro pursued her, stumbling over the chairs, and shouting foully.

"What are you doing there on your knees?"

She paid no attention.

"Ave Maria . . ." is all he heard.

Before the lighted lamp in front of the Virgin her figure was a sad silhouette, bent head, bent shoulders, hands clasped under her heavy bosom. Gennaro looked at her, his anger mounting.

"So, you won't come to a party you're invited to? You leave me when I return?"

"Ave Maria . . ."

"By Saint Jerome, Rosaria . . . talk to me . . . don't you think I, too, am suffering?"

She resumed her monotonous mumble, never once changing her position.

"In my heart, too, is sorrow," Gennaro continued. "I know . . . you are praying for me to be forgiven . . . it was me sent him into the war . . . I . . . I . . . killed him . . . I, his own father who loved him once. . . . Rosaria, you know I loved him once."

THE GRAND GENNARO • 177

He shook her shoulders.

"Ave Maria . . ."

"And then I hated him. . . . I don't know why . . . you, too, I hated . . . you came, all of you, out of the past. You spoiled my new life . . . what I did alone . . . you reminded me of the old days . . . I . . ."

Rosaria rose to her feet.

"Down on your knees, *scellerato,* you foul man, and pray the Sweet Mary to have mercy on your black soul. . . . You, you have made America! Bah! The debts back in Capomonte were better than all this money you have piled up. What for? Do you need it? Do you know what to do with it? On women you could spend it . . . but you could not see Domenico do the same . . . sure, the debts were better . . . for you far better . . . the work in the fields when you came home tired and ready for a crust of bread with a bit of cheese . . . that was better . . . that was our life . . . not this . . . trying to be important. . . . Make America! Pray to God, wretched man, on your knees, ever and ever. . . ."

Gennaro was too stunned to answer. He gazed at her as she talked. He gazed silently after her as she left, and then in the half-darkness of the kitchen he, too, kneeled before the form of the Holy Virgin. He beat his chest with his fist.

"I . . . I am a murderer . . . that's what she wanted to tell me. . . . Pray for me before God. I will make amends. I will make amends. . . ."

He got up and quietly went to bed.

4

Life slipped away from Rosaria. It left her shocked and silent, gazing about her dumbly but without appealing for recognition or sympathy. Her actions became as automatic as a human being can make them. The children looked after themselves. Emilio, fifteen years old now and grown to be almost the replica of his father, chunky, broad-shouldered, with deep-set eyes that had the piercing quality of one always on the alert to seize the immediate advantage, took over the management of the household. Zia Anna tried to help. She rushed in as soon as she could in the morning and looked after the cleaning and getting lunch for Elena and Emilio when they returned from school. That was, however, only on such days when Rosaria did not drive her out.

"You here, you crone, you here again? Go home, I can take care of my own, I say."

Zia Anna knew better than to put up any opposition. Placing her shawl on her head, she left without a word, making only the sign of the cross and uttering in her old heart a fervent prayer to Saint Anna, mother of Mary, to help the poor thing.

"She is out of her mind, the wretched woman, she knows not what she does...."

But when she had left, Rosaria did nothing. At first she would begin to putter with a broom or the utensils on the stove, or she would sit in her chair and begin to shell the peas or string the beans. In a few minutes she had abandoned all activity, sat down in a chair, head bent forward, eyes blank, motionless. Elena found her so, and in the wisdom of her eight years just stared and waited for Emilio to return. Emilio had come to realize that his mother had put them out of mind, him and Elena, as if neither he nor his sister existed. He got the lunch for both his sister and himself, and soon after sent her off to school once more. Then he went to his mother, took her by the hand, and led her upstairs to her room. There he sat her down again, and pleaded with her to get undressed and go to bed. Sometimes it would take the whole hour, sometimes much longer, and he would miss his lessons. In the end she would obey him, take off her clothes and go to bed. He brought her food—broth with pastina, a piece of chicken, or a salad. He insisted that she eat.

"There, now, ma, you know I made it all myself—for you. Eat, do eat."

The rose and tan of her skin had turned to a yellow pallor, the clear light was gone out of her eyes, and the fine brown hair had lost its gloss. It was no longer piled in braids over her head, but caught up in any sort of knot. Emilio sat on the bed with her, his arm about her shoulders, talking to her while she ate. She would now and then turn to look at him, the spoon in her hand, all recognition gone out of her eyes. She scanned the boy's features closely, smiled, then shook her head, and her face set once more into its expressionless pale agony.

Gennaro became kinder and kinder to her, but it did no good. She pushed him away from her and fixed strange penetrating eyes upon him. Once she held him by the shoulders while the light in her eyes focused into a searching insane glance.

"Where is Domenico?" she asked slowly, as if now the anguish in her heart were intensified a thousandfold so that he would be aware of it, and return her son.

"*Rosaria, per l'amor di Dio santo!*"[5]

She continued to eye him, waiting for an answer. Tears came to his eyes.

"You know," he whispered, beseeching her to accept the cruel fate.

"Murderer," she shrieked, and threw him off.

He appealed to Donna Maria. Maria, very stout now, could barely get about. She had become the butt of a thousand comments.

"America has gone to fat on her," they would say.

"Well, by the dear saints, she eats like a man. What do you expect?"

Donna Maria, despite the long painful climb it would require on her return, went to see Rosaria as often as she could. It meant being exhausted, not only from the numerous stairs up which she would be compelled to pull her enormous weight, but also from the pain of being with Rosaria for an hour. At first they would talk rationally enough. Yes, Rosaria had noted how well Emilio and Elena were thriving. Praised be heaven, they were getting on. Soon they would be ready to marry and leave her. It would inevitably result in some mention of Domenico, and then a long shrill tirade against Gennaro, the shameless man, murderer of his own son. As to Donna Sofia, Rosaria would not see her at all.

"What do you want here, in my house? Go away, go away, I say."

"You go," Gennaro asked Carmela. "You are young and sweet to look at . . . you may help her."

Carmela was overcome with horror at the request. Her startled eyes showed it.

"I should want to, Gennaro. I wish I could help. I would do anything. But don't you see? It would do her no good."

She was persuaded to try. Her father opposed it strenuously.

"She is demented, Carmela. Who knows what she would do?"

But despite her mother and her father the young girl decided to visit Rosaria. Gennaro had in some fumbling simple fashion divined that the visit would not be fraught with danger, that it would indeed be some form of solace for his wife.

5

Carmela had developed into a large well-built woman. She showed her seventeen years only in the clear red of her skin, the flash in her eyes, the quickness and agility of her movements. She might easily have been taken for a young matron, settled and experienced in the ways of life, capable of sweet understanding and sympathy. She had become serious, saying only a few words. And if asked for advice, she would be inclined to shake her head and shrug her shoulders as much as to suggest that she had nothing to offer.

But she spoke English so fluently, she went about with so much assurance and poise, she must certainly understand a good deal. She had been educated in the American way, dressed in the American way, held herself up in an unmistakable American way, easy, self-contained, always unembarrassed. She must be capable of a greater insight than they all had. Besides, were not the reports from the asylum always more and more astounding, and had she not been made one of the officials? The whole of the Parterre, adults and children alike, looked upon her with admiration and deep respect. But as if the experience through which she had gone had conferred an unusual gift of silence upon her, she rarely had anything to say except when pressed beyond her ability to hold out.

"You talk to my wife," Gennaro pleaded. "You ask her things, and you counsel her. She will listen to you. I know she will listen to you . . . as I would."

The meeting was only between Rosaria and Carmela. Rosaria was seated in a chair in the backyard. Gennaro had kept the yard exactly as Mr. Muller had sold it to him. There were two narrow plots of flowers, one behind the other in the middle section. At the sides, the narrowest ribbons of lawn skirted the fence. In each of the far corners a linden tree threw a light flickering shade into the yard. From the doorway leaned a small porch, and up to this porch lilac bushes grew in profusion. It was now the lilac season and the soft all-pervasive odor of the blossoms mingled with the warm wind that came off the river.

"You know who I am?" Carmela questioned, kneeling at the older woman's side and putting an arm about her shoulder.

Rosaria stared blankly.

"I am Carmela."

Still Rosaria stared with open uncomprehending eyes.

"You remember? I knew Domenico."

Rosaria put her hands to the young girl's face.

"You are beautiful. You are very young. You must never forget Domenico. I cannot forget. He went away."

"Yes. I know. A long time ago it was, even before I went away."

"Yes. Ah, once we lived on a mountain side in a hut of stone, and I took care of goats and pigs, and in the fall we made the salami from the pigs, and we made cheeses from the milk of the goats, and we put them away in a cellar under the earth. And we made wine, and we kept the wine in large barrels, and we drank it mostly on feast days when we joined in the processions to the church. Over the stones we went in our bare feet, and the good Don Vito and the boys in their cassocks marched with us, too, and we lighted candles and bore the image of Saint Elena high in the air. Domenico was young, and he liked to be all dressed up, and so I made breeches for him out of his father's pants and a red sash to wear across his body and the feather of a rooster in his hat, and he put out his chest and he stuck out his legs, and he marched like a big man, and his father held up one side of the saint's image, a great honor. So we all had honor in the family, but mostly because we were good farmers. Our pigs and our goats were the best, and when it came time for the priests to bless them, we tied ribbons on them, and we made a beautiful thing of the old cart, too, and the donkey—ah, the lovely old beast, how funny and grand he looked with bells on his harness and ribbons all over. But Gennaro did not like it, for there were heavy taxes and he came here, and he called for me . . . and look, my sweet one, look . . . what have we? This . . ."

She took the girl by the hand and showed her around.

She pointed at everything in the house, the new coal stove, the electric lights, the oil-cloth on the floor, the ice-box on one side of the kitchen, a table with a marble top. But as she said "this," "this," her voice became sadder and sadder, tinged more and more with contempt.

"These things are not for me. . . . I have nothing. I want nothing. Domenico is gone . . . that is all I know. Ah, you knew him?"

"Yes. I knew him."

"He is dead, you know, dead in the wars, sent out there by his father who has eyes only for young girls. . . . You beware. . . . You are beautiful . . . you are young . . ."

She shook her finger at the girl, slowly, back and forth, in a gesture that said, "No, no. . . ." Then she relapsed into her silence with her hands folded in her lap. That evening she told Gennaro that a lovely young woman had come to visit her.

"She knew Domenico. But she is not for you, you hear?"

Gennaro escorted her with great gentleness to her bed. There she turned on her husband, seized him by the shoulders, and cried, "Look, look there! See, the blessed virgin herself with the lamp burning at her feet. Tomorrow, Gennaro, we must go to church."

6

There followed many weeks when they went to church together for the first early mass. Gennaro knelt with her at the lowest step of the altar.

She prayed quietly, her head bent, in an undistinguishable monotone. He prayed, too. Then she climbed to the next step on her knees, sometimes catching her skirts about her ankles and falling over. He helped her rise to her kneeling position again, and he, too, would climb the steps on his knees.

People heard of it and came to see. Little groups of women collected in the morning, standing off to one corner of the church where it was dark. Neither Don Anselmo nor the fat little sacristan could induce them to go away nor to kneel seemly in prayer and be quiet. It was a sight that in some obscure manner thrilled them with drama, this spectacle of a demented woman and her arrogant money-making husband, a *contadino* who had amassed a fortune in rags, humbling themselves before the Holy Sacrament. They stood and watched, some with fingers to their lips, others leaning against the wall, others weeping. Gennaro saw them and became angry. One day he went to Don Anselmo and demanded that it be stopped.

"But I can't keep them out of the church, Gennaro."

"*E' 'nna infamia*—it's a crying shame."

"Yes, I know." The priest stroked his hand. "Perhaps there is a way out. Could you not have the doctors examine her?"

Gennaro declared that he would not have her taken away and placed with the cracked persons in the hospital.

"Let her be examined nevertheless . . . maybe they will know something to do."

Dr. Giovanelli strutted into Gennaro's home, tapping his cane importantly and exposing the great area of red sash across his breast. He made his examination. It consisted of holding Rosaria's head between his hands and gazing into her eyes with a kind of smiling sympathy that was supposed to soften the fatigue of the posture. He stared into her eyes and shook his head.

With a shrug of his shoulders he got up and insisted on delivering his message in the other room.

"At Aspromonte, I knew what to do. Here . . . it is a matter for God."

After many consultations with other physicians, it was finally agreed that Rosaria was to return to Italy where the change of air and environment might recall her from the deep darkness into which she had fallen. She was to travel with a group going to Calabria and take Elena with her. She seemed willing, and brightened a good deal while waiting for the necessary preparations to be concluded. She spoke with Elena about Capomonte.

"Do you remember, lamb, the old stucco house, and the lovely old donkey we had? Do you? Ah, there you will not need to talk the strange language of this country."

Several weeks after she left, Gennaro received word that she had not landed in Italy. One night, the letters from his friends and the reports of the steamship officers declared, she was taken with a chill, was sent to the ship's hospital, and died on the day before the boat was to put in. Gennaro had the letters and the reports read to him by Don Tomaso. As each word corroborated the story, he merely kept taking his pipe out of his mouth, thrusting it back, rising and stamping back and forth across the room. He asked no questions, just listened. When it was over, he stopped abruptly.

"Don Tomaso," he said in a tone much milder than his wont, "for seven years I said 'No, do not send for her.' For seven years my friends they say, 'Yes, send for her.' I don't say I knew what would happen. But some of us can't be just pulled out of our nests. We die like the birds. Some, they become strong and fly high in the wind. Like me. Poor Rosaria...."

He sat down, placed his head on his knees and wept gently.

"About Elena," he said at length. "You write this, see, to Don Vito, or anybody, Don Emiliano, maybe, the lawyer, and you say, 'Here is money. You put the girl in the convent school in Reggio. She will become a sister, and she can always have money from me. But if she wants to be like other girls and marry, she will find money in the bank for a dot ... but let her remain in the old country ... that is all ... that is best, no, Don Tomaso?"

With Zia Anna installed in his home, Gennaro continued to live in the Parterre. Every morning before going to his work, he visited the church and prayed for the repose of Rosaria's soul. He prayed for himself too. He donated a sum of money toward Don Anselmo's new church. And from that day on, he bent all his efforts to collecting funds for the erection of the sacred edifice.

7

His business might be nothing, but he worked at it harder than ever. He drove his men on harder. He added this to his shrewdness and meanness in bargaining with the junk and rag-collectors. For some time he had been content to accept the current valuations that were placed by the buyers on all of his offerings of metal and cloth. He reverted now to his old practices of jumping on the seat with the drivers of his wagons and riding the whole length of the city to the sections downtown where the jobbers had their warehouses.

"What you mean, Mr. Rosenman, you give me so small pay?"

He took them by storm, accusing them, without preliminaries, of cheating him.

"You pay the bale ten dollars . . . I say you give me fifteen for the cheap one. No, so I don't sell . . ."

He organized the strongest dealers into a group bent upon higher prices. He bull-dozed, teased, cajoled his fellow rag-men. When they passed his business place he called out to them,

"Hey there, you scared rat, hey there? You still afraid? Why?"

He was tireless. He followed up his instructions to his men with merciless persistence. Rocco had taught him to tamp down the bales with a great deal of force, making them tight and heavy. He found it possible to put fewer bits of rags in each bale and yet obtain as good a price. The ropes he used were somewhat heavier, he employed one and a half as much burlap again for the outer covering, he wrapped the bales in newspapers and then in cloth. He resorted to the most ingenious methods for cutting down the actual weight of the rags themselves and yet making the total bale weigh as much as ever. Because the assortment of the rags was always excellent there were few complaints, and he followed up one clever practice with another. He was simply and decisively minded upon building up a fortune for the church.

The church might do a great deal of good. It would bring the stray-ing back into the fold. He talked it over with Don Anselmo.

"It's something in here, padre."

He pounded his chest.

"It tells me, 'Gennaro, you build a church. Gennaro, you do the good deeds now. You help your neighbors.'"

Struzzo offered objections to Gennaro's new activities.

"You'll go broke, old man. You're not the kind to do this sort of thing. Only a millionaire . . . like Martin."

Gennaro turned on him quietly, but nevertheless with a pleading look in his eyes.

"What'll I do, Struzzo? Tell me that."

"Rosaria's death has got you now. I know. But time, man, time . . . that'll make it all right."

"Sure, it's got me. Don't I know? It's opened my eyes. It's like I see where I am going, but not altogether, not clear and straight. Who am I, after all? A clod-hopper from the mountains of Calabria! What have I done? Piled up the money, soaked it into houses, strung up a big business . . . well, what of it? What'll I do now? See what I mean? What's left? So I build the church, and when I build that, there maybe will be nothing left. Maybe then heaven . . . maybe . . ."

He shrugged his shoulders, and pulled long and thoughtfully on his pipe.

"Sure, Struzzo. I look in the glass. I see my face. Wrinkles getting there now, and gray in my hair, and I say 'You're different now . . . your face, just a twist of wrinkles . . . Only your earrings. They don't change. They shine . . . like they shined on your grandfather.'"

"It doesn't make sense to me," Struzzo persisted. "Sounds like you're just milling around trying to find your way out of something."

"But it does make sense. You see, they say to me what you got with all your money, what's the good? And so I answer watch those piles of granite . . . watch them getting piled up . . . high into the air. That'll show them. Gennaro isn't just snuffing around like a pig in the money-heaps . . . doing nothing good."

"Stop talking like a church-going fool."

Gennaro stood up. His face was pale.

"Maybe, Struzzo, I am an old fool. There are fools get wise things done."

"You're in business. There's where you belong."

"And I'll stay in business. But I'll do more than that. Watch. I'll show them. A *cafone* with earrings I may be . . . but I'll show them, I'll show them."

8

The lonely Emilio worried him. It was not good for a child to be left without guidance.

"What can Zia Anna do with him? She has her own troubles. Take those nephews and nieces of hers. What a bad lot they are."

Carmela listened attentively.

"You see, he's a bullock, that Emilio of mine. There's no saying just whoa there, whoa there. And he just keeps home. You have seen him . . . making friends with nobody . . . head down, looking neither left nor right nor up . . . just down. . . . He'll follow his mother."

Gennaro rose from his chair quietly and rested his knuckles on the table. He was making swallowing motions with his neck to keep his emotions in check.

"I'm not one to cry like a woman, but you see, Carmela, how can I ask you? Be a mother to him . . . you were good and came down to help Rosaria. That was nice. With all that's happened, that was very nice."

"I'll do my best."

"There's no one else I'd ask. You have a heart and brains."

Carmela reddened. Gennaro saw it, and leaned over closer.

"You think it's funny this, no? Here I ask you these favors. And what have I done for you? I have brought you nothing but sorrow . . . first one son . . . and now this one."

"Please, Gennaro," she whispered. "The things that happened are all past."

Gennaro turned away abruptly. He had wanted to approach even closer to the girl. She had noticed it and drawn back slightly, but he was even more frightened than she. He sat down at once and drew his chair up close, spreading his small heavy-knuckled hand out before her. He kept looking at the tips of his fingers in an effort to avoid her eyes.

"Yes," he said, "all those things are past. What's happening now is a new sowing. The grain comes up in good time, and let us hope it will be tall and the shocks full. Ah, I keep sometimes going back to the old farm days in Capomonte, especially these times, with Rosaria gone, Domenico dead. That was a different life, harder work and nothing to show for it. It's over, it's like it never was. I'll be busy, the church, the rags . . . and I won't have much time . . . there's the boy . . . he's closer to you than me . . . he likes you . . . you look after him like. You have things to do, too . . . the shop upstairs and your own family . . . but maybe you can spare a moment now and then. He'll snap out of this slow bull-like way he's got into. Just talk to him . . . you will, Carmela, won't you?"

She looked up at him with wide-open eyes as if she was trying to find in his features some marks of the impulses behind his request. He looked back at her frankly, while his wrinkled little face brightened with a pleased awkward smile.

"You will, won't you?"

She nodded without removing her eyes from his. A pause followed and their eyes continued to meet.

"I like you, Carmela," he finally blurted. You're like me. You're made over. The soil is not in you as it was in Rosaria. You don't look back like your mother. You don't whine like that big bellows upstairs, Monterano. You look ahead like me . . . and you're a good girl."

But there was hardly any need for Gennaro to have asked Carmela to befriend Emilio. More and more she had become the center of life for the young people in the Parterre. Not only her brothers, but Gilda and the Monterano boys carried their troubles to her. With her they planned games and excursions. Of her they asked assistance in their school work.

Nevertheless, it was true that Emilio was evincing reactions to his mother's death that included general and specific rebellions against all the modes of life about him. It was with him as it had been with his mother when the news of Domenico's death had come and made all the urban grandeur that her husband had provided her seem but a bloated show-off's work.

His father went to his room the night when the fatal cable arrived. Emilio had already got into bed, had turned off the light, and was about to fall asleep. He saw his father standing near him, only his earrings glinting in the faint light from the backyards.

"Emilio," Gennaro called to him. The voice was softer than Emilio remembered and faraway. "Emilio. You can read. Read this."

Emilio turned up the light hurriedly. It was so good to be asked to do something, late at night, too. He smiled as he took the telegram.

Gennaro stood at the bedside without moving or uttering a word. The boy read the telegram through. Gennaro saw that he had finished. But Emilio did not take his eyes off the letters. What was it? He was still and drooping, his head fallen low. Was the child weeping? Such a young child to understand so quickly!

Gennaro crossed himself. "Saint Elena, Saint Elena, I beg you, give me strength."

The child's tears unnerved him. It was the rarest sensation for Gennaro. He felt as if the props he had been accustomed to—the respectful good-mornings of his workers, the waving hands of his acquaintances on the street, the feel of rolled bills in his pockets, the sight of the Parterre rising delicate and narrow, like a signor's mansion—all these had given way and left him groping for something more substantial and real. He fell slowly to his knees and fumbled for the child's hair. He forced his fingers through it and at the same time placed his head in Emilio's lap and sobbed.

So they remained, the boy now tearless, the father weeping. Finally Gennaro rose and looked his son in the face.

"One thing," he said quietly. "Just one thing, I ask, Emilio. You're your own boss now . . . alone in the world. What can I do? Food, a stupid man like me can get and give to you, and a few pennies for your pockets. That's all. The good Lord knows that's all. But I ask you . . . you're capable and you got something up here (Gennaro pointed to his own head).... Study ... study hard ... learn to be somebody ... a doctor or something."

He allowed the boy to do as he pleased. However, more and more the lad withdrew into himself.

On first coming to New York, Emilio had been fascinated with his father's rag and junk shop. There was no end to his tours of exploration through it. He had salvaged for his own use old gilt frames, copper pots of strange designs, odd pieces of machinery, gadgets of one kind or another which he kept himself busy repairing, several ormulu clocks, and useless battered watches. He was especially taken up with their machinery. His desk was filled with numerous little cases and each contained wheels or screws, hair-springs, pivots, bits of jewels he had found in the timepieces, dial hands and faces, a multitude of winders and crystals. The child's collective instinct expanded day by day. There was not a thing he decided to keep that he had not labeled and put away in a proper classification. The workmen put all sorts of things aside for him. In fact, there sprung up between them and him a bantering sort of trading system, the principle of which was that Emilio could obtain none of the items that had been saved up for him unless he managed to retort more cleverly, or more sharply, or even more sarcastically than any of them could taunt and bait him or, for that matter, his father, Gennaro.

But when his mother died, he all but ceased going to the rag-shop. It was not so much the feeling he had of wanting to avoid his father as much as possible. He was bewildered and depressed, and all his keen strength of muscle and mind fought back against the events of his life. There were hands pressing him down, putting him into a corner, clapping foul fingers over his mouth. In some way the shop was to blame for it all. His father might burst out with ever-increasing displays of affection. He hated it. Gennaro only made him feel suspicious and uncomfortable, and the shop was Gennaro and Gennaro the shop.

And the boy fell into the bullock-like sullenness that Gennaro had described to Carmela. That is why he appealed to her and hoped she would help. He could not help his son.

"By Saint Jerome, I tried. What'll I do now, carry him around town pick-a-back?"

On numerous occasions he had sneaked in where Emilio was seated at his table, strewn with books and gadgets.

"Well, you little owl, how goes it, hey?"

He handled first one thing, then another, raised a book and put it down.

"Geography, is it? Well, well, and this green spot is Italy? There's no green here in the United States. That's why we're all greenhorns that come across, hey, Emilio?"

He laughed at his own joke.

"Learning about bugs, too, hey? Come over to the shop again, they're millions there. But don't let them get away or they'll be trying to see what you're like yourself."

Emilio liked it, but only if Gennaro remained but a short time. Otherwise he became restless and ill at ease.

"I'm in your way, hey, you young pup?"

And with that and a timid attempt at another joke, Gennaro would leave.

It was really only with Roberto Monterano that Emilio kept up some measure of liveliness. They had become friends from the beginning, waited to go to school together, lunched together, nominated and seconded each other for the officerships of all the clubs in school or in the Mission. In recent months they had joined the chess and checker group at Miss Reddle's. The new playground with the handball and basketball courts did not interest them. They had ceased to attend the Baptist Sunday school, and despite Gennaro's suggestion Emilio for one would not join the Catholic school. With Don Anselmo he remained on kindly terms despite the priest's constant if genial protests to Gennaro. With the death of his mother, these activities appeared even less alluring.

For the most part he wanted to be alone.

"Emilio, what a way to behave!" Carmela hinted. "Why don't you go out with the boys?"

Emilio hunched his shoulders and let his head slump forward. There was no word to be had out of him.

9

In the first days of the Parterre, Emilio, a boy of ten, had been very fond of Carmela. In some vague childish way he realized that she had become the center of the family concern. During the time when she and her brothers had been going to Miss Reddle's Soup School in preparation for their departure for the juvenile asylum, Emilio would wait for her to come down the stone stoop. He would go up to her shyly, and if he had nothing but his hand to offer, he would stretch that out, or take hers. As a rule he had a piece of his coffee cake, or a fruit, sometimes a flower. But when Carmela returned from her three years' absence, Emilio all but ran away from her. He hung his head in her presence, or bolted the room entirely. No matter how she tried to get him to speak, he kept his lips shut and refused to look at her. Something in her expanding beauty, touch of strangeness or suggestion of loveliness too much for him to comprehend, threw up a barrier between her and him. With the death of his mother, Carmela had attempted to be loving and kind. She ran down when Zia Anna was not in to help him with his lunch. She took his clothes and mended them. Once he had been ill. Gennaro had not yet returned from his business, and Zia Anna was worried. She ran up for Carmela.

Emilio, his thick, jet-black curls, shining in the light, lay on his bed. He had refused to allow Zia Anna to undress him. His own efforts had wearied him. At the side of the bed lay one shoe and a stocking and on the chair his coat and cap. He had drawn the blanket over him and was huddled under it, knees close to his chin, elbows and hand together pressed up by his thighs.

He opened his eyes slightly when Carmela placed her hand on his forehead.

"He's so hot," she whispered to Zia Anna.

"Some cold water and vinegar," Zia Anna suggested. She went out to fetch the liquid and the cloth for the compresses.

Carmela sat down near the boy and felt for his hand under the blanket. She was surprised that he allowed her to take it. He came closer to her and looked up.

"My throat's sore," he gulped.

"Ah . . . we'll make it better."

"You won't call in the doctor? What'll he do to me?"

"Sh . . . you mustn't talk. He'll give you something."

"Will it taste bad?"

"Maybe not. Some medicines taste good. But lie quiet."

She turned him on his back, adjusted the blanket under him, and put her head close.

"First, Emilio, you've got to get your clothes off."

"All right," he whispered.

"Then we'll put the cold cloths on your head, and you must keep quiet like a little mouse and go to sleep."

"All right."

"And I'll call the doctor."

"You ain't going away, Carmela?"

She had no recollection of having heard him call her by name before this. It was said in the same tone he might have called his mother, and it pleased her. She stooped over and kissed his cheek. He seized her hand as she did so, and began to cry softly.

"My throat's so sore . . . you won't go away."

"No, no, but let's get undressed."

Zia Anna had come in, and together they got him under the sheets, and with Carmela at his bedside he fell asleep.

When he was able to sit up, she ran down as often as she could and read to him. She sent Gilda and Roberto and her younger brothers to play with Emilio, and when she finally joined them, the party became a free-for-all to obtain her attention. Emilio became his old rollicking self.

It was inevitable that both he and Roberto should be in the school play. There were just three parts. Roberto and Emilio were the bad boys of a school determined on welcoming the new teacher with a lot of ingeniously conceived horseplay. The result was that the new appointee, much smaller than either of the boys, turned the tables on them. Emilio had coached the act. But he had decided in the end not to put it on until they had rehearsed it for Carmela.

The table in the middle of the living and dining room in his apartment Emilio pushed to one side. The chairs he ranged at one end in two rows. He pulled the shades down and placed heavy cardboard around the electric lights. One door was designated the entrance for the stage, the back door for the audience. But the audience was to consist of only Carmela, Mr. Monterano and the children. Emilio and Roberto had pooled their resources in money and had arranged with the café-keeper for steaming thick chocolate, a slow-pouring syrup-like drink, the richest *boccotoni*, cream-filled heavy *sfogliate*, and almond confetti.

The party was a huge success.

"Oh, you're a real actor, Emilio, and you, too, Roberto . . . and this little fellow, your friend . . . he is, too. You'll give the school a treat."

Emilio became voluble. He was elated with the praise, but insisted upon discussing every phase of the presentation.

"Do you like the way I twist my mouth and make faces?"

"Fine . . . fine. . . ."

"But do you think Roberto should look like me? Shouldn't he sort of screw up his eyes, and pull out his mouth, and look even more scared than I do?"

Carmela wondered.

"Sure, sure he should," Emilio persisted.

Mr. Monterano took a hand in the discussion.

"Of course he ought to be different. But if you can't coach him to be different, he has to try his best."

"No, it isn't that . . . he won't follow my ideas. See, I say, do this, like this, see?" Emilio spread his mouth into a wide slit, elongated his eyes, and in some way or another contrived to bring the upper part of his face and the lower much closer together than was normal. Everyone laughed.

"But, look, look, Carmela," he pulled at her sleeve as he called. "This is what he does. Watch now. See, like this."

He screwed up his face, puckered his lips, beaded his eyes, and at the same time managed to give his cheeks a suggestion of puffiness. Again they all laughed.

Roberto, a quiet lad and a real admirer of his energetic friend, laughed too, and made no effort to defend himself.

"All right," is all he said, "I'll try."

That evening Emilio followed Carmela about, asking endless questions, confiding untold things, offering assistance in whatever she was doing. He accepted Donna Sofia's invitation to eat with the Dauri family and without waiting to be directed took a seat next to Carmela. Between mouthfuls, he and Roberto laughed and giggled at everything said or done. The whole table was in an uproar of merriment, especially as Emilio found time between courses to give graphic accounts of school life, mimic the teachers, the principal, and his classmates.

"Look, Carmela, see, he's got a part middle and back, and in the back his hair looks like it was a butterfly stuck on his head, and he has whiskers right in front of his ears, and every time he talks they shake like feathers, and this is how he talks, see, like his nose was being pinched, and somebody else had stuck a cherry in his throat and he couldn't get it out. Like this, 'And now, children, always mind. Be ever so neat, and drink your milk. . . .'"

Emilio had stood up and had pressed his hands together and pointed them out as he spoke, holding his head down in a mimicry of solemn and austere dignity.

"But surely he teaches you good manners," Don Tomaso interrupted, "and it is not proper to make fun of your teachers behind their backs."

"You wouldn't dare do it under their noses, would you, Roberto?"

"You bet you wouldn't, they'd soak you one in no time."

That brought on a discussion of the Juvenile Asylum, in which Emanuele and Giovanni outdid each other in vivid narration.

"You got the strap there on your bare bottom, not a little ruler on your hand."

"And a pin stuck into you at night if a monitor didn't like you."

10

Evenings such as these were not numerous, however. For the most part Emilio kept to his own quarters, rearranged his collections, performed his homework at his own leisure, and saw little or nothing of Carmela, except in so far as she herself came downstairs and assisted him or Zia Anna in running the household.

With the Monterano children Carmela had many more contacts, but they were of a more natural kind. They came home from school, Roberto, Ernesto, and Gilda and almost immediately plumped themselves down anywhere in the workroom and studied their lessons. It had become understood that that was the established arrangement. There was no going downstairs unless the homework was first done to the satisfaction either of Don Davido, the mother, or Carmela. Ernesto, with his little peaked chin and eyes like a chipmunk's, buried himself at once in his books. It was not from any excess of zeal in his studies, however. In a half hour he had rushed to Carmela, thrust a sheet under her chin, cried, "Sure, it's done, I always get them right," and away he bolted, not to be seen or heard from again until time for dinner. Gilda would rather annoy the girls than do her work. She had to be driven into the sunshine. Her homework could always wait.

"Gilda, how do you get along at school?"

Carmela asked in vain. Gilda would rather tie ribbons and gather the paper petals into flower-like clusters than sit down to her daily stint of arithmetic. She shrugged her fat shoulders and flounced her little skirts saucily as she rummaged in the needle box for implements and materials.

Roberto was the only one of the three who took the work at school with becoming seriousness. He sat at the window, using a collapsible shelf for a desk. The first thing he did was to pile up his various books with extreme neatness, set out his paper, sharpen his pencils, and then lean over the desk, elbow on it, head in his hand, his fingers in his hair. The pose was so characteristic that at a much later date

Carmela associated it with difficult problems that worried him and threw him into fits of thought.

And yet Roberto was never too busy with his school work not to give up many an afternoon to shouldering huge packages of finished work and journeying downtown by elevated train to deliver them to various houses. On such afternoons he returned late for dinner, tired enough to be sent to bed after his meal. However, he insisted on staying up to complete his school work. He found these afternoons more profitable than the ones when he remained home. For the trip back and forth was long, and invariably he had a book under his arm, no matter how heavy the package of material, and there was enough time to read hundreds of pages. Dumas[6] provided him more sights than the thousand tenements that lined the route. By thirteen, he had devoured Cooper[7] and Henty.[8] He had ferreted out every life of Napoleon in the neighborhood libraries. His hair showed it. He allowed a good-sized forelock to fall over his forehead. Could he have planned it, he would have allowed even a noticeable corporation to develop. He contented himself with the habit of clasping his hands behind his back. Then he came upon chemistry and physics. In his moments of solitary study, he took poses like those he had seen in portraits of Faraday[9] and Maxwell.[10] But he learned so readily that he stuffed his mind with a hodgepodge of facts that he later found it beyond his powers of memory to thrust aside. The result was that he caused his teachers untold annoyance when he demanded answers to questions based on older and discarded theories. And yet, unlike Emilio, he made no egotistic display of his accomplishments. He was in reality shy to the point of silence and was moved to put questions to others only when definitely desirous of clarifying matters in his own mind. But like Emilio, eventually, and like his sister Gilda, he threw off all his defenses in the comfortable presence of Carmela, unbosomed himself of all his burdens, confiding his dearest ambitions and his most secret longings.

CHAPTER FIVE

1

Progress on the church was slow. Gennaro fretted and fumed.

"Every time you move you get something signed, every time you get something signed you peel off money from the pile, every time you peel off a thousand bills you got to collect a thousand more and every time you collect a thousand more you know you'll be able to collect a thousand less the next time. Nobody in America wants to go to heaven if it costs them money . . . bah!"

But plunging headlong into this added activity seemed only to create new energies in him.

"I got more than twenty-four hours a day, Struzzo."

"Oh, yes, you're the Almighty."

"Well, pretty near."

To his general beneficence toward the church, he added specific acts of charity—coal for families here and there, a wedding dress for the daughter of a worker, steamship money for the wife of a neighbor who could not send for her out of his own savings.

"Show-off stuff," his old friend Rocco commented. "I bet you he's raking something off on everything. He doesn't give without taking. Look at the houses he sold me. Tumble-down shacks that needed more money to fix up than they paid rents."

Gennaro approached him one day.

"Rocco *bello,* I never did thank you in person for the wine you sent when my Rosaria of blessed memory died. That was very good of you and Elvira."

"It's the least an old friend could do."

"And Elvira, she likes America?"

"It's where our children were born."

"Well, you're piling it up."

"Not so fast as others."

"There are those that would be thankful and set up a shrine to Saint Anthony or Saint Francis."

"The way a certain big shot is erecting a church, getting others to contribute."

"It's something, at any rate, my dear Rocco. There are some do things and some don't . . . and it's best for those that don't not to say much about others."

Rosaria's death had sobered Gennaro. Rocco understood that and realized that it was possible to badger him beyond the usual limits of his patience. He went a trifle beyond that point at this time. He particularly wanted to report to Elvira that for once at least he had let Gennaro know that he, Rocco, was not being deluded like the rest of the community.

"Anybody can be kind if he makes an honest cent or two out of it."

Gennaro stuck the pipe he was holding in his hand back into his mouth, glared at Rocco and then once again removed his pipe, and held it out, close to his fellow ragman's face.

"There was a time when I'd bash in your teeth, Rocco, for less than these careless words of yours. Death has a way of softening one's temper. But this I'll tell you . . . I have given you a lot as a penance already. I don't want to lay more on my soul and be forced to shell out more money to hush my conscience. By the thousand saints, you're a whining ass in need of the horse doctor. But take this from me now, stop your braying about the town, and just stick around your dear wife Elvira and don't venture many steps away from her apron-strings."

He thrust his pipe once more into his mouth, laughed in his throat, and walked off.

Davido Monterano was one of the first to feel the fervor of Gennaro's new enthusiasms. It happened a year or so after Rosaria's death. Something had to be done for Monterano and through Monterano he hoped finally for Carmela. The young woman, with her upstanding carriage and frank lovely face, her efficient ways, her affectionate companionship with all the youngsters of the Parterre, occupied a larger and larger portion of Gennaro's thoughts. Through the captain and his wife he had planned a brilliant career in business for Carmela.

The captain had prospered in New York. His wife's cleverness had resulted not only in a fine millinery establishment but even in a partial transformation of the captain himself—difficult as that task was.

Indefatigable, eager, she had dropped all the illusions of greatness inspired by her origins and her marriage. She saw the reality of her American life through no hope-tinged glasses, nor minimized her descent into the ranks of the workers with arrogant displays of nostalgia. Where her mother was buried, she never wearied of exclaiming, was the fit place for her children to grow up, to be married, and to die. And where should she go then? Back to Naples? No. America had received them living, America would receive them dead. And so she worked, and she caused her husband to work. She realized from the outset that it was from no love of effort nor of its rewards that Davido applied himself to the millinery business they had developed in their flat in the Parterre. Out of it Davido hoped not so much for individual comfort as for Roberto's future. It was to be the means of fulfilling ambitions, justifying himself in his own conscience, proclaiming himself capable of a great son if not of personal genius. And so he, too, applied himself.

The one indulgence the family of the Monteranos allowed themselves was the *cena*—the evening meal. Breakfast for the adults was but a cup of black coffee, at times with rum, and possibly with a hard sweet biscuit which they steeped in the strong liquor. The children had enormous chunks of black bread and coffee diluted with enough milk to render it a straw-like tan. They ate their lunch hurriedly—on the work tables, moving the material and equipment to one side. At the best, it was a larger edition of their breakfast, more coffee, bread and cheese, and fruit. But their evening meal was an affair that partook of a jubilee. They seemed joyful that they could eat.

They always found dozens of reasons for adding this or the other to their meal. Davido would walk the length of the avenue, swinging his cane importantly, in search of a special cheese, or if he heard of an importation of snails he would leave work early to make sure to obtain his share. He spent many evenings preparing his own cordials, while Donna Maria, seemingly untired from the day's exertions, thought nothing of pickling mushrooms and peppers, egg-plant and carrots, beets and onions. When they had tickets for the opera, they ate a light repast—possibly a dish of macaroni covered with cheese and tomato sauce, fruit, and coffee. On their return they put in two solid hours at the postponed meal of the day, running the gamut from an antipasto of salami, ham, peppers, and olives through meat with vegetables, and rich pastry topped off with coffee and cheese. Generous tumblers of wine washed it all down pleasantly, and the night was a comfortable season of sleep.

The family fattened—but especially Donna Maria. She had increased in bulk to the point where it was painful for her to move with ease from place to place. She discovered she could do her work in the same room where she ate, while the food could be prepared by one of the girls. This young woman would be released from her real task as a milliner several hours before closing time and sent into the kitchen. As reward she was permitted to have her meal with the family. Davido superintended not only the shop in front but the cooking in the back of their narrow railroad flat.

One day Dr. Giovanelli called for Signor Monterano, and induced that gentleman to don a special suit, select a dashing cane, and promenade with him along the avenue. It was warm enough for the doctor to unbutton his frock-coat, stick a hand in his pocket, and so reveal the great red sash of honor spread across his chest. As substantial citizens of the locality they were recognized by many, and their hats were always bobbing superiorly into the air.

"*Carissimo*[1] Don Davido," Dr. Giovanelli began, taking the captain's arm. "You must yourself have thought it surprising that I should ask you to take a stroll with me. I have never done it before."

"If it is to give me an opportunity of showing that I realize how patriotic . . ."

"Ah, no, ah, no. I am asking for no loan. I just managed to float one with my dear friend, Mastro Ciccio, you know, the grocer. . . . No, thanks to my friends who are willing to lend an old patriot on such easy terms, I manage, I manage. . . . No, it is not that. It is something not really to do with me . . . it is about your wife. . . ."

Davido's cane hung suspended on its upswing while he himself came to a dead halt. What could it be?

"You see, your wife has become enormously stout. . . . No?"

"But, doctor, what of it? It is no business of yours."

"Ah, yes, ah, yes, but it is."

He turned to face the husband, stroking the long flow of his beard with reflective gestures.

"*Bello* Don Davido, do not be alarmed. I was not alarmed on Aspromonte. . . . I saw my duty and I did it . . . you must, too."

Monterano became speechless. He moved his cane and free hand about in the air beseechingly.

"Let us walk . . . slowly," the doctor suggested and resumed his explanation. "You remember the other night. I spent the afternoon with you. I watched her closely. The puffs under her eyes—surely you have noticed them—they alarmed me, and she complained of a swollen foot . . . you recall? Well?" He held up his cane in both hands by way of climax.

"I recall, of course, but what of it?"

"I am afraid Donna Maria is developing serious symptoms."

"Symptoms of what? She seems happy, does her work. You should hear her sing in the morning, starting the girls off, it's a glorious moment."

Dr. Giovanelli thought fit to stop walking and turn to his companion.

"As a friend only, you understand. I am an old man now, and this is a country where they practice medicine differently. The time was I could hold my own with them all. I staunched the wounds of our great general—maybe that is not something to my credit. In the way of duty, mind you, not as is done in this beastly land, money down first, and then the cure, and what a cure it is apt to be! So I say, my good friend, your wife has serious symptoms . . . she complains of being tired, too."

Monterano gazed helplessly at the old doctor. He seized his cane in the middle with both hands and pumped it up and down as if to convey by that method the dread feelings that were starting up in him.

"But what is it, doctor, what is it?"

Giovanelli was as direct now as he had been roundabout in getting started.

"Your wife, I fear, has diabetes . . . the sugar sickness."

The captain still held his cane by the middle, aloft. For a minute he maintained the position.

"But that means death," he cried hoarsely.

Suddenly the pounding trolley, the cries of youngsters, the hawkers bawling, the whole chaos of a city street became a terrific din that deafened him into insensibility. He could only stare open-mouthed and wild-eyed while above the confusion about him he heard the word "diabetes," and following it, the echo, "Death. . . ."

Dr. Giovanelli took the man's arm and advanced several paces forward.

"Not really. We can put it off a long while. It means care, eternal care."

"Anything, doctor, anything."

"No wine, no meat, no macaroni . . ."

"But that does mean death . . . to go without all those things . . . it does mean death."

The announcement had come too suddenly for Monterano. He forgot to demand how the doctor could prove his statement. The only idea that came to his mind was to rush at once to the house and ask Donna Maria herself. Oh, he was going to do it skillfully. She would never learn

what all his questions meant. He would insist upon a thorough examination. But when he reached the foot of his stoop, he halted in fear. He
dreaded looking at Donna Maria. He would examine her to note the
puffy yellow bags under her eyes. He would glance at her feet to see if
they were swollen. He could not go upstairs and face her. He made an
about-face and ran away from the Parterre. Almost without knowing
why he had hastened to the door of Gennaro's rag and junk shop and
rushed in.

2

"Whey there, Monterano, what brings you here?"

Gennaro was in an expansive mood. The pipe stuck up at its
sharpest angle emitted assertive cloud-bank of smoke that screened
him effectively.

Monterano sat down quickly and leaned forward. Without preliminaries he plunged into an account of what he had just heard.

"You say, serious?" Gennaro inquired.

"If it's true, it means death."

Monterano forgot his dignity long enough to burst into tears. For
want of a better reaction Gennaro let his visitor weep.

"Oh, this is shameful, a soldier weeping, I, a soldier. . . ."

"We all do it once in a lifetime," Gennaro responded. "But listen
here. Why think the worst at once? People get sick, recover. . . ."

Monterano shook his head.

"No, Gennaro . . . no. Her father had it, too. You should have seen
him die. In a year, he went . . . what agony. . . . Poor Maria, poor Maria!"

Gennaro re-lighted his pipe slowly. It was best to let the man talk.

"What will become of me? Gennaro, what will become of us?"

"That's what is in his mind, hey?" Gennaro thought, but felt
ashamed the moment he realized it.

"She loves to live, Gennaro. A cup of coffee to her is a miracle. It
makes her happy. A new walnut—it's something that sets her heart
flaming. By the good Saint Stephen . . . it is a hard thing for her to die."

"Ah," Gennaro finally answered, "this is America, not Italy. The doctors here will cure her."

Monterano would not be convinced.

"Not this illness, sir, not this. It is death."

He rose to his feet and held out cane and palms as he had done with
Dr. Giovanelli.

"Maria dead!"

He spoke as in a trance.

"What will the end be? The end of us all? It is she who has worked. It is she who has done things. Without her, Gennaro, I am a lost man . . . and the children, the children! How shall I look after them? Gennaro . . . you must know . . . you, too, are a man without a wife."

Gennaro burst into a shout of contempt.

"Stop mewling like a kid," he cried. "She's not dead yet. And if she was, why, you'd go on with the business. Let's say she is dead . . ."

Monterano was listening. At least, so Gennaro thought. It seemed that he had found a way to ease the pain of the bewildered man.

"Well, then," he continued, "she's dead. In a manner of saying, I mean. Now what? Take my advice. You start out in business for yourself. Learn it all. Right now. Let your wife do nothing from now on. Rest she needs, and care. No worry. See? Come with me."

He gave the dazed man no time. With a shout to his workmen to announce that he was going out, Gennaro seized his hat and was rushing out of the dingy office, Monterano trying with difficulty to keep up with him. They reached the corner of the thoroughfare lined with the most pretentious brownstones. They had for the most part belonged to the established Irish and German families who had supported the half-dozen churches that faced the tree-flanked sidewalks. Tracks for a trolley were being laid and the macadam of the pavement was a powdery mass that left its stains on leaves, windowsills, and stoops.

"See this corner house," Gennaro exclaimed. "I'm buying it. See that other corner over there. Struzzo and I have bought that. Guess what's going to happen in that corner. A bank—a big bank is going to open in that corner. By Saint Jerome and the Holy Calendar, the Italians in this part of New York will be showing the Americans a thing or two. Yes, sir, yes, sir. With my church up soon, a bank here . . . we'll have a showplace. And now what do you think I brought you here for? Take this corner. I'm going to break that wall open, see, and make a store out of it—a wide, gorgeous store. And here's my idea. All the girls are beginning to go around like Americans with hats on their heads. See what I mean? You start a store. . . . In the back is the shop, you see, in the front you sell. Hats in the window, big electric lights, all fine. Hey, Monterano, a scheme, no?"

"It is," Monterano agreed, lost in the dream conjured up by Gennaro.

"There'll be money for you, plenty."

"Yes . . . if my wife will consent."

"Consent! She will have to . . . a sick woman. . . . Sure."

He rushed off, Monterano following. On the way, he stopped to shout out ideas that came to him. First it was the shop, then what doctor to call in, then about the three children, and who was going to look after them.

"I'll tell you, Davido, *mio bello,* I'll tell you. There's Carmela. A pretty girl that. But she has brains, too. You will take her in the business . . . part-owner with you, and manager . . . a fifty-fifty job. . . . I'll pay all expenses the first six months. We'll get it started. . . . With Carmela, the thing will go big. Sure. Come, we'll talk to her."

The dusk was coming on. As they neared the Parterre, they already smelled the rich cooking of the Monterano family. It filled the whole house like a mist of incense.

"Poor Maria," exclaimed Monterano. "She'll have to give up all that."

Gennaro shouted up for Carmela to come down. In the dining and sitting room in front of the kitchen Carmela sat stiff in her chair, facing Gennaro and her employer. At nineteen she was a large woman, rounded into a ripe fulness of beauty. Gennaro stared at her, speechless for a minute, his breath gone, unable to account for his silence.

"Hey, there, Zia Anna, some coffee . . . coffee for three of us."

Then he turned to his guests.

"Carmela," he called, "you know the hat business, no?"

"A bit," she answered, taken aback by the question and trying to puzzle out what was coming.

"She knows it very well," Don Davido interrupted. "As well as any of us. She is accomplished. . . ."

"Oh, Don Davido, hardly."

"Well, you know it enough," Gennaro announced as the coffee pot came out. "A bit of rum for me. And you, Don Davido, a bit for you, too?"

The coffee was poured, and they all took the small cups in their hands and blew on the steaming liquid.

Gennaro gulped his down at once.

"Carmela *bella,* we're going to move the hat shop. To One hundred and sixteenth Street. On the corner. We're going to make it big. You and Don Davido are going to manage it and own it."

Carmela looked stunned, and turned first to one then the other of the men.

"How can this be? There's Donna Maria. What will she be doing? I couldn't, I couldn't."

"She's a sick woman, Carmela, very sick, needs to rest. . . ."
Monterano tried to protest.

"You told me yourself," was Gennaro's comment.

"But supposing she isn't?"

"She is," Gennaro persisted. "A person as fat as that who eats as much as she does! Of course, she's sick. I want Carmela in this business."

The repercussions of the discussion reached throughout the whole of the Parterre. Don Tomaso, as well as Donna Sofia, was as stunned as the daughter.

"You're well enough off as you are," Don Tomaso asserted.

"Let things take their own course," Donna Sofia said in agreement.

"If it is true that Donna Maria is sick, I do want to help out," Carmela said. "I've noticed recently she has been always tired. In the evening especially. And she looks yellow, like a lemon."

"Don't go meddling," Donna Sofia persisted. "We have had enough of meddlesome people."

That night Donna Maria had her first attack. Dr. Giovanelli was right. While at dinner she complained of dizziness.

"It's all black, Davido, black."

He led her to her bed. The doctor was called in.

"As I suspected . . . as I suspected . . . tomorrow we examine the urine, and she must remain in bed."

Dr. Giovanelli rubbed his hands until his whole body seemed to warm up. Here was his first important case since Aspromonte. The sick woman, lost in the depths of a featherbed, looked at him beseechingly.

"Ah, Donna Maria, you must not be alarmed. Nothing serious, in all reality. We shall pull through. I did not fail my chief at Aspromonte. Shall I fail my dear friends now?"

3

Gennaro divided his time between the creation of the Italian millinery center and the erection of the church of Saint Elena, the Blessed. He rushed from one to the other several times a day. His short animated figure became a daily spectacle as he hurried through the market district, exchanging comments left and right with the push-cart vendors and the storekeepers.

It became necessary to have either Don Davido or Carmela accompany him on many of the visits to the millinery shop. Technical questions of space and arrangement, the mechanical equipment, the cutting-tables, the machines, the pressing-boards he could not settle by himself. It was not long before he realized that the captain had been properly dismissed from the army. Mr. Monterano was a delightful companion but an abominable organizer. Most of the time he spent with Gennaro he devoted to long and glowing expositions of the Monterano family and its importance in Italy, of the disastrous campaigns against Menelik ten years before, of his imposing colonel who had presented il Monterano with a pure ebony cane mounted in gold. If the weather should turn to a dark muddy murk, heavy with heat and clogged with moisture, he was reminded of Dante's description of the intolerable winds that blew Paolo and Francesca about in the regions of purple air.[2] A chance remark by a pedestrian, overheard above the noise of the streets, would stir untold associations in Monterano's memory. If he did not burst into long quotations from Ariosto,[3] he broke into impromptu doggerel of his own, flamboyant praises of the sun, the sky, the very noise of life.

"Ah, my marvelous Gennaro, you create energy within me, great and growing flames of life, as if my whole being is being remade in the furnace of American ideals. And it is, sir, it is. You have known how to subdue the inclement winds of adversity to your own purposes. That, I take it, is the American ideal, pinnacle of our modern thinking. You have shown those of us who derive from successful stocks of the aristocracy what indefatigable energies, applied to the service of an unbending will, can unfailingly achieve for one of lowly birth. Despite the fact that you have chosen to retain, unabashed and unembarrassed, the signs of your origin—your earrings, and I admire you immensely for your courage and independence—you have risen above the common herd, distinguished yourself by signal achievements. Take this store we are jointly creating. What a thought! The essence of business acumen! It moves the stars, Gennaro, and all the other worlds, for it is greater than all things, business ability, greater even than love."

Gennaro was realist enough to understand the difference between grandiloquence and actions. Talk of this kind set his teeth on edge. In his mind he reviewed the words and the acts of the lawyers and the mayors and the notaries and the landowners of his native Calabria and compared them with those of the important captain Monterano. The more he did so the more he believed in himself as the type of doer to whom all things finally must come. He began to feel uneasy and embarrassed in the company of Monterano. He wanted to tell that windy gentleman to take the next boat back home, and regretted having been taken in by him to the extent of going through with the millinery shop. Donna Maria, Gennaro knew, could have handled the enterprise and made it a going affair. There was the stuff of the doer in her. But she, poor thing, was now in pain. She had interposed no objections to the removal of her workshop from the top-floor of the Parterre to the spacious corner store on the avenue.

"It will be a grand thing, Gennaro, a grand thing for all of us. I do hope my husband will appreciate all you are doing for us. He will try. I know he will try."

Gennaro understood, and as the days passed he found one excuse after another for calling Carmela and not Don Davido to his assistance. The tall straight figure of Carmela became as well known on the avenue as that of Gennaro. The old story about her was raked up, passed on from mouth to mouth, so much so, in fact, that several of the young blades of the neighborhood began to have ideas. They tipped their hats over knowing smirks.

"What's the jackass after?" Gennaro demanded of Carmela, when one young man boldly accosted her, hat raised.

Carmela shrugged her shoulders and walked on.

One day the young pharmacist, Salvatore Manzella, sent a note to her mother.

"You do not know me," the note read, "but I am the gentleman who has opened a drug store on the corner near you. I am interested in your daughter in a serious way and should like to have you meet my mother to talk about it. I got a good business started, I am twenty-six years old, and I want to say that I am a sober man, and hard-working as all my good friends will guarantee. So if you will meet my mother maybe we can arrange it, and I should be glad, too, to come whenever you say and meet your daughter. She is a beautiful girl and I would not care if she had no money. If you will let me know soon, it will be a real kindness as I am in agony waiting for a reply."

"What kind of person is this man?" asked Donna Sofia of her husband.

Don Tomaso put a hand behind his head and scratched for a long time as he thought. He was getting gray and the hair in the front of his head was falling. This new gesture, his wife averred, was to assure himself that he still had some bit of hair remaining.

"Let me see, I bought something in the store the other day. Oh, yes, a plaster for my back. Gianni and I were in there. A nice fellow, a white-haired boy, an albino, I declare, eyebrows all white like fuzz, and little cat eyes, round and blinking and pink, and a sharp, very sharp nose, and he looks at you hard and answers in a nice deferential way . . . a nice boy."

Donna Sofia folded up the letter very slowly and placed it in the pocket of her apron. Without another word she went to the stove and turned the red peppers sizzling to the accompaniment of crackling sausages.

"We'll see what Gennaro thinks of it," she called out to her husband as he sloshed himself with water at the kitchen sink.

At the same time, Gianni and Giovanni banged the door wide open and shouting at each other and slapping each other's backs they stormed into the place. They were working one as a carpenter and the other as a mason on the same job, and returned each night in the wildest mood of horseplay.

"Sit down, both of you, and keep quiet for a second, I got something important on my mind and want your advice."

There were times the big-boned youngsters knew when their mother was in earnest. They evidently felt so now, and each took a seat. Gianni had grown into the bigger boy of the two. Just turned seventeen, he was big-shouldered and heavy-chested and insisted upon wearing a mustache, a device that made him look older and bigger. Giovanni was big-boned, too, but he ran to thighs and legs. Both of them had masses of the thickest black hair and eyes equally black. They had regained a smattering of Italian, just enough to talk to their mother. Dressed in their Sunday best, despite their swarthy features and the jet of their pupils, they could have passed for young American mechanics.

"Sounds awful, ma. Go ahead. What's on your mind?"

"What do you know of this druggist on the corner?"

"Why?"

"What do you know?"

"I hardly ever said even hello to him," Giovanni confessed.

"But you heard things about him?"

"No."

"All right . . . here's dinner ready."

They ate.

"Why all the questions?" Gianni wanted to know as he stuck pieces of sausage and peppers together and stuffed them into his mouth.

But Donna Sofia said nothing. She hoped Gennaro would drop in that evening. As a matter of fact, he was just returning from the new store. Carmela and he had just inspected the counters being put up in the front part, and tested the new gas-heated pressing apparatus installed in the rear. Carmela opened the door with the decisive gesture with which she did everything.

"Come in, Gennaro," she called, "and eat a bit with us."

Gennaro followed quietly. For a minute both Donna Sofia and her husband were surprised at this sudden exhibition of quiet movements on Gennaro's part. There was never a time when he did not burst in without ceremony and shout at the top of his voice.

"We've just been looking over the new store," Carmela explained.

"Yes, and what a store it will be," Gennaro added.

Donna Sofia laid out two more plates. The younger children had already eaten and were now inside quarreling and shouting over their homework. Donna Sofia dispatched the two older ones to the front room to keep the peace and compel them to study.

Gennaro had just drunk a full glass of wine and smacked his lips in approval.

"Sausages, pepper, and wine . . . the grandest dish."

"What do you know about this new druggist?" Sofia asked.

"Hey? The new druggist? Oh, yes, a fine boy."

"He comes from a good family . . . no?"

"Like my own. People from the country. They've made America, all right. Yes, nice people."

Don Tomaso began to show his irritation at these tactics of his wife. He could see no reason for the sudden outburst of excitement she manifested and would much rather have taken the whole thing calmly. He had studied his daughter carefully ever since she had returned from the Juvenile Protective Asylum. During the two years and more, she had grown into a steady, serious-minded young woman who seemed more interested in the work she was doing as a milliner than in anything else. There had been other offers for her hand which he had induced his wife to keep from her. There was no telling how many young men had approached her personally. After all, she was a beautiful young woman and attracted attention wherever she went. She had gone for the past year to an evening school where she had studied not only English but also hat-designing. She had spoken of several men who had insisted upon walking home with her. But her manner of referring to them had reassured him from the first. Her experience as a child and her three years in the asylum had given her a weight and a dignity which proclaimed her self-sufficient, thoroughly able to take care of herself. If she had a mind to marry she would bide her time and choose her own man.

Certainly she would not be inclined to respect her mother's desire that she marry in the manner of the old country, allowing her mother to select the most eligible of the young men and accepting him as a matter of duty. And here was Donna Sofia now, agitated out of her skin by this new offer! Let her watch her step, he thought to himself.

He was relieved and at the same time made even more fearful when Carmela asked, "Why all these questions? Who is the young man anyhow?"

Gennaro looked from mother to daughter, then saw the serious expression on Don Tomaso's face.

"Say," he shouted, "you don't mean he's been asking for your daughter?"

Donna Sofia betrayed the truth in her embarrassed laugh.

"Yes, he has sent me a letter."

"You?" Gennaro queried. "The goat. . . . Hasn't he got spunk of his own? Say, we're not in the old country now—let him come over himself, I say, and talk to the girl."

Carmela rose from her seat.

"And tell me, ma, since when do we discuss such things . . . like this in public?"

"Oh, I'm no stranger," Gennaro answered. "I'm one of the family. I was your father for a while."

He realized that he had muddied the waters rather than settled them. He felt the need of making other remarks in the hope of ending the embarrassed silence.

"Sure, that's why I can talk the way I do. Why, if I was the pup, I'd get to know you, I'd follow you up to your door, I'd bang on it until I got in, I'd up and tell the world I wanted you for my wife, and I'd lay down a stack of gold to prove to you that I had a right to ask, see, that's what I'd do."

He was making matters worse. On the faces of the whole family he saw the ravages of painful memories, but he could not stop. Always a forthright man, he had no capacity for measuring the intensity of his statements in proportion to the demands of any occasion. He continued blurting out his feelings.

"I'd do more than that."

He had an impulse that now he ought to try humor.

"I'd camp on your doorstep, and remain there all night. Sure, I'd sing songs for you . . . that's what I'd do. By Saint Jerome and all the thousand saints in heaven, you'd know I loved you!"

This tack did not work and so in the prevailing silence he stuck his unlit pipe in his mouth, rose to his feet, and paced to the far end of the room.

"Besides," he finally turned around angrily, "who is this pharmacist? A weak little puling cat looks like he never seen the sun all his lifetime, no color, nothing, got a voice like a sick baby ... *miiaa* ... *miiaa* ... like that. What you want to marry a man like that for, hey?"

Don Tomaso's pride of family, long dormant in the leveling atmosphere of America, began to play upon the impulses of his anger. In some manner he sensed that Gennaro had not meant to go to the extent to which he had reached, and that it was impossible for him to stop now without creating even more painful scenes. At the same time something had to be done to bring the situation to an immediate end.

"Gennaro *bello*," he called out sharply. "I will thank you if you say no more."

"No offense intended, dear Don Tomaso, let's get straightened out on that point. I intended no offense. You understand, Carmela? Sure you do. I expected you to understand. I admire you myself. I would not willingly—you know—with my heart—hurt you."

There was a rush of blood to his face. The wrinkled eyes flamed. Gennaro saw himself transformed.

Out of the hard-headed business man amassing a fortune, out of the lustful power-drunken reveler he had been, out of the disappointed disillusioned man, first a rebel against the conditions of his youth, then a seeker after something else besides the fortune he had made, he emerged, in the twinkling play of the rapid emotions flowing and surging within, the man he had always wanted to be, devoted to an objective beyond his reach and yet obtainable, filled with love and adoration for something earthly and yet touched with beauty and mystery. That was Carmela. In a crude, dramatic way now he seemed to understand one reason why he had turned against his son, Domenico, why he had failed to respond to the sad yearning love of his wife Rosaria, why he was so frantic in his efforts to justify himself in the eyes of Don Anselmo, and through Don Anselmo in the eyes of God. And therefore why should he not speak out? But he was overwhelmed by the force of his new perceptions. He trembled inwardly, and he felt his whole face redden.

"No offense," he blurted out. "*La voglio troppo bene a Carmela, sa....* I love her too much your daughter, you know...."

And there he stood, thrusting his pipe in his mouth and removing it immediately after, only to thrust it back once more.

He smiled awkwardly, and then turned to Carmela.

"Tomorrow we'll go over the amount we need for supplies," and without saying another word he left.

4

The Dauris looked at each other in silence and in dread. Carmela was the first to break the pause.

"At heart he's a decent man, no matter what he's done."

Donna Sofia flared up now that her daughter had spoken.

"He's a scoundrel at heart, all he can do is make money. Is there a decent thing he's done?"

Don Tomaso sat down and rested his head between his hands. He whistled low to himself.

Ever since the children had been placed in the Juvenile Asylum, Don Tomaso had rarely interfered with his wife's wishes and plans. She had taken the separation to heart so deeply that she had railed against him, against America, against Gennaro, against the church. "Imprisoned is what they are," she kept exclaiming. "Shut up like a lot of criminals. Who cares if they learn to be Americans and speak the language? They've been snatched from my breast, the babes!"

Don Tomaso was well aware now that Donna Sofia had been captivated by the respectful old-world note written by the pharmacist. She had been hoping ever since Carmela's return for a favorable match. Here was the opportunity come to hand. He realized with equal force, too, that Gennaro's words had not been just the words of any ordinary friend of the family much older than Carmela. "I love her," meant just what the words said. They were not just friendly, homely words. They were words of passion—the passion of an older man for a young woman, deprived for a long time of companionship. Tomaso whistled to give himself a chance to think. In the meantime he would not interfere in the discussion between mother and daughter.

"Ma," Carmela said quietly, "tonight I am going downtown to that designing school. Gennaro has been very good, and I want to see the millinery shop go big. For his sake, too, besides for the good people upstairs. Besides, it will be a good thing for me."

"You're a young girl, you don't need to work like that. Here's a nice man with a business, he wants to marry you. Why not? It's the place of a young girl to get married."

"We're not living in the old country."

"No, but a pretty girl is a pretty girl everywhere."

Donna Sofia crossed herself and then bit the side of her hand.

"I don't want to say anything. The good God give me strength not to say anything. But only this I must say, Carmela. They'll be after you, first one scoundrel like Gennaro and then another. You'll get no peace. . . ."

Carmela put her arms about her mother's waist and pressed her cheek close.

"You dear. What a way to talk. I can take care of myself."

She kissed her mother and went inside to her brothers. They adored her and she them, and she knew she could always have a few minutes of fun and relaxation in their company.

"And you sat there and never said a thing," Donna Sofia shouted at her husband. "You, the great man who was going to own half America in no time. . . . A pretty mess you've made of it."

Don Tomaso reached over for a piece of the cheese. He filled himself a glass of wine and drew up to the table. These movements angered Donna Sofia to the extent of forcing her to take a seat, draw it forcefully up close to her husband, lean over, arms akimbo, and cry out, "So, that's your answer? Ignore the whole thing, hey? You listen here. Carmela's too ripe a prize for some gentlemen in this country. She's got to be saved from them, you understand. We had enough of a scare once. That was bad enough. I want you to go right now and invite this Salvatore Manzella and his mother to come here Sunday."

Don Tomaso drank his wine slowly, listening attentively, but showing no emotion. When he was through, he set the glass down and drew his napkin across his mouth.

"It's not a bad plan," he consented mollifyingly. "If we were back in Villetto, I'd be the first to see it through. A girl would have minded her parents in Villetto. But you heard Carmela."

"She said nothing."

"No, nothing direct, I know. But she meant a lot. Do you suppose she would consent to this pharmacist chap? If I know her at all, she doesn't seem to want to have anything to do with men or marriage. You say we got a bad scare once. We did. And what do you think it did to Carmela? Tell me that."

Donna Sofia had no answer. She gathered up the dishes and placed them in the sink. Don Tomaso removed the checkered red table cloth and shook it out of the window, took a chair, and lighted his pipe.

"Ho, there," he shouted, and in a few seconds the younger boys had rushed into the room.

"There's your job ready," the father said. "Get those dishes cleaned up."

5

The next morning Mr. Monterano was not in a position to go to the store. It had been arranged that Carmela and he were to meet Gennaro and go over the list of purchases they were to make and draw up final plans for the opening of the combined work- and sales-shop. Small groups of shoppers and passersby stopped in front of the store and gazed in.

"Little Italy is making progress," many a man would say.

The women for whose benefit the store was being opened entertained more doubtful attitudes.

"Hats, no less. Won't our shawls do well enough? What a country? You got to tighten your dresses, and cut down your blouses, and then you got to stick a flower pot or a big bird on your head or you ain't nobody."

"You're in America now."

"The more should the good Lord protect us."

"Oh, well. We make a crust of bread here at least."

"But what have you with the crust, hey? Where's the good wine of the old country and the bit of cheese? Bread you have, if you slave, but for the wine you've got to be a sharp one to get a mouthful."

Donna Maria had not moved from her bed since her first attack of dizziness. Her feet had swollen to abnormal proportions, her energies had flagged to the point where she raised her arms with pain, and the fine clear color of her face had changed to a pasty yellow. She became frightened as much at the physical distresses of her disease as at the prospect of her death, the children motherless, and her husband, no matter how well-meaning, floundering helplessly.

"I know it's important for you to go, Davido, but you stay here. I am so much alone—the children all at school."

"There are the girls inside working."

"No . . . I don't hear them any more. I want to shut them out, out of my eyes, my mind . . . it's the last few months on earth, Davido, and I want you here with me always . . . Carmela can go . . . she knows what to do."

In the semi-dark room the tall figure of Davido Monterano, hat and cane in hand, looked even more somber and forlorn than the extended form of his wife in bed, the muscles of her face pulled with pain.

"How you talk, Maria. I shall stay, of course."

He put his things down on a chair and sat down, taking his wife's hand in his.

"You have a long time to live, and to enjoy America. We'll prosper in the store. With Gennaro's backing, surely we'll prosper."

Carmela came in from the room where the five milliners were working. She wore a small jacket that flapped off her hips and fitted close about her bosom, outlining her large full figure and its pleasant roundness. Over her mass of reddish hair, pompadoured in front and pulled up sharply from her nape, was a large hat with a dark-blue plume swung debonairly across it. She breathed her adolescent vigor into the sick room and by contrast lifted the heavy sick frame of her employer into dread relief.

Davido Monterano looked up and shuddered. It was as if for the first time in the three years he had known the growing girl he had witnessed the full quality of her beauty, and he shuddered. He shuddered because he was quick to realize that Carmela's charms had become exciting in the presence of Maria, sick now and revealing the first signs of a wasting that was destined to be rapid and final. As life was going out of Maria, the full tide of its appeal was mounting in Carmela. He turned away his head with a sense of shame and placed his lips in the palm of his wife's hand and kissed her.

"Carmela, darling," said Maria. "You must represent us today. I just cannot let Davido go . . . let him stay here with me."

"Why, yes . . . you are not very well today then?"

Carmela asked the question with fear in her eyes.

"The whole world seems slipping away, swimming off from my eyes. You remember how we looked for the ships at sea? You crossed over, too, and you were old enough."

Carmela went up close to her, and leaned over the bed.

"Yes, I do . . . but you mustn't talk this way . . . you will be well. . . ."

"And remember how a ship came up and then passed us and then it slipped down and away, out of sight, and left us alone once more . . . so it is, so it is. . . ."

She wept, and Davido wept. Carmela did not know which one to comfort first. She leaned over the sick woman and dried her tears and kissed her cheek. Monterano's hand she took in hers and squeezed.

"No, Don Davido, no, you will see, it will be all right."

The man did stop weeping, and gazed at the girl. Again her ripe young beauty danced before his eyes. It bewildered him, and it frightened him again.

But the girl was calm and possessed, unaware of the impression she was making. He passed the back of his hand across his eyes.

"Carmela, you better go. Gennaro will be waiting for you."

When she had left, Maria turned to her husband.

"She is a peach tree in full bloom," she whispered. "I have noticed her as she grew. What a lovely, lovely child."

"Yes, a real type, a real beauty."

"And capable, Davido, how capable. She will manage very well for you."

6

The mid-October days were warm and bright. The push-cart market through which Carmela had to make her way to the new shop rioted in its abundance of fruit and fish, colorful vegetables and racks of tin-pans and stalls of cheap crockery, long carts stuffed with remnants of silks and woolens. The sun enriched their tinges and their shapes, but it also gave their odors, single and harmonized, a heavy mellowness. Depressed as she was at the sight of her friend and employer lying helpless in bed, Carmela walked through this maze without much interest. But she was stopped so often by friends of Gennaro and acquaintances of her father that she made slow progress. The scents and the sights bore in on her, the unusual keenness of the sun touched her cheeks with pleasure, and the central vigor of her youth was aroused. She had dismissed from her mind the scene of the previous evening—Gennaro with his sudden exclamation of admiration for her, the letter of Salvatore Manzella.

"*Oh, ch'e' bello,*"[4] she heard the fishmonger as he raised his hawker's cry, and held up a fish with open gills.

"It certainly is nice," she turned around to say.

The old fellow, with a neck like a flattened accordion, was overjoyed.

"It is beautiful—hey, oh, beautiful," he sang out the words, and then, smitten with the girl, he cried louder than ever, "And look, and so is she, and so is she. Oh, what beauty in the world, oh, look what beauty in the world!"

She hurried. But not fast enough. At her side walked Salvatore Manzella, a thin anemic young man with flat buttocks and narrow rounded shoulders. He was raising his hat when she turned to look at him. She had made purchases in his drugstore and so recognized him at once. She flushed.

"It's not like we are strangers," he said as he quickened his steps with hers.

"Well, no," is all she answered as she walked on even faster.

"I mean. . . ," he stammered as he, too, flushed up to his white eyebrows. "I mean, pardon me . . ."

"Yes. . . ." But she did not turn.

They walked on for some seconds in silence.

"Signorina, if you will only say a word. . . ."

"Good-morning, signore."

"You see," his voice was deep, despite his small chest, as if it were part of an extensive cough. "You see, I wrote your mother. Your mother told me you know about it. So I left the store, hoping to see you. You see, I saw you passing so I thought why not, and I talked to you. I mean, I wanted you to know . . ."

"Mr. Manzella, of course I am pleased to know. You are kind, but please leave me now, and do not write again."

The young man reddened even more than before.

"I have been hoping for so long."

She was glad that they had reached the store. Its broad plateglass windows sparkled in the sunlight. The workmen laying the mosaic threshold moved away on their knees to make room for her.

"Good-bye," she cried in a low voice, and left him standing, a gray thin shadow with hat raised.

Gennaro's voice was all over the place. He was shouting at the workmen imbedding into the mosaic floor deep show-cases that were to receive the hats Carmela was to make. In the sun his hair looked jet black in spite of the gray that was beginning to streak it. But more than his hair, his earrings stood out bright and shining. For the first time, Carmela saw them as not incongruous ornaments. They seemed part of the man, and she felt the strength in him that laughed at those who thought him laughable because of them.

Salesmen began arriving at once. They were busy all the morning with their ordering. When the men had left, Gennaro, animated into greater vigor by the exertion of commanding the workmen, shouting out approval at each suggestion of the salesmen, despite Carmela's insistence upon caution and moderation, turned at once to Carmela and yelled at the top of his voice, "A great day, Carmela, a great day! We open up soon."

"And now I had better go back. The girls will need me."

"Donna Sofia is still in bed then?"

"She's very sick."

Then, for seemingly no reason whatever, Gennaro took Carmela's hand and asked her almost at the top of his voice, "You're glad you're moving here, aren't you? You'll be your own boss."

"But the place is to be the Monteranos!"

"Yes, and no," was the answer. "An excuse only. I want you here to be the boss. He's an old fool. With his wife sick or dead he'll be a worse fool. A big bag of wind, that chap, kicked out of the army he was for it. Talks big, but he's got no sense. He make America! By Saint Jerome, no talking idiot can make America, he's got to have the guts—like me. I'm sorry for his children. Nice kids."

"Oh, I can't, I can't," Carmela whispered.

"Can't, can't? Can't what?"

"Come here the way you said. It won't be fair. Mr. Monterano has put his whole heart into it."

"What of it? So have you, so have I. We'll tack his name up there. He'll have a job here, sure, but it'll be you, you'll be the brains. . . . It wasn't going to be like this. It just came to me. I wanted to put him up in business. He's of fine stock, so he says. He is. A gentleman like, and his wife's nice. I like her, and the children . . . that boy, Roberto, for instance . . . very bright. How he studies! Sure, he'll be the boss—on the window like, you know. But you'll be behind it. You are the real boss. I saw it all when he and me tried working up this place. A wind-bag, but you have the stuff, see . . . and you own the business. It's yours. We'll pay him off."

He took her hand again and shifted off to another tack. If his attitude toward her had surprised her the previous evening, it frightened her now.

"I like you, Carmela. I like you . . . by Saint Jerome and the Holy Calendar, you're the kind I ought to have had from the first."

Something in Gennaro's heat and eagerness evoked the figure of Domenico—his debonairness, the utter self-centeredness of his passion, the animal-like directness of his demands. She stepped back, scared.

"Carmela, when I saw you—six years ago and more—you were beautiful then, too. . . . I know what you think . . . but don't . . . I'll not bother you after this. You just say keep your damned mouth shut . . . see . . . and I will . . . what's happened is between us . . . but I, I love you. . . . Saint Jerome pray for me, I love you."

7

After the first weeks of intense fear, Donna Maria had come to realize that it was possible, despite the sugar in her body, to continue living for a long time. In fact, she was busy calculating the expense of a trip to

Italy. There she would hie herself at once to the famous mineral baths; on the money she would take with her, once more would she live like a *signora per bene;* have a little villa off the main spa, an attendant or two constantly administering to her comfort, and so would look forward to a return to America, a well woman, plunge once more into the fine business that Carmela and her husband were making of the millinery shop, and end her days in delightful affluence, her children married and established. On occasions she would pay a visit of several months to her own home in Castello-a-Mare, equipped to stun the town, sporting the newest American styles and showing off her grand-children to the astonished world.

Possessed of good common sense, she had understood that Dr. Giovanelli, of whose merits as a physician she had made just appraisal from the very beginning, was enjoying her illness rather than contributing to her welfare. To him it had come as a dramatic event. He found it perpetually self-inspiring to expatiate upon the manner in which he had discovered it, and moreover he derived unlimited self-satisfaction in outlining in minute detail the probable course of the disease, employing in the progress of his oration on the subject such lengthy and recondite terms as to scare his listeners into states of inward paroxysms. At such times Donna Maria would give herself up for lost. But she repressed her greatest fears, in a genial parade of brave and exultant plans. Her husband, however, completely bewildered by the turn of affairs, harbored the most paralyzing dread.

Dr. Giovanelli came daily, and although he followed minutely the prescribed methods of treatment, undid all his good work by stressing the nature of the symptoms, the probable oncoming of coma, the distressing loss of vitality, the not unusual development of gangrene in the body extremities, and all the various secondary phenomena of torture that the disease displayed.

"Ah, my dear friends, my dear friends," he exclaimed one morning, "I must counsel you against any form of worry. It would not become me, a physician who administered to the great general Garibaldi in his high moment of combined wounds and victory, not to exert all my energies in behalf of even the humblest patient. And so I cannot overstress, you understand, Donna Maria, the importance of serenity, of calmness. You do not wish, I am sure, nor does your good husband, to see you in the collapse of a coma. Ah, no! ah, no! And so, no worry. A strict diet, mind you—no macaroni, no bread, no *dolci*[5] . . . but above all, cheer, cheer, always cheer. What care we then for lipaemia, for choroeditis . . . ah?"

Donna Maria had gone him one better, as a matter of fact. She followed Giovanelli's directions all too rigorously. In several weeks she looked shriveled into fantastic thinness.

"But I feel better, my good doctor. It's this thirst, though . . . this interminable thirst. . . . I could drink the Atlantic dry . . ."

"Ah, my dear," the old patriot said, ecstatically, as he rubbed both her hands in his, "ah, my dear, but you are doing beautifully, beautifully."

Donna Maria made up her mind to attend the opening of the millinery shop. Gennaro had momentarily relaxed his attentions to the church-building and was devoting all of his energies to the humbler enterprise. The day of the opening was to be in his finest form of entertainment. The societies of the order of Saint Jerome and Saint Elena were to march, and there was to be the usual fanfare of bands and fireworks. Donna Maria had no intention of missing it.

An added interest attached to her getting up and being about. Don Davido had received a letter from his old colonel. Colonel Umberto di San Martino was now retired, had been retired for several years. In his lengthy letter he had bemoaned the fact that a hearty upstanding man like himself should be compelled to spend his last decade or two of life in utter idleness. But always and always his main concern had been to assist the fatherland to achieve the undoubted grandeur that was implicit in its history and development. Italy, the land of beauty and of the arts, had need of the aid of all men. He, for one, had decided to devote his last years to the glorification of one portion of the marvelous peninsula. In the small town of Castello-a-Mare from which they both came, he had reason to believe existed some of the finest examples of the art of Italy during the past several centuries. He reaffirmed his belief by careful investigation, and his discoveries simply went beyond even his most sanguine expectations. He had collected, at great cost it must be asserted, a group of paintings by masters of the eighteenth and early nineteenth centuries. Valuable canvases they were. He was now on his way with them to New York. Without doubt Don Davido was acquainted with important people in that large and wealthy city who would be only too anxious to acquire such remarkable representations of the noble art of Italy. Don Davido could expect him in the next few weeks, as he was sailing at once.

The effect of this curious letter on Don Davido was one of immediate well-being. It was as if for his whole life he had been awaiting just the moment of di San Martino's arrival in New York.

"Ah, *cara* Maria, you must be well, up and about, when my old commander places foot on these shores. It will be a great day for me. How I long to see the dear man!"

Roberto, now thirteen years old, plied his father with questions about the colonel. Gilda, a fat-legged child with plaited hair hanging down her back, insisted upon knowing what the colonel looked like. Ernesto, unlike his brother and sister thin, morose-looking, who never at any time showed much eagerness for anything except the amount and quality of his meals, merely lifted his eyes off the paper he was scribbling on and listened.

"As an engineer, the colonel must understand mathematics," Roberto asserted. He was to enter high school in six months and considered himself a learned fellow.

"And he must have big mustaches and a beard maybe," Gilda cried.

"Both things are correct," their father assured them.

"And has he been in any war?" Roberto wanted to know.

"In the hapless war in Abyssinia.[6] He was one of several dozens—yes, dozens—who escaped from the butchery the Negus Menelik inflicted upon a whole army corps. What a dreadful experience . . . dreadful. The good colonel can tell you the story himself. He is capital at narrations."

"Is he a big man, papa, like a real soldier?"

"Big? No. A slight man . . . very small, really, Gilda. But you will know he is a soldier at once the way he stands, straight, shoulders out, head high."

The whole family hoped that the colonel would arrive just before the opening of the shop. Then they could merge the two celebrations into one. Donna Maria was determined that she, too, must take part in it. So she called another physician, a young Italian by the name of Rosillo, who took himself if not as importantly as Dr. Giovanelli, at least with such seriousness as to preclude any display of good humor. A stout little fellow, he had a round puffed face that was always slightly red. He said but a few words, affirmed the diagnosis, prescribed the same treatment, but assured Donna Maria that she had a long life ahead of her.

"Daily examinations for three months, signora. No sugar, no bread, no *pasta*. Live otherwise as you always have. Rest, of course."

The whole family was relieved and looked forward to the day of the great celebration. Donna Maria laid in supplies for the colonel, assisted in the dismantling of the shop in her front rooms, bought new furniture in keeping with the impression they all desired to make on their military guest and as befitted a household whose head now owned a great business. Carmela devoted all of her time to the store, but she found opportunity to visit Donna Maria and help her with the refurnishing of her home. Mr. Monterano lived in perpetual ecstasy, first because of the coming of his commander and second because of the rapid completion of the business. He skipped from his home to the store with extraordinary frequency, swinging his cane in perfect abandon, shouting good-mornings and bowing gingerly to everyone who merely glanced at him, acquaintance or not. But an even subtler sense of importance crept into the attitudes of the captain at this juncture. He was thrown into constant contact with Carmela. The first reaction he had had to the sudden recognition of her beauty was to forget about it. He was getting on in years, he had a wife and children. Carmela and he were to be together a great deal. It would never do to allow himself to think about the charm of the budded young woman. Nevertheless, it was not a simple matter of the will.

8

They had worked late into a November twilight. The glass of the showcases had to be washed to a high polish. The nickel along their edges had to be even more lustrous. Huge cases had to be unpacked, the contents noted, the stock set out in the shelves, and the windows had to be dressed. All the girls had worked the whole of the day. Gennaro had bobbed in and out, shouting with joy at the progress that was being made. Now as the light was going out of the sky, the girls had left, and Carmela, in the rear room, was putting on her hat.

Monterano had just thrown the bolts in the front doors, turned off the lights, and entered the rear room that was to be the shop just as Carmela's arms were raised to her head as she inserted the hatpin with one hand and held the hat with the other. She stood in the path of the only clear light in the place, a broad stream of gray that came from the translucent glass in the rear door. He stopped short. Her fine bosom outlined in the dusk, her statue-like body, the contours of her arms and shoulders, stimulated feelings beyond the resources of his will.

"Carmela," he cried, "*sei bella.*"

It was a clear cry out of the silence, and filled with an admiration that was unmistakable. He heard himself as it filled the room, and he stepped back amazed. He was startled more because of the effect it might have on the girl than the fear that came into his own heart.

"I am sorry," be whispered. "What a thing for me to say. But more and more I see how beautiful you are. Just now I could not help it. I had to shout it out. Carmela, I should shout it out to the whole world. But I must not. I must not...."

Carmela turned to him, pleased and frightened both.

"Don Davido," she said, "do not let us stay here longer. It is getting so late. We must never again work so late."

They left together and proceeded to the Parterre in silence.

He felt a pride in walking beside her. He held his chin higher and swung his cane with greater decision. All night the feeling continued, coursing through him like the heat of a light wine, spreading through his dreams with a quiet radiance as if he had become an adolescent once more and was enjoying the pleasure of a new and confident love. "A true beauty," he kept telling himself, "a heavenly creature that deigns to walk in these wretched places of the earth."

9

The colonel kissed Donna Maria's hand with an elaborate bowing of his body. When he straightened himself it was to seize the long ends of his mustaches and caress them affectionately to the very tips, tips that extended to the line of the chin. They were the hugest thing about him of a physical nature. Nothing was huger than his conceit. But he had brought over with him a whole parade of memories, and the elder Monteranos at least felt grateful. They spent the whole evening after the dinner in his honor in nothing but talk of the times when they had all been stationed with the troops and social life was glitter and show from one year's end to the other. The colonel never spoke without clearing his throat, so much so that Gilda took up the mannerism and the whole hour before falling asleep she devoted to the exquisite pleasure of mimicking him before her brothers. Gales of laughter broke in on the solemn reminiscences being recounted in the other end of the apartment.

Donna Maria's pleasure was unbounded. She made the most of it. The laughter and charm of the meal more than the simple starch- and sugar-free foods she had allowed herself restored her animation. She spoke definitely of making the Italian trip. But it was not until Don Tomaso came up with his wife, and not until then, that she began to feel the utter fulness of her joy.

The colonel, a short man like Gennaro but wiry and sharp-nosed, with mustaches like a Mongolian, jumped to his feet with comical alacrity on the sight of Carmela. He bent stiffly from his hips, and when he rose he stroked his mustache as if licking his chops. Donna Sofia threw a sharp glance in his direction and wanted to inquire who the queer popinjay was but thought better of it. Don Tomaso plunged at once into flattery and outdid even his host in florid descriptions of the colonel's calling, the colonel himself, and his mission in New York. In fine fettle, the military gentleman felt called upon to display his wares. The children had been compelled to go to bed, but Roberto had been given secret permission to rise once the others were asleep and join the adults. He and Gennaro happened to open doors at the same time and just at the moment when the colonel, expostulating volubly upon the remarkable quality of his canvases, was in the act of displaying the first picture. It proved to be a fleshy Venus surrounded by equally fleshy Cupids floating in an indistinguishable welter of blue waters under roseate mists.

"What's that?" Gennaro shouted without waiting for preliminaries. "A picture for a brothel?"

The colonel straightened up.

"I do not know who the gentleman is," he answered brusquely, "but from all appearances he seems to lack any understanding of art."

"No offense intended," Gennaro laughed awkwardly, pulling his pipe out of his mouth, "but I got just as good stuff on my walls."

Donna Maria saved the evening by performing a quick series of introductions, mentioning in passing how eminent a figure Gennaro was among the well-to-do Italians of New York.

"Ah, really, really?" the colonel inquired, stroking his mustaches. "If that is the case, you must let me show you indeed what exquisite things I have brought with me. And I hope, sir, I shall have the honor of selling you one or two?"

Gennaro shrugged his shoulders incredulously.

"What do you think, Carmela?" he asked by way of stating his own position.

"I think they're lovely, but what do I know of art?"

She blushed as she saw the eyes of all the men turn to her eagerly.

"They are lovely, most lovely maiden," the colonel responded, making another deep stiff bow. "The lovely should possess the lovely."

"It is as if Dante might have said *Amor che a null'amato amar perdona* . . ."[7] Don Davido interrupted, pleased to be able to interject a line from his famous poet, no matter how incongruous or far-fetched, and admiring quite openly the happy phrase of his former commander.

Gennaro felt too much out of it, and sat himself down next to Carmela. The little Roberto wandered to a corner and looked on the scene with enormous eyes, kindled not only by the sight of the colonel but also by the sight of the pictures that that gentleman busily placed about the room. There were half a dozen, all small enough to be carried under the arm, and all on classic themes sterile in conception as they were rococo in execution.

Surrounded by so many people, the colonel felt disposed to orate on the exhibition at great length. Donna Maria was at her wits' end, for she saw at once that Gennaro was terribly bored and could not be held back much longer from making some outburst or other. Don Tomaso, however, was immensely interested and followed the colonel's remarks attentively.

"You ought to be able to sell these to any millionaire. The problem is getting to see them."

"We'll manage that, hey, captain?" the colonel declared quite solemnly. "You and I will start out tomorrow, and let me tell you we'll come back with a fabulous sum . . . we ought to get ten thousand apiece . . . ten thousand is nothing . . . nothing for these grand, unusual masterpieces."

"Tomorrow nothing," burst out Gennaro.

"And why not?" the colonel asked.

"Davido is to be at the store where he belongs when it's opened," Gennaro answered. "He'll be sure of his bread and butter there."

"So?" The little colonel looked around offended. But he realized the ridiculousness of changing the plans about the store and contented himself with suggesting the day after.

"Not even then," Gennaro insisted. "It'll be the first big sales, and he'll have to be around . . . and the day after too . . . no fool business of calling on millionaires . . . bah!"

"But this gentleman is insulting." The colonel held himself erect, red in the face, hands trembling in mid-air.

Donna Maria stepped forward.

"He really means well, my dear colonel. Davido will have to stay in the store for a while . . . Let us have some of these excellent cordials . . . Come, come, Davido, get the glasses, let's get them poured."

She drank with the rest.

"Why not? One glass won't harm."

She ate some of the hard sweet cakes. She even demanded another glass of the fine *strega*,[8] and followed it with a glass of anisette.

"*Un biscottino*[9] with this," she pleaded of her husband. "How can one drink anisette without a bite of a cookie, hey, tell me that?"

The colonel expanded.

"Listen here," he cried. "I have bought some real *rosolio*[10] from Naples, and two flasks of the finest *Lachrymae Christi*[11] . . . Let's open them tonight and drink to the pictures."

"And the store," Gennaro added.

"And Donna Maria's continued good health," Carmela climaxed.

Cheese was brought out, and whole salamis. Gennaro went downstairs and returned with flasks of wine that he asserted were unsurpassable. He had Roberto run to the café on the corner and have a whole tray of the finest *dolci* brought over at once.

Donna Maria drank and ate with the rest. Her husband rubbed his hands effusively.

"It's like the old days, colonel, the old days of merriment when we had gala parties nightly, and the wine flowed, and there was dancing. Come, let us drink."

He burst into the drinking song from *Lucia*,[12] and followed it up at once, just as soon as the applause had subsided, with an army song, and then the *brindisi* from *La Cavalleria*.[13] He bowed to the applause. "A really excellent opera, that, my dear colonel . . . I have not seen it yet . . . but they say the young composer himself will soon be here in New York. We shall all go. No? There will come with him his lovely prima donna." He turned to Carmela, abruptly.

"Ah, you are more beautiful than any prima donna, you are beauty made real, you are heavenly."

"Hey, there," shouted Gennaro, "going crazy?"

"And why not? Why not? Who would not go crazy over such a marvelous creature?"

The colonel clapped his hands.

"Very well said," he cried, "very well said, captain."

"Very well said, nothing," shouted Donna Maria and slapped her husband smartly on the cheek.

She followed it with another slap on the other cheek.

"I never thought to live to see such a day. In my very presence, under my nose, making love to . . . to . . . Now I know it, once a woman tastes it, always she wants it."

She screamed at the top of her voice. It was so unlike her that everyone was too dumbfounded to speak. Roberto, alarmed at the wild tones, ran to his mother and cried helplessly, "Mama, mama."

Don Davido turned from one person to another, his hands stretched out pleadingly. All he could say was, "She is sick, she is sick."

Don Tomaso and Donna Sofia rose to their feet.

"Come, Carmela, we'll go."

"No wonder you spent hours at the store," shrieked Donna Maria. "Get out of here, get out of here, all of you . . . low-downs, the lot of you. You see, colonel, you see what good families get, mixing with a crowd of country yokels . . . you see, get out . . ."

"The fool woman's crazy," Gennaro shouted. "Drag her to bed, Monterano, and sit on her. That's the way to handle that kind."

Donna Maria was about to turn on him. She opened her mouth to speak. But a thick viscid spume of saliva gathered at the ends of her mouth and strung like gum from lip to lip. The color went completely out of her skin. It had become cold-looking, parchment yellow. She tried to raise her arms, but they would not flex. Before anyone could go to her assistance, she had fallen to the floor in one piece, as if her knees had refused to crumple under her and her fingers would have broken with keen torture had she tried to ease herself down. Her eyes were wide open but unseeing, uncoordinated, focused nowhere, blood-shot and yet not red, only a diluted pink. Hoarse outpours of breath, forced out with increasing noisiness, were the only visible sign of energy in a body that had once been a vibrant eager bulk.

"She—phewed up, you know, like yeast, and then—she phewed down. A chunk of shrunk dough."

That is how Gennaro described it later. He was the only one present who knew enough to call for a doctor.

"Put her in bed, I'll go and fetch Giovanelli."

10

Davido remained at her bedside the whole night and the whole of the following day. Carmela helped with the children and saw them off to school. When Gennaro came to fetch her to attend the opening celebration for the millinery shop, she said simply, "I ought to stay here."

"Well, you aren't staying. She's as good as dead, and what can you do? We got to live if we're living. It's too damned bad."

"There's so much to do . . . their guest . . ."

"By Saint Jerome, he'll look after himself, the old plucked rooster. . . . Zia Anna'll be here soon, and the girl that used to help cook, you know, Rosinella."

One band at the head of the society of Saint Jerome and one band at the head of the society of Saint Elena, proceeding from opposite directions, fifteen blocks or so away, finally met at the corner of the street where the *Cappelleria*[14] *Monterano* displayed its gold-lettered windows and its dozens and dozens of hats, each upon a stand, rising from a broad base to a sharp apex. As the bands joined in a combined outburst of Italian and American patriotic selections, Gennaro was busy superintending the laying out of hundreds of yards of cracklers and detonators. At his signal a fuse was to be lighted, and immediately after a thunderous proclamation, couched in terms of gunpowder, was to mark the formal opening of the business.

Crowds had collected. When they were sufficiently large to suit his purpose, Gennaro drew a string. From the double-doorway there fell off a canvas curtain that had been shrouding it. The doors were thrown wide open despite the late fall chill. The figure of Don Anselmo in full cassock and beret with a surplice and censer in hand marched solemnly up and down the store. The words of his Latin benediction were loud and intoned in all the sacredness of the mass. As he moved past the door, choir boys followed him, singing softly; and bringing up the rear, stunning in a tight-fitting, full-length dress buttoned in the back from neck to hem, Carmela walked, and behind her the girls who were to work in the shop. After they had paraded back and forth two or three times, Gennaro, his pipe in his mouth, his little wrinkled face shining with smiles, brought up his right hand and then pulled it down with great vigor. The signal set loose a petty hell of noise, a sizzling, crackling, booming series of explosions that ended in successive thunder-claps. The bands took up the noise-making no sooner had the fireworks ceased, and the huge crowd shouted, laughed, and applauded.

In her windowless room Donna Maria lay as inert as she had fallen. Her eyes had not shut the entire night. One looked sidewise, the other straight ahead, and both were filled with a thin, pallid pink. The only effort she seemed capable of was her regular noisy breathing, a continuous procession of long-drawn hoarse sounds that died away into whistled echoes. Dr. Giovanelli had prescribed opium powders, but Davido Monterano had become too alarmed at the mere mention of the drug. He refused to administer it. Zia Anna hobbled back and forth, making the sign of the cross and calling upon one saint after the other. Donna Sofia had promised to fetch Don Anselmo and was even now waiting for the ceremonies to be over to accompany him to the presence of the sick woman.

Monterano had not relinquished the hold of her hand.

"No fever, Zia Anna," he would say, shaking his head as if he could not understand it, "not a bit of fever. She is getting cold. A stick of ice— that's all her arm is, a stick of ice."

To everyone who entered the room he vouchsafed the same information.

"See, Rosinella, just a chunk of ice, see."

He heard the noise of the celebration. It was too distant to be distinct and clear, but large masses of music and the hurrahing of the crowds detached themselves from the remote air and floated muffled and diminished into the sick room.

"Did you hear, Maria? Colonel, you see, she does not speak. She does not hear. Maria, Maria!" He shouted her name as if she might hear it that way. "It's the opening of the store, it's going to make us rich. . . . Do you hear, Maria, rich, and we'll go back to Castello-a-Mare and live the way we should, the way people like us should. Maria. . . . Oh, colonel, colonel, she won't talk."

He rose to his feet and turned to the colonel who had just shuffled into the room.

"A little longer time, my dear captain . . . just give her time."

"She will die, die before she speaks to me again. Colonel, do you hear, she will die."

He whispered it defiantly with clenched fists shaking, eyes staring, his face, pale from lack of sleep, filled with the horror of death.

"She will die . . . and leave us."

The first slow crackling sound of the fireworks worked itself in and out of his words.

"She will leave us, colonel, the three children and me. I have been useless, useless in this country, colonel . . . she's the one who fed us, clothed us, made America for us . . . she . . . she . . . and now . . . now. . . ."

Only her steady raucous breathing, as if she were playing with bubbles of heavy liquid in her throat, answered him.

"Maria," he turned again to her and took her hand. "See, cold! Ice cold . . . life going . . . dying . . . !"

He only made the words with his mouth without sound, as if he, too, were losing his strength forever.

Outside in the bright autumn day rose explosion after explosion.

"Hear, hear, Maria . . . the store is opened. . . . It'll make us rich. . . . Maria, Maria, you must not die! You have worked too hard, you must not die . . . no . . . no . . ."

Now he was shouting, and he kept shouting, shouting louder and louder, and with each shout it seemed Gennaro had timed the bursting of a detonator. A muffled boom filled the room. The whole of the Parterre seemed to shake with each new explosion.

"Now, the store is open . . . you must be there . . . tomorrow . . . tomorrow . . . tomorrow. . . ."

Zia Anna had heard the shout and rushed in. The colonel went up to his old friend and held him gently by the arm, not knowing what to say or do. Rosinella, a little stout bandy-legged girl with a fat pimply face, stood at the door jamb, her eyes filled with tears, biting her finger-nails. Another boom.

"Look colonel, look. . . ."

Don Davido caught the colonel's hand as in a vise.

"The saliva, thick like a horse's. *Dio Santo, Dio Santo.* Zia Anna . . . call Don Anselmo, quick . . . see, colonel, her eyes, they're half-shut now."

He threw himself over the bed and wept.

Donna Maria died without absolution, and was buried two days later, her coffin borne behind a slow-moving band of musicians provided by Gennaro.

PART THREE

Carmela

CHAPTER ONE

1

At the age of twenty, Carmela had become a leading business woman of Little Italy. What was more, her fame as a milliner had spread downtown. A year after her shop had been opened, she began talking to Gennaro about going entirely into manufacture and abandoning the selling end of the shop. The salesmen had carried the report of her good looks far and wide. But it certainly was not that alone that earned for her a signal reputation in the trade. The three years she had spent at the juvenile asylum in charge of the younger girls and their sewing had given her the ability to command. It had given her, too, the ability to instruct. And she added to her experience not alone the three years of practical work with Donna Maria in the capacity of what was to all intents and purposes general manager. She brought to her new enterprise more than two years of faithful night-by-night attendance at a designing school. The methods she learned there were not mere theory with her. She put them to the test as soon as possible. With Donna Maria it had to be cautious experimentation. After all, the work in that shop was contracted for. The designs were set by the original firms and deviations were not tolerated even when they might be improvements on the initial pattern. But in the new *Capelleria*, Carmela became interested not in the selling of hats but in developing her own ideas. Gennaro became overawed by her skill and ingenuity.

"You ought to've been a man. No question. You got the stuff."

He had been true to his word. Words of love never passed his lips. He made it his business to visit her store at least once a day, but limited himself to shouting "Good morning to everybody. And what's the song going to be today?"

The girls immediately launched into a full-throated chorus. It was either the newest Italian popular hit, or, as they called them, the English songs of the day.

"And so this is the new hat, hey?" he asked, picking up the latest display. "And somebody's going to wear this? Suppose the bird flies off?"

"The bird's dead . . . can't you see?"

"By the calendar of all the saints, it is. Funny thing to wear all the same. Let's see how it looks on me."

There was laughter as Gennaro strutted about, hat on head, pipe in his mouth, his earrings dangling and shining. The girls all realized that Gennaro had been bewitched by their forelady, and watched the progress of his crude, silent love-making with sentimental interest.

Young salesmen stayed longer than there was need. Gennaro interrupted the visits on several occasions, but said nothing. It was his same shouted time-of-the-day and then good-bye. Possibly the next morning he would take Carmela aside.

"I'd keep an eye on those bright roosters," he would say. "They're too sharp for some of us."

One day she announced to him that a large department store had taken the original of one of her hats, and paid her fifty dollars for it.

"Here's the check."

Her cheeks glowed with pride. Gennaro rustled the paper in his hand.

"Fifty dollars, hey? A lot of money . . . is that what it says here?"

"Yes, see, there?"

"I can read enough for that. Young woman, you'll make America, by Saint Jerome, I swear it."

2

Because of her success with the shop, Carmela found herself designated by the whole of Little Italy as "*l'Americana*," but more often than not she was referred to as "*quella buona buona*."[1] There seemed to exist the need to express their wonder at the ability of the girl and at the way in which she had assumed the responsibility for the development of the children of the Parterre. These were not really a problem because she did not regard as a problem the relationship that had grown up among them. Quite naturally she had become both companion and sister to the entire group and it seemed as if there never had been any other arrangement. But with the death of Donna Maria, whatever was exacting and serious in the situation converted the harmonious free-play of the young personalities into a major difficulty.

Davido Monterano, windy, grandiose, and self-centered, collapsed into a self-pitying, helpless old man sustained only by his passionate adherence to Old World conceptions of greatness. Throughout the days when his wife's body lay in its ice-filled coffin waiting for the time of its interment, Davido could play the big fellow. He gloried in the presence of the numerous visitors. His friend, the colonel, mustaches sleek and well-combed, clothes worn with an air, remained close to him. No sooner had one visitor come in and viewed the corpse, expressed his formal regrets at the calamity, than he was introduced to the colonel.

The men kept to the rear room, the women remained with the body. All night long they stayed awake, listening first to the ex-captain and then to the colonel. If the talk was not about the army days of their youth, it shifted to the masterpieces the colonel was seeking to sell in America. Davido rose from his chair and strutted back and forth, describing how unfairly he had been cashiered from the army.

"What could my good friend here, the colonel di San Martino, do? I had enemies, envious of my reputation, the devices I invented. Ah, my saintly wife—may she find a place in heaven—she realized my true worth. She was always sure of our future. We came here to America. We set up a large business—a very promising one! I chose a competent, a most competent person as manager. Carmela Dauri will make the place hum, I'm telling you. All one needs is to find the right persons to do the routine work. That accomplished, what is there to a business? It goes on and on. Oh, yes, we have great plans. We shall make money out of it. When I have had enough, back to Italy shall I go with these darling children of mine. They need the Italian environment. They are Italians of the Italians. They need a land of culture and of beauty."

"And it may not be so long as you think, my dear captain," the colonel volunteered. "Let us once sell our pictures...."

"Really, we should retain them for the glory of Italy. But we'll sell them, we'll sell them."

And so on through the night. But once Donna Maria was lowered into her six feet of soil, next to the mother and the child whom she had brought with her from Italy, Don Davido broke down. Alone, he wept like a child. His children were off at school; the flat where there had always been girls at work, his wife moving about, Carmela busy, was now empty. The colonel had finally decided that it was an imposition to live in the Parterre, and took rooms in the Knickerbocker Hotel.

"Besides, sir," he confided to Gennaro, "I shall be able there to meet important persons. I shall sell my pictures more readily. I cannot cart them around with me like a dray-horse, can I? And really, I could not ask prospective buyers here. What would they think? That I had stolen them."

Don Davido refused to go to the shop.

"How can I, Gennaro? It will kill me. Remember, it was my wife's business. She was to be there in charge. . . . I could not bear it."

Gennaro gave him up.

"He's a whining jackass, Carmela. Let him alone."

In the end, despite his display of grief, Davido Monterano found it possible to dress in his finest attire, select the most dashing cane, and go downtown to meet the colonel. Likely as not he would not return in the evening. What they did no one actually found out in detail. They did advertise in the American newspapers that they had for sale several unusual paintings by Italian masters. It was known that they visited the art-dealers. Only on Saturday evenings would Monterano be sure to be present when Carmela came home from the shop. He would then ask for an accounting of the business for the week. He laid aside a substantial amount of the profits for himself. Gennaro became enraged, and showed it.

"Say, big shot," he cried one night, "by all the thousand saints, you're not getting one cent more."

Davido rose his full height, pulled down the lapels of his coat with both hands, and balanced himself back and forth on his feet.

"And may I ask you by what right you interfere in my business?" he demanded. "My wife, Donna Maria, made it possible. You have been repaid for what you laid out. It is not your concern."

"The hell, it isn't! By Saint Jerome you've got the nerve of the old landowners and lawyers in the old country. It isn't my concern, hey! Well, I'll show you, you blow-hard. . . . You're the kind I spit in the eye. Bah . . . Carmela, no . . . not a word from you!"

Don Davido appealed to Carmela. He knocked on the door of the Dauri apartment one Sunday morning with a vigor that startled the whole family. Don Tomaso was polishing a fancy wooden table he had made. He looked up with a mock frown, and then shouted to his wife loud enough for the stranger outside to hear.

"Sounds like a police inspector or the Lord God himself."

Don Davido strutted in. On his arm was slung a new black cane with a huge dog-head in silver and a silver band shining with initials. He had acquired one of the long coats affected by sporty gentlemen, tight around the waist and split in the back from the middle to the hem, with pompously padded shoulders. He bowed deeply, holding his brown derby in the crook of his arm. He was condescending to pay a call on the Dauris.

Don Tomaso lifted his eyes.

"Good morning, Don Davido, and to what do we owe the honor?"

Monterano suspected a note of unfriendliness. He cleared his throat.

"I have come for a few words with my manager."

"Manager, manager?" Don Tomaso sang the word questioningly.

"Your daughter," Monterano bowed low as he spoke, "whom I have engaged to supervise my *capelleria.*"

Don Tomaso shrugged his shoulders. What was the use in being subtle with a fool? "It would seem you are assuming too much."

"It is just a word . . . a word of instruction."

"Carmela is at Sunday school."

But she had appeared in the doorway to belie his words.

"No, I have just returned. And what is it?"

"A word in private?" Monterano's question had implications of a command.

"Shall we go to the store?" Carmela asked. "We're so crowded here."

3

On the way, the ex-captain threw out his chest with immense assertion. With equal energy he flung his cane ahead of him, twirling it two or three times in the air before drawing it back. When he was greeted, he came to a complete stop and bowed profoundly, and then, assuming his erect posture once more, lifted his hat far above his head. Carmela, he ignored.

In the store, he sat himself in a chair, crossed his legs, arranged the folds of his coat over his knees, cleared his throat, tapped two or three times on the floor with his cane, and spoke in a definite basso, evidently chosen for special effect.

"Carmela, I have honored you in making you sole manager of this shop. You understand that?"

She could not make out the man, so she merely nodded.

"You realize that it was because of your ability, do you not? Not for any sentimental reason? Oh, there was a time when . . . shall we say your beauty, your attractiveness, your youth made a certain impression upon me. I do not deny it. It was in this very place, as I remember, that I confessed to you the feelings which you inspired. Be at ease, be at ease . . ."

Something in his manner had frightened her, and she had stepped back a few paces.

"I have no intention of renewing my confessions. Many things have happened since then to sober me—events of which you have some knowledge. There is the return to my regiment. You understand, that is a great, a marvelous thing for me. There are these art treasures which we shall soon dispose of for fabulous sums. Ah, you have no inkling, Carmela, of the millions—yes, I do not hesitate to repeat—millions that will come to me from these masterpieces."

"Really? No, it would be too wonderful."

"But it is a positive possibility within the week. A millionaire will see us tomorrow in his private museum on Fifth Avenue. It is a palatial residence, Carmela, in the Italian style, a magnificent marble edifice, a fit place to house our canvases. A positive possibility, and within the week, within the week."

He felt called upon by an inner urge to rise and walk rapidly back and forth, swinging his cane and smiling with pleasure.

"But, Carmela, and this is why I have decided it was necessary to have a talk with you."

He swung himself around vigorously.

"Look." He pointed with his cane. "There is my name, in gold letters—Monterano, *La Capelleria Monterano* . . . a firm with my name. It is an honored firm. I mean that it shall be a first-rate establishment. It must become a name that shall be a beacon for business. . . . You can do it. But only you."

He looked at her steadily, laughed quietly, and then resumed his seat.

"You see, you have a self-imposed assistant . . . a certain Gennaro Accuci, a veritable clodhopper, a country yokel. . . . What does he know? He is fit to pick rags from the garbage pails—and that is all."

He hit the floor a smart rap with his cane.

"He must stay out of this . . . you hear, Carmela, out of it entirely. These are orders, mind you, orders, and they must be obeyed."

His voice rose sharply and quivered in mid-air.

"You will turn over your money to me—all of it. I am engaged in a work—outside of this little place here"—and he pointed deprecatingly to the windows, show-cases, and models—"of great importance. I shall have need of considerable resources. In fact, I must have two thousand dollars at once. We must raise it somehow."

He snapped his fingers two or three times.

"There is that much money in the bank. No?"

His sudden demand startled her. From the first she had listened with respectful interest. Her employer—as he styled himself—seemed to have business of real importance—what, she had been unable to fathom until now.

This was the first time that he had been in the shop since his wife's death. More than three months had elapsed, and he had made no effort to assist in the business. All his time he spent in what Gennaro called "this mule-affair of the colonel."

Although no papers had ever been drawn up as to the ownership of the millinery shop, it had been taken for granted that it was to be the joint enterprise of the Monterano family and herself. That was the open agreement. Actually, Gennaro looked upon her as the sole proprietor. He had told her so when he had confessed his love.

And on another occasion he had repeated it.

"How else could I do anything for you? You see, Carmela, now all there is for me is the church and you, you and the church."

She remembered how he had leaned over the table in his dining room the first time that Monterano had demanded an accounting of the money and a share of the profits. The night had come early. They had failed to turn on the light, but through the kitchen door there came enough for them to see each other's features. He leaned over the table and looked at her with eyes wide open, the earrings gleaming in the dim illumination.

"You see, I have nothing else," he repeated.

They were alone and it was getting darker and darker, so that the light from the kitchen and the noise of Zia Anna puttering around with the evening meal were thrown into sharp outline.

"Emilio—yes, and you. But Emilio—he does not really like me, no, I would not say that. But he will not talk to me. . . . I hoped years ago I should have sons . . . I killed one . . . so his mother said, and I killed her along with him . . . and now there's what left? The girl in the convent . . . she writes . . . but she will forget me . . . and then . . . no one . . . just more years coming on . . . more money. . . ."

She had listened to him unable either to answer at any point or to add remarks of sympathy or understanding. In the six years since the frightful experience with his son, the girl in her had been suppressed entirely. She had leaped into adolescence at once, but even her adolescence was only a matter of physical expansion, a rounded body, a fine figure, a lovely face. In responsibilities and outlook she had become a woman immediately. Pressing upon her memories and crowding into her consciousness, displacing the quiet of her sleep with resentful dreams, was always the agony of that harrowing escape through the snow, the mad attempt to seek shelter, the young man pursuing, his hot breath, his animal strength, the quick sharp agony of a second and the bone in her arm pulled out of joint with its sequel of pain.

Marriage had been rendered hateful to her, and the eyes of men, glowing with the sight of her beauty, abhorrent. She understood in the simple way of young women that Gennaro's feelings for her were the truest that he had ever had for anyone. Something crude and heavy in his manner was transmuted into genuineness and sincerity because the feeling in him was strong and real. She felt, too, for his loneliness, the sense of failure that kept sweeping over him. She knew, besides, that his work in building the church was an effort to cover up in an insulation of mere activity the despair he was experiencing. She would not have put it that way. She groped in her mind for a way of explaining him, and she pitied him in doing so, and desired to see him as he was revealing himself, not as he had been in the beginning, determined, rough, high-handed.

All this came back to her as Monterano made his preposterous demand. The store was making enough money to have afforded Monterano the two thousand dollars. But Carmela, having found peace from the central pain of her memories in the work of her shop, had developed the business acumen necessary to realize its full possibilities. It took no great foresight to see that the money was needed now if the business was to expand, if her cherished dream of having it moved to the downtown districts where she intended to set up a fashionable shop and be a leader in the trade were ever to come true.

But she desired the success of the store not so much for herself as for Gennaro. She envisioned an enterprise that would be in itself an accomplishment as noteworthy, as prosperous, as immense as the great business that Gennaro had, but one somehow that had more than mere size and money-making elements. She desired to be closer to the ideal of the church which he had in mind. She sensed that it was not the religious quality of the erection that fascinated him and drove him energy and soul to hasten its completion. It represented something apart from whatever others had achieved, something unique, explanatory of his deepest self. Her business might be such a thing—possess a sort of soul. That she could give.

And so it was that she was frightened by the curious request that Monterano was making. She recoiled from him as if he were holding a sledge hammer ready to strike. It would not so much harm her as it would wreck the store. That must not happen.

"Mr. Monterano," she said at length, quietly, drawing a chair close to him, and for the first time sitting down. "If you need the money, I suppose you must have it. In some ways, of course, it is yours. . . ."

Monterano tapped his cane impatiently with all his ten fingers going at once.

"There can be no doubt of that. But are you presuming, young woman, to catechize me. I do not like"—he waved three or four fingers in the air—"I do not like the tone you are assuming. Not in the least. As your employer, the owner of this establishment, I demand that you turn over two thousand dollars to me, and at once."

Not for the first time, but more distinctly at this point, Carmela noted a lack-lustre steady glare in the man's eyes. He appeared to be perpetually smiling at her, and yet there was no happiness in his features. A pompous self-satisfaction in the way he held his chin, an air of assured authority in the way he sat, and a hint of contempt for all these details into which he found it necessary to go—these, and the joyless smile, the shineless eyes alarmed her. She began to feel strange in his presence, as if she were not speaking any longer to the affable gentleman she used to know, given to wordiness and grandiosity, of course, but pleasant. Here there appeared another person, altogether different, who wore Davido's features but was not Davido.

4

She hastened to talk. Only in that way, she felt, could she succeed in pacifying him momentarily and prevent him from bursting into a fit of dangerous temper or into action that might be disastrous to them both.

"Why, naturally, you shall have the money."

"The business can afford it?"

He spoke with confident arrogance.

"Oh, yes. It can. It is a good business. Only . . ."

"Anything with the Monterano name attached . . . it must be good . . . and there can be no 'only,' no 'only.'"

"What I wanted to say, Mr. Monterano . . . do let me speak."

He threw himself back in his chair, tilted it on its hind legs, and rolled his eyes toward the ceiling.

"Proceed, proceed," he laughed as if he were immensely pleased at the humbleness of the request.

"It's this. You may have the two thousand. Of course you may. But if we take out the two thousand now, you will be ruining the future of the store. Really, this is a fine business. It has started very well. It is making money. We shall continue to make money. But if we spend all the money we make instead of putting it back—"

Monterano jumped to his feet and struck the floor with his cane. Instinctively, Carmela rose, too, and moved away. Gradually, as he approached her, she worked her way behind one of the counters and managed also to throw the latch in the swinging door closing off the aisle.

"You will not presume, young woman . . ."

He had no chance to complete his speech. The door was thrown open and Gennaro, furbished up in his Sunday serge, his hat aslant, his pipe at a contrary angle, his earrings dancing with light, shuffled slowly into the store. He cleared his throat before saying a word. Monterano turned about.

"What is it that the young woman presumes?"

Monterano, swinging his cane with debonair facility, eyed the new-comer from head to toe and back again, smiling contemptuously as he did so.

"And who are you?" is all he asked.

"Carmela, what's all this?" Gennaro questioned as he strode past the other man.

"What right have you, you country dog, to interfere in my affairs?"

Gennaro was shrewd enough to realize that Monterano could not be in his right senses. He saw from the first the queer absence of light in the man's smile, heard the dull flat quality of his laugh, the high-pitched shrill tones of his voice. At the offensive question and epithet, therefore, he said nothing.

"After all, Mr. Monterano, I am a friend."

There had been no warning and there were no preliminaries at all. Mr. Monterano made no cry, shifted no step, raised not an eyebrow, gave no indication in gesture or sound of his intentions if the intentions existed at all. With a sudden swish, he raised his cane and bore it down across Gennaro's cheeks and temples.

"In the old country, this is how we treat low-down curs who dare question a gentleman. This way, this way, this way . . ."

He slashed with his cane at Gennaro's ear, at his cheeks, with long sidewise strokes. The cane whirred and whistled in air. The blows had come too swiftly for Gennaro to have stepped aside to avoid them. The pain of them was too intense for him even to scream. He had just suffi-cient consciousness left to draw up his arms as a shield.

It was some seconds before Carmela was aware of the frightful thing that was happening. She fumbled for what seemed an eternity to open the aisle-door, not crying out either in fright or horror. She saw at once that shouting would attract a crowd. She would handle the whole thing herself. She finally got past the barrier of the door.

Gennaro had fallen in a heap. She ran to him and threw herself between his prostrate form and the upraised cane in Monterano's hands. Monterano was laughing to himself.

"It's that way, Carmela, we treat them in the old country. And to you, I issue final orders. I need the two thousand dollars, and tomorrow."

He strode imperially to the door, bowed profoundly, and left, swinging his cane with the most audacious insouciance.

5

Carmela shut the door fast behind her and ran back at once to Gennaro. He lay bleeding and unconscious, his face welted on both sides, his lips thick and viscous, one of his earrings imbedded in a mass of spongy gore. She realized at once the need for assistance. Quickly she slipped out the back way. As if nothing had happened, she waited patiently for the trolley. It made slow progress through the crowds going to and coming from church. Finally she reached Dr. Giovanelli's office. It was another half-hour before she got back. On the way she had ample time to explain the whole incident to the aging doctor.

The old fellow kept stroking the full-flowing panel of his white beard with open fingers, bowing his head deeper and deeper as he listened, almost as if he were on the point of dropping off into profound sleep. The broad, dirty red sash under his frock-coat, his picturesque white head with its green-tinged ancient top-hat, attracted the attention of all their fellow-riders. One would have thought he neither saw nor listened. But throughout the entire explanation Carmela was making he kept whispering, "Softer, child, softer . . . show no excitement— we might have lots of trouble to clear the thing up . . . softer . . . no excitement—quiet, child . . ."

He took her word for it. The marks of the cane were too definite and striking to have been inflicted by any other instrument and to have been wielded by any other hand than that of an anger-crazed man. Dr. Giovanelli went about his work slowly.

"You see, Carmela, I am now eighty-three. It was in sixty-eight that I was the surgeon—the only one, mind you—with the forces of that great and good patriot, Garibaldi. Just like Gennaro here, he lay bleeding on the field of battle. His head reposed on my knee. My uniform was drenched with the chief's own blood. But I—did I falter, did I hesitate? I staunched the dear man's wounds, I bound his head—I did my best—all I can do now."

Gennaro had been injured beyond hope of quick recovery.

"His jaw is broken," the doctor announced.

Carmela wept. For the first time since the dreadful episode, she allowed herself to relax from her state of muscle-binding tension.

"This is nothing, child," the old doctor assured her. "Nothing . . . a jaw heals . . . but this, this is not so good."

He held up the lobe of Gennaro's right ear with the earring still in it, a red glob. The cane had cut it completely off.

"This will not grow back. It will heal . . . I shall wash it at once and sew it up—but it will be a blow to him. How proud he has been of those things in his ears! Proud that he was of the soil, of the old mountain stock without letters! After all, Carmela, he has done things . . . here in this country."

6

It took several months for Gennaro to recover. Carmela assumed full charge of the sick man. His head was bound in such fashion that his lips could barely be opened to allow for his nourishment. To talk was a special agony in itself, and he made no effort to talk.

The only thing he seemed to recognize was the figure of Carmela. He put out his hand for hers, and held it clutched like a child. His eyes followed her as she moved about the room, and when she left in the morning to go to the store he relapsed into sleep, waiting for her return. Evidently he had learned to judge in a semi-conscious way how long she might be gone. For a half-hour or more before she returned for the lunch hour he became restless and uneasy. Zia Anna might offer him water, Donna Sofia might arrange his covers and bathe his hands. Nothing mattered. He kept uneasily stirring about, trying to lift himself up. Sounds of footsteps on the stairs gave him unusual energy. He managed to raise his head, although the doctors had forbidden it.

Emilio came to see him frequently. He would sit at the side of his father and tell him what was happening.

"I am getting fine marks in school. This morning it was funny. The teacher told a story and she asked could anybody repeat it. She read out of a book like ... I don't know if she did, because she kept looking up so much. Maybe she was making it up. But she asked who could tell the story, and I did, and guess what? I told it almost word for word the way she had, and she brought me to the principal and said it was a hard thing to do and she gave me a fine mark."

Gennaro stroked his son's hands, but it was quite evident that he had not paid much attention. He was expecting the arrival of Carmela. All other things dropped out of time and place.

The loss of his earrings she herself took as a fine act of fate. She hoped it would be the last of the monstrous ornaments. Not that she thought them ridiculous. But they were such easy marks for smart wits to shoot at. Who would understand the subtle symbol of destiny which they represented to his mind?

"Just a slash across the face, Gennaro," Carmela explained, holding his hand and smiling at him. "Really, nothing in comparison to your jaw. The bone is broken in it, but the doctors say it will knit ... soon."

He raised his hand to his head and tried to cry out.

"No talking ... it isn't permitted. You must give your jaw a chance."

"Here ... here...," he muttered, pointing to the bandaged ear.

"Nothing."

"But, Carmela!"

It was unmistakable. He was beginning to understand. His eyes questioned her with such an intensity of feeling that she turned her face away from him.

"You will have to have some broth. It's time ... every two hours."

"The pain, Carmela ..."

"I know ... I know ... here, hush now."

"Tell me, tell me."

But it was not until many days after New Year's that she revealed to him what had happened to his ear and to his earring. The winter day was filled with the kind of sunshine that gives a false impression of warmth even in the late afternoon. As Gennaro lay in his bed, looking out across the newly-built park covered with snow, Carmela and the nurses were getting ready for the coming of the doctors. The bandages were to be completely removed, the jaw bone tested once more, the wounds dressed, and if possible the patient was to be permitted to sit up and eat solid food.

The three vacant streets, stretching out under a pink-gray sky in front of his windows, gave the room a feeling of isolation. The lights had not yet been turned on either in the houses or outside. A low hum of activity—the occasional roar of the gas-tanks, the passing of a trolley, footsteps hurrying out of the cold—pressed in upon the room but not noisily, rather as another layer of the silence which enshrouded the growing dark. Gennaro had dismissed everyone. He wanted to be alone. In a few minutes Carmela would be coming.

She, too, looked forward to being alone with him. She feared that what she had to tell him might hurt him more than the physical agony of the wound, and she wished to comfort him. As she moved about the room she was always aware of his eyes upon her. She had sensed the meaning of the confidence he reposed in her when he begged her to take a look now and then in the rag and junk shop.

"See that they do some work. They needn't kill themselves, but don't let them kill me. See?"

She had assured him she would do her best. And so she added a daily inspection of Gennaro's business to that of her own. In the last few years Gennaro had been gradually motorizing his transportation service. His stables were being slowly transformed into garages. Instead of the sixteen horses he kept, he was intending to have four huge trucks. Besides the trucks, he was ordering a car for his own use. As he lay in bed the thought of all these things which he could not himself supervise, troubled him.

One night he had spoken to Carmela, between his teeth—as he must because of his bandage—so that he sounded like one issuing a dramatic challenge to the world.

"Imagine this thing happening now. By all the saints, now ... with all this new work on my hands."

Carmela attempted to reassure him.

"Sure, it'll be right in time. But it isn't now. . . . Say, Carmela. . . ."

He called her name impulsively.

"By rights you ought to be my partner—in my business—I need a partner."

"You're a funny person, Gennaro. That's a man's job. Hats are my work."

"But I do need a partner."

He had seized her hand in his and held it tight, thinking. Then, slowly, the pain of his talking mingling with the pain of his memories, he told her of how he had come to America, how he had wrested the business out of Rocco's hands, and how it all seemed to him now something about which he stood in need of atonement.

"Rocco does well . . . he has a going business . . . but it's only fair, it's only fair."

She listened intently. A father confessor, blest with the gift of listening, could not have accorded him a quieter, more understanding, attention. And as he spoke she sensed the inevitable surging in him of feelings for her which he had already confessed but which had become broader, deeper, fuller. They bewildered her and flattered her, they gave her thoughts about herself a feeling of stability and definiteness. But that was all. She felt grateful to him for that, but she was nevertheless confused and agitated. Whatever it was she might be to him in his mind, in her own she knew from the outset that it could be no more than just what he had suggested, a partner, one who had an interest in what he did. No more. It made her sad as she listened to the slow deliberate words that came from his tight, pain-locked lips.

"We should have been together always, Rocco and me, grinning goat though he is. He hates me now. . . . He must . . . and yet, why? I paid him . . . gave him a store free, helped him get more money. . . ."

Carmela was compelled to hold him down. He had begun to speak too freely and to rise on his elbows—all against orders. She bent over him.

"Gennaro, you must be careful. The jaw will never knit."

He sank into his pillow deep in thought.

"Carmela," he called at length. "What you think? Maybe I can ask Rocco to be my partner again?"

"Rather late now to do a thing like that, isn't it? He's getting along."

"In a way. He has bought a lot of rotten houses in a rotten section."

"Hush. That's not your fault."

"Muddle-headed mutton that man is."

"Gennaro."

Carmela spoke sharply.

"Don't get yourself excited. You're not too well yet."

He placed his hand on hers and let it rest there, patting it gently with his fingers, irregularly, quietly lost in a maze of memories.

"He's blaming me for lots of things, Carmela, and I don't blame him. No, by Saint Jerome, I don't blame the sickly old ram. He's got the kind of wife keeps stirring him up."

"But it's all over now between you."

Despite his pain, he sat up suddenly.

"By the thousand saints of the calendar, Carmela. You would think I'm afraid of the fool."

Carmela attempted a merry peal of laughter as a final answer.

"You remember he came to see me the other day? Always distrust an old friend who comes to see you once in five years. Something's up."

Carmela rose to her feet and placed her hands on his shoulders. She made an attempt to force him back on his pillow.

"If you don't stop talking, I'm leaving."

"Carmela, I must talk, I have been to Father Anselmo and talked in the confessional . . . but never freely. . . . By the saints, if you're really penitent you can't confess . . . not in a church. The candles—like the ghosts of the saints, they look at you. The images, they stare at you. The place is dark and you're alone and you're afraid. . . . But to you I can talk . . . you're a living saint . . . you know . . . Rocco blames me for selling him the house he's in . . . isn't worth much these days . . . blames me for that more than for the way I stole his business . . . he hates me. . . . By Saint Jerome . . . he's glad to see me in bed this way . . . and I won't say he's wrong . . . if I got out of his way . . . that's how he's thinking . . . I saw it in his eyes. . . ."

Confidences like these strengthened her belief in herself. They made it possible for her to assume an interest in Gennaro's affairs that otherwise would seem incongruous with her years and her relationship to him.

Therefore she felt it devolving upon her rather than upon Giovanelli or her father to relate to Gennaro what had happened to his ear and earring. She wondered how he would take it. But no matter how he took it, she was prepared to accept his reactions as they were, neither console him unduly nor attempt to put an emphasis upon the situation different from his own.

She leaned over his bed and arranged the pillows.

"You're looking so much better, Gennaro. A good thing, too. You seem stronger and ready soon to be getting up. Tomorrow they will give the final verdict . . . tomorrow, and maybe you'll be called all better. You will know the worst, and the worst won't be bad at all. Suppose they tell you you lost a bone or an ear."

He looked at her quizzically.

"Would you mind?"

He felt for the earring in the good ear. It was there, hanging definitely by the side of his neck.

"I have lost an ear?"

He asked it, and she knew she must answer.

"Yes . . . half an ear, the half with the earring!"

"No wonder, no wonder I had so much pain."

He said no more for a second, but seized Carmela's hand in his, and held it tight.

"Funny, Carmela," he said at length. "Very funny. You see over there. Houses were up there once, a great many. How they were dirty and close together and sort of no use. But do you know, when they were torn down, I felt sad. I was making lots of money, too. The city, they paid me big for the houses I owned. I bought up cheap, me and Struzzo, and the city paid us big money. See what I mean? There they were, dirty, rotten houses, everybody getting sick in them, full of rats, and you couldn't walk up the stairs, they creaked and had big troughs in them like, you know, worn down. They ought to have come down and the park it ought to have been built and it is built, see, but I am sort of sad anyhow. Those houses, I knew them. That's how New York was to me when I came here, see what I am thinking? But they're gone now, and my wife is gone, and Domenico, and little Elena—you remember her with her curly hair, don't you?—she's gone . . . and I look out there and it all seems empty space, something cut out of it that belonged there and thrown away."

He stopped, and propped himself on his pillow. He was stronger, as Carmela had said, ready to be up and about. But one saw that he would rather have remained where he was for a while at least. The empty space he saw had no beckoning elements for him any longer.

The darkness had deepened. The big brass bed in which he lay glinted in the stray lights from the gas lamps outside.

"So," Gennaro laughed slightly, "so, the captain slashed off my ear and my earring. Well, well . . . that's that."

Carmela began to understand what the long speech meant. Like the New York he had known on his first arrival, he, too, had changed. The old had been cut away. No matter how much he kept improving his business, he kept reverting in his mind to the early years of his coming. It was an echo in his words that would not be muffled, a far-flung memory that lay its shadow over the present.

"Carmela, I am not like you . . . educated. I'm what the captain said, a country dog, see . . . that's why I kept those earrings. I wanted to show them a country dog could do things. I did. I am going to do bigger things yet. The church will be up. I am going to have my business run by machines, automobiles, machines to pack down the rags, machines to break up the old junk . . . electricity in the shop, everywhere, see."

"Everybody knows you will, Gennaro."

"By Saint Jerome, earrings or no earrings, I'll show them."

And then he patted Carmela on the cheek.

"You've been very good to me, Carmela, very good . . . and so, look, I want you to have them."

He took off the one earring that remained, and put it into her hand.

"The other, you know where it is. That's yours, too . . . they are old . . . what's it now, 1903? My father he put them in my ears way back in 1850, and they were his father's . . . when he died they took them for the grandson . . . that's me, see . . . and he had them in his ears all his life . . . they're yours now."

A wry smile lit up one side of his face.

"Tomorrow I'm different . . . no earrings. . . ."

He laughed and looked far out across the spaces where the old filthy tenements had been, old hovels that had made him a fortune.

7

Davido Monterano had obtained his two thousand dollars. Undaunted by what he had done, he had boldly accosted Carmela the next morning and demanded what he considered his rightful money. Unwilling to prolong the painful debate, she consented to go at once to the bank and let him have the sum he requested.

The last she saw of him was when he counted out the money with extreme care, made a neat little pad of the bills, put them in the inside pocket of his jacket, buttoned up his overcoat, brushed his hat with his sleeve, turning his arms about and about over the hat, smiled benignly, swung his cane high in air, and walked out on his heels into the cold winter morning.

The children kept asking about him. Between them and their father, during the life of Donna Maria, there had been true affection and a warm sweet intimacy. What had happened to snap the cords of love between them no one could understand.

Gennaro possibly came closest to the explanation.

"He could never be an American. He could never make America. His life was in Italy, and to that could he go back? I ask you, by the holy calendar, could he, now, could he?"

The police brought his body to the Parterre some months after Gennaro had finally recovered and was again going about his business. They had found him, ragged, penniless, starved, wandering the streets. The report had come to them frequently that a distinguished-looking man on Fifth Avenue, on Broadway, sometimes outside the Museum of Art, would stop passersby and offer to sell them some remarkable works of art. They for the most part had simply shaken themselves free of him and left him shouting in a strange tongue.

"He had a friend," Carmela told the police, "an Italian colonel who did own some pictures. Have you seen him?"

The police knew nothing.

At the Knickerbocker Hotel it was ascertained that Davido Monterano had been registered with the colonel. The day after the money had been turned over to Monterano, the colonel had disappeared. For more than a week, Monterano had continued to receive callers to whom he exhibited a set of paintings, or he induced occasional loungers and guests to view them. When he had failed to pay his bills over a period of two weeks, they had insisted upon his leaving the hotel. More than that they did not know except that he had returned now and then, each time looking less and less presentable, but always swinging his cane, to make inquiries about the colonel.

Now his body was returned to the Parterre. A crowd collected to view the coffin taken upstairs—the coffin ordered by Gennaro. Many of the spectators followed the bearers into the house and remained to have a glimpse of the dead man's face. The girls in the shop in particular insisted upon paying their last respects to the dead man. Carmela had pleaded with Gennaro not to have the body brought to the house. But Donna Sofia had advised that it be done.

"Your mother, Carmela, well, she ought to know. It would be disgraceful having the police bury him. Besides, the children—they ought to have one last look . . . he's their father."

"Have it your way—both of you," Carmela cried. "The disgrace is to have the man buried with a hearse, and curious neighbors coming to take a peek at his face, and to talk about him. In the presence of the children! Dreadful, dreadful, dreadful! And of course he's to go to the church, and there will be a big show!"

Chubby Gilda, twelve and big for her age, refused to look at her father's face. She buried her head under Carmela's arms and begged to be held and kept away. Roberto, quite manfully, showing his seventeen years in a kind of arrogant reserve, went up stolidly to the coffin, laid his hand on it, and quietly surveyed the emaciated, hollow cheeks, the thin long hands, yellow now and curiously more hairy than he remembered. Then he collapsed utterly; fell over the coffin and shook with his sobs. The uninvited mourners all held their handkerchiefs to their lips, trying to repress their feelings. Ernestino ran in at this moment, calling for his brother disconsolately, as if there were no one left to whom he could appeal.

Carmela, downstairs, upbraided her mother for having allowed it.

"The darlings—subject them to this scene. If their hearts are not broken, it won't be your fault."

The night when Davido Monterano was buried, his son Roberto, feeling his full responsibility as the oldest of the three children, knocked at the Dauris' door.

"May I speak to Carmela?" he asked.

When they were alone, he sat down and leaned toward her.

"What are we going to do?" he asked at once.

Carmela realized how important, if distressed, the boy felt, and concluded that it would be best to engineer the conversation so that what she had decided to do would appear the very thing he himself suggested. So she asked him in her turn, "And you, what do you think you ought to do?"

"Go back to Italy, I suppose."

He tossed back with his hand the mass of his silk-like hair that refused to be combed, and looked at her steadily.

"It's an idea. Do you think it's a good one?"

"Well, we have relatives there, you know."

"Yes. And of course they would have to find some way of providing for you."

"Sure," he said eagerly. "They would, wouldn't they?"

"Would you care to go? If you do, why, I think we can arrange it."

"Really, Carmela, I haven't even thought of it. But I'm thinking. What would we do? We can't talk Italian, really, not good Italian, you know."

"Of course. That means you can't do that."

"And besides, look, I'm in high school, Ernestino—he's been bad but he ought to wake up to himself now—and Gilda, they go to school."

"So, you don't want to go back to Italy?"

"Not really." He smiled sweetly as he said it, as if it were a charming little joke. "No, I wouldn't."

"They say it's a lovely place. Why, they never stop talking about it. There's nothing here like it—the skies, oh, my, they're just not blue at all here, and the air is damp and full of sickness, the people are ill-mannered and don't know their place, they have to work too hard and can't enjoy themselves. Oh, I suppose they're all homesick, and here the

Americans keep saying what a wonderful land it is we're in, and how well they've taken care of the foreign people who have come here. Oh, yes, sometimes I think I should like to go back. I remember it, Roberto. Hills with woods, and sheep on the sides of them, and slopes covered with grapes, and square stone houses with green doors, and the weather always warm, and when it hailed it was even more beautiful afterward, looking like a picture in a mirror that has been polished, oh ever so bright. But I wouldn't go back . . . not any more, and I don't blame you either."

"Sure," Roberto assented, "I can see that. This is where we have lived, like, all our lives."

"Even Gilda."

"Oh, she told me she'd hate it."

"Well, that settles it. Have you any other plan?"

"Yes." He spoke eagerly, his brown eyes flashing, pleased that he had found so sympathetic and willing a helper. "You know, Gennaro might give me a job, or maybe you, see, and I could go to school nights. Only you'd have to let us live here for a while anyhow."

"You hadn't thought of going to Miss Reddle and having Ernesto and Gilda sent to the asylum, the way I was, and my brothers?"

Roberto stared at Carmela. The smile left his face entirely. He looked blankly at his friend, shaking his head slowly. Suddenly he put his hands to his eyes and wept. Carmela took a seat next to him, and put her arms around him.

"Oh, how glad I am that you are crying. Of course, of course, I knew it. You'd want to take care of them yourself, wouldn't you. Tell me, wouldn't you?"

8

But the problem was not so easily settled. Donna Sofia insisted that the three children should be returned to their own relatives in Naples. That is where they belonged. Blood with blood, that's the rule. Don Tomaso had fallen into the habit of saying nothing in opposition to his wife. The thirteen years in America, in which he had done nothing except stain and varnish pianos, had left him without courage to oppose anyone, much less his wife. Every argument ended with her remarking, "Well, we're in America, and what can you do about it? You brought us here."

It was Gennaro who found the solution.

"I'll make them my children. I'll adopt them and send them to school and all. Why not? I have money. What'll I do with it all?"

Thinner, quieter, more subdued since the loss of his earrings, Gennaro still possessed the same tricks of energy, the same rapidity of impulse. He seemed to divine ultimate success from a quick show of action, and was willing to abide the decision of events. Nobody displayed any real understanding of the situation, so by the calendar of all the blessed saints why not just adopt the young people? Sure, he was getting old and the days were cutting deeper wrinkles in his face. Yes, but he had seen many a tree on the slopes of Capomonte shake in the wind, roaring with the glee of it, lose a mass of twigs, and yet stand up in the sun afterward just as strong as ever. By the saints, he would show them!

He had plunged once more into his business and into the erection of the church. Building the church had been a slow process. It was simpler to extract a promise than to collect the promised funds. The old buildings had to be demolished, but to be demolished had first to be bought. To induce the owners to sell at the prices dictated by the pocketbooks of the subscribers was not so simple a matter.

"By the miracle," Gennaro stormed at Father Anselmo one night. "By the thousand and one miracles, they call themselves Christians, these people. Of course, they're not good Christians, these Protestants, but it's the same God or isn't it, hey, Padre, you know? Well, then, are they going to make money on the Lord God, too?"

In the end the foundations got themselves laid down. Some months after the adoption of the Monterano children, the super-structure started to rise.

"Real American stuff, Carmela," Gennaro shouted, pipe waving in air to indicate an incomprehensible grandeur. "Steel beams . . . not your old wooden frames . . . this is a building, I tell you . . . it's going to be standing up there long after the dust of these bones"—and he pounded his chest—"gets mixed up with masons' cement."

"The people will have to thank you."

"An old country lout, Carmela, with earrings."

He stopped short and felt for the missing lobe, now a rough red scar. He laughed uneasily.

"But I tell you, Carmela, they're hanging there all the same, just as sure as the church is there now. It's not like the fireworks we have at the feast of the Blessed Saint Elena. One match and up that goes, and it puffs and snorts and then goes black. It's my heart got this started and by Saint Jerome it'll stand up."

Often he took Carmela to see the huge steel network. In the flush of an early spring twilight, he was standing with her on the sidewalk opposite.

"It will be beautiful," he was saying. "We'll bring over the fine image of Saint Elena they have in my home town. I have promised to have another one built for them, a brand new one, and it will cost plenty, but the old one I'm going to buy, and have it here."

As he walked away with Carmela, he crossed himself.

"Lots of things have happened to me since I left the old country," he told her, "and whatever is good in it all was her work, Saint Elena's work. I should bring her here."

They walked on in silence. Everyone recognized him and called out his name. He waved back his greetings and walked on.

"Well, when the church's up, that'll be the end. I am not really an old man, but I feel old. I ought to stop, and maybe just sit around and do nothing.... Unless, Carmela...."

She divined what were going to be his next words, and so hurried her steps.

"No," he said with finality. "I promised ... I won't speak of it."

It was that evening that he declared that he would adopt the Monterano children. No sooner had he stated his design than he decided that the children must be consulted at once. He and Carmela went upstairs where the three of them were studying their lessons. Roberto had assumed full control of his brother and sister, and under his firm young hand the others felt it necessary to work out their salvation.

"Hey, there, you people," shouted Gennaro, "don't you see you got guests? What do you do when you got guests?"

Roberto jumped up to turn the lights on. Ernesto offered his chair to Carmela, and Gilda snuggled up close to her.

"Fine," Gennaro cried. "And now, you go down, Roberto, and bring up with you that big boy of mine."

When Roberto had returned with Emilio, Gennaro turned to his son at once.

"Come here, you old curly dog," he shouted, while Gilda laughed. "Do you know these people? Roberto, there, with his pepper of a nose, and that little fellow, see, that one holding his head down because he don't want people to see his thin little chin, and this round potato of a girl? You know them?"

"Sure," Emilio replied, looking around sheepishly as if he thought he was being made the butt of a vast joke.

"Well, then, do you like them?"

The boy smiled.

"What do you say then, Emilio, if I made them your brothers and sister, and how would you all like it, hey, tell me, tell me!"

Carmela explained.

"And you don't have to call me papa or nothing, just Gennaro, the way you used to. How about it, young rooster there, come on, speak up?"

Everybody laughed. No one knew what to answer. It was taken for granted that the arrangement would stand, and in due time the papers were drawn up.

"Tell me, Gennaro," Carmela asked him that evening. "Why did you do it?"

"It'll be something to do when I get the church up."

She seized both his hands in hers, and pressed them.

"You know," he said as she looked at him, full of admiration, "I have never done anything just because I knew what I was doing. Things got excited inside of me, and I saw there was something straight ahead and I went and did it, and that's all. But now I see clear like, straight. I see you—you are not like the women in my life, and you aren't even like the women I know. You are not just a woman—I can't say it, Carmela— you're not a man, of course, but the things women want most you don't want them most, see, you'd rather be doing things and being some-body."

"Gennaro," she told him, smiling, "you ought to have your earrings back."

He disengaged his hands and, seizing both of hers in his, drew her closer to him, smiling in his turn.

"You can't talk straight without them."

"Oh, yes, I can. I'll tell you now. You know why I did it? You're not the kind of a girl's going to get married if she can help it, see. In the old country, even here, a girl's gone and had her six children the time she's your age. So I went and got you three children . . . see . . . they're mine, but they're yours, too, and you haven't had to get married to get them . . . and that's the truth."

His face had become warm with smiles as he anticipated that she would regard his explanation funny enough to laugh over it. All she did, however, was to withdraw her hands from his, and turn her head.

"Carmela," he called after her as she moved away.

She stopped, and faced him.

"I would have done it, if you had not," she said. "And yet I am afraid of it all."

"Oh, they're grown up. They'll be out of the house soon, married and starting life on their own. All we do for them is give them a roof and a couple of meals. That's all."

CHAPTER TWO

1

The complications that arose could never have been foreseen by Gennaro nor Carmela. Their lives were to be completely transformed. The presence of the three young people attached to them now by ties of a responsibility not born of the flesh but of bravery was a definite delimitation of all their activities. To begin with, it necessitated a change in the physical arrangements of the Parterre. The kitchen in the Monterano flat was torn out and the room made into a bedroom for Gilda. The dining room was abandoned and turned into a place where the children, including Emilio, kept their books and studied. Ernestino slept with Roberto in the large bedroom with its lone window opening on a narrow airway. The front room, in which the millinery shop had been kept, was converted into a bedroom for Carmela. She insisted upon it. The three young people could not be permitted to be alone on the top floor.

The arrangement precipitated a quarrel with Donna Sofia.

"What foolishness! You ought to be thinking of rearing your own family! What kind of life is this? The store by day, and looking after a family not your own by night! There, my grand Don Tomaso, there is your dream come true . . . your beautiful daughter has finally achieved her great success."

No matter how gently Carmela remonstrated, Donna Sofia argued and argued hotly against the whole scheme.

"He's tightening his claws around you. It would be fine if he were a young man, and what happened once never had happened. But now! He ought to give you a chance. There's that druggist—he's still willing to marry you, and many a message I have had from others, but what do you do? Bah!"

Don Tomaso merely patted his daughter's hand.

"Do what you think best, my dear, what you think best! Of course, it agitates your mother. She has had a hard life, never got over coming here, you know. I'd like to feel that something, some little thing here in America would really please her."

"Mother doesn't know just what she wants," Carmela answered. "I want to please her, want to do everything I can. But I'm not thirteen any more. Marrying somebody only to satisfy her, well, that is another thing . . . we've come far away from that here in New York."

"All right, darling, all right. I won't be the one to quarrel with you. I have always said the heart and the head should come before custom. Only so we progress! We throw away all fixed habits—we have to, provided—and this is my advice—provided our sentiments and our reasons are of the best."

"That's just it, father," she answered, and for the first time in years took his hands in hers and came close to him. "I do not want to marry just because I ought to be married or mother wants me to be married."

Her father placed his arms about her shoulder, and said nothing else. But the quarrel with her mother was by no means over.

"Carmela," Donna Sofia announced one night. "I know you have no use for my advice. I know it . . . and so we will not talk about that. But I'm still your mother. . . . What I do I do for your good. Please be sure of that. There is nothing selfish in me, just my good mother's heart."

"Well, well, what then?" demanded Carmela.

"We are alone, fortunately," Donna Sofia answered. "And we can talk. I have invited Salvatore Manzella and his mother here for dinner—the whole family, in fact."

She spoke rapidly so as not to be interrupted. Carmela, however, had no mind to interrupt. She wanted to have it out once and for all.

"His father will come, too—a very nice man, very nice. He's been in the contracting business for years and all his children have had a good education. It's a very nice family, one that we should respect. Carmela"—she laid her hand on her daughter's knee—"do it for my sake, meet this man and his mother and father, see if you can't get to like them, he's so gentle and refined, has such lovely ways. He'll make you a real husband, a real loving, cultured husband. I don't want to speak of others."

Carmela placed her hand over her mother's and pressed it.

"Oh, still at it, mother? Still?"

"Why not, Carmela? Believe me, I know what's best."

"Yes, I know, and I would be the first to say yes if things were not so changed. You see, I have a business, I am interested in these orphan children, they need me . . . I have no feeling for this man. Oh, he's nice."

"A gentleman, not like this boor, this country dog, this fool man you're bewitched by . . ."

"No more bewitched, mother, than you are. Gennaro does say he loves me. . . . He said it only once, and he has said nothing since. But because he loves me doesn't make me love him. I tell you, mother, it's the truth. Do I have to go into things that hurt? I have put away all the dreadful memories, but I can't put away my feelings. I have no wish to be married, and what's more I do not need to . . . and that's all I can say."

In the end she consented to be present if the Manzella family came to dinner. But the dinner never took place. Donna Sofia let the matter drop. In letting the matter drop, however, she did not forgive her daughter for her obstinacy, nor herself for her softness, as she put it.

"I've been soft, soft, from the first day I married you," she complained to her husband. "This, though, is the end. I am not going to be soft any longer. I allowed you to drag me from my mother's home, where I was born, to this land, this place of work and misery and no manners. What happiness have I had, washing your clothes, looking after your children, watching you go off to work day after day? None. None. And now this thing—my daughter making a fool of herself with an old yokel who can't sign his own name, the father of her first husband—he was her husband, nothing can prevent that, in the eyes of God he was her husband! It's going to stop. The shame of it!"

Her plan matured long before either Don Tomaso or Carmela could understand what she was designing. Her oldest boys had been working steadily. The two younger boys, like Roberto and Emilio, had gone to high school but left after a short while. They had noticed how their older brothers were making money, dressed well, went out, and had many friends. They developed the desire to do the same. One had forthwith got himself a job with Salvatore Manzella and set about becoming a druggist; the other joined Giovanni as a carpenter's helper. Donna Sofia had no control over Carmela, but over her younger sons she exercised real power. They gave her all their earnings, consulted her in all their doings, begged of her for the money they needed, and listened to her advice with child-like faith.

Gianni and Giovanni had been employed for a long while now on a construction job in Cornwall-on-the-Hudson. A large Catholic seminary for girls was in the process of erection, and Don Anselmo had used his good offices in obtaining positions for the skilled young men. Industrious, steady boys, they applied themselves not only with zeal but with real intelligence to their jobs and were retained even when the work fell off in the winter months. In the first warm spring weeks they had organized an excursion to the job. Donna Sofia, Don Tomaso and the children all took the boat up the Hudson and prepared to stay in

Cornwall for a week. The sight of the mountains, green with new life, the flash of the sun on the water, the meadows atop the heights—these were the first sights of open country that Donna Sofia had had since her coming from Villetto.

They had just got off the truck that the boys had borrowed from their employers. It had wound its way through dirt roads flanked by elms and maples flush with the new leaves of the year, caught glimpses of pools bright with sun, and looked upon hillsides heavy with the growing brush. A silence had fallen upon the older people—a silence compact of memories that hurt and stung. The wooded slopes of Villetto quivered like distant uncertain shadows, and the whole countryside of their native place, dotted with copses and alive with little lakes, came trembling back into their consciousness. The laughter of Immanuele and the rough-housing of Carlino and Modesto were faraway echoes without content and meaning. The truck drew up against the farmhouse where the boys had planned to have their family remain, and the boys and their parents descended. Giovanni was leading his mother to the porch when he stopped short.

"You're crying, ma!" he exclaimed.

She wept now without shame.

"What is it, Sofia, what is it?" Don Tomaso inquired, alarmed.

"Oh, nothing, nothing," she laughed now through her tears.

"But why are you crying?"

They crowded about her.

"Because it's so beautiful . . . so beautiful."

Don Tomaso alone understood, and he took out his handkerchief and pressed it against his eyes. The boys just roared.

"And we stayed in New York all these years! No one ever told me about this—look, all these marvelous things, trees, and sky, and over there the river."

She had risen as if enchanted and possessed, her handkerchief to her mouth.

"Tomaso," she said, "we're not going back. We're going to find a place here."

The plan was discussed and finally approved of.

"And Carmela?" asked Don Tomaso.

"She will come here, too."

"And if she doesn't—then?"

"She will come where her parents are."

"Yes, but she has her own business . . . and her own mind."

Donna Sofia said nothing.

Once back home, she outlined her plans to Carmela, and spoke as if she were taking it for granted that Carmela would pack up and go along.

"Your brothers will have work for two or three years. Carlino will open a drug store—we have the place selected already—and your father will not have to work any longer. It'll be like being back in Villetto. We'll have a little house—you should see it, Carmela. It's old, of course, but the boys said they'll make it look like new ... and there'll be a bit of a farm for your father ... oh, how lovely, how lovely it's going to be for all of us."

"How marvelous!" exclaimed Carmela with genuine interest.

"Isn't it? You will like it so much after all this." Donna Sofia made an inclusive gesture of the hand to denote the whole of Harlem.

Carmela was silent.

"When will you be going?"

"In less than a month. The boys have already bought the property and are now fixing it up, working after their day's job and on Sundays."

"And the money?"

"We have enough. Do you know we still have the money we brought with us from the old country—all saved up in the bank, and what you gave and the boys—oh, there's plenty."

"If I can help out ... let me know. The business is doing well and I can help."

"But you'll be selling it!"

Donna Sofia threw her bombshell into the conversation boldly. She watched her daughter's face. It whitened, and her eyes filled with tears.

"No, ma," she said, "no ... that I am not going to do."

"But we can't leave you here."

"And why not? You have found a place you love, and you ought to go. I am not going to stand in your way."

"Of course not. You will come with your parents."

"No, ma, I am going to stay here with my own boys, and with my business."

The fight was on again. It concluded in a peculiar fashion.

2

Gennaro had heard of the arrangements the Dauris were making for moving to the country. They saddened him. He listened, and said nothing. The whole fabric of his life seemed suddenly to be undergoing a vast change. What had seemed fixed was shifting. He had become so close to the family that the intimacy had taken on the aspect of permanence.

What he dreaded most, however, was not so much the lonely floor in the Parterre, the coming in of new tenants, but the departure of Carmela. She had said nothing of her plans, but he divined that Donna Sofia was insisting that her daughter go with her. He decided to ascertain the truth.

He had invited Carmela to come into his car and drive to the church with him. The whole of the outside walls were up. Granite had filled over the network of steel, and the steeples, a gleaming brace of glinting stone, sprang boldly into the air.

"Just a month more, Carmela," he said to her as they at in the car looking at the building, "and the interior will be finished. Next week Saint Elena is arriving from Capomonte, and the cardinal is going to consecrate it."

"Wonderful!"

"We'll have a big celebration."

"Not fireworks?"

"Sure. The whole town's going to be on fire. Bands and everything, and a long procession. Don Anselmo's inviting all the priests. It'll be a great day. You'll be here, won't you?"

"And why not?"

"Then you are not going to this place in the country?"

Carmela did not answer.

"You are?" Gennaro asked it without disguising his anxiety. "What'll I do alone with all the kids?"

"They're grown up."

Gennaro in turn was silent.

"You must not go," he cried, after the pause, taking her by the shoulders. "You must not go. What's more, you are going to stay here, and marry me. We'll be married in the new church, the first day it's opened. You hear? We're going to be married . . . you and I. I have loved you all my life . . . Carmela . . . that is, since the day I saw you first."

Memories clouded about them and pressed them into awkward silences. There was the noise of hammering coming from within the body of the church. Carmela heard it and listened to it, hoping to escape the notes of the distant pain sounding in her mind. Gennaro listened to them, too, following the taps with eager interest, as if with the diminishing echo of each one diminished, too, the time between now and the day of a fulfillment longed for over many years.

"If for nothing else, Carmela, for the children—I need you for them, they love you, and I love you—you must not leave us now. Say you will, Carmela, here outside the church."

"Yes," said Carmela simply.

She looked up at him with a quiet smile, her eyes glowing and yet timid and withdrawing. She expected to greet his face smiling, too. Instead, she met a face startled into a fixed wonder-stricken gaze. Tears were in Gennaro's eyes, and his lips quivered. Slowly he placed his head on Carmela's shoulders, not touching her at all with his hands, and wept softly.

"There, there," she said softly, patting him. "There. . . ."

He raised his head quickly, smiled awkwardly, brushed the tears from his eyes with his fist, took a stiff position at the wheel, and started off. Only after he had gone several blocks did he say a word or show any further sign of emotion.

"I am not so old, Carmela. You'll see, we'll be happy . . . sure. We'll do big things, you and me. . . . You tell your parents now . . . hey?"

She merely looked ahead of her, evidently incapable still of understanding what she had consented to. The mention of her parents caused her lips to flicker with a smile.

"Sure," he cried, "they got to know right away. . . . We'll get married the day after the church is consecrated. And by Saint Jerome, they'll get the damned church up before the month's gone!"

3

Donna Sofia knew what Gennaro's mission was. He had sent Emilio up that evening with a message. Would she and Don Tomaso come downstairs or should he come upstairs to talk over an important affair?

Carmela had previously taken her aside and told her. She had been busy at the stove, stirring and stirring with a wooden spoon the huge cauldron of tomato sauce for the macaroni that night. When Donna Sofia cooked, it was with the sight of a whole squad of voracious adolescents encircling her. Nothing was ever prepared except in quantities that would outlast the appetites of the entire family. She had just turned over the solid chunk of beef with shredded onions and tomato-pulp clinging to it, savory and steaming.

"Ma," said Carmela to her, "I have something to say."

Donna Sofia put down the spoon and wiped her hands on her apron. Her face betrayed the fact that she sensed something serious in the tone of her daughter's voice. For no reason, she removed her apron, folded it slowly, and placed it on the table. She sat down in a chair near the window and opened the window wider, breathing in the fresh air.

"Well, I'm listening."

Carmela sat opposite her, her hands in her lap, waiting. She turned to her mother quickly, putting her elbows on the table, and leaned over spiritedly.

"I am going to marry."

"Gennaro?" Donna Sofia hardly uttered sound. She just framed the word with her mouth.

"Yes, Gennaro."

Donna Sofia put her hands on her hips. But the gesture was one expressive of thought rather than belligerence.

"So," she said, "so."

That was all. She remained in her seat for some time, saying nothing else. Carmela tried to make an explanation. But each time she leaned over closer, Donna Sofia raised her hand, motioning her to say nothing.

"Well, if I don't turn that meat, it'll burn."

With that she rose, replaced her apron, tying it behind her with some vigor, and resumed her operations at the stove.

She was prepared therefore to meet Gennaro.

"Tell your father, Emilio, he'd better come up."

In a few minutes Gennaro came. As usual, he threw open the door without knocking, strutted into the room swinging his shoulders, constantly removing and replacing his short-stemmed pipe.

"Here's a seat," Donna Sofia placed a chair before him. "Tomaso," she called to her husband in the outer room, and while she waited for Don Tomaso to join them she took a seat and stared at Gennaro. The silence between them was painful. It increased Donna Sofia's breathing and caused the erect shoulders of Gennaro to go gradually limp. She looked him over without concealing the contempt that she had hidden for more than a dozen years. He stole a glance at her now and then, feeling smaller and smaller each time. Don Tomaso walked in breezily and happily.

"Gennaro *bello*," he shouted. "Just on time for a bit of cordial I made myself. Last year I made it and only now opened the bottle. It's capital. A Sicilian drink—the *Quattro Compari!* A fine drink for parties. Here's the bottle."

He had opened the kitchen closet and reached up for a bottle. The splendid nut-brown liquid grew luminous as he raised it for Gennaro's inspection.

He poured the drink and offered it to his visitor.

"The fragrance alone, Gennaro, the fragrance—it, well, it reminds me of the spring in Villetto."

Gennaro assented that it did remind one of spring.

"It's warming, at any rate."

"Yes—like sunshine."

"Gennaro has something to tell us," Donna Sofia interrupted in a tone of voice that caused her husband to turn from his guest to his wife and back again with a bewildered look.

Gennaro thought it best to plunge into the subject at once. Evidently Donna Sofia had decided upon obstruction.

"Don Tomaso," he spoke without misgiving of any kind, "Carmela has promised to marry me, and I am going to marry her next month."

Don Tomaso had bent over to listen. He retained the position as if he had been molded into it, speechless.

"Carmela told me," is all Donna Sofia answered, and then said not another word.

"Well, I suppose," Don Tomaso found his tongue, "she knows best."

"She knows nothing," and with that Donna Sofia rose and left the room.

Gennaro stuck his pipe into his mouth and drew a long puff. The smoke circled in thin clouds about him, ribboned off toward the window, and disappeared into the vivid twilight of May.

Don Tomaso shrugged his shoulders.

"What can I say, Gennaro? You have my good wishes. I wouldn't have wanted this thing to happen. It has happened, though. Time moves on, and each day brings new fashions. That is what I have always said. I repeat it. I don't venture to say I understand. But you have my good wishes, my best wishes—both of you, both of you."

He looked steadily at Gennaro, but there were the signs of tears in his eyes, and his voice quavered.

Gennaro rose and took Don Tomaso's outstretched hand. They shook silently and long. Gennaro put his hand on Don Tomaso's shoulder and said, "She'll be happy."

Don Tomaso turned about and filled the cordial glasses once more.

"Just between you and me, Gennaro," he announced, raising his glass. "I want to confirm my good wishes—this way. Let's click. *Salute!*"[1]

4

Mother and daughter greeted each other for a month without once alluding to the impending marriage. While Carmela made preparations for her nuptials, Donna Sofia busied herself getting ready to move to Cornwall. Day by day the apartment looked more and more shorn. Gianni and Giovanni did not come home weekends, and had sent for Modesto. They were occupied in a feverish attempt to remodel the old farmhouse in time for their family to move in by the first of June. Don Tomaso had already informed his employers—he had worked for them for thirteen years—that he was quitting his job for good. As a token of their good will they let him have the whole month off with pay and he helped with the dismantling. Practically everything had been crated and was ready for shipment. Gennaro offered his trucks.

"Tell him," Donna Sofia answered through her husband, "we don't need his charity . . . neither his, nor . . . well, that good-for-nothing daughter that's going to eat at his trough."

Don Tomaso could not mollify her, and Carmela dared not speak for fear of arousing her to overt action that might be disagreeable for all concerned.

"The things are all ready to go. Why don't you get them off?"

Donna Sofia was hurrying matters.

"You persist?" her husband asked. "You will not stay for the wedding?"

"We're going to leave at once."

Don Tomaso seized her by the arms.

"You will do nothing of the kind. We're both of us going to stand in church, next to our only girl—do you hear, both of us, you and I, and we're going to have the boys there, too. She has been a friend to them all, more than a sister, and she has loved us and been a fine daughter."

Donna Sofia shook herself loose.

"Another long speech—always long speeches!"

"And I say, long speech or not—"

"You have said enough. You said enough fourteen years ago. You were going to make a fortune—buy up the whole of Villetto in a few years on the money you made in America! And what did you do—just get your hands stained red for the rest of your life."

Carmela interrupted them at this point. She had left off work early. For days she had been troubled by her mother's unbroken silence and by the sad look in her father's face.

"Ma," she spoke at once. "I came back early because I could not stand it in the store. I am going half crazy. Do you understand? You have no business to do this to me . . . no business."

She fell into a chair and wept.

"You have chosen your own way—it's in the other direction from mine. What shall I do, keep you in swaddling clothes all your life?"

Carmela jumped up, furious and red.

"You have no right to talk this way. You made me go through with something that I did not want—that was many years back. But what's happening now I want. It's my life. If you do not approve of it, that's one thing; but to treat me like a criminal—ma, ma, you can't, you can't!"

"All right, my good girl, I won't. I'll treat you like the grand lady you have become. Marry this one-eared jackass if you must, but don't come whining like a lashed bitch seeking my blessing. I should have thrown you out—"

Don Tomaso slapped his hand over her mouth.

"Quiet, quiet! Not another word!"

She struck him over the hand sharply, and turned upon him.

"So," she cried, "I'm always in the wrong, she's always in the right. So ... well, this time, I repeat, do as you please, both of you, but leave me out of your plans, now and forever."

She was as good as her word. The next day she caused all the household goods to be shipped to Cornwall, and with the help of the druggist, Salvatore Manzella, she boarded the train and was off.

Don Tomaso was alone in the empty flat. He paced up and down, disconsolate and unhappy, not knowing what to do. Carmela came in and said, "Come downstairs and have a bite to eat."

He shook his head, and continued walking.

"But you can't go without food, and without rest. There's not a chair here, not a bed. Come downstairs."

"No, I'll go out."

He wandered about the streets the whole night. Carmela and Gennaro set out to find him, but it was in vain. Emilio and Roberto had taken up the search, too, but they returned equally unsuccessful. He appeared in the store the next morning, pale and worn-looking.

"Carmela," he said to her. "Come out. I want a word with you."

They walked to the Parterre. On the way he did all the talking.

"Carmela, I love you. I want you to be happy. You are young, and you have many responsibilities. I am getting old ... you see, gray hair, my shoulders stoop. ... Where can I go? Back to Italy, with my tail between my legs, beaten? I can't, can I?"

She insisted that he have coffee and something to eat. Zia Anna, withered into a thin, bent reed, shuffled about, getting things for them. Her voice had become even more whispery than ever, and cracked more frequently.

"Fortunate daughter you have," she kept telling Don Tomaso. "He'll make her a good husband—he's gone through so much."

Carmela ordered her to remain in the kitchen.

"Pa," she said, "I know what you mean . . . and it's right. We intend to have a very quiet wedding anyhow . . . very quiet . . . and if you are not there, I shall not mind . . . you belong with ma and the boys—you must go there . . . today—after you rest . . ."

He seized her hand and showered it with kisses, weeping silently.

5

Emilio was now in his graduating year at high school. Because he had arrived in America when he was over seven years old, he had lost several years at school. At twenty he was a senior and preparing to enter college. His career had not been an easy one. He had learned English well, but there was something in the high school work which failed to enlist his solid enthusiasms. The things he had done throughout his childhood were entirely apart from the values put on them at school. Algebra, mathematics in general, interested him—as a matter of fact, he was interested in all the subjects, even in the Latin he had been required to take. But he questioned them at every point. The study of geometry possibly least only because he associated with the figures in his book the collection of wheels and pivots, screws and washers he had managed to salvage from the wrecks of old watches in his father's junk emporium. Some subtle fraternity seemed to exist in his mind between the drawings of Euclid[2] and the ingenious contrivances of the watchmakers.

In some mysterious way, likewise, he found in the work in chemistry—a very slight course, a dabble in vague theorems and slightly thicker fumes—some correlation with the transformation of the multitudes of rags and scraps of metal into other molds and fabrics. But Latin, and later even French, seemed without point. It was not until he progressed into the upper terms and began to understand his Latin authors that his interest in that language became an effective, abiding thing.

It was the same with French. He was irked by the patient need of conning rules and studying syntax. Once embarked upon the reading of stories in French, his interest flared into something steady and real. The curious thing about the whole course in high school, however, was the fact that his grades, as put down solemnly on official-looking cards, bore no relation to the progress he himself thought he was making.

When he studied with least zeal, as in the preparatory grammatical work in Latin and French, he received the highest marks. But it was just during that period that he despised the work. Later, when he had become so interested that he went outside the school texts to find material to read, he achieved even lower standards in numerical points. The consequence was that he was thrown in upon himself.

"Ah, I don't like it, Carmela," he kept repeating. "Why study all the junk? I'll get into papa's business and I don't need all this."

Carmela listened. She adored his powers of mimicry. He took off his teachers with just enough malice to make his caricatures impressive. But more than this, she enjoyed his little storms of rebellion against the whole curriculum and regimen of the school. He became intense and excited, found queer words of heat and opposition for his sentiments. He plunged her with him into his experiences and made her relive them as if they were her own. She led him on until he got to the point where he would launch into his most solemn denunciations. Then she would burst into good-natured laughter, ridicule his ridicule, and cause his whole program of criticism to tumble into confusion. He resorted to argument.

"You don't believe me? How would you like sitting up all night boning up on a bridge Caesar built? We don't build bridges like his today, we never are going to build a bridge like his again, and here we are learning the names of the joists he used, the foundations he sank. Why don't we read about how they built the Brooklyn Bridge, and now they're putting up that other bridge—what are they calling it, the Manhattan, yeah, the Manhattan—why don't we go and read about it and see how they're doing it? Sure, that's the way they ought to teach you . . . but this stuff *proelio facto, agmen*[3]—bunk!"

"Maybe your elders know better than you. These men who tell you what to study."

"What? That lanky bean pole, Reynolds! Say, Carmela, a man with a beard like his—on the tip of his chin—he doesn't know what it's all about. He's the only man in the world with a chin like that. He hasn't got eyes . . . see, he doesn't know anything."

"Oh, come off your perch, young blow-hard! I suppose you know a lot more."

"I can talk rings around him about watches and the kinds of metals and all about rags and how they make paper and where things are in the city—where they fought the battles, and where you can go swimming and row a boat . . ."

"You silly—oh, you silly. Where'll that get you? Anybody knows his own trade and where he lives. Why shouldn't he? But that's not getting an education. You know what I think is getting an education? Learning the things you would never want to know all by yourself."

Emilio threw his hands up to his matted curls and made a gesture of tearing them out.

"Oh, oh, oh . . . Carmela—what a definition! What a definition! It's just the opposite. Education's getting to know all you need to know about what you want to know, and that's all there is to it."

So they argued, and discussed, and considered. His problems became hers, and he did few things without consulting her. It was together with her that he saw his first play and his first motion picture. He had come home from school, he and Roberto, and announced that the teacher was selling tickets for Henry Irving in *The Merchant of Venice*.[4]

"We have to go. You know we're studying the play. Get papa to give you the money and we'll all go."

Carmela piloted the four of them to the play. The Harlem Opera House[5] had begun to enjoy a burst of belated glory. The population of upper Manhattan had taken a spurt forward. Once empty lots were being covered with immense apartment houses. Cliffs that had lined whole streets and been hangouts for gangs and goats, and been, here and there, solid foundations for squatters' rackety frame-houses, had been razed to the ground. There had been constant dynamiting for years and the youngsters from all the neighboring streets found it a pastime to assemble at a distance and watch the muffled explosions break down the gneiss and slate formations upon which they themselves had often played. The cinema was still showing short crude pictures of inaugurations and the launchings of ocean liners. The Opera House, refurnished as if for a long run of classics, had already brought *Rip Van Winkle*[6] to Harlem, followed it up with *Stanley in Manila*,[7] *Nellie, the Beautiful Cloak Model*,[8] the blood-curdling *The Bells*,[9] *Uncle Tom's Cabin*,[10] and now Henry Irving in a repertory of Shakespearean plays.

Gilda was as much of an actor as Emilio. When they returned from the theatre they made immediate plans for transforming one of their rooms. They hung up as heavy drapes as they could find, painted old boards with splashes meant to be the canals of Venice, found themselves feathers to put in their caps and vividly colored coats and dresses from Gennaro's inexhaustible stores. For months they played and played over again first one scene and then another from *the Merchant.* Gilda, in long red dresses, insisted upon being merciful on the least provocation. She loved to hear Emilio go into a passion of anguish, asking in melodramatic whispers, "Hath not a Jew eyes? Hath not a Jew hands?"

"Say it again, Emilio," she asked him over and over. "Well, say the speech in *Caesar*[11] then."

If it was not these passages from the works of Shakespeare, it was a dramatic rendering of *Bernardo del Carpio*,[12] or the *Skeleton in Armor*,[13] or *Inchcape Rock.*[14] First Emilio recited, then Roberto, or Gilda or Emilio both. She was untiring in her search for poems for them all to learn. She chanced on Browning quite accidentally. At fifteen, to her *In a Gondola*[15] was the quintessence of romance. She successfully begged Emilio to stage it for her. It was a grand affair.

The teachers at school had never discovered the young people's passionate interest in these things. It was only in Miss Reddle's mission club, where entertainments of all sorts were constantly being held, that Gilda and the boys developed their histrionic arts.

It was quite evident to Carmela that Gilda's main interest, however, was not strictly in the mere conning and spouting of the lines, nor for that matter in the intricate and elaborate preparations she made for them. These necessitated costumes and crude sorts of drops and gave her an opportunity to display her fine needle work and her consummate ability in depriving Gennaro of his best castoff dresses, rugs, tapestries, and table-linens. If required, she thought nothing of spending whole evenings in an astounding concentration on washing and dyeing, starching and ironing, patching and darning. It was the only labor into which she entered with all her energy.

But Carmela doubted whether she would have put as much thought and effort into it if it did not bring her into constant companionship with Emilio. As a matter of fact, Gilda seemed to begrudge every second that Emilio was not at hand or had no reason for spending his time with her. She was up in the morning long before he was, helped him pack his books and hurry with his breakfast, and walked with him the few blocks to the rendezvous of himself and all the neighborhood boys who walked to their high school. In the afternoon she was waiting for him.

"Want me to copy anything?"

He had got into the habit of depending on her and with her assistance maintained superb notebooks in history and chemistry. She copied out all his notes in a fine stiff hand, like miniature print, very beautiful to look at. She underscored important passages in various colored inks, and generously touched with red crayons the tips of the Bunsen burners otherwise conventionally indicated by rigid outlines. If he found fault with any page, she took his criticism to heart, weeping over it, but never threatened to withdraw her aid. In the end, when he declared with utter brutality that he had no use for all her work on his books, she did the offending page over, even if it meant staying up beyond her bedtime.

6

Carmela discovered her late one night rewriting a whole outline of medieval history from the Crusades[16] to the Hundred Years War.[17]

"Gilda, you ought to be in bed."

Gilda's heavy black hair had fallen over her eyes. She shook it off with a weary toss of the head.

"Oh, I can't go yet."

She answered resentfully.

"I don't like you to stay up so late."

"But I got to finish it . . . I have four more pages."

Carmela sat down beside her. Gilda was a very large girl. At fifteen her bust had filled out to adult roundness, her shoulders were full and square, and she was almost as tall as her friend. With her black pompadour she made a startling contrast to the auburn-haired Carmela.

"Let's see what it's all about."

Carmela looked at the notebooks and turned several leaves.

"Why, this is Emilio's book. Are you copying it for him?"

"He hasn't the time to do it himself."

"Nonsense. He has more time than you. Here you are up so late . . ."

"But Carmela, he has to have it in tomorrow morning."

"Well, for once he will have to do without handing it in."

"I promised."

Gilda had become belligerent.

"No, dear, promise or no promise, it's after twelve, and all little girls—"

"Oh, let me alone, I'm not a kid . . . and I want to do it. Don't come interfering."

Carmela found it futile to reason with her, and thought better of provoking the child into tears. But in the morning she spoke to Emilio. She made him walk with her to the store before meeting Roberto and his other friends. Emilio seemed more than delighted to walk with her. She walked fast and he kept up with her rapid strides.

"What is it?" he asked.

"Wait until we get to the store."

"Is it so serious?"

"Very. You ought to be ashamed."

"Ashamed?"

"You're nearing twenty . . . Yes, ashamed."

He took her by the arm. "What do you mean?"

In the store she made him sit down beside her.

"About Gilda, Emilio. Last night she was up until after one writing out your notebook. It's not right."

"She wants to do it."

"You do your own work, and let her do hers."

"Can I help it?" He was prepared to launch into an extensive defense.

"No talk, Emilio. There are other reasons too . . . she's doing twice as much work as she ought. She has her own work. . . . But there's more to it than that. . . . You really are not very nice to her. You don't take her to the games. She has to invite herself. And sometimes you chase her home."

"Sure. She can't be sticking herself into everything."

"Of course not. She's a child. She thinks you're the grandest thing in the world, and it's not right for you to take advantage of it."

"But, Carmela, I haven't done anything."

"I know. You don't really care for her."

"But I do. I like Gilda. She's ever so nice . . ."

"It's so sweet of you . . ."

"But I don't care for her in a serious way. Carmela, you know that."

He hung his head, and then looked up at her, his eyes troubled. She was sorry she had spoken.

"Well, that's all," she said, patting him on the hand. "It's funny the way I scold you."

Before she had time to take her hand away, he had seized it.

"Carmela . . ."

The word seemed to have sprung out of him like a cry. Something in his manner, his posture, frightened her. The same wild look, the same sudden pallor, had been on his face before. But before today she had not been frightened. Now the wild look was filled with intensity and strain, the pallor was like the loss of blood in a flurry of shock. What at other times had been adoration touched with a sweet awkward embarrassment was now young manhood passion horrified at itself.

"You run off," she said gently, disengaging her hand. "You're late, and the boys will be getting impatient."

He dashed out of the store, leaving her to think about him. She was five years older than he and a grown woman. It could not be a real nor a lasting feeling, this outburst of his. She had never thought it possible that such an attitude could manifest itself, much less develop at all. How had it all come about? It must be a boy's passing fancy. He would think better of it, put it out of his thoughts. If not Gilda, some other girl nearer his own age would soon take up his interest. She would mean-time show no sign of having understood what he had attempted to blurt out. She continued to treat him exactly as she had always done, never avoiding him, listening always to his accounts of the events in school or in Miss Reddle's Mission House.

7

Toward the end of his high-school career, they found themselves involved in a long discussion of their religious beliefs. It was Emilio who started it. Unlike Roberto, he insisted on explicit explanation, argument, analysis. Nothing seemed to reach a conclusion in his mind unless it had come as a result of a series of complicated wranglings that ran the total gamut of feeling from hot partisanship to even more heated opposition.

Emilio had concluded along with Roberto no longer to attend the Protestant mission, the church in connection with it, nor any form of religious practice. He was driven by the force of a newfound idea. It fell into the peace of the Parterre with the detonation of one of Gennaro's celebrations. It seemed to mark the beginning of a new life for Emilio, and he was determined to carry out its implications to the full.

"This church of my father's—what money he's sunk into it— whew!—it's crazy!"

Carmela invariably took the role of listener and rarely entered into debate. This time she was taken aback by his open assault on his father's ambitious scheme, and in her heart became alarmed. Gennaro had devoted eight years to the project. It had taken the place of stimuli that had called forth unwholesome energies. It had succeeded in reestablish-ing his individuality in his own sight, affirming as if in perpetual stone what he asserted to be the fundamental goodness of his aspirations. It was a concrete confession of sins which would otherwise have been so constant a torment as to have released the demon in him if only from a spirit of sheer obstinacy. He had squared himself with the world. But here was his son—to whom he was attached by a love so passionate that it was difficult for him to speak about it—ridiculing the accomplished fact.

"Rather strong language, young man!"

She smiled as if to indicate that she was not taking him too seriously.

"But I mean it, Carmela. It's crazy. What's it for? To worship an ancient deity that has no scientific basis—"

"And the boy's using long words."

"Well, it hasn't," he retorted sharply. "Have you read—"

"So much reading you do! What's the use of that?"

"It makes things clear. This question of God, for instance. You take God for granted. So does papa. Sure, I see why he does. What does he know? All these immigrants—right off the soil, what do they know? The priests have kept them ignorant for years. My father—"

Carmela watched the eager lad rather than listened to him. His round face, so much like his father's, glowed. His eyes—small and close to the nose, as bright and restless as Gennaro's—closed halfway, exactly as Gennaro's did, when he became animated. The black curls, too, were like the elder man's, a well-knit crown of hair. As he talked he moved about, or leaned over sharply, banging his fist, and at times stroking his mouth, just as if he missed the short pipe without which his father could never talk. She wondered as she watched—so close a parallel in physical points, so distant in habits of thought. And yet were they so different? They both thought with their emotions, and they packed into their emotions all the dynamite of their energies. Should they collide, she dreaded the ensuing explosion. It must not occur. She bent all her power of sympathy to the task of preventing it.

"Maybe you are right, now I think of it."

"Right! Well, I should say so. The church is an instrument of darkness for science, for truth, for social progress."

"To people who see it that way, it is."

"Then it must be so for everybody."

"I'm not so sure, Emilio."

Carmela spoke in a kindly way, suggesting that she agreed with him and indicating at the same time that there were things to which he had not given sufficient consideration.

"Don't you see, Emilio? Look out of the window. What do you see— the park, no? In a few years how tall the trees have grown, how perfect and big and shady. Now, if you lived in this room and never went out—"

"But I don't."

He detected the beginning of a counter-argument and wanted to forestall it at once.

"Suppose you did—you'd never believe that the water from the river really made those trees grow, the river you can't see from here, the river over there."

"What an argument! What an argument!"

"Maybe, Emilio, not so good as yours—but that's how those people reason. It's a comfort to them—why disturb them? It would kill your father—almost—"

"Oh, he's a tough egg."

"But you'd only get into a terrible row with him, and what good would it do? Listen, Emilio . . . you do like me a little, don't you?"

She took his hand and pressed his fingers.

"You do, don't you?"

During the pause that followed, he looked at her steadily, then lowered his eyes.

"You know . . . ," he muttered under his breath.

"Well then, will you promise me one thing?"

He did not answer, and she stroked his hair, combing it back with the flat of her hand.

"You're a man, Emilio."

He lifted his head belligerently, and his eyes blazed at her.

"A young one, of course, and you are away beyond your father and . . . us others who haven't been to school and read books."

"It's not books—I'd have the same ideas without them. You have. You have given up the mission and the church, and you don't go to the Catholic church either . . . you have the same ideas. I got them from you really. I watched you, ever since I was a little boy I watched you. I copied you . . . I . . . ever since my mother . . . Carmela . . ."

Once more the same fright came upon her. She wondered with a suddenness of apprehension at this developed attitude of Emilio's, unable to break it down in him, realizing that to talk about it was to bring it to a head, to ignore it was to keep it fanned, to accept it was madness, and in addition impossible. But her main concern at this point was to prevent an open rupture between father and son.

Emilio deep in his heart carried a kind of desperate love for his father, compounded of admiration and of fear and of memories of tenderness which seemed always charged with the hope of imminent renewal. Carmela had studied him closely. There was no mistaking the vigorous undercurrents of this feeling, prevented by the egotistic assertion of adolescence and the timid reserve of old age on the part of one and the other, from manifesting itself in overt acts of affection. She had attempted to fashion events that would call it out, but without success.

Now, in the midst of a more fearful agitation, she made up her mind that the two men must never come face to face in anger on an issue dear to them both. Only in a vague way did she sense that this agnostic passion of Emilio's was a mechanism of a self-assertion having for its main purpose drawing the line between him and his father with utter definiteness, so that she, Carmela, might be compelled to make a choice between opposites, that she might see in him some strength, too, as much as Gennaro's, but of another quality and directed to entirely different ends. She sensed it vaguely but refused to think about it. What she wanted most was that the issue would never be fought out in words or acts.

"It's sweet of you, Emilio, to think so much of me. But maybe you don't understand. I can see you like me, and I like you ... very much ... and that's why I am going to ask you to be nice and do something for me, for me alone."

He looked up quietly this time, become conscious of her desire to return to the previous topic, and anxious not to displease her.

"Never, Emilio, discuss this with your father—I mean about the church—never. Will you? For my sake. Just don't say anything."

8

Emilio kept his word. There were provocations enough for him to break it. Keenest of all was the strutting boastfulness of Gennaro as the church building neared completion. The services of Gilda, Ernestino, and Carmela had been enlisted in getting out invitations to the celebration. Don Anselmo, grown ruddy-faced and corpulent, exuding a good-natured air of a great and solemn bustle, bobbed in and out of the house. He knew all about Emilio and Roberto, but let neither of the boys become aware of his knowledge.

"Ah, we could never hope to have your services, Emilio, nor yours, Roberto. You do well to keep plugging at your studies. The last year, isn't it? Ah, that's a difficult year. Well, we are all praying for you ... and how are you getting on, Gilda? Dozens more to write?"

Don Anselmo's Italian had become mixed with numerous English words. He spoke neither language by itself. No sentence he uttered but started off in one language only to finish in another.

"Ah, *Gennaro, bello bello, evviva evviva, lo possiamo sgridare, sai*[18] . . . yell it out to the world, we've completed a great, a great job."

How he burned—but Emilio maintained his self-control. He had promised, and he would not speak. But when he learned of the marriage that was to take place between his father and Carmela, he clenched his fists in an agony of silence. He heard it first from Gilda.

He had drawn his chair near the window, tilted it back against the side of a book-case, had placed his calves on the back of another chair in front, and in that position of precarious balance was absorbed in reading his history lesson. Gilda had rushed into the room, shouting.

"Emilio, Emilio . . . oh, guess, guess!"

She was out of breath.

"You might give me one of the chairs."

She sat down and leaned forward.

"Oh, Emilio, you'd never know—the grandest news!"

In Gilda's presence Emilio behaved on all occasions as if he were a granite statue. He said little, looked stolid, and seemed forever immovable.

"Well, come on out with it! Don Anselmo's gone and got married, I suppose."

"Oh, don't be so nasty. Wait till you hear . . . Carmela . . ."

It was Emilio's turn to sit up, all attention.

"Is going to be married!"

Gilda shouted it joyously.

"And guess to whom. Guess—guess—"

Gilda saw Emilio turn pale, but she could not stop the impulses of her buoyant proclamation.

"Gennaro—your father. . . ."

"Oh, get out of here."

She thought he was joking. He had got up and gone to the window, pressing his face against it. She tried to continue.

"Get out, get out!" he screamed.

Realizing that he meant it, she withdrew timidly to the door. The silence lifted the ache out of the drooping shoulders of the young man and sent it like a dull reverberation through the room. Gilda, despite her fifteen years, understood. She, too, grew pale. She placed her hands over her face and wept.

"Get out!" She heard Emilio shout it again, wildly, in anguish, and she rushed disconsolately out of the room.

At the window, he clenched his fist and fell into utter silence. The gas-tanks that hid the river loomed enormous and opaque, boundaries between him and a distant area beyond the immediate through which he was searching with firm, painful gaze. All the activity of the streets, ordinarily so tense and real, fell into a discordant hum that attempted to attract his attention and then scatter it. But with clenched fists, his forehead pressed against the window-pane, he looked out into the far reaches of the May afternoon, unhappy and alone.

So Carmela found him. She did not know whether he had heard her enter the room. She stood behind him and called his name, softly.

"Yes," he answered, swinging round quickly.

"I meant to tell you myself. But Gilda, the old gossip, went shouting it around to everybody."

"She told me."

He brushed past her, and went out. And for some reason she could not put in words, she fell into the chair, buried her head in her hands, and wept. Fear clouded her mind. She dared not think. All she understood was that some indefinable pain had come to her with the suddenness of light, and pierced deep.

9

"About the wedding, Carmela," Gennaro said, taking Carmela aside on one of his daily visits to her store. "We'll have it nice and quiet—sneak into the church, like, and slip out, hey? There'll be plenty of fireworks when we consecrate the church."

To Carmela it came as a merciful decision. She had been dreading what might have been the effect on Emilio.

Her mother's removal she accepted without rancor and without indignation. There seemed to be within it a quality of inevitability which excused it and took the pain away. Her father, she knew, was going about his new duties in the genial pacific silence he had developed as a protection against his wife's continuous bitterness. And as he did so, he was blessing her, and thinking about her, and being with her. That was soothing. Her brothers and she had drawn apart. The older ones, successful at their work, had risen to the stature of adults long before the normal time and had fascinated the younger ones. The troop of them wheeled and marched about to the tune of Gianni and Giovanni's mastery. Carmela seemed to have been forced out of the circle, and there had come about no common point of intersection. Definitely she was in the orbit of Gennaro's family. Her own was a thing of the past. She accepted it sadly enough but without the sense of irretrievable loss.

But it was different with Emilio. For several years she had looked after him in a real way, been companion to him, and the center of his thinking. She had watched him develop and loved him as one does a person for whom one has expended one's greatest effort. What had occurred she could not have foreseen. Despite the episode of her childhood that even now was capable in retrospect alone to render her limp with fright and shame and anger, she was so completely lacking in the seemingly instinctive coquetry of her sex that she did not consider herself either attractive or able to command attraction by any wile or art. She was overwhelmed and shaken by the feelings Emilio had displayed, and now more than anxious to make sure that he forget about her and take to the normal lines of his own age. She realized the agony it would have been had Gennaro insisted upon all the young people attending the ceremony. Gilda as her maid of honor and Struzzo as his best man, and the bridal group was complete.

But on her return from the honeymoon, things took on a more ominous aspect. Gilda had been cherishing the homecoming as an event that must be as gala as the ceremony of the marriage had been simple.

"We must, we must do something, Emilio," she cried.

"Leave me out of it."

"But why? He's your father."

Roberto took Gilda aside.

"I think we had better do nothing. I don't think Carmela herself would like it."

Roberto was as soft-spoken a young man as Emilio was assertive and forceful. His long pale face, and his long smooth neck, and his long arms and fingers gave him an ascetic aspect that accentuated a dreaminess that the quiet blue eyes and the soft hair falling over them created. He allowed Emilio to take the lead in all things, feeling keenly the anomalous position of foster-brother to the originally well-to-do boy, and deciding that such a course of conduct was best. The only matters upon which he took a four-footed position and stuck to were his own ideas. Like Emilio he had become imbued with a freedom of thought that had cleared out of his mind and heart whatever religious habits had developed in him. But he went farther in his thinking, though he spoke less.

For Emilio he had a real love and affection, and so understood exactly what was happening to the boy. More so, possibly, than Emilio or Carmela could have realized. For he himself, ever since his first contact with Carmela, had been in love with her, too. But only he knew about it. And he was understanding enough to admire and to worship her as if she were a distant star far beyond his powers to reach. There was nothing he would not willingly have done for her, and that was ultimately the reward he gave himself.

Emilio's reactions to Carmela's wedding had filled him with dread. And now of all things, the worst was to have a gay party at which Emilio must be present. That he would do all in his power to prevent. He spoke to Gilda.

"No. Carmela would not be pleased. Why did she have a quiet wedding at the church?"

Gilda wept. "Oh, you're all against me . . . you and Emilio, and even Ernestino, though he likes parties . . . only Zia Anna and me . . . we can't have a party if you boys won't pitch in."

"Well, we're not going to have one."

But Gilda's mind was made up. Just so long as Emilio did not command her to do nothing about it, she was going to have one. She ran over to Struzzo and persuaded that gentleman to organize an impromptu celebration. No one was to know about it. It would happen, and that was all. Roberto and Emilio remained completely in the dark.

Largely because of the example of Roberto, Emilio had become absorbed in his studies for the final examinations. They spent their entire afternoons and evenings reading, making outlines, quizzing each other. Gilda was in a ferment, but managed to conceal it. She begged permission to stay in the same room with them when they were studying on the promise of being perfectly quiet. They allowed her to remain one evening, but decided against it after that.

"You're in the way," Emilio informed her.

"How? I don't do a thing."

"That's it. You don't seem to fit."

She accepted his decision without question, and, in a sense, gladly. She began working in her own room on a great floral wreath of artificial flowers. She had learned to make them in her mother's millinery shop and now she was in a veritable stew of ecstasy over using them this way. Afternoons she spent shopping, and in the evenings, bolting her door, she worked with feverish speed. The piece was going to be a double pillow of white roses, each with a center of mignonettes to spell out PEACE, HAPPINESS.

On the day of Gennaro and Carmela's return she helped Zia Anna make the bridal couple's bed, smoothing out every wrinkle, polishing the brass knobs until they glowed like lamps, flicking out of the room every grain of dust. On the bed she insisted on spreading the crocheted coverlet that Carmela had herself made—a combination of lace panels and crocheted strips without the usual flower patterns so dear to the Italian, but arranged in patterns that were strange and arresting.

No sooner had the telegram come announcing the homecoming than Gilda ran to Struzzo. Struzzo called for Giovanni Sardi to collect his guitar and mandolin orchestra. From the big café of Don Felippo were to come huge trays of sweets and confetti. The choir boys from the church and the girls of the choir were all dressed up in their church vestments—the girls in white veils, carrying candles, and they marched through the streets, gathering a crowd of followers as they did so, and took positions in front of the Parterre. They lined up on each side of the stoop and formed a lane for the home-comers to march through. Giovanni Sardi's string band waited in the parlor to knock out the gayest tunes they knew.

10

The June day was sunny and hot. The park was filled with strollers and sitters. The sidewalks opposite were lined with pushcarts laden with mounded vegetables and fruit. The whole neighborhood had poured into the streets in a fervor of summer happiness.

Emilio stood at the window of the second story, Roberto at his side, looking down, saying nothing, clenching his fists and pressing them hard against his thighs.

"Struzzo did it, Emilio," Roberto said. "Not Gilda, I am sure."

"What are you telling me that for?" cried Emilio angrily. "You would think I'm against having a party for them. . . . It's the thing. Why not? I wasn't present at his first wedding. He's going to try to show me what he thinks a wedding ought to be like. Sure. . . . I know my father. There's no one can do anything just like him. . . . Look, look at that crowd of men over there, see—all the café loungers . . . with bags of confetti. . . . I wouldn't be surprised if they were filled with nickels and dimes, too, and if my father had his way I bet there's a five-dollar gold piece in every bag. . . . Playing the big boy . . . largesse, you know . . . like in the old days . . . setting himself up for a big guy. Ah, it's disgusting . . . but let him have his fun."

Roberto listened. He even laughed when he thought it would be proper. It might soothe Emilio's feelings. But he felt at the same time he must change his friend's attitude.

"You ask me, though, Emilio, I don't think it was your father did this. Struzzo must be responsible for it all. And what of it? Carmela—"

"Why drag her in?"

"Not dragging . . . don't be so snappy. I was saying, she deserves . . ."

"Sure, she deserves it. After all, look whom she married . . . my father—biggest shot in Harlem—money—everything. I'm going out!"

Without another word he bolted the room and was gone from the house before Roberto could catch up with him.

Gennaro and Carmela drove up in one of Struzzo's new limousines. Dozens of business men of the neighborhood, Dr. Giovannelli, and Dr. Rosilli, Rocco at the head of a ragmen's group, and a delegation from the society of Saint Jerome, had gone to meet the couple at the station. As they drove into the block, the crowd shouted. Gennaro stepped out on the running board and waved his hat to everybody. Carmela rushed up the steps between the lines of boys and girls, and as she did so, men on the opposite sidewalk threw into the air handfuls of confetti of various sizes and shapes, handfuls of small coins, while the crowd in the street scrambled wildly, shouting, jostling, laughing to gather the scattered coins and candies. Giovanni Sardi's string band played the march from *Aida*.[19] The strains floated outside and a dozen voices took up the melody. Gennaro, still on the running board, shouted along with the rest and kept waving his hat.

"Grand, Struzzo, by Saint Jerome . . . grandest thing ever. Hurrah!"

Carmela had embraced Gilda and was holding her close. Roberto stood nearby sheepishly, but smiling with happiness. Ernestino, as usual, made no special point of the affair. He remained where he had been from the first, near the bandmaster, turning the pages of the score.

Gilda was weeping in Carmela's arms.

"I'm so glad, so glad to be back," she said, patting the girl, "and to be with my boys and girls again. Hello, Roberto, have you been studying!"

"Sure. You look marvelous."

"Oh, it was so good, but I am, I am glad to be back. And who got all this shouting crowd together? We didn't expect it, and didn't want it. But it's nice . . . it's so sweet of everyone."

"I did it," Gilda cried happily.

"You darling, you darling," and Carmela kissed her cheeks over and over again. "But where's Emilio?"

Roberto could see that she had been looking around for him ever since she came into the room. He saw that she was pained at his absence, and uneasy because of it.

Gennaro rushed in, pipe high in air, the scar on his ear red from the flush that spread over his entire face. He shouted wildly to everyone, calling them by name and embracing each one. He was about to take out of his pockets things which he had bought.

"Where's Emilio?"

"Out," Roberto said fearfully.

"Out, out, when I'm coming back from a trip? What's the young scamp mean, out? Fetch him, Roberto ... tell him I command him to be here. By Saint Jerome and the Holy Calendar, out at such a time."

Carmela realized how pained her husband was by his son's absence, but said only the obvious. "Oh, he's bound to be nearby. After all, we set no time."

"He ought to have been at the station. By Saint Jerome ..."

"He'll be here soon."

Gennaro turned savagely on Roberto.

"Where did he go?"

"Out...."

"Out, hey, out? Is that all you can say?"

He obtained no more precise information, and so he stuck his pipe in his mouth, puffed madly at it, then quieted into an ominous silence. Without a word, he went downstairs where Zia Anna's dinner was to be served. Emilio's chair was empty. Carmela attempted to fill the silence with a continuous narrative of her experiences. Roberto, as desirous as she of avoiding any further reference to Emilio's conduct, kept plying both her and Gennaro with questions. The dinner ended, but the joy that was to be part of it had not touched the hearts of anyone. Gilda, excited and happy as she was at Carmela's return, ate little, held her foster-mother's hands in hers, kissed her now and then, and tried to sit up brightly and listen to the running story that Carmela told. Ernestino, sitting next to Gennaro, ate voraciously, but found it possible to talk with his mouth full of food about everything that had happened to him in the absence of his parents. Gennaro's account of his trip, given only in answer to Roberto's questions, did not interest the boy at all. When he was through with his dinner, he excused himself.

"I have an engagement."

"So," said Gennaro, "even this young whelp's got things of his own to do. You and I don't count any more, Carmela."

He rose and left the house. On his way out he met Emilio on the steps. He transfixed the young man with a stare, a stare filled with anger and sadness both, but said not a word. Emilio looked up at his father, his eyes trembling and uneasy. He, too, passed on without uttering a syllable.

In his own room again, he pressed his face against the pane and gazed out over the park. He wondered how long would it take the dusk to blot out the saplings rising within it like soft, pencil shadowings. He counted them—one, two . . . three. He wearied of it soon, and looked beyond them. How quietly the cluttered tenements merged into the serene pink-toned gray of the evening air. Why could he not fade as they did, or be lost like the scattered cries and murmurings of the neighborhood? Subdued to the lowest cadences, they quivered in random notes and fell into the pattern of the evening. Emilio looked out upon it in the deep silence of his unhappiness and trembled.

At the river's edge where he had gone, he had sat down on a pierhead and gazed into the water. He seemed to be doing that now, and all the sights ahead of him appeared swimming in the depths of moving water, distorted momentarily only to achieve newer and newer outlines. At the river's edge he had wept in a baffled, exhausted way. There were tears now in his eyes, and it was through those tears that he was aware of the scene ahead of him. But once he brushed them from his eyes, the trees, the houses, the expanses of the street assumed their normal lines, and the agony of his experience seemed newly intensified.

Carmela found him thus.

"Emilio," she called to him quietly.

He turned around abruptly and exposed his wild, tear-stained eyes to her.

"Oh, Emilio, Emilio." She shook her head.

He clenched his fists and gazed at her, expecting her, like him, to burst into tears. But she did not. She merely continued in the same tone of voice.

"It was so mean of you . . . so mean of you. You hurt your father terribly."

That was all she said. Then she left him. He followed her form into the darkness of the stairs, made a movement to pursue her, but dropped instead on his knees at the foot of his chair, buried his face in the warm rough plush, and sobbed.

CHAPTER THREE

1

*H*ome life by its very nature brings about adjustments which achieve a surface comfort and the illusion of stable peace. Gennaro and his son met and talked and lived in the genial acceptance of each which is the mark of friendship between father and son. Carmela's tact and charm, acting like a rich clear solvent, filled the Parterre with a new life and the young people fell quickly into its spirit. She continued her personal interest in each one of them, discussed their college plans and their life at college, and as treasurer of their establishment provided them with sufficient funds for them to enter into all of the activities they were minded to.

She never went to her millinery shop in the morning without first seeing Roberto and Emilio start on their walk to Columbia at the other end of the town. When they were to stay out late, she waited for them, and had coffee and food ready. She was in bed only when Ernestino, Gilda, and the older ones had gone to theirs.

Gennaro accepted the regimen without question, content as he had never been before, and showing his contentment in numerous ways. He rarely returned from his business without having his arms filled with all manners of tid-bits from the stores. He had never been a man for going to the opera or the theatre. Noticing that Roberto and Emilio discussed plays and music, he proposed family parties, and was not hurt when the boys refused to join in a whole caravan, as they called it. Instead, he went with Carmela, and for a week afterward sat around with the family, listening to the talk of the music or the production, interlarded with strange terms that the younger members had picked up in their studies. They baffled and annoyed him, but he listened. Occasionally he shouted, "All I know, it was fun," but that was the extent of his comments.

So passed the first year of his marriage. It was as quiet and happy a year as was possible. A disturbing factor was the constant messages from Salvatore Manzella, the druggist. Not successful in obtaining Carmela for his wife, he turned to Gilda. His mother, a brisk little woman with an unusually sharp chin and a sharper voice, called personally.

"Signor Accuci, your foster-daughter . . . I come about her and my son. There is no use being long-winded—that's what I always say. An affair is best concluded, not when it's strung out, don't you know? Well, my son, he's a splendid man, a fit husband for anyone. Shall a mother praise her own children? That is not fitting. Everyone knows him—you may find out for yourself. He wants to marry your girl, Gilda. A fine girl . . . and he's a fine man. There could be no better match."

Gennaro shifted his pipe to the other side of his mouth, blinked, and looked at Carmela.

"Should we not ask her first?" Carmela wanted to know.

Mrs. Manzella, who was so thin and angular that she found it more comfortable to sit forward in her chair, stiffened up at the question and at the same time opened the collar of her coat.

"I am sure she is willing. She comes to the store often enough."

Carmela was as amazed at the information as Gennaro was, but made no show of it. Gennaro took a long puff on his pipe and shot up from his chair.

"By Saint Jerome," he muttered, "the girl's certainly put something over on us. So . . ."

"Of course, signora," Carmela interjected, "if she wishes to marry him, the affair is concluded, as you say."

It disturbed Carmela to her depths, however. Gilda might be going often to the drug store and meeting the druggist. It meant nothing. Ever since her own marriage to Gennaro, it was quite obvious that Gilda had ceased throwing herself at Emilio. But it was equally obvious that Gilda's love for her foster-brother had become if anything deeper and fuller. Gilda was now seventeen, and through high school. The problem of what to do for her had not come up. It was taken for granted that she would enter college like the rest of the young people. Gennaro had expressed in his own forthright way his disbelief in further education for the young woman, but as usual had acceded to Carmela's wishes. This question of Salvatore Manzella was another matter. Was the girl finding an easy way out of the tragedy that was growing in her heart?

Gilda knew that Emilio loved not her, but Carmela. Why had he grown quieter and more serious since Carmela's marriage? Why did he try so hard to fit himself into the general scheme? Certainly he revealed in no overt particular the feelings he had for his foster-mother. But he could not hide it either from Carmela or from Gilda. Gilda, always in advance of her years, was at seventeen mature in thought and feeling

and capable of conduct actuated by sensible motives and fine understanding. And she was capable, too, by a like token, as Carmela divined,
of quixotic conduct as well. Unable to have Emilio, and unwilling to
remain constantly not only in his presence but also in Carmela's, was
she resorting to the device of a decent marriage as their friends would
call it, to cut herself off from the scene of her unhappiness? Carmela
decided to find out.

On the night of her graduation from high school, Gennaro had
insisted upon a huge party in one of the downtown Italian restaurants.
He had also insisted that Emilio must present Gilda with a purse filled
with gold coins, a gold chain and pendant—a pendant imported from
Italy and holding a cameo of great age and beauty. Emilio had balked.

"By Saint Jerome and the thousand miraculous saints," his father
shouted. "There's only one thing got a stubborn will like yours, and that's
the old donkey I had in Capomonte, way back in my youth. By the horns
of the devil, you're going to do it. What the hell do you think you are?"

Carmela laughed as if she had taken the irate remarks as a form of
intended joke.

"He stubborn, Gennaro? No, indeed, just timid, that's all. You know
Gilda would like it, Emilio. Why not please her and me?"

It was done, and a pretty speech he made. Everyone admired him for
it. And Gilda took the pendant and the money, and rose on her tiptoes
and kissed him while all the table applauded.

But that night Carmela found her lying on her bed weeping.

"I know, dear, I know...."

Gilda sat up.

"I'm sorry, but it's been such a marvelous evening. Oh, I'm just too
happy. All the money I got, and the gift, too, and the speech, and the
dancing afterward.... Oh, I'm so happy. That's why I cried, Carmela,
honest, that's why."

She wept on Carmela's shoulders.

After a while, Carmela helped her to undress. Gilda sat on the edge
of her bed, removing her stockings and talking gaily.

"Oh, I'm so glad the party was so nice. All the girls I invited loved it.
Did you see how sweet they were on Emilio and Roberto, too?"

"I certainly did."

"They're nice girls—awfully nice girls. Some of them are going to
Europe, Carmela, and did you see that sweet one with the big blond
pompadour—it's all her own hair, too ... well, she's going to get married and go to Europe, too."

Carmela seized the opportunity.

"You're not planning the same thing, are you?"

Gilda looked up bewildered.

"I mean, only the other day, you know, the Manzella woman came here and said something about it. Darling, he wants to marry you."

"Oh, really?" Gilda laughed. "He's never said a word to me."

"Still an old-fashioned Italian! Sent his mother as a special pleader. Would you marry him if he did ask you?"

Gilda gazed directly at her questioner, trying to be as steady as possible.

"I would think about it," she answered.

"And finally?"

"Say yes."

The two women looked at each other. Carmela was afraid that there was a sort of accusing rancor in Gilda's brave, upright manner. She saw through the girl, however, and realized that the controlled, assured manner was but a pretense, not a sign of the spirit within. The depths of the girl were troubled and restless, a maze of painful conflicts, conflicts which, despite her maturity and good sense, she was not altogether capable of either resolving or concealing.

And Gilda looked at Carmela with a flickering smile playing about the corners of her mouth and eyes alert to catch whatever display of emotion Carmela might make. She loved Carmela with all the affection of a younger girl who has admired a skillful beautiful woman all her life. That Emilio should have loved her, too, seemed only natural, if distressing to all of them. She did not blame Carmela in the least, but at the same time Gilda had always hoped that Carmela might never know of her own affection for Emilio, or, if she knew, might never allude to it. In her heart she prayed now that Carmela would make no mention of it. It would be too terrible. Something of this fear was in her attitude and her silence, but she resolved it must be kept hidden. Carmela knew what was in Gilda's mind, and she on her part was determined that it must not appear in the open. And so they looked at each other silently, smiling with thankfulness for each other.

"You're sure, darling, you love him?"

Gilda nodded.

"Of course, if you're sure."

"I'll make sure."

"Make sure? How?"

"Do you think Gennaro would let me go to Europe . . . alone? You see, I'll have a chance to—" she looked up smartly—"forget and remember. If I forget Salvatore entirely—then it's off. If I can remember what he looks like and still like him—maybe I'll say yes. . . . Isn't that some scheme?"

It was left at that. The whole Struzzo family was going to Europe, and Gilda joined the party. She was to leave them in Naples and proceed to her mother's family for an indefinite stay. As usual, the family celebrated. Preparations went forward with ever-increasing fervor.

Gilda and Emilio engaged in numerous discussions as to the value of a stay in Italy.

"All Italians should go back and renew their love for their past."

"Love for their past? Which past? The Roman past and the past of the sixteenth century? Or the past of their miserable enslavement? Or the past of their recent history—the betrayal of Garibaldi and the republican hopes of Mazzini? The kowtowing to this country and that?[1] Let Italians forget. That's what I say."

"You're just getting stupidly serious, Emilio. First it's one thing and now it's this idea. Oh, I'm not going to Italy to study art and history and all that. I'm just going to meet people and learn about them and what they do, and if they are the same as we are in America, and I'm going to have some fun, and that's all."

"You might better stick around here and forget you're an Italian. . . . Oh, hell! You'll have more fun here."

"This'll be different."

"It's all right with me, and lots of luck."

The morning of her departure she ran into Emilio's room. He had just completed dressing save for the tie he was pulling through his collar. He was startled to see her standing in the doorway, her full form in a tight-fitting traveling suit, the skirt of which reached to her ankles. The strange tinge of red that ran through the otherwise solidly gray cloth was a effective foil to the jet black of her hair, and to the small toque-like hat with its wreath of quiet, distinguished cockades of red. She looked excited and uncertain, and hesitated before entering further. After a pause, she shut the door behind her and stood against it. Emilio was so overcome by the sudden invasion of his room that he could not proceed with his tie-knot. He saw how flushed and high-strung she was, and stood stock still.

"Emilio," Gilda called to him. "Oh, forgive me. I did not want to do this. I kept telling myself all night that I must not do it. But I couldn't help it. My mind was made up to run past your door and downstairs and never talk to you . . . never, until we got on the boat."

"What are you talking about?" Emilio said. "What's all this that you didn't want, and you wouldn't and you're doing and . . ."

"You would be brutal."

"Gilda, Glida, what's got through you?"

"As if you didn't know! Oh, Emilio, how can you stand there and keep staring at me when I'm burning up—burning up, do you hear, with shame, for being such a fool."

Emilio went to her. "I don't mean . . ."

He was close to her, and she put her hands out.

"Emilio, I'm going away. For good, I hope. I don't want to see you again, but I want to tell you, now . . . I love you . . . I love you . . . that's why I'm going away."

She had kept him off at arm's length as if she were in mortal terror of touching him or being touched by him, standing the while stiffly against the door.

"I hate leaving New York. I hate leaving this house. I hate leaving you. You can't help it. If you don't love a person, can you help it? I know . . . but I . . . I love you, and I'm going to obey your instructions . . . let Italians forget . . . I'm going to . . . I'm going to . . ."

And without another word, she turned around and fled. Emilio stood quietly for a while, thinking. A second later he shrugged his shoulders, and, going to the mirror, finished knotting his tie.

2

During the year the Accuci family—children and all—settled into a jog-trot happiness. Gilda's animation had always set the key higher than it became during her absence, but happiness even at an octave lower proved a sweet blessing.

Emilio and Roberto had only two years more to go before completing their studies at the university. These studies always awed Gennaro. Pipe in mouth, feet spread out, arms behind his back, he would stand at the side of one of his sons and pore over the books spread out on the table, smiling if he could make out a number, grinning with unabashed delight if he saw a picture.

"God hasn't got so much in his noodle," he confided once to Carmela, "as those boys. Notice what big books they got, and how they keep writing all the time?"

"It's precious little they really know," Carmela confessed to him. "Emilio doesn't want to know any more."

"What? Wants to quit the college? He's got a splinter in his brain, that boy. It keeps him yelping all the time at this, at that.... First it's the church, then ..."

"But it's mostly talk."

"Not with him. When he talks he means it ... like me ... I never had an idea I didn't talk about, and I never talked about it only ... see? Like marrying you. I knew I wanted to marry you ... I have told you ... from the first ... you must be getting tired hearing me talk about it."

They sat at opposite ends of the table after their evening meal. Zia Anna was too old to clear things off, and so she had trained her grandchild to help. She and her grandchildren now occupied the top floor of the Parterre and did all the work.

Carmela had been trying to reclaim the three of them ever since their father had been imprisoned along with the younger boy. She made trips now and then to the reformatory where the little fellow was and to Sing Sing where the father was imprisoned. Zia Anna was so grateful that she never passed Carmela without seizing her hand and kissing it, with a sucking motion of her toothless mouth. She insisted that Gemmina do the same thing. But the girl, close to eighteen, was sullen and withdrawn, a heavy-bosomed shambling-gaited young woman who never looked one in the face. She was practically compelled to remain indoors by the machinations not only of Zia Anna but also of Carmela. It was Gemmina who now was pulling the table-cloth, on Carmela's side, with a jerky, rebellious gesture, plates, bread, salt-cellars, forks, and half-emptied bottle of wine. She had heard Gennaro's remarks and something of their sentiment had annoyed and irritated her. She was easily annoyed and irritated and made sure that everyone about her knew that she was.

"Why, there, by Saint Jerome, that's no way," Gennaro shouted. "Take it easy, take it easy."

Gemmina cleared the table finally, and stalked out, slamming the door behind her.

"That's a hot-blooded mare for you," Gennaro jerked out to Carmela. "A stallion or two ..."

Roberto and Emilio, if not Ernestino, flashed into her mind.

"Don't talk like that," she said.

"Oh, no offense, Carmela ... no offense. Using strong words again, am I, hey? Ah, but you know we Southern people got to stick a bit of garlic into all our food."

He made a quick transition back to Emilio's attitude toward his college work.

"You talk to him, Carmela. No use my doing it—better be priming an empty well than talk to that boy. But he listens to you."

He put his hand upon hers and drew it across the table to where he could stoop and kiss it. The fall evening had become darker than usual with the feel of snow in the air and the gathering of clouds over the river. The outside noises penetrated into the unlit dining-room with individual distinctness and were louder than ordinary. A tug, expending exceptional energy on a long heavy tow, chugged harshly over all the sounds.

Carmela was pleased at Gennaro's gesture, and allowed her hand to remain in his longer than she normally did. There was a sweet exchange of understanding between them at all times, but their love lacked the quick flare-ups of passion that Gennaro might have desired and even the occasional drop into just laughter and a jolly sort of silliness that she on her part might have welcomed. Except for the discussion of common interests there was little or nothing of the intimate play of love that endears and strengthens affection. This gesture of Gennaro, therefore, came as an unexpected thing, timid as it was, but welcome.

"Gennaro," she called his name softly, and in the crowded moment of the dusking the name sounded like an echo of far-off music nearing and nearing.

He stopped to kiss the hand again, but this time she withdrew it.

"What is it, blessed one?" he asked.

There was the slightest suggestion of a tear in his tone. For some subtle cause not definable in language he was moved by her voice, and he felt himself urged to fuller expression than he ever had employed before. "Carmela, my dear one, what is it? Your voice sounded then so strange to me . . . it made me sure I love you, and I want to get on my knees and pray to Saint Elena who gave me to you, thanking her with all my heart."

She ignored the tenderness and sweetness of his speech—moved though she was by it and grateful to him for the feeling. They were now in total darkness and in total silence save for the slit of light under the door to the kitchen and the whispery voice of Zia Anna behind it.

"Gennaro," Carmela called again. "I am with child. . . ."

Gennaro's immediate reaction was to jump up with his usual vigor, and shout, shout with the suddenness of joy, shout so as to force the lump out of his throat, shout so that the world might hear. Instead, he bent his head lower than before and pressed Carmela's hand closer to his lips.

Gently she withdrew it once more, and rose.

"I am tired, Gennaro. I am going upstairs."

He, too, rose without a word. There was something he wanted to say to her, something in the nature of the prayer he had thought of for his patron saint. Instead, he laughed awkwardly.

"You won't forget to give that big fellow a talking-to, will you, Carmela, about his college?"

3

But it was just that that had cast a cloud upon her spirits—the necessity for still mothering Emilio. From the day Gilda had left, Carmela had divined a change in the character of the young man. Gilda had been an outlet for him. He could cuff her around with his words, as it were, take out on her the feelings that now and then became pent and close within him. Now he merely became quiet and unhappy, and stared at Carmela as she moved about the house with a longing for affection that went through her like a shaft, a thin blade of pain that cut deeper and deeper into her feelings. She had begun to be frightened and uneasy. She knew that this new outburst of criticism, directed this time against the college education he was receiving and not against the church, was of a parcel with his adolescent infatuation for her. She could no longer sit with him and discuss his plans and his ideas. The mere nearness affected him and he burst into angry noisy talk . . . a wild mocking bravado with which he battered down all ideas that seemed reverent both to her and to Gennaro. In fact, the more she espoused them, the more she hinted at what Gennaro felt about them, the more reckless he became in denunciation.

"What do I need to go on with all this flum-flummery? It's just a feather to stick in one's hat, and who wants it? The old fellow would like to go around slapping his chest and yelling, 'Look me over, the big shot, I got a son out of college!' You'd like it too . . . your step-son a Columbia graduate!"

"That's just stuff and nonsense, Emilio. It's for your sake . . . you don't want to stick in this sort of place all your life, baling rags for a living?"

"Why not, why not? Suppose I know the binomial theorem and the dates of Galerius[2]—what the devil?"

There had been sweet afternoons between them when he had merely sat with her and read to her. He had become proficient in his Italian and attempted translations into English of the Italian poets. Leopardi[3] became his favorite. One afternoon he sat at his window and she in a chair nearby. The Sunday was a pleasant one and the park was filled with strollers and children shouting at their play. Gennaro was asleep, and Roberto had gone out with Ernestino. He read to her first in Italian, and then in English, the most bitter of Leopardi's laments. *The Evening before the Feast Day* he read with lyrical fulness, as if it were the expression of his own feelings.

"That's too sad, Emilio."

"But so true. . . . Be happy . . . it lasts a minute . . . and listen . . . 'that time of life when the road of memory is long and the road of hope is short' . . . that's great!"

"Oh, that's for an old man. Not a boy of twenty-one."

"Well, that's how I feel!"

"Ninny . . . but why."

"I do. I don't know why. I do. Maybe because I'm still a big baby."

"You're a nice enough baby, but a big baby you are."

"And listen to this: 'how sweet it is to drown in such a sea' . . . the sea of the evening like now . . . notice how the sounds get fewer and fewer, the kids are going home with their mothers, they're all tired and it seems just too much to keep going."

He had dropped his book at his side, and his eyes felt through the soft evening twilight for hers. A silence fell between them—a silence that was all echoes of muffled heart-beats. She rose and left him. From then on he had avoided her, and she him in part. Now he kept to his room studying harder than ever but rarely taking whole-hearted part in the family doings. She knew why and shuddered. What would happen when he heard of what was to happen to her? She shuddered as she left Gennaro, went upstairs, and prepared to go to bed.

4

As Gennaro and she lay in bed that night, she shuddered again, perceptibly.

"Not feeling right?" he asked her.

She merely stroked his hand.

"You got to give up that shop . . . that's too much now, looking after that and this house and everything."

"Oh, never, it'll take care of itself. . . . As a matter of fact, Gennaro, I was thinking of giving it up—up here in Harlem, I mean, and moving it downtown in the fine sections."

They talked of that. Gennaro made some feeble objections. Actually, he could not have opposed her. He was too proud of her ambitious projects and believed too deeply in her ability to carry them to a successful issue. He would have been pained had she listened to his arguments and abandoned her plans. As she lay at his side, quiet with the confession that she had made, she seemed more than ever the shining miracle of his life. A great contentment fell over him. He lay motionless, following his thoughts.

Always they came back to the lovely woman at his side, young and intelligent, sweet and yet capable as a man, yielding and yet upstanding and strong-minded. For once, the sense of a deep security, a charmed and sun-filled serenity filled his heart. He had come to his fulfilment. Let his hair turn completely white, the wrinkles about his eyes grow numerous and cleft-like—his slipping into old age was going to be as gentle and sweet as his first years had been harsh and turbulent.

His business was running itself. It could keep running without him. He was the possessor of numerous buildings paying good rents. There was nothing he wanted that he could not have. The old wounds had healed. His wife's death and Domenico's death he had atoned for. There was the fine granite church to witness it, and the daughter he had dedicated to God. Her letters had become fewer and fewer. The memory of the girl was becoming dim and indistinct. The whole episode was merging with the shadows of the days far back. Life was beginning anew. It was a new day beginning in the twilight of an old one, and it was going to be warmer and brighter.

He chose not just these words to make the feeling clear to himself, but in the movement of his blood coursed the assurance of its existence. He turned to kiss Carmela. She was asleep. And so he gazed upon her face in the dark of their room. Light slanted in upon her from the electrolier[4] on the corner.

It was good to took at. It seemed both familiar and strange. It was familiar with memories not only of her, but of all the other women he had known. Their countenance seemed merged into hers and at the same time seemed to have written their peculiar traits into the resultant face. There were the soft, fleshy cheekbones of his mother, the straight chin of Rosaria, the madonna-like contours of Dora Levin, and even—by Saint Jerome and all the saints—even the worldly qualities of those other women—so many that they had no names, the women that eased the overflowing energy of his early days, that were the noisy, brawling prelude to this peace, this beauty, this fulness.

And the face was strange, too, stranger than he cared to admit. It was filled with lights that he could not understand, with quiverings that marked the passage of thoughts hidden from him. Something was troubling her, and it became a part of that loveliness upon which he gazed. That she might not be happy did not occur to him. That she might have memories out of a tortured past, of course, he knew. That she had been left alone in New York by the family for whom she had worked all through her young womanhood he knew, too. But it was not that. It was a different species of anxiety, something he could not put into words of his own, something which both excited her and subdued her, animated her and calmed her into a deep seriousness.

He could not know. All he understood was that she lay at his side, and was his, in all the exquisiteness of her youth. He kissed her softly and fell asleep.

Two events marred the immediate future of Gennaro.

There was the matter of Rocco Pagliamini. It was almost twenty years ago that Gennaro had floored his employer and wrested the business from Rocco's hands. The relations between them had naturally not been without an undercurrent of suspicion and uncertainty.

Rocco Pagliamini had remained content with his rag and junk shop put up for him by Gennaro. For more than fifteen years he had even remained friends with the man who had driven him from his original business and compelled him to establish another one. True, Gennaro had been a powerful ally and a willing one. The terms upon which Rocco had rented the space for his new store had been not only generous, they had been without any burdensome quality whatsoever. If Rocco could not pay, he did not pay, and for several years Gennaro allowed him to go without making suitable advances on his arrears. Rocco played a kind of game of it. He falsified, deliberately and unshamedly, whatever slight books he kept so as to give the impression that his business was always in a precarious condition. With the money he saved from rent in this way he contrived to establish a fund for real-estate operations.

These he conducted through his wife—the Elvira he had been sending for, over a period of years. She had come, he had married her, they had a large family, and he had prospered. She proved to be a sharp business woman, seeing eye to eye with her husband in all matters and imbibing from him the spirit of animosity and opposition to Gennaro which Rocco had nursed for years. But like him she, too, had discovered the proper formula for postponing whatever action might bring them the satisfaction of revenge, but also possible disaster to their business and their home. As time passed, the hatred for Gennaro seemed to have passed too. They accumulated money with the years, they had become substantial house-owners, their children were doing well at school— why bring on trouble? So they were friends with Gennaro.

And then came the depression of 1907.[5]

Like all depressions, its central Wall Street explosion had its reverberations in such a remote place as Little Italy some months later. After all, the mass of workingmen had been accustomed to slack periods, and this seemed but another slack period. Their grocers and their landlords, their furniture dealers—who had sold them their plush chairs and big brass beds on weekly instalments—and their insurance agents, still collected their dues. The family savings were in most cases adequate for a period of months, and so throughout the winter and the spring life moved at its customary pace.

The cafés were lighted; the saloons blazed into the late darkness; the Christmas week was gay with wandering bag-pipe players, and the newly erected nickel shows—in which irreverent tramps threw custard pies into bloated faces leering under radiant top-hats—were crowded. On Easter day palm-bedecked hats hurried home to heaping plates of macaroni and roasted chicken.

But in the beginning of the summer, at the time when Carmela was expecting her baby, things changed.

Rocco seemed to have had the instinct of a bird about the severity of the economic storm. He felt its first tremblings and began to scurry to cover. His real-estate operations had been in the realm of the most ramshackle type of tenements, tenements that were dirtier, more run-down, darker and smellier than the car-barns they faced. Only the lowest of the so-called "submerged tenth" of the period were without sufficient pride—or, as the radicals of the day hinted, funds—to seek the flimsy malodorous shelter of these insect-corroded places. Their dirty infants sprawled in the mud-caked hallways or sat in the offal piles in the streets. Filth pails crawling with vermin, piled up tier on tier, fire-escapes flapping with soot-streaked washings, roofs with cornices battered away, gaping windows often stuffed with ancient rags— no running water except from a common rusty pump in the hallways, often no bannisters for the rickety creaking stairs, no paint for the walls—tinder boxes stuffed with the refuse of years and the poorest dregs of men and women! Such were Rocco's houses. But while there was work, the rent-money rolled in. And it meant almost one hundred percent profit—no repairs were ever made, new window panes never put in. By a like token, the first severe onset of unemployment showed its initial ravages in these pestilential lazaretti.[6] Rents stopped almost at once . . . and the courts refused to dispossess. Rocco became truculent, to his own damage.

There were the foul items of a small family's household effects piled up one day outside one of his houses. It had been the second and last case of successful dispossess. Crowds of children stood around, touching the sunken sofa, the backless chairs. Their elders stood around, too, cursing the courts, the landlords.

Rocco, as usual, his face smiling, somewhat debonair in a new suit, his large-boned Elvira at his side, emerged from the house when they had seen the last of the articles of furniture taken out. At the same time a huge car drove up, and several dapper, tight-trousered young men dropped out of it. One of them, sallow-faced, with a scar from the right side of his mouth running semi-circularly to the chin, wearing a winged collar and cravat, made more conspicuous by a huge brilliant horseshoe stud, shuffled up to the pile of chairs and pans.

"What the hell?" he asked.

Everybody hushed and looked up.

"Well, what's the noise?" the sallow-face repeated while the tight-trousers crowded close.

A slat-chested woman with a scrawny baby pawing at her neck raised her head. She was seated in a rocking-chair enjoying the tragedy of her eviction. Everybody had vied in language that became constantly fouler.

"They put me out."

"Couldn't pay no rent, hey?"

"Sure, my husband ain't worked and so he ain't give me a cent, and I ain't got no credit no more and so he ups and leaves me, see, with all them kids."

Four of them without shoes, their little bodies showing through gapes in their blouses and dresses, pressed close to her.

". . . going off, he says, maybe he'll find work somewhere but we ain't heard for a month and this guy . . ."

Rocco and Elvira had worked their way to the front.

" . . . this guy, he don't mean nothing, he's got to live, too, see, but he won't wait, he wants his rent, so he says get out . . . and so they come . . ."

"They do, hey?" Sallow-face came forward, slim, eager-eyed.

"Yes, they do."

"Got another place to go?"

"Yes, down the block, but I ain't got the money."

"This'll do the trick," he said, and placed a bill in her hand.

"She ought to pay me first."

Rocco said no more. The sallow-faced gentleman had a fist, and the fist catapulted through the air and Rocco fell to the sidewalk.

"You're getting yours now."

The crowd moved away, open-mouthed, too awed to make a sound. The tight-trousered followers of the sallow-faced gangster took gratuitous kicks at Rocco. Elvira shrieked. Some seized her and tied a handkerchief about her mouth. Others dragged her and her husband into the car. They were deposited in their junk-shop, and the doors ordered shut. Rocco had come to.

"You say a word of this, and you'll get more."

Rocco's money was going fast. He had no plans, trembled at the future, but did nothing. Elvira, however, prodded him until he appealed to Gennaro.

"Gennaro, I'm going broke. You got to do something."

"Well, rents aren't everything. You got the shop."

"The shop! Hell, it isn't paying. You got all the business. What we small fellows got, hey? We have no chance against you. You got to help me out."

Rocco was prodded further by Elvira. The old fires sprang up.

"Look at him," she kept saying. "It isn't because he has more brains than you. He's got the corner you had. He's got the customers you had. All he owns by rights belongs to you. He's got to give you something."

But Gennaro himself was beginning to feel the pressure.

"What do you want me to do? You have your troubles . . . I have mine."

Rocco's houses went on the auction block.

Elvira shrieked. "You cheap coward. You have the man in your power. Go to the courts . . . it isn't too late."

But Rocco had fallen into a grim, silent mood. The rag-business had decreased to the point where he was barely making enough to pay expenses. It went from bad to worse. He could not meet the mortgage charges on the house in which the shop was located. Gennaro had sold it years ago, making a handsome profit out of it. It had seemed to Rocco then a good buy. Now the transaction haunted him. Rocco figured that

Gennaro had foreseen what would happen and had played a low trick on him.

"A shrewd bastard, that, Elvira."

"Sure, he must have known. Has he sold other places?"

"He's held on to the good buys. Sure . . . he sneaked it over on me. God. . . . Elvira, I took him in, gave him a job, good money. . . . He'll have to do something for me now. He's got to."

So Rocco again called on Gennaro.

"Gennaro, you got to take the house back. Do you want to see me in the street?"

Gennaro removed his pipe and held it up between him and the scared-faced man.

"You're talking rot. Hold on for a while."

"Hold on! That's easy to say—if you got something. Mine's gone . . . trying to hold on to the other houses. . . . Gennaro, by the saints you hold dear, don't make me go crazy."

"I got my own troubles."

Elvira and Rocco decided to let the house go. They sold it at a loss that eventually ruined even their old rag-business. There was nothing to do but to sell that, too.

Rocco again appealed to his old friend.

"Once, Gennaro, you remember, I almost stuck a knife in your throat. You have stuck one in my heart. I have four children. What's this handful of dirt I got for my store? It's nothing . . . look what you got . . . look at this place . . . all brick now . . . and the trucks you own . . . the buildings you own . . . they ought to be mine."

Both men were now gray-haired, and both now were deeply wrinkled, and their eyes—even those of Gennaro, filled with the content of his new life—were the eyes of men who had faced a strange world under many difficulties and wrested power from it. But there was a real sadness in them as they looked at each other. Gennaro's in particular lost their spark for the moment. His friend's distress cut into him. Something of the old doubts crept into his mind. He wondered whether he was now not faced with a real problem of atonement, not one that could be solved by pointing to the church, or explained away because it had brought him Carmela. Should he tell her of it? What would she say? He dreaded that. And yet, deep in his heart for many years, he had thought over the bold act of piracy that had netted him the thriving rag-business. Not that he could not have started on his own and achieved the same results. By Saint Jerome, you bet he could!

Sure. But he had kicked Rocco into a back street. He had pushed him down to a poorer section for the business they were in. As long as Rocco had done well, Gennaro could overlook the decided wrong that he had perpetrated. But now that Rocco was going to smash—that was different. Yes. But times were different, too. And he had paid Rocco ten times over for the old shop. What did he want now?

In view of his own happiness with Carmela, the situation distressed him. He had no envy in his make-up. He was not really mean—only forthright, he seized what he wanted. Gennaro had reasoned it all out. It was too late to do much now, no matter how sad he felt about his old friend.

"I'll tell you what, Rocco . . . I'll do something for you."

He threw off his coat, he got so excited. He stuck his pipe into his mouth and walked up and down the room he now called his office. It had a desk and typewriter, filing cabinets, and a rug on the floor. On the walls were photographs of his trucks and photographs of the old horses he had given up for them. Under one he had had printed "OLD," and under the other "NEW." There was a frame with a pattern of old rags of many bright colors and designs—the work of Emilio, of which Gennaro was very proud and to which he invariably called attention. The late June afternoon poured heat and noise into the open windows. The cries of the men at work in other sections of the building mingled and floated off with the strains of the assorting women's songs.

"Here's what I'll do, Rocco. By the thousand saints—yes!"

Rocco too, rose, in expectation of something miraculous.

"Carmela's going to have a baby, and I'm happy, Rocco. I'll do something for you. In her honor. I don't need to, you understand. I got as many men now as I can handle. I'm keeping lots on, though I should fire them. I don't need a manager. I'm that, and Emilio could take it over, see. But by Saint Jerome and the blessed saints I'll make you manager . . . at a good sum, too . . . sure . . . come here . . . let me show you."

He dragged Rocco by the hand.

"See this room? Remember that was the old second story—old frame house . . . rotten wood . . . see now . . . steel, this beam, and these doors iron . . . and the bins, notice the bins . . . all . . . what they call it . . . cargated . . . yeh, cargated iron . . . no fire'll ever happen here . . . not on your life . . . big place, hey! And here, Rocco, look . . . changed, hey? Remember we had wooden frames to hold the big baling cloths . . . they're steel pipes now . . . and see this . . . look . . . over your head . . . the pulleys . . . sure. . . . Look, you pack a bale, you bring the hooks of the pulley down, you jab the hooks into the bale, you turn this handle, watch . . . hear it whirr . . . machinery . . . rrrr it goes . . . up comes the bale . . . and watch . . . it slides along those beams up there . . . see . . . like rails . . . and whew, out of the window it goes . . . and it hangs there . . . then the men on the street back up the trucks . . . look . . . lean over . . . care, there, ho . . . see that drop . . . men stand on the bale and go down with it into the truck . . . a minute . . . another bale . . . the truck's filled. . . ."

Gennaro was exhausted. He turned on Rocco and slapped him over the shoulder. Rocco reeled, and became pale. His eyes stood still in their sockets and glared out at Gennaro like live coal.

"What the hell, Rocco? Frightened at looking down?"

But Rocco continued to glare. He could say nothing.

"What's scared you?" Gennaro asked. "You're pale as an egg-white!"

"Nothing . . . maybe the heat. . . . I was thinking . . . imagine getting buried under those rags . . . in a bale . . . a hot day like this. . . ."

Gennaro roared with laughter. Once more he slapped Rocco on the back.

"You damn fool, what ideas! Well, how about it?"

"About what?"

"Being manager? Having charge of all this? You'll make more than having your own shop. Hey?"

Rocco laughed uneasily. "Seems like getting kicked downstairs."

"Fortune, Rocco *bello,* the great dame fortune . . . *Com' pium' al vento* . . . you know . . . Verdi . . . the opera . . . sure . . . *Com' pium' al vento.* . . ."[7]

"Is it easy . . . getting kicked downstairs."

"Between friends? Rocco . . . hell! It's coming back . . . back to your own . . . and there'll be more money in it . . . sure . . . By Saint Jerome, I'll pay you a salary and give you something besides, so much per bale, per pound of metal . . . see. But don't go and get buried in one of those bales."

5

That evening Gennaro was in one of his merriest moods. He came home with his arms weighted down with every conceivable fruit and tidbit of cheese or salami he could find in the stores. But he found Carmela in a mood completely different.

"What is it?" Gennaro asked, placing his packages down.

"Dr. Giovanelli . . ."

"Say anything wrong?"

"No . . . they found him . . . dead in his office . . . it was so terrible . . . alone he was, Gennaro. . . . He was dressing . . . he did not have his coat on . . . he was just putting on his scarf . . . the red sash of Garibaldi . . . it fell out of his hands on the floor . . . and he fell down over the chair . . . struck his head . . ."

"Not like what he wanted, hey?"

They decided to take charge of the funeral and all of its concomitant details. Nothing would do for Gennaro but to have a parade. He assembled all the Italian societies, especially those that affected various uniforms of the Italian army and navy. Bands were hired. Huge limousines were filled with local celebrities. The stores were festooned with black crêpe. In one of the limousines he and Carmela rode. She had not wanted to, but Gennaro had insisted.

"Sure . . . what will I do without you at my side in the carriage, hey?"

Emilio, however, had flatly refused. No amount of urging by Carmela prevailed.

"Why do you talk to me like that? You must think I'm a baby in arms?"

"Oh, Emilio," Carmela pleaded. "You haven't been nice . . . nice to your father . . . nice to me. . . . What's the matter?"

"Does it matter?"

"Yes. A lot, Emilio. After all, we're very fond of you."

He bolted the room without saying a word and left her stunned.

After the funeral, Carmela and Gennaro returned at once to their home. She had already begun to complain.

"We must hurry, Gennaro. Tonight, I think. . . ."

Gennaro insisted on her going to her bed at once. It was evening. The stairways were dark and quiet. Zia Anna, bent over double almost with her eighty years, had taken advantage of their absence to pay gossiping visits in the neighborhood. Roberto had not returned home from the funeral. He pleaded an engagement that evening, not knowing what was to happen to Carmela. The Parterre was vacated. The stillness of it seemed like the absence of all life.

"Call Dr. Rossilli at once," Carmela pleaded.

"I'll have to leave you alone. Everybody's out."

"No matter, go," she cried.

Gennaro rushed out.

Carmela alone in her room, the first pains of her birthing upon her, looked vacantly into space. The scene with Emilio that afternoon had distressed her. It kept building itself up in her mind in fantastic forms, each one different. First it seemed that Emilio struck her violently and threw her from him with all the force of his young strength. She lay huddled against the bed now in pain. That was the pain she was feeling. And as the pain increased, she wanted to scream out his name, and ask him "Why, why did you do it?" The next moment, with a subsidence of her agony, the scene changed. Emilio had taken her into his arms and wept against her shoulder. It was he now who had fallen to the floor, his head in the crook of his elbow, sobbing in pain. Again she wanted to cry out his name, and then stroke his hair, his forehead, softly, soothingly. Then all pain went away, and calm settled upon her. The darkness was falling rapidly and filling all the corners of the room. Only the clock— the huge clock that Emilio had salvaged and repaired and given to her for her room—pounded into the silence. She counted each one of its heavy ticks . . . and then it seemed to stop. There was the sound of laughter . . . the laughter of Gemmina, coarse, self-pleased laughter, not ordinary laughter, but laughter like that of lovemaking, like that of one being caressed and stroked. . . . She shuddered . . . and listened. It was unmistakable. . . . It was Gemmina and Emilio . . . she heard his laughter now . . . and hers . . . mingled . . . she shrieked. . . .

"Emilio, Emilio . . ."

And as she called, the pains of her body seized her as if in perverse sympathy. She grasped the rods of the bed-stead with her hands and clutched with the force of a vast despair. But the agony of it was good. It shut her ears to the sound of the laughter upstairs. It blocked the path of her vision, and the shambling-gaited coarse figure of Gemmina receded behind curtains upon curtains of mist.

She called again—sharply, with jet-like suddenness. Her voice hung in the silence. She heard it like a thing apart, apart from the wallpaper ahead of her that squirmed in fantastic whorls, apart from the long brass rods of her bed that shone like vivid pencils of flame and ran and broke into the mists, gathering, forever gathering about her. Oh, it was so difficult to hold on with her hands. The cool brass rods had become streaks of heat. It burned into her flesh. But she must hold on, only so could she fight off the unearthly grip that had seized the middle of her body and drawn the rest of her muscles and nerves about it. She must hold on . . . there was that laughter still upstairs . . . fainter surely . . . but it swelled and rose with her pain and fell off only as she held tighter and tighter and called and called. . . ."Emilio" . . ."Emilio."

Now all noise had ceased. All pains had gone. She relinquished her hold. What blessed peace! How her body sank into softness, the limbs relaxed, the muscles quiverless and reposed, her skin delightfully moist and cool. And, oh, the whole world had fallen away! There were no walls crowding in on her, there were no flaming rods at the foot of her bed, there was no flooring beneath her. Oh, that forever and ever she might float thus on the receding waves of a refreshing morning mist, and hear nothing, see nothing, care for nothing.

The noise of the door downstairs! The noise of a door upstairs! And the pain once more—a sudden massing of hands about her entrails, pressing them together, not once slackening their grip, not once easing the pressure, relentless, steady, fiendishly strong. Would no one come to help, help her pull away from her this fury of constriction, tightening ever and ever? She tossed her head from side to side, she threshed the covers with her hands, she bit her lower lip with her teeth to keep the shrieking pain within her, and then she fell back exhausted, moaning, not caring any longer what the long agony was doing to her, indifferent to the sounds of the doors, the footsteps on the stairs, the murmur of numerous voices . . . it was all so much like the activity of a dream, clear and meaningless, here and gone again, reshaping itself into ever odder and odder forms.

All she wanted now was Gennaro, his rough gentleness, his hesitant caresses, his timid anxiety . . . all so sure, all so ready.

"Gennaro," she called, "Gennaro . . ."

She looked up with wild pain-filled eyes. There in the doorway stood Emilio, his frightened face pale and distorted.

"He's on the steps, Carmela . . . he and the doctor . . . they're coming. Oh, God!"

He covered his face in his forearms, and ran.

6

The baby was still-born. She had wept when they first told her about it. But now the sadness of it was too great for her to believe that tears would help. She was conscious only of a void that would never again be filled.

Gennaro was at her side in the faint light of the dawn. He held her hand in his and said nothing about the child. It had already been taken away. Dr. Rossilli promised to see to its being properly buried. Gennaro would have nothing to do with it. He wanted Carmela to forget—to forget and get well.

"I am lucky to have you, my blessed one."

He made the sign of the cross.

"All night I prayed to Saint Elena, on my knees, Carmela, down in the kitchen. All the boys, too, were on their knees, and I called loud for that little girl in the convent in Italy to be on hers and be praying, too. It was the only thing we could do, my darling . . . while you suffered here . . . fighting death . . . you dear one, you dear one. . . ."

He laid his forehead in her hand, and remained so, quietly, trying not to disturb her. Sometime later he heard her saying something. She was too weak to move.

"Yes?" Gennaro called, bending over her.

"It's Gemmina."

Gennaro was startled.

"Gemmina—what about her? Want to see her?"

She nodded. He could not understand it, but he sent for the girl. When the big shambling young woman, with her animal-like slanting eyes, stood at her bedside, holding her apron nervously in both hands, Carmela motioned Gennaro to go away.

"Gemmina," she whispered softly, "bend over."

Gemmina came closer to the bed.

"I may die, Gemmina . . . and I want to say . . ."

She paused to catch her breath.

". . . something to you . . . listen . . . no more . . . last night something happened . . . I know . . . it must not happen again . . . you will work somewhere else . . . not here . . . it must not happen . . . you hear?"

Her voice had become momentarily strong. Gemmina drew back, her hand in her mouth, not daring to speak.

"You hear, Gemmina? No more . . . no more . . ."

After that, she fell back asleep. They thought her dying. The next morning she was brighter, and she let the women of the neighborhood crowd into her room. They made every possible sound of sympathy without actually uttering a word. And they placed on the table and on the floor bags filled with fruit, boxes of sweetmeats from the café, a brace of dressed fowl, a huge cake, little wicker baskets containing soft creamy cheese.

One old woman with a vivid yellow kerchief over her head and shoulders, and her face alive with wrinkles like water in a breeze, stood at her bedside and prayed to the Madonna for her speedy recovery.

"All the workpeople in the rag shop sent me. They wanted to send a gift. But the good God saw fit to take the infant back to him at once . . . blessed may he be unto eternity, Amen. So what can we do? Just pray to the Holy Virgin for your good health.... Oh, Virgin Mary..." she broke into a clear loud cry ..."thou who hast had the agony of a suffering child, thou wilt understand when we pray thee to be merciful, to go before thy glorious son and tell Him to be kind to our Carmela."

Late that evening, Emilio stood at her bedside, alone.

When he saw that she recognized him, he fell to his knees at her side. She lay still, conscious of his presence, saying nothing. She felt his hands on the bed, trembling, agitated. The tired feeling became intensified. The room dropped out of her existence. She was far away on a high place, and far off Emilio kept calling into the wind.

As soon as she was well and on her feet again, she managed to procure Gemmina work with another family. She gave no excuse except that she thought it was better for the girl. To assist Zia Anna she employed a woman who had just arrived from Italy only to discover that her husband had run off several days before her arrival.

Carmela busied herself, too, with the removal of the millinery shop. For months she had gone about in the district around Thirty-fourth Street, looking for a suitable place for her establishment. The salesman who had been instrumental in creating the idea in her mind was her constant companion on these business trips.

One day Gennaro said to Emilio, "Emilio ... you know what? You are doing nothing. College is all over ... you don't work or nothing.... Why let Carmela go by herself? We got the car. You drive. Why she must use the subway, ha?"

Emilio turned pale.

"You no want do it?" Gennaro asked angrily.

"I would be getting into her way."

"I no think so. She will like it ... we got fine car ... we use it ... that's all."

"She's got plenty of help, papa. She doesn't need me around."

"All right ... all right ... you feel that way ... all right."

Emilio sensed that he had hurt his father, that there was something troubling the older man and that he had by his refusal troubled him all the more.

"I drive her myself," Gennaro said at length, "but the business is in a mixup just now ... things are bad.... I must be in the shop."

Emilio consented. He took the place of the salesman, and day in day out drove his step-mother about. After the store had been selected, it became necessary to order fixtures, display devices, mirrors, rugs. They went about together, arguing, disagreeing, reaching conclusions only after thoroughgoing discussions. Young man that he was, he brought to the debates all the off-hand theories of esthetics he had imbibed in his literature classes and the sketchy survey course of art. She listened intently, but chose her own articles. Occasionally she made a concession. The white alabaster jardinière, holding crisp giant ferns almost stiff as metal, was his selection. He declared it gave the quiet softly-lighted store its peculiar distinction. That was the only ornament, that and the essential lines of the fixtures themselves.

The changes in the family began to disquiet Gennaro.

"Carmela," he called to his wife one evening. Summer had set in early, the streets were crowded, the park noisy, and every sound floated into the Parterre. "It's so empty here, the noise rushes in like water in a bottle."

"I know," she said. "Everybody's gone."

"Emilio could at least eat home."

"Well, he's a young man . . . I'm glad he's going out so much."

A shade of a cadence into a lower note seized his attention, and he looked up alarmed, almost hurt.

"Seems you miss him, too."

"I do. . . . Here we are alone at dinner."

Gennaro was not accustomed to the casual caress within the pauses of conversation. He wanted to, but he did not rise and walk softly behind her chair, put his arm around her and place his cheek against her. Their life together was a magical union to him, a compound of unreal dream and exciting realities. The shadow of any bewilderment or uneasiness on Carmela's part put heavy hands upon his emotions and pulled at them until they jangled out of all quiet and harmony. But he could do nothing to soothe her, nor himself. His ways had been rough and boorish, and his caresses forthright and forceful. Could he now fall into sweet whispers and lay gentle fingers upon her? Ever since her childbirth she had seemed to him changed from the steady, poised creature she was—like one of the masterful eagles hanging above the farms in old Calabria—into a person somewhat feverish, too quick in decision, too active in execution, putting too much energy into her new enterprise. It absorbed her completely, shutting him out, tinging the dream of their marriage with faint clouds of doubt. What was happening? It never occurred to him that it might be the daily meetings with Emilio. It must be the departure of all the children for distant places.

"But, we're together," he managed to blurt out, puffing strongly on his pipe to conceal the adolescent vigor of his emotions.

"Of course, Gennaro . . . but with all the young ones gone."

She patted his hand and looked at him as if she beseeched him to understand. She wanted to believe it herself. It was not Emilio . . . Emilio who seemed to gain a dramatic animation in her presence, a bubbling of spirits, like still waters suddenly stirred into boiling . . . Emilio who seemed to live only when he was with her, and to hate the rest of the day, to bolt the house because he would not be alone with her. Oh, it was not Emilio—not he alone. Her body ran cold as she thought of him, the deep pooling of desire in his eyes, the flushed quivering lip, the sudden break in his speech as he gazed at her, unashamedly adoring for a second, and then turning away hurt and miserable. She wanted to brush off with rapid all-encompassing strokes of her hand this sensation of shivering fear. Gennaro looked uneasily at her as she touched his hand.

"What is it, Carmela?"

"Just that we are alone . . . everybody out . . . as if they had thrust us out, you know, or we them."

There was some touch of truth in her words. Gennaro acknowledged that as he squeezed her hand, and puffed long and steadily on his pipe, his eyes blinking unhappily.

"Seems like you crawl into the stall where your favorite jackass died," he finally said. "By Saint Jerome, the place is just as quiet and just as sad."

7

Roberto, immediately upon graduating from college, had found work as a chemist in a Pittsburgh mill. He had left at once. Ernestino had been allowed a trip to Europe where he was to meet his sister. It was a gift for fulfilling a solemn promise exacted from him by Carmela.

He had been dissatisfied with school and desired to quit at once. No reason why he shouldn't enter his foster-father's business. Why not? What's wrong with storing up rags? What's wrong with being a ragman even? He wanted to go to work. What did he care about all the junk one picked up at school? What about Roberto? He liked it. As for himself, Ernestino, he hated it. And look at Emilio. Sure, look at Emilio. He hates to go into the rag-business, he hates to study any more, he hates to stick around home, he doesn't want to travel, he doesn't know what to do with himself, he's all up in the air, like a man without a cent in his pocket and standing around in a big hotel with restaurants and all kinds of places to go to. "You know, Carmela, that's what happens sometimes when you study too much. You don't know what it's all about because you got too much in your head. All the kids that stick in school don't get anywhere. Take that fellow . . ."

"All right, Ernestino. I agree with you," Carmela had said. "I see that you simply don't want to go on."

"I want to quit, that's what."

"But give yourself a little time. Get through high school first."

"That's a whole year! Have a heart, Carmela. You don't understand. Look, it's this way. I got to do this, this blasted intermediate. . . . Now I can't. I hate it. And English! Whew! Did you ever have to tell about the most exciting incident in your life? Every six months—and then read a lot of stuff and spend a whole week talking about it? Why did Macbeth kill that king? Who cares? And you got to read about what this fellow— what's his name—oh, yeh, Ruskin,[8] and some other guy, Tennyson,[9] got to say about women. . . . Who cares? And the Latin . . . oh, Carmela, have a heart."

She was overwhelmed by his long speech. Despite his spare little frame, to her Ernestino had always appeared to divide his day into the three sections set apart for meals and think of nothing else but how the time could be passed until the lines of demarcation were reached. He rushed down to breakfast with the speed of a rabbit, he ate with the voracity of a day-laborer, and rushed off again somewhere to be lost to view until the next meal, when he would repeat his performance of the morning. After that he would vanish once more and miraculously reappear for dinner hungrier than ever. He listened to everybody and said nothing unless it had some direct concern with himself. Even on such occasions his words were limited and his requests modest, if altogether selfish. To hear this living symbol of indifference explode into such violent objections and at such length was a minor revelation and a major miracle. He was too much in earnest for her to put him off or altogether to deny his request. But she had been led to believe that there were magical values in the education he was receiving. She had somewhat of the same wonder Gennaro felt in the presence of Latin paradigms he could not read and chemical formulae he could not even decipher.

"Listen here, Ernestino," she cried, sternly, attempting one more tack. "Suppose we make a bargain. Finish school—for my sake. You don't want people to say you haven't had an education, do you? Go to school this year. Finish. Get good marks. When it's over, I'll give you such a gift . . ."

"Oh, the only thing I'd want 'd be to get on a steamer and whiz way off to Italy . . . oh, boy!"

He had jumped off his feet and wiggled his thin legs in midair at the prospect.

"All right . . . Italy."

For a second he was too stunned to utter a sound. But it was only a second. The cry of jubilation that he let out after that slight pause seemed to negate once and for all the common belief that Ernestino possessed no real emotions. And so on his graduation he had been shipped off to Italy as gaily as his sister had been the year before.

8

Gennaro's business kept him too busy now for him to rush all the way downtown for a daily visit to Carmela's new shop. But he had promised to run down before it was opened and pass judgment on its appearance. Work on it had progressed with unusual vigor.

A few last touches were required. Hats had been assembled in the window. The stock had been stored away in the proper drawers and shelves. The rug had been swept down and the mirrors polished. Notices had gone out announcing the opening of CHEZ MONTER-ANO. Gennaro entered the store timidly, holding his hat in his hand.

"By Saint Jerome," he whispered, "you got the place so fixed up, it scares me. I feel like I ought to get on my knees and pray."

Carmela laughed.

"It isn't like the two-by-two shack we had in Harlem."

"It certainly isn't," Gennaro agreed. "And how's that big fellow been—a help, hey?" He pointed to Emilio, who was standing on a stool, placing a box on the topmost shelf.

"He has been . . . and what a help! See that jardinière . . . that's his."

Gennaro took his pipe out of his mouth and surveyed the pot and the plant.

"Big enough," he commented, and puffed again. "Big enough—but by the cross it sure is fancy."

Carmela put her arm through his and drew him close to her. The old fellow looked at her askance and then patted her on the cheeks.

"You're an American, all right," he said. "You and that big scamp up there. I made the money . . . I made America . . . no one can't say I didn't . . . but, good God and the Holy Calendar, I never fixed up a place like this . . . this looks like America . . . my old rag-bins look like Italy."

And then he sat down and leaned over.

"Listen to this, though. I've been having my hands full with my men, and the women, too. You got it smooth and easy here . . . I haven't. I think Rocco's been kicking up . . . but I can't prove it, and I don't want to chuck him out. You know what, Emilio? I think I'll hand the business over to you. You're young . . . unless you want to be in this business of Carmela's, hey? That fool Rocco—by Saint Jerome, I ought to throw him out on his rump and let him starve with his whole family . . . advises me, advises me kindly, mind you, like a brother—advises *me!* . . . the men ought to get more . . . they'll go on strike otherwise . . . all the men got into a union. . . . He's not with them out and out, but he's not with me either. Of course, I can't prove it. . . . And guess what!"

He rose and paced up and down on the deep velour rug. It was so noiseless that he looked down two or three times to make sure he was on level ground.

"Can't hear yourself moving," he grinned. "Guess what . . . that Joe Fornaro . . . the strong-arm guy . . . they got him head of the union. . . . Truck drivers and everybody. . . . What's a union? By Saint Jerome and the thousand saints . . . do they have to join a union? I been friends to all those men . . . like in the old country—haven't we exchanged gifts at Christmas time and haven't I been godfather to all their babies and bought them things! Union! Blessed Saint Elena, if it's Rocco got them stirred up . . . I'll fix the puppy-yelper. . . . I'll do what I didn't do once."

He caught himself up. He was not going to let Emilio know what happened more than twenty years back. That was an episode that had shown him his strength and because of that fact alone he was not ashamed of it. But it had been like the sharp point of a splinter he had not been able to pull out. He shrugged his shoulders and tried to put the thought aside. But when he least expected it, the point touched a tender nerve and he jumped. For all the other things he had done, he had made proper atonement. Making Rocco manager was at least partial atonement for the original theft of the business. But Rocco had come back to torment him, to brew up trouble. By Saint Jerome!

"I'll get him by the gills like a fish," he shouted. "I'll trounce the last trickle of blood from his little puppy heart."

"That'd be a fool stunt," Carmela interrupted.

"I'd just take the wind out of him, if I was doing it," Emilio cried as he jumped off the stool. "I'd let him keep his job, and yet take the wind right out of him."

"How'd you do that?"

"I'd sign up with the union! Oh, I wouldn't give them all they asked for . . . half only. That'll satisfy the men and what could Fornaro and Rocco do then?"

"I'll wring their necks first."

"And in the end give in."

"Me? By the howling sinners in hell, never!"

Carmela said nothing. It was good to hear father and son debate a common issue without quarreling, without all their emotions set to a full gale. They would eventually reach a decision. In the few months during which she and Emilio had been engaged in the task of setting up the millinery shop, they had arrived at fuller mutual realization.

For Emilio she had always had the love of an older woman for a boy who suggests the full grown man without boldness, with a certain touch of diffidence and sweetness that endears him. This love for Emilio was fanned into a dangerous glow during their two months of constant association.

But along with it came to her, too, a deeper love for Gennaro. Originally it had been the reaction of admiration—admiration for his behavior with the Monteranos, admiration for his strength and success, his sincerity and his forthrightness. There had been pity for him, too—a sense of the frustration he himself felt, a sense of the way he fumbled to reach out for something above the sordid details that darkened his memories, a sense of the bit of poetry in the center of his peasant roughness.

Now her love for her husband was the love of a deep experience shared, of possessing between them the life of others whom they loved. The rough man, moreover, had become a tender lover, dependent upon her and measuring himself constantly by the light of the affection he bore her.

Of Emilio she had lost her fears and yet in some fashion had begun to realize that they should be stronger. Throughout these months he had been caught in a whirl of action. He had had no time to think about himself and his step-mother, but by a like token each act had been animated by his love of her.

He was happy as he had not been for the last year. He walked in a colored mist of dream and faith and hope. Every word he uttered, no matter how routine, every thought he expressed, no matter how utilitarian, every deed he performed, no matter how pedestrian, seemed touched with fervor, inspired with worship, trembling with wonder. He breathed his love without giving it tongue, he sang it without music, he shouted it without sound.

Finally, in the last few days, she dared not allow him to take her arm to help her into the car. She dared not sit close to him. She dared not meet his eyes. He sensed it all, and respected the impulse behind her caution. He himself permitted no pause to intervene in their talk. He maintained a steady stream of comment and observation. He was always at pains to find something else to do, and remained in the store with her only if the workmen were about.

She was glad it was going to end soon, and she hoped he would soon be carried away in an interest of his own. He had refused to follow a profession, and he had always held the ragshop—at least in the last few years—in utter contempt. Would this new turn in his father's business arouse him? Would he now accept some of the responsibility that should by right be his? She listened with all her soul to the debate between father and son.

"You'd have to give in," Emilio rejoined. "Sure, you'd have to, sooner or later. A man like Joe Fornaro you can't fool with."

"Oh, I'll show them, I'll show them. Joe is no saint. He isn't in this thing for his health. I made America one way, he makes it another. Show him a wad, and he'll come across."

"That's a mean way to do it," Emilio protested. He had stuck his hands into his trouser pockets and stood nonchalantly against the all-glass showcases. "It's a cheap way, too, papa. . . . After all, the men believe in this Fornaro chap. All these rag-pickers and assorters, what are they but a lot of downtrodden peasant workers who stole away from Italy, hoping to find something better here? What are they getting out of all their hopes? Long hours in the shop and short rations at home . . . and what homes . . . filthy, crowded, worm-hills! Give them a chance . . . you can afford to raise their wages and make a handsome profit, too . . . and I'd even lower the rents of the men who worked for me. . . . God, you'd spike Rocco's guns and make Fornaro look like a piker."

"Listen to the chap," Gennaro cried, taking his pipe out of his mouth and using it for a pointer, "Listen to him, will you? Talks like a king!"

It was evident that he was as proud of his son as he was surprised by the sentiments. He was not really surprised. He just wondered why they had not occurred to him. Although he had put into effect high-pressure methods of buying up and selling the rags and metal scraps in which he dealt, he had never worked his men on the basis of any thought-out scheme of social economy. He paid them what he thought right and they took it.

He gave them more as he made more or as they asked for more. Had the men approached him in a group, or in smaller groups, or as individuals, he would have settled the whole problem exactly as Emilio had suggested. But that his son should finally evince an interest in his business troubles—that excited him, and his latent pride for the boy.

So he kept repeating, "Talks like a king . . . be generous to the small man! Not a bad idea, though," he exclaimed finally. "And I'll do just what you say . . . but listen to this. This is my last day as the boss by myself . . . tomorrow you come into the shop . . . no more moping around the house—you don't want more education . . . maybe you can do some work. . . . Now you listen here. . . ."

He had become tremendously agitated, the more so as Emilio seemed by his silence and seriousness to have accepted the offer of the partnership. He stuck his pipe back into his mouth, sucked on it thoughtfully, and then filled the store with the thin acrid smoke that it always emitted.

"Listen here, Emilio. Tonight—right now—I'm going to the men themselves . . . their wives, see, and the men too . . . and tell them . . . form a union . . . sure . . . I'll give them a raise right now . . . but don't be listening to men like Fornaro . . . tomorrow, Emilio, my son, he will be in charge of the men, and later when Ernestino comes back from Italy he'll be in charge of the outside work. . . . I'll be in the office and take in the cash."

He exploded into laughter at his little joke.

"That'll be grand, Emilio," said Carmela, seriously.

Emilio looked at her searchingly. Her earnestness was sweet and tender. Her smile and the quiet brightness of her eyes were urging him to say yes. She yearned for his decision, as if in some gentle fashion it would end the turmoil of their own unhappiness.

"All right," he said. "It's a go."

"Fine!" shouted Gennaro. "By all the thousand saints, by Saint Jerome, it's good to hear you say it. Hey, Carmela, we'll see this chap stop hanging around like a sick cat . . . work . . . that's the stuff . . . we'll do big things, Emilio. By the miracles, I feel young again! Who says I got gray hair? Who says I got wrinkles? Who says I'm an old timer? Emilio—"

He stopped with a shortness that alarmed them.

"Listen," he resumed. "Years back, before you came to this country, Emilio, I wanted to have my son with me . . ."

He talked as if in a trance.

"That's what I wanted most . . . now I have it. Carmela, it's great. . . . You know, Emilio, the rag-business is not so bad. Not now any more. We got a big clean place and you just hang around bossing people . . . different now. . . . Tomorrow, then, hey, you college-boy?"

They all laughed, and Gennaro, waving his pipe and shouting he was going to take care of that stinking Fornaro, left Carmela and Emilio alone.

9

"I'm glad, Emilio," she said.

"It'll be all right," he muttered.

"You'll do something with the business—modernize—put some of your ideas . . ."

"Are you serious?" He asked the question hotly, defiantly.

"Why not?" she laughed.

"You know why I'm doing this, don't you?"

"It's the only thing for you to do, Emilio. You were brought up in it. You spent your childhood in the rag bins and the metal piles. It means more to you than all the fine things you have learned at college . . . it's going to be your life work."

She refused him the opportunity to answer.

"Let's get this box of pins out of the way, and these ribbons, and all this stuff, and then back to Harlem. Come on . . ."

It was not so simple as that. The silence that fell on them was filled with the murmur of their thoughts. Emilio worked quickly, quietly, but she knew that he was fighting as she was fighting, fighting against the gallop-forward of their impulses. Like him, she, too, was feeling the first real surge of passion—passion such as she had not felt before. She knew it was not like the feeling she bore for Gennaro, and she knew it was not like the feeling that had been aroused in her years back by Emilio's brother.

It was in one sense revulsion, in one sense exaltation. It was an alternation between an awed hush of all her energies and a trembling rise of desire. But it was relentlessly driving her to a moment that she sensed must come, and yet which she must by all the power she possessed prevent. The hot day wore on and the time for their departure seemed never to arrive. She dreaded each lagging minute. She dreaded not so much its effect on her as on Emilio. The quiet with which he worked was more compact of danger than if he had turned about and faced her with his eyes lighted and unhappy, his muscles taut with fear and with yearning.

The time to go came at last. They rode home in a slight shower of rain. In the car they were as silent as they had been in the store. And then they reached the Parterre.

But the silence of the empty house was too unbearable. It echoed back the enforced silence of the afternoon, the further silence of their ride home. It mocked their controlled purpose; it challenged all their fears. The straight narrow stairs, carpeted and dim, were ahead of them. They both had to go up, each to a separate room. She knew she must hurry, and he hung back, knowing what she knew.

"Your father will be back soon. When he comes we'll go out for dinner."

She started to climb the stairs. As she raised her flowered voile dress to climb the stairs, she looked back at him. In the half-light of the hall her face seemed to emerge out of the soft material of her clothes with the flush of blooming petals. Her eyes shone and quivered. Her mouth opened as if she wanted to call his name, softly, dearly, begging him for her sake not to think of her, to forget, to mold his young life to a pattern not so complex, not so fraught with danger and horror and tragedy.

And he looked at her, and his eyes, too, shone, but with the desperation of his youth, and his mouth opened and she knew that he, too, would call her softly and dearly and beg for the mercy of a moment's ease, for at least the touch of her hand, the closeness of face to face, in an agony of a farewell from all this billow of fire that must destroy them both.

"Carmela," he said, hardly audibly.

She turned.

He seized her hand and drew her to him, and as he did so he stepped on the stairs, and there seized her whole body in his arms, and pressed his head into her bosom, and cried, "I love you . . . I can't help it. . . . I have fought it . . . just let me stay this way . . . a minute . . . you are all to me that ever mother was and so much more . . . how can I help it?"

She put her arms about him, and held him close, pressing her lips gently upon his hair.

"You dear boy, I know."

"Nothing counts, Carmela, except you."

"You must not, darling, you must not."

"I love you . . . I love you. . . ."

He wept, and the sound of his weeping was both a pain and a joy. It intensified the silence about them and seemed to isolate them from the noise of the world and time. Once more she leaned her head on his and softly shut her eyes.

The door opened. In the light of the vestibule Gennaro stood, watching them. The light coming in from the street roused her from the momentary peace she had found in Emilio's arms. She raised her eyes only to confront those of Gennaro. They stared at each other in dread silence. All she saw was his face twitch, and the pipe hang from his lips. He shut the door and left them.

Emilio had sensed what had happened. He struggled to be free of Carmela's arms, but she held him tight to her, unable to do anything else.

When they heard the door shut, they separated.

Stroking his head, she said quietly, "Dear boy . . ." and ran upstairs.

10

When Gennaro had left Carmela and Emilio in the early afternoon, he had gone at once to carry out his expressed purpose of suppressing the strike which Rocco and Joe Fornaro had organized. His first stop was at the shop. He had expected to find the men and women at work and he had intended to call them singly and in groups, depending on the several workers, and offer them individual raises and privileges. The four wooden shacks that had originally formed his business— dilapidated, weather-corroded old stables—had been faced with brick. The floorings had been reinforced with steel beams, and the walls of the interior plastered roughly and then white-washed. Order had been brought out of what had at first been a chaotic assemblage of all the various types of cast-off materials that he bought and sold. There were classified sections and in each section booths and stalls. The whole place was kept clean and even carefully dusted. Gennaro had discovered that the rags could be kept longer if they were given some light and air.

The back of the frame buildings, however, was still as it had been in the beginning. The old clapboards were still doing service, unpainted, cracked, and charred. The yard was still of earth, covered with the collected leavings, scraps, papers, rags, and metals. Heaps of hoops, old barrels, iron pipe, all the numerous forms of waste of an industrial civilization. In the center was a cleared space.

In this clearing all the workers had collected—about ninety men and women. The men for the most part were in dirty overalls or in trousers patched and repatched and held up by strings or ropes. Their arms and necks, bared and sweated, had none of the vigorous musculature of dock or building laborers. They were colorless from being confined within doors, flabby, thin. The women, for the greater part old and dried-up, had wrinkled faces and emaciated bodies. Only several of them were as young as forty, and one was a flat-breasted, strong-looking person with fine straight hips and a mass of hair pompadoured boldly off her forehead. It was she whom Gennaro saw first as he entered the yard.

Mounted on a barrel, she was making a speech to the working people. Rocco, standing by, sullen, head drooped, hands limply thrust into his pockets, listened, did nothing.

"What's all this, Rocco?"

"You got eyes and ears."

"And so have you. Why don't you drive them back to work, hey?"

"I can't," Rocco retorted grimly.

"You're lying," shouted Gennaro.

"And you . . . up to your old cut-throat tricks, hey?"

The vigorous woman on the barrel-end interrupted.

"We don't want no fighting. What we want is our rights . . . what's coming to us, hey, people?"

There was a shout of approval.

"Gennaro thinks he's been good to us," she continued, "All right. He has. But the Madonna knows we ain't got much to feed our kids. That's the matter. We work, Gennaro, and what for? Can we save enough to send a bit of something to our people in the old country?"

"No," came an answering shout.

"We can't go back ourselves," an old fellow trebled.

"We can't pay rent."

"We can't call in the doctor."

"All right, by Saint Jerome," Gennaro yelled above them all. "Let me tell you . . ."

He forced the woman off the barrel and mounted it himself. Silence. Everyone stared at Gennaro. He hitched up his trousers, and glared. Then, deliberately, he took his pipe out of his pocket, filled it, and lit it. The puffs of his smoke issued like a series of muffled menaces. Suddenly, before they had a chance to express their impatience, he burst into an angry shout.

"By Saint Jerome, I'll tell you what, I'm giving you all a raise."

They could not believe their ears. His words seemed to give the lie to his tone, and his voice to his words.

"A raise to all of you. I made America, and you'll share it with me. You, Tomasiello, and you, Ciccio, and you there, Tonno, and you, too, Angelino. And you over there, Concetta, stop making the sign of the cross. I mean it. Now what?"

The response was deafening.

"What's more, right now, outside, is a wagon with two kegs of beer. We're going to celebrate, celebrate because we all belong together."

He singled out Rocco with his eyes as he said this. Rocco in his turn was unable to remove his eyes from Gennaro. For a second they stared at each other, Rocco, sheepish, uneasy, Gennaro grinning unhappily.

"No, Rocco," he said slowly. "Don't hate me. I hate you to hate me. We've drawn blood in our day . . . let's call it quits now."

Tears stood in his eyes.

"Since the earrings," old Tomasiello mumbled to his neighbor, "he ain't been the old bear."

His friend cackled. "No, 'tain't that . . . it's the young thing in bed with him these nights . . . that'll soften any old rooster."

"What say, hey?" Gennaro shouted to Rocco. The crowd once more burst into a shout of approval.

Gennaro turned to them once more.

"And Joe Fornaro . . . your president. I'm donating a year's salary to him. You won't have to pay it out of your wages."

Another shout.

Beer had been brought in, and with it great chunks of salami, cheese, and bread. A clearing was made at once. Improvised tables were set up. Somebody shouted for an accordion or a mandolin. Instruments were produced and the afternoon became a merry one.

Rocco stalked up to Gennaro, chest out, smiling as if amused.

"You pulled a fast one. Well, it's better than getting a soak in the teeth. All right, I lost again."

"By Saint Jerome," Gennaro whispered, "I mean you well."

He put his arm affectionately around Rocco's shoulder.

"What's the use, Rocco, making so much trouble, hey? Call it quits. I don't want to see you out of a job, out of the business."

Rocco merely grunted and smiled awkwardly.

"All right, it's over."

But he did not remain for the feasting. Nor did he go home. Elvira, his wife, had become embittered to a higher degree than Rocco. She nursed the belief that all the success of Gennaro would have been her husband's had not Rocco been defrauded of his original business. She could not regard Gennaro and his position in the community without suffering the pangs of an unmitigable jealousy. For some reason she had been cherishing the hope that there was still time to recover the business. If to wrest it as boldly out of Gennaro's hands as it had been out of Rocco's was not so simple, possibly it might be done by ruining him. She had thought of arson, and confided her plan to Rocco. He would have none of it. Then he remembered the beating he had received at the hands of the gangsters at the time he had dispossessed a tenant. He made inquiries about the men and discovered it to be a gang of strong-arm men who preyed on the lawless and even the law-abiding whom they could intimidate.

Joe Fornaro was already the head of a rockmen's organization. He might be induced to employ the same destructive methods against Gennaro's business which his gang had used against the building contractors of the neighborhood. It was that way the strike became organized, and the plan had Elvira's endorsement. Gennaro's shrewd capitulation had prevented the violence that Rocco had been hoping would take place. He was left beaten again. He dared not report to Elvira. He felt broken and saddened. The offer of a raise in pay was, if anything, more galling than his defeat. Like all generosity on the part of a conceited giver it seemed like an act of gloating. "Licking his damned chops, is he?" thought Rocco. For a second he clenched his fists, and thought. The impulse that came to him was as sudden as it was unaccountable to him. It just came.

He hurried upstairs to where the rag bales were packed. He selected one of the iron-piped cages nearest the window from which the bales were swung to the trucks below. He adjusted the crane over the cage. Then he hung the cage with the burlap bags that eventually formed the covering of the bales. He arranged the ropes under the lower layer of burlap. He chose heavy but easily handled rope that he could bring over the side of the bale he was contemplating, and tie with ease. That done, he threw armful after armful of rags into the case, tamped them down, and when the bale was about one-third completed he stopped. His next procedure was to pile a quantity of rags against the nearby wall, sufficient to fill the cage entirely and make a compact bale, ready for shipment. On top of the pile, he placed the sharp hooked spike used to move the bales from one place to another. He mopped his forehead and laughed. Then he went down to call Gennaro. But the feasting was over, a slight shower of rain was falling, Gennaro and the rest had left.

11

Gennaro had opened the door to the Parterre and, at first, had seen nothing. That is, for just a second. Then he understood what the shadows were ahead of him. He was on the point of crying out, "Hey, there, the strike's all over, by Saint Jerome!" His mouth opened, his pipe almost falling out. That was all. He shut the door after him and went down the steps. He walked quietly, his head hung down, seeing no one until he reached the ragshop. He unlocked the office door and walked in. But it was unnecessary to have unlocked the door. There was Rocco seated at the desk, going through price lists and account books.

"Whey, there, Rocco!" Gennaro tried to shout. He was aware, however, that he had not quite got the pitch and the vigor that characterized his words. "You here?"

Rocco grew pale, and stared at Gennaro.

"What's the matter? See a ghost? By the Holy Calendar, you look afraid as a cat."

Rocco got up. "No, Gennaro, I'm not afraid. I had a plan and I was thinking about it, sitting there, and you came in unexpected and I got sort of confused."

His pale face filled with smiles, awkward, frightened smiles.

"Thinking up plans, hey?"

"About the business."

"Yes? By the thousand saints, everybody's thinking up plans today."

He drew out his bandanna handkerchief and wiped his brow.

"Everybody's got plans . . . all kinds . . . now, that plan about paying the men more . . . you want to know where that comes from, hey?"

Rocco was silent. He realized that something distressing had occurred and that Gennaro was troubled. He spoke with so much laughter in his words, so jerkily, so fast . . . something must have happened.

"But never mind, Rocco, never mind . . . it worked, and how it worked! Now, what's your plan?"

Rocco became even more silent than ever and smiled even more awkwardly.

"Come on, what's your plan? Got a notion you'd kill me, ha? Come on, that's it . . . the others, too, Rocco, sure . . . the others, too . . ."

"Not going crazy, Gennaro?" Rocco whispered.

Gennaro laughed. "Me? Crazy? Say, I'm not one to go crazy. I got a steer's heart in this chest."

He pounded it. "Strength's there . . . big strong bones . . . and the heart inside . . . you can't just smother it . . . and the brain in this hard head of mine. . . ." He pointed . . ."You can't twist it so easy. . . . No, by Saint Jerome . . . I'll work the thing out somehow . . . you bet. . . ."

Rocco stared at Gennaro and said nothing. The pause was intense. But Gennaro's thoughts were far off. For no reason, Rosaria's image came to him, and he smiled.

"You remember Rosaria, hey, Rocco?"

Rocco nodded.

"Oh, hell, why think? What's your plan? Come on, business first. What's this plan of yours? Not about the workmen?"

"No."

"About clearing up the yards?"

"No."

"Getting bigger trucks?"

"No."

"By the holy shroud, then what? Come on, what's it so secret for?"

"It isn't secret."

"What's it, then?"

"You see, the bales . . . the way the men pack them . . ."

"The bales? Why, they're packed fine . . . the way I worked out . . ."

"But . . ."

"You have another way?"

"Quicker."

"Let's go and see."

"All right."

Rocco could barely utter the word. He had trembled all through the talk and had wanted to escape. Now he could not. The impulse that had begun in the afternoon received an unexpected impetus from Gennaro himself. The hatred for the man achieved the momentary urge of an agony he must at once assuage.

"All right, I'll show you," he repeated, gaining courage with each sound. "A better way . . . we'll save money."

They went upstairs and walked down the silent second floor without another word.

"Look at these rags," Rocco began.

But before Gennaro could so much as turn about, Rocco had seized the hooked spike. With a sharp cry, he dug it into the base of Gennaro's neck. It was too sudden for Gennaro to know what was happening and too deep a stab for life to continue one second longer.

Working fast, Rocco fixed the crane over Gennaro's body. At first he had tried to drag the body and raise it himself into the bin, but finding that too great a task he thought of the mechanical lifter. The body was swung lightly into the cage, small jets of blood splashing about. With quick fury, Rocco threw in the rags that he had piled up. After that, he himself jumped into the bin and with a huge tamping iron packed them tight, forcing in with his feet portions of the dead body.

He tied up the bale, being very careful to make perfect knots, and then swung it out of the window, and allowed it to hang half-way down. He shut the shop and went home.

Carmela and Emilio saw it in the early morning soaked with blood, hanging against the blue sky over the East River.

12

Struzzo had returned from his Italian tour in time to accord Gennaro the most elaborate funeral in the history of Little Italy. It was just such a funeral as Gennaro himself would have wanted. The streets were lined with huge crowds. A President or a King might have been in the gold-encrusted coffin that was borne on the shoulders of Gennaro's most stalwart fellow-officers in the various societies he had headed. No mean fellow was being escorted to his narrow resting place in the distant Brooklyn hills. This was no peasant, wrapped in a cheap cloth, boxed in a pine-wood oblong, to be lowered into a hole below scraggy fig-trees on a Calabrian slope. Bands with their bass drums hung with black crêpe ribbons, musicians with black bands on their sleeves, flags at their head furled and cased in black, passing slowly between canyoned tenements with their fire-escapes crowded with onlookers and festooned in black like the stores, like the doors to the tenements themselves—such were not intended for an ordinary forgettable figure, a man who had merely been born, and had eaten day by day, and worked in the ditches alongside railways or carried bricks in hods to wind-swept rooftops, and then fallen sick and died with no money left to bury him! The music of the bands swelled like that of a great organ, and the crowds on the sidewalks were stilled and gazed at the procession and made the sign of the cross.

"What a string of automobiles!"

One dared just whisper his astonishment.

"A backwoods country lout he was! Think of it! Not even Umberto himself had such a turn-out!"

"He'd 've loved to be looking on. You know what he'd say?"

"By Saint Jerome and the thousand saints, but I, I made America!"

There was low laughter among the men. The women made deprecatory noises with their mouths. There was silence again and the slow surges of the funeral marches.

"What did it get him?"

"A young wife ..."

"And a murder ..."

"Sh ..."

The sound was passed around.

And so the procession moved on to the church, the fine granite pile that Gennaro had worked so hard to have erected. Don Anselmo wept as he intoned the service. Only Carmela knew that. In complete black, veiled from head to waist, she knelt at the altar rail and slowly struck her bosom with her fists closed nervously tight. It was the first time since her wedding and only the second time since she had been sent to the Juvenile Asylum, that she had been in a Catholic church.

It was as if she had walked out of light that blinded and unnerved her into a darkened stillness that soothed and composed her whole being. The shock of her discovery of the blood-soaked bale was resolved in the rising fragrance of the incense and in the deep-stirred voice of the priest. It seemed to lose significance, to be not of the earth, but formed apart from the ordinary modes of life, like a memory of a fear that never happened, like the thought of a future that never was. She lowered her head and allowed the sense of the timelessness, the earthlessness of her present feelings to take complete possession of her and to shut her in from the noises of the world. And then she heard the catch in Don Anselmo's voice and the sob and the tears that followed. And for the first time she wept, wept long and quietly, wetting her veil.

13

Between Carmela and Emilio not one word passed about the last time Gennaro had seen them and they Gennaro.

As the door closed behind them, she kept staring as if through it. She dropped her hands at her side, and stood. Then she heard Emilio trying to speak to her. She was afraid of anything he might say. She wanted the minute to be lost in silence, no word spoken, no thought even suggested. All too vividly she realized what a unique act of control had been Gennaro's departure, his head slumped, his shoulders narrowed. The energy of anger in him had diminished in the steady love he bore her. There was

a time when the ego in him, nurtured in a culture that allowed no limitations upon its pride, would have broken forth with the fury of tem-
pest, and he would have sought immediate satisfaction in an act of
savagery. But he had gone, quietly, conveying the impression that he had
not entered, that he had not seen. She wanted no defense from Emilio,
she wanted herself to say nothing, speak nothing in extenuation. What
had happened was to her own shame! Not Emilio's! Poor lad—so forlorn because of her, so yearning, so unthinking!

But Emilio was about to speak.

"No, Emilio . . . say nothing. It *was* your father."

She climbed the stairs to her room, fell into a chair, and sat there
looking out vacantly, limp, her whole body loose. Not even when they
had seen the huge bale, swinging gently from its chain, blood-soaked
against the clear summer sky over the river, did they say anything.
Somehow, they guessed the gruesome contents bound up in the rags.
Neither had the courage to stand by, while bit after bit of linen, of wool,
of silk was taken out, slowly, carefully so as not to disarrange the horrible package. They heard whose body was in the center, and what must
have happened to him. They left the matter in the hands of the police,
and Struzzo later. That was all. But no one who looked at either
Carmela or Emilio would have failed to see how deeply into their lives
the dreadful event had cut.

14

Some days after the funeral, Gilda returned from Italy. Ernestino cut
off his stay to come back with his sister. Roberto had come for the
funeral and soon after went back to his work in Pennsylvania.
Carmela's family had refused to come. A letter from her father told her
how saddened they were by the news. Between the lines she read how
much he felt for her. As for her mother, Carmela understood the
absence, shrugged her shoulders over it, and forgave them all.

She went to meet Gilda at the pier. The girl had grown into decisive
womanhood. Large and full, with a firm, steady carriage, she walked
with the assurance and poise of a matron but with all the life and grace
of her youth.

"You're so charming, Gilda, so charming! Oh, my darling, how glad I
am to see you. We've never forgotten you—not a bit."

They wept in each other's arms.

"Emilio did not come down, did he?"

"He is at home—waiting."

Gilda smiled unbelievingly.

"Is he very sad?"

"Poor boy. . . ."

Then, like a shot out of the clear, she asked bluntly, "What are we all going to do now? We can't all live together."

The two women looked at each other, and both understood.

"No. I thought you'd bring home a great big handsome husband."

Gilda shook her head, and put her arm under her step-mother's.

"Guess!" she said coaxingly.

"He's coming on the next boat?"

"No . . . he's here already!"

"Not here already! Came ahead of you?"

"No, darling . . . he's been here waiting . . . I am going to marry Salvatore. He was so sweet in his letters. They're such dear letters, Carmela. . . . Oh, he'll be a fine man to me!"

She shut her lips tight, disengaged her arm, and walked stiffly alongside of Carmela. After a second she said, "So, I know what I'm doing. But what about Emilio, Ernestino, you?"

"We'll settle all that."

It was arranged among them all. Emilio and Ernestino had decided to continue with the rag and metal business. The younger boy became serious and even quieter than usual, allowing his voice to drop into appropriate basso depths with each phrase he uttered.

"That's just what Gennaro would have wanted," he declared, "and let me tell you, Roberto, we'll run a grand business."

Carmela was to live downtown near her hat store. Gilda was to marry at once. Immediately after her wedding—quiet as was fitting after Gennaro's death—she stood on the landing of the Parterre while Salvatore shook hands with everyone, his pink face, under its wispy albino hair, flushed more than ordinarily. Emilio pushed through the crowd and stood at her side.

"Good-bye," he said, holding out his hand.

"Good-bye, Emilio," she smiled and gazed at him steadily.

"Lots of luck."

"Right. I'll send you a postcard."

"That'll be great."

"Maybe two."

"Twice as great."

"Good-bye. . . ."

He waved, and bolted back into the house.

"Walking way down to the Battery and back," he shouted early that evening and slipped out of the house.

15

Carmela waited up for him. He had evidently kept his word about the walk. The evening was cool enough, but it was still summer and the heat was not out of the air. It had fatigued him so much that now he looked pale and worn, and appeared altogether unwilling to talk.

"Going to hit the hay," he announced, and was about to go upstairs.

"Come here, Emilio," Carmela called after him quietly.

Unlike the women in her station, Carmela had refused to wear the prescribed black dress. In her starched muslin, open at the neck and loosely belted at the waist, she looked much older than she was and larger and taller. She stood at the mantelpiece as Emilio returned, her neck with the hair tightly combed up from it reflected in the mirror.

"What is it, Carmela?"

"You know tomorrow I move."

"Yes, I know. Anything I can do?"

"No. Just this. Will you take some things from me and keep them always?"

"Why not?" He tried to smile.

"These things were not mine. They belonged to your father. They once belonged to his father."

"And to his father."

"Yes, that's true indeed. I don't know how far back they go. But Gennaro prized them. I know he'd want you to have them. Please . . . you must . . ."

She placed Gennaro's gold hoops on the table between them. The electric light caught them and flashed back their sheen in the mirror, on the ceiling, back and forth across the room. Especially when Emilio raised them in the air to look at them did they scatter the radiance of their smooth surfaces up and down the long narrow chamber.

"Of course, I'll take them—" he answered. "For luck."

EXPLANATORY NOTES

Part One

Chapter One

1. In the late nineteenth and early twentieth centuries, the area of East Harlem, New York City, between 125th and Ninety-sixth streets to the north and south and Fifth Avenue and the East River to the west and east was a solidly Italian neighborhood.
2. The Panic of 1893, caused by the overexpansion of the railroad industry and its dubious financial backing, was, at the time, the most serious economic crisis in the history of the United States. Unemployment soared, and the value of the dollar plunged as foreign investors and U.S. citizens alike pulled their money from American financial institutions. A similar financial downturn in Europe, accompanied by crippling agricultural conditions, spurred many Italians—mostly from the overtaxed and underdeveloped southern regions of the country—to emigrate to the United States in greater numbers than ever before. From 1881 to 1930, over 4.5 million Italians escaped the conditions of *la miseria* ("the misery") and traveled to the United States—roughly 73,000 in 1893 and over 285,000 in 1907, the peak year of Italian immigration. This wave of immigration was part of a broader wave of "new immigration" of peoples from southern and eastern Europe then considered inferior to the "old immigration" from northern and western Europe. Concerns about southern and eastern Europeans' supposed racial inferiority, tendency toward crime, and unfitness for American democracy caused Congress to pass immigration restriction acts in 1921 and 1924 that would soon all but end the flow of immigration from these regions of Europe. The Immigration Reform Act of 1965 would end this policy of restriction.
3. Saint Helena (ca. 250–ca. 330) was the mother of Emperor Constantine I, the first Christian Roman emperor. Gennaro here engages in the heterodox practice, common among Southern Italian Catholics, of praying to patron saints, who were often associated with specific regions of the country and categories of requests.
4. Gennaro refers to the destructive colonial wars that a young Italy—unified in 1870—fought during the late nineteenth century in order to enhance its status as a world power. As a Southern Italian *contadino* (agricultural peasant), Gennaro expresses a typical class antagonism toward the *galantuomini* (gentlemen) class of professionals and landowners—often absentees from the more economically, industrially, and culturally developed north.

5. At this early stage of Italian national history, education was considered to be for the rich only, and literacy rates in the south of Italy were notoriously low: roughly 30 percent at the turn of the twentieth century.

6. King Humbert I, born in 1844, was king of Italy from 1878 until his death in 1900, when he was assassinated by anarchist Gaetano Bresci.

7. Beautiful Gennaro, son of the sacrament of Jesus!

8. *Scuti* is the plural form of *scuto* or *scudo*, a kind of coin used in Italy until the nineteenth century.

9. Fellow countryman. At this early stage of Italian national history, though, when Italian immigrants were more parochially and less nationally minded, the term also applied to those from the same village, or at least region of the country. Italian Americans now use the term more broadly to refer to others of Italian descent.

10. A standard curse or insult: literally, "devil's pig."

11. A celebration, party, or feast.

12. An honorific used when addressing gentlemen (*donna*, for ladies) in Italy.

13. Such household shrines were, and to a lesser degree still are, commonly found in Italian and Italian American homes.

14. Holiest Mary.

15. Literally, "mother of mine," but a standard interjection.

16. Saint Jerome (ca. 347–420) is perhaps best known for his famous Latin translation of the Bible. The Holy Calendar can refer to the calendar of holy days observed by Roman Catholics, but it can also refer to the calendar of feast days for the many venerated saints in that tradition. Thus, Gennaro is invoking not only Saint Jerome, but all the saints also.

17. Aunt.

18. Saints Roch, Blaise, and Anthony.

19. Giuseppe Garibaldi (1807–1882) was most famously a military commander during the *Risorgimento*, or the nineteenth-century unification of the Italian states, which were previously controlled by Austria, France, Spain, and the Papal States. The Battle of Solferino was fought on June 24, 1859, between France and Piedmont-Sardinia on one side and Austria on the other, and the former's victory is viewed as a pivotal step toward unification.

20. *Bello* (masculine) and *bella* (feminine) literally mean "beautiful." Placed after a given name, the meaning is closer to "dear."

21. A very small pasta.

22. Scoundrel.

23. You're beautiful.

24. Father.

25. Literally, "English." Italian immigrants often referred to Anglo Americans this way.

26. Sir.

Chapter Two

1. The majority of Italian immigration of this time period came from those regions of the country south of Rome. Northern Italians had greater access to the social, cultural, political, and economic advantages offered by cities such as Milan, Bologna, Florence, Verona, Padua, and Rome and were generally better off and better educated than their Southern counterparts, who came to be thought of by Italian sociologists as not only culturally but, *racially* inferior to their more solidly Nordic counterparts. The mutual animosity between Northern and Southern Italians persists even into contemporary times.

2. Gioachino Antonio Rossini (1792–1868) and Domenico Gaetano Maria Donizetti (1797–1848) were famous composers of opera, a favorite musical form among Italian immigrants.

3. A meat sauce, or *ragù*, consisting of, among other ingredients, beef, carrots, onions, and celery. Lapolla is likely drawing a distinction between this sauce, which traditionally uses only a bit of tomato paste, and the more heavily tomato-based "red sauces."

4. South America was another likely destination for late nineteenth-century Italian immigrants. For instance, Argentina has seen so much Italian immigration, that the culture and language of this once Spanish colony have been indelibly altered by it.

5. "Hooray," or "long live."

6. A lout or boor—or in contemporary parlance, a "jerk."

7. Coins, pennies.

8. Literally, "holiest devil." A relatively mild blasphemous Italian curse.

9. A very nice person.

10. Master.

11. Ice cream.

Chapter Three

1. Such mutual aid societies were common among immigrants of all national backgrounds.

2. The Madonna of Mid-August refers to the Marian Feast of the Assumption, observed on August 15 in honor of Mary's ascension to heaven. Lapolla's description of the Feast of Saint Elena seems to refer to the July 16 Feast of Our Lady of Mount Carmel, which, in New York, featured a massive march and celebration

centering around the East Harlem church of the same name. Far and away the premier Italian celebration in New York for many years, its history and cultural implications are masterfully explored in Richard Orsi's *The Madonna of 115th Street: Faith and Community in Italian Harlem, 1880–1950* (1985). The evocative description that follows in the text holds true to actual accounts of Italian immigrant faith, devotion, and charity during this celebration.

3. Canopy.
4. Nougat.
5. Terrible rascals.
6. *Morta cristo* and *Mazza cristo*—roughly "Christ killer"—are Italian slurs for Jews.
7. A wig worn by orthodox Jewish women to cover their hair in accordance with biblical law.
8. Gentiles.
9. Whore.
10. Holiest whore. Gennaro invokes this Italian blasphemy likely due to his insistence on comparing Dora to Saint Elena.
11. A losing battle Garibaldi waged against the Papal States in 1862 during the wars for unification.
12. The suffix *accio*, plural *acci*, added to some nouns means that they are especially bad. Thus, it is far worse to be a *cafonaccio* than a *cafone*. (See Part One, Chapter Two, note 6.)

Chapter Four

1. For the love of God, what are you doing?
2. Holiest Mary, don't do anything, Gennaro.
3. It's a shame, Don Anselmo . . . a stupid life.
4. Disgusting.
5. I love her very much.
6. The plural form of *pizza*.
7. Stromboli, Aetna, and Vesuvius are active volcanoes in Italy, the first in the Aeolian Islands, the second in Sicily, and the third near Naples.

Chapter Five

1. This reflects the old Greek and Italian tradition of using a definite article *the* (*il*/masculine, *la*/feminine) before surnames.
2. "Country," but to the more parochially minded Italian immigrant not yet accustomed to thinking of himself or herself as Italian at this early stage in that nation's history, this also could mean "village."
3. My beautiful.
4. Slacker.

5. My beautiful and holiest Mary.
6. Holy Mother.

Part Two

Chapter One

1. Sir Captain.
2. Peasants, farmers, agricultural laborers.
3. Plural form of *cafone*. (See Part One, Chapter Two, note 6.)
4. Respectable.
5. In the style of King Humbert.
6. Giuseppe Giusti (1809–1850), Alessandro Manzoni (1785–1873), Dante Alighieri (1265–1321), Francesco Petrarca (1304–1374).
7. Literally, "my good one": a term of endearment.
8. Holy God, dear, I can't do it anymore.
9. Dear. The feminine form is *cara*.
10. Greek for "Lord, have mercy." This prayer is an essential part of the Catholic Mass.

Chapter Two

1. Emperor Menelik II (1844–1913) defeated Italy in the First Italo-Ethiopian War (1895–1896), a failed Italian attempt to colonize the African nation.
2. It was customary for Italian immigrant families to have such an arrangement in which the mother handled the finances and all gainfully employed members of the family turned over their earnings to her with every payment.
3. A little Madonna, you know.
4. My God.
5. Mary of mine.
6. Holy God.
7. For the love of God, Sofia.
8. Don Tomaso is using standard Italian, which, developed from the Tuscan dialect, was the language of the political, economic, and cultural elites, rather than the Lucanian dialect he would likely speak coming as he does from Basilicata.
9. A *comune*, or municipality, in the province of Naples, region of Campania.
10. I love you, but it's true, it's true.
11. *Sfoglatelle*, a layered pastry.
12. A sweet, pretzel-like snack.
13. An obscure reference, probably to another dessert dish given its placement in the text. Roughly "big mouthfuls," it may be related to *bocconcini*, a cheese dish, or *boccone*, a dessert featuring chocolate and strawberries in a meringue.
14. Villain.

15. "For pleasure or for pain." The reference is to Canto IV of Dante's *Purgatory*, and the "misquote" likely stems from its irrelevance to "the bitterness of exile," a common theme of *Inferno*.
16. Beauty.
17. Strong, warm, and dry Mediterranean winds from North Africa that contributed greatly to the agricultural crises of nineteenth-century Southern Italy.
18. Holiest pig Mary.
19. But I love you very, very much.

Chapter Three

1. The narrator here relates the conflict between the Irish power structure of American Catholic churches, which observed a more traditional and clerical version of Roman Catholicism, and the newly arrived Southern Italian immigrants, who observed a more heterodox, even improvised, version of the faith that featured, among other heresies, worship of Mary and the saints and belief in the efficacy of pagan practices such as *malocchio*, the evil eye.
2. A common practice of the time.
3. Protestant missionaries provided much material and cultural assistance to Italian immigrants adjusting to urban America, though they often misunderstood the culture of those they sought to help.
4. The Spanish-American War (April 25–August 12, 1898) began when the United States intervened in the Cuban war for independence, which Spain had refused to end peacefully. The event that immediately precipitated U. S. involvement in the conflict was the February 15, 1898, sinking of the USS *Maine*, which had been sent from Florida to Cuba to help defend U.S. interests.
5. Jesus, Joseph, and Mary.
6. Plural form of *lasagna*. (*Lasagna* refers to only one such noodle.)
7. Stuffed lasagna.
8. Italian dry-cured ham.

Chapter Four

1. George Dewey (1837–1917) was a highly successful admiral of the United States Navy, who was perhaps best known for his victory in the Battle of Manila Bay, in which the United States remarkably suffered no combat fatalities.
2. Provolone is a similar cheese.
3. Lavish, luxurious. The word is derived from the name of Roman military commander Lucullus (ca. 118–56 BC), who was renowned as a decadent gourmand.
4. Literally, "sharpshooters." A corps of the Italian army that once had a showily distinctive uniform.
5. Rosaria, for the love of Holy God.

6. Alexandre Dumas (1802–1870), biracial French author of the novels *The Count of Monte Cristo* and *The Three Musketeers.*
7. James Fenimore Cooper (1789–1851), American writer of *Leatherstocking Tales* and *The Last of the Mohicans.*
8. George Alfred Henty (1832–1902), British historical novelist.
9. Michael Faraday (1791–1867), British chemist and physicist.
10. James Clerk Maxwell (1831–1879), British physicist and mathmetician.

Chapter Five

1. Dearest.
2. Tragic lovers featured in Dante's *Inferno.*
3. Ludovico Ariosto (1474–1533), Italian poet.
4. How beautiful it is.
5. Sweets.
6. Refers to the First Italo-Ethiopian War. (See Part Two, Chapter Two, note 1.)
7. Francesca here describes her intense love for Paolo in Canto V of Dante's *Inferno.* "Love that releases no beloved from loving" in English, the famous line, like Don Davido's previous misquote has little relevance to the discussion. (See Part Two, Chapter Two, note 15.)
8. A liqueur once thought to be effective as a love potion, hence its name, which means "witch."
9. Little cookie.
10. A liqueur.
11. Literally, "tears of Christ." A Neapolitan red wine.
12. Gaetano Donizetti's opera *Lucia di Lammermoor.*
13. *Brindisi* means "drinking song." *La Cavalleria Rusticana* is an opera by Pietro Mascagni (1863–1945).
14. Hat store.

Part Three

Chapter One

1. That very good one.

Chapter Two

1. "Cheers," or, literally, "health."
2. Greek mathematician and geometrician active in the fourth century BC.
3. The battle ended, the army . . .
4. Henry Irving (1838–1905) was a highly acclaimed English stage actor who played Shylock in Shakespeare's *Merchant of Venice.*

5. A once legendary opera house on 125th Street.

6. An 1882 operetta by French composer Robert Planquette (1848–1903) and British librettist Henry Brougham Farnie (1836–1889).

7. An obscure reference.

8. A 1906 melodrama by American playwright Owen Davis (1874–1956).

9. 1871 English translation, by English playwright Leopold Davis Lewis (1828–1890), of the French play *Le Juif Polonais*, by Erckmann-Chatrian.

10. During the late nineteenth and early twentieth centuries, there were so many adaptations of Harriet Beecher Stowe's (1811–1896) antislavery novel *Uncle Tom's Cabin* (1852)—many of them riddled with stereotypes common to minstrel shows that badly undercut the anti-racist thesis of the book—that they became their own genre: the "tom show."

11. *Julius Caesar*, by William Shakespeare.

12. Mythical Spanish hero whose legend, long a part of Spanish oral tradition, was first published in 1624 by Bernardo de Balbuena.

13. 1841 poem by American poet Henry Wadsworth Longfellow (1807–1882).

14. 1820 poem by British poet Robert Southey (1774–1843).

15. 1842 poem by British poet Robert Browning (1812–1883).

16. Wars waged by European Christendom against Muslims and other mostly non-Christian religious groups from the eleventh through the thirteenth centuries.

17. War fought from 1337 to 1453 between two French royal houses, Valois and Plantagenet.

18. Hooray, dear Gennaro . . . we may yell it out to the world, you know.

19. An opera by Giuseppe Verdi (1813–1901).

Chapter Three

1. The "betrayal" of the nationalist ideals of military leader Giuseppe Garibaldi and political philosopher Giuseppe Mazzini (1805–1872)—both instrumental in the attempt to establish Italy as a democratic republic—could be any number of things, including political corruption, the gross disparity between the north and the south, the economic upheavals that drove so many Italians to immigrate, and misguided colonialism. The "kowtowing to this country and that" could refer to Italy's 1882 entry into a Triple Alliance with Germany and Austria-Hungary—an arrangement whereby two of the powers would come to the military aid of the third if it were attacked.

2. Roman emperor (ca. 260–311).

3. Giacomo Leopardi (1798–1837).

4. Electric chandelier.

5. The Panic of 1907 resulted in a wave of "bank runs" that crippled financial institutions and halved the value of the stock market.

6. Scoundrels.
7. "Like a feather in the wind." The line appears in "La donna è mobile" ("Woman Is Fickle") from Giuseppe Verdi's *Rigoletto* (1851).
8. British poet, critic, and artist John Ruskin (1819–1900).
9. Alfred Tennyson (1809–1892), British poet.

ABOUT THE EDITOR

Steven J. Belluscio teaches English at Borough of Manhattan Community College/CUNY and is the author of *To Be Suddenly White: Literary Realism and Racial Passing.*

Printed in the United States
152363LV00001B/3/P